MERRY MONARCH

BIOGRAPHIES BY
HESKETH PEARSON

CHARLES II AS KING

MERRY MONARCH;

The Life and Likeness of Charles II.

by
HESKETH PEARSON

HARPER & BROTHERS
PUBLISHERS, NEW YORK

This book is published in England under the title of
CHARLES II: HIS LIFE AND LIKENESS

Contents

Contents

Illustrations

The portraits in this book are reproduced by kind permission of the National Portrait Gallery.

To
My Friend
CASS CANFIELD

'*Kings are not born: they are made by artificial hallucination. When the process is interrupted by adversity at a critical age, as in the case of Charles II, the subject becomes sane and never completely recovers his kingliness.*'

BERNARD SHAW (1903).

MERRY MONARCH

[1]

A Bad Beginning

AT ABOUT THE AGE OF FIFTEEN Charles Stuart, Prince of Wales, was with the King his father at Oxford. Attending divine service in St Mary's church, the youngster became bored with the sermon and amused himself by joking with the girls in his immediate vicinity. Noticing this, the King rapped him sharply on the head with a staff, checking his laughter. The incident reveals their characters. Father and son were opposite in nature, the one solemn enough to be stupid, the other gay enough to be intelligent. Charles I took himself so seriously that he believed everything he said. He had no knowledge of people, no imagination, no common sense; defects that were remedied in his son. The Civil War would never have been fought if the grown-up son had been in the father's shoes. Unfortunately Charles I was married to a Roman Catholic, Henrietta Maria, daughter of the French King, Henry IV, and her ignorance of the English national character, her miscalculation of the strength of Protestant feeling, reinforced her husband's obtuseness and obstinacy, the combination of the two resulting in a disaster which their son as a young man could have predicted. They were married in May 1625 when Charles came to the throne. For about four years they remained childless. Then Henrietta Maria had a son who was born, baptised and buried on the same day. The birth of their second son, Charles, took place at St. James's Palace on 29 May 1630, one of his godfathers being Louis XIII, King of France.

The baby did not take after his parents, being dark and un-

1

comely. 'He is so ugly that I am ashamed of him,' wrote Henrietta to her former governess, 'but his size and features supply the want of beauty. I wish you could see the gentleman, for he has no ordinary mien; he is so serious in all that he does that I cannot help deeming him far wiser than myself.' A little later she noted his growth: 'He is so fat and so tall that he is taken for a year old, and he is only four months. His teeth are already beginning to come. I will send you his portrait as soon as he is a little fairer, for at present he is so dark that I am ashamed of him.' But he remained swarthy all his life and in the years to come was often toasted as 'the black boy'. As a child he displayed vivacity and a will of his own. His first governor was the Earl of Newcastle, who preferred sport to literature and encouraged the boy to study men instead of books. His tutor was Dr Brian Duppa, Bishop of Chichester, a gentle, tolerant soul, very much to his pupil's taste. The only peculiarity recorded of the child's earliest years was that he became much attached to 'a wooden billet' which he carried about wherever he went and always slept with. It was the precursor of many bed-companions.

At the age of nine he broke an arm, the accident being followed by a serious illness. With a wisdom beyond his years he refused to take some of the medicines then thought necessary to allay fever, receiving a reprimand, addressed 'To my dear son the Prince', from his mother: 'Charles, I am sore that I must begin my first letter with chiding you, because I hear that you will not take physic. I hope it was only for this day, and that tomorrow you will do it, for if you will not I must come to you and make you take it, for it is for your health. I have given order to my Lord Newcastle to send me word tonight whether you will or not; therefore I hope you will not give me the pains to go, and so I rest your affectionate mother, Henriette-Marie R.' That the young Prince was not merely indulging in a fit of boyish stubbornness is proved by a note he sent to Newcastle: 'My Lord, I would not have you take too much physic, for it doth always make me worse, and I think it will do the like with you. I ride every day, and am ready to follow any other directions from you. Make haste to return to him that loves you.' Newcastle resigned his charge when the Prince reached the age of eleven, and the job was entrusted to the Marquis of Hertford, an amiable fellow who preferred literature to sport.

By this time the folly of Charles I had caused universal unrest. With a lack of discernment that would be unbelievable if it had not been manifest, he tried to force his new prayer-book on the Scots, who united against the imposition and drew up a National Covenant, hostile to popery and episcopacy, whereby all the signatories were bound to resist any attack on their religion to the death. That started the trouble. The Scottish resistance stiffened the demands of the English Parliament; and Charles sacrificed his loyal lieutenant Strafford, the one man who might yet have saved him. A combination of feebleness and imbecility then drove the King to the House of Commons, where he intended to arrest five refractory members, but they had fled to the City for protection; and now the fat was in the fire. No man in history had worked so conscientiously for his own undoing as Charles, and his attempts at appeasing those whom his policy had provoked ended inevitably in war.

The King went north to collect an army in January 1642, his eldest son being given the command of his bodyguard at York two months later. Not many heirs to the throne have started soldiering at the age of eleven. Hostilities commenced in August, and as both navy and seaports were on the side of Parliament the King could receive no supplies from abroad, his only hope being to win a quick victory. This he nearly succeeded in doing because his young nephew, Prince Rupert, had seen service in Germany, had studied Swedish cavalry tactics, and quickly became a brilliant if rash leader of horse. At Edgehill in October '42 a charge by Rupert appeared to give the royal army victory, but it was more of a display than a decision. Prince Charles and his younger brother James, Duke of York, were present at the battle under the charge of the King's physician, William Harvey, who

3

had discovered the circulation of the blood. A cannon ball passed close enough to the Princes to send up the doctor's circulation, and they were placed under the protection of Sir Edward Hyde, with whom they were nearly captured through mistaking a body of the enemy's horse for their own. The Royalists then marched on London, but were checked at Brentford, and the King retired to Oxford, which became his headquarters for the rest of the war. In order to gain the assistance of the Scots, the English Parliament took the Covenant, with the result that Rupert sustained a serious defeat at Marston Moor in July '44, his cavalry being no match for Cromwell's Ironsides.

For the next six months the King's campaign in the west was fairly successful, and the Parliamentary army under Essex surrendered at Lostwithiel in Cornwall. Prince Charles saw a good deal of active service, but the King thought it advisable to give his son more responsibility, 'to unboy him', and in March '45 sent him to Bristol, where there was much disaffection among the Royalists. Though nominally under the governorship of the Earl of Berkshire, a man so feeble that when captured at a later date he was released by Cromwell on the ground that he was harmless, the Prince was created Duke of Cornwall and appointed General of the Western Association. As Rupert, now at Bristol, refused to take commands from any of the King's generals, the Prince was also made generalissimo of all the royal forces in England and Wales. He was told by his father to act on the advice of a council composed of various peers and Sir Edward Hyde. The latter treated him as a schoolboy and expected him to be on his best behaviour at council meetings. He chafed, but did as he was told. Hyde was a member of the squire class; also a shrewd and witty lawyer whose sarcasm and honesty aroused much enmity, but whose ability, loyalty and religious orthodoxy ultimately earned him the highest office in the kingdom. He had been on the Parliamentary side until, perceiving that Church and State were imperilled by the extremists, he joined the King and quickly became a trusted counsellor.

A Bad Beginning

At Bristol everything was at sixes and sevens; the officers were quarrelling, the troops were given over to violence and rapine, and discipline was at a discount. Attempts were at once made to bring the western counties into some sort of cohesion, and the Prince summoned their representatives to meet him at Bridgwater. Here he came across his one-time nurse, Mrs Windham, now wife of the port's governor. She wished to display her old influence over him, and succeeded in diverting his mind from business. She kissed him publicly at dances, made fun of his father, encouraged him to scoff at his council, and fostered his more sensual tastes. Noticing his indifference to their opinions and irreverence for themselves, the council reported his attitude to the King, who recalled him to Bristol. Driven thence by the plague, he went to Barnstaple, where in June '45 he heard of the crushing defeat of the royal army by Cromwell at Naseby. Soon afterwards he received a letter from his father instructing him to leave for France, where he would have to obey his mother's wishes in everything except religion. His council, hating French influence, opposed the King's design. While staying at Exeter in September the Prince heard that Rupert had surrendered Bristol, and another letter from his father repeated the command that he should go to France. But Hyde and the rest continued to withstand such an action. Parliamentary forces were now reducing Royalist garrisons all over the country, and the Prince retreated to Truro, whence he made an effort to relieve the now beleaguered city of Exeter, marching by Bodmin to Tavistock and so to Totnes. Another note from his father insisting on his immediate departure for France was answered by his council, who promised to send him to Scilly or Jersey, as it was essential that he should not leave the King's dominions. The final action of the war took place at Torrington in February '46, and the Prince was driven to his last stronghold on the mainland, Pendennis Castle, Falmouth. With the capitulation of Oxford in June the Civil War came to an end, and the King took refuge with the Scots, who eventually sold him to the English Parliament for

5

enough cash to settle the arrears of pay due to their army.

At ten o'clock on the night of 2 March 1646 the Prince set sail in a frigate for the Scilly Isles, accompanied by Hyde and others. They arrived at St Mary's in a forlorn condition, and as there was little food on the island, and nothing at all to be bought for money, their residence in the castle was uncomfortable. Soon the Prince received an invitation from Parliament to visit London, the ostensible object being that he should help them to reach an amicable arrangement with his father. The true object became clear when a Parliamentary fleet arrived off the Scilly Isles; but a storm dispersed it, and some days later the Prince, unallured by an invitation backed with force, embarked on a small frigate, and attended by two other vessels managed to elude the fleet, arriving at Elizabeth Castle, Jersey, the residence of the governor Sir George Carteret, on 17 April, with a retinue of three hundred persons, including the members of his council, the grooms of the bedchamber, the gentlemen of the privy chamber, the cupbearer, carver and master of the robes, the pages of the backstairs, the pages of honour, shoe-makers, tailors, laundresses, equerries, chaplains, and a barber.

There is circumstantial evidence that the Prince's first serious love-affair occurred during the ten weeks he spent in Jersey. A seigneur of the island, Amias de Carteret, had a pretty daughter, Marguerite, by whom Charles, aged sixteen, may have had his first son; at least in a letter he is believed to have written many years later there occurs a statement that the child was borne by 'one of the most distinguished young ladies in our kingdom, more from the frailty of our first youth than from evil intention'. It seems that he pensioned his offspring and rewarded the Carteret family, and there is nothing in our knowledge of him to make the episode in the least unlikely; but the whole affair was surrounded by enough mystery to make the biographer cautious. Whether or not his first amorous adventure occurred in Jersey, he certainly revelled in his early nautical experiences there, sailing a yacht that had been constructed at St Malo and equipped with twelve pairs of oars and two masts. In this way he passed many happy hours, developing a passion for ships and the sea which never left him.

Though the young man's chief councillors had set their minds against it, his father and mother entreated him to leave Jersey for France, and after much debate he acted against the advice of Hyde, whose main objection was that, as many Englishmen believed Charles I a papist even though he was seen daily at a service in the English Church, they would certainly believe the same of the Prince 'when he shall have no church in France to go to', their presumption being strengthened by his residence with a papistical mother. But the Prince had made up his mind and would have crossed to the mainland in a small rowing-boat if the wind had not changed and enabled him to sail in a larger one. On 26 June he landed on the French coast with a considerable suite.

2

Uncrowned King

HAVING ESCAPED FROM ENGLAND two years before, Henrietta Maria was now at St Germains, where, as daughter of the great Henry of Navarre, she received the respect of the populace and a pension of twelve hundred francs a day, enough to maintain her with regal dignity if she had not spent much of it in helping her unfortunate husband. She was on good terms with Anne of Austria, Queen-Regent of France, and with Cardinal Mazarin, the real ruler of the country and the amorous ruler of the Queen-Regent. At that time the boy-King, Louis XIV, was eight years old.

Following the usual manifestations of joy over the reunion of mother and son, the reality of the relationship between Henrietta Maria and Charles became apparent. Henrietta loved to exercise power, and her son was soon made aware of his penniless position. Although mature at the age of sixteen, he never had more than ten pistoles (about £8) in his pocket, and whenever in her presence his head remained uncovered. Such of his friends as she disliked were compelled to look elsewhere for their subsistence; and Charles was nagged into a courtship with his rich cousin, Mademoiselle de Montpensier, known as 'La Grande Mademoiselle'. But he was attracted neither to her beauty nor to her money, and refused to appear at his best in her company. He gazed at her but hardly opened his mouth except to make brief replies. As a rule he was fairly fluent in the language of love, but in her presence he could not speak the simplest phrases in

French. Henrietta did her best to persuade Mademoiselle that the strength of her son's feelings made him tongue-tied, but the lady was vexed, feeling that there were other ways of demonstrating affection besides standing dumb and looking unhappy.

Some weeks, however, elapsed before Charles was received into Court circles. Several points of etiquette had to be decided before that happened. But when in August '46 it was at length agreed that the French King Louis should sit down before his cousin the English Prince Charles could take a seat, the two with their families met in the forest of Fontainebleau, a more formal reception taking place at the palace there. The manners of the English Prince were approved; but as he could scarcely speak or understand French, and Louis was ignorant of English, their conversation was restricted. The Court was in Paris for the winter of 1646–7 and Charles passed his time agreeably at balls, concerts, masques and plays. Then he returned to St Germains and the jealous tutelage of his mother. While there he heard that his father had been sold by the Presbyterian Scots to the English Parliament, and had become a prisoner in the hands of the English army, that the Scottish Royalists under the Duke of Hamilton were about to intervene on the King's behalf, and that a Royalist rising was expected in various parts of England. Asked to join Hamilton's army, the Prince refused to do so unless he could bring his English chaplains with him.

In April '48 his brother James, Duke of York, managed to escape from England to Holland disguised as a girl, and in June a part of the navy declared for the King. Charles left France for Holland to take command of the fleet, much to the chagrin of his brother, who was titular Lord High Admiral of England. The ships were victualled by Charles's brother-in-law, the Prince of Orange, and in July they sailed for the English coast. Divided counsels caused the failure of the expedition, though several prizes were captured. A deputation from the Scots inviting Charles's co-operation annoyed his sailors, who wished him to attack the Parliamentary fleet. To avoid a mutiny Charles agreed, and at length came within range of the enemy. Before the action he was begged to go into the hold, but he replied that his honour was dearer to him than life and that he would take his chance with the rest on deck, which made him popular with the sailors. The two fleets were about to engage when a strong wind blew them apart, and as supplies were running short the Royalists had to sail for Holland, where they arrived early in September to the great relief of the Prince's secretary, Sir Robert Long, who declared: 'If ever they get me into their sea-voyages again, I am very much mistaken.' Under Prince Rupert a thorough re-organisation took place, and the Royalist fleet sailed for Ireland in January '49.

Charles went to the Hague and was well received by the Dutch, being invited to spend the winter with the Prince of Orange. But disquieting news from England made him uneasy. Everywhere the attempts of the Royalists were frustrated. One episode was particularly tragic. For over two months the King's supporters were besieged in Colchester by General Fairfax, and when the town surrendered at the end of August '48 the two leading defenders of the garrison were ruthlessly executed. In the same month Hamilton's army of Scots was routed near Preston by Cromwell, and the prisoners were sent as slaves to Virginia and Barbadoes. Not all the English Royalists were in sympathy with their northern allies, one of them writing: 'It is a wonderful thing and God's just judgment that those that sold their King not two years ago for £200,000 should now be sold for 2/- a piece to be carried to new Plantations.' Hamilton was executed, his brother, who now became Duke, being with Charles at the Hague.

In the latter part of the year 1648 Charles solaced himself with a lady named Lucy Walter. She was the mistress of Colonel Robert Sidney, who apparently raised no objection when she wished to change her master. Charles admired beauty and bold-ness in a woman, and as Lucy possessed both he was easily capti-vated. Their son, born in April '49, was afterwards created Duke of Monmouth, and Charles became devoted to him. In the days to come Lucy stated that she had been married to the Prince, but he persistently denied it and no proofs were forthcoming. Though he later renounced her on account of her scandalous behaviour, she continued to make vexatious demands upon him, and for the sake of their child he provided for her support until she died in 1658.

The winter of 1648–9 was not passed wholly in amorous dalliance. Soon after the Christmas festivities at the Hague, the refugees heard of their King's trial at Westminster. Although Charles I had commanded his wife and son not to allow pity for him to jeopardise his heir's future right to the crown, the Prince at once disobeyed him. Not only did he beg the Dutch authorities to do all in their power to save his father, but he offered to surrender himself if the conditions of the English Parliament demanded the sacrifice. Further he entreated Mazarin and the Queen-Regent of France to use their influence. Both countries sent protests to London, but neither was willing to adopt extreme methods. While recovering from an attack of smallpox Charles wrote a personal appeal to General Fairfax, and finally he sent to Parliament a signed and sealed *carte blanche* which they could fill up with whatever terms they cared to impose in return for his father's life. Parliament replied with a proclamation that all who recognised the Prince as the King's successor would suffer the death of traitors. The dignity of Charles I at his trial and execution made converts of his enemies, and it may be said of him that 'nothing in his life became him like the leaving it'. The act of regicide was broken gently to his son, by the simple method of addressing him as 'Your Majesty'. On hearing the words he burst into tears and rushed to his bedroom, where he could weep without restraint. The populace as well as the rulers of Holland and France expressed horror at the act, but they had their own troubles to divert them, the Dutch being concerned over the interruption of trade with England if Charles remained in their country, the French being busy with a civil war of their own, the

Fronde, caused by Mazarin's unpopularity with a section of the nobles and the *parlement* of Paris.

Charles was in a difficult position at The Hague, the fact that he had been proclaimed King in Scotland and Ireland making his presence awkward for the authorities. His sister's husband, the Prince of Orange, was always generous to him, but the arrival of a representative from the English Parliament would create an unpleasant situation. Charles discovered that there was danger in a multitude of counsellors, some of whom advised him to take command of the army in Ireland, others urging him to be crowned in Scotland. But he could not agree to the conditions laid down by the Scottish deputation which had been sent to treat with him: namely, that he should accept the Covenant, which meant that he would have to suppress all forms of worship except the Presbyterian, persecute papists and prelatists, forswear his own faith, and disown those of his father's followers who had remained true to their religion. He found it impossible to reconcile the pro-Covenant Scots with their anti-Covenant fellow-countrymen; and as both sides had a great deal to say, the members of his Privy Council being far from dumb, their conferences might have continued indefinitely but for an incident that compelled him to cut them short. An envoy arrived from the English Parliament at the beginning of May '49 to make a treaty with Holland. The man, Dutch by birth but long resident in England, had acted as prosecuting counsel at the trial of Charles I. As The Hague swarmed with Royalists, he was warned of his danger as a regicide; but he took no heed of the warning, and one evening half a dozen men entered the inn where he was staying, ran a sword through him and decamped. Though the act was approved by the average Dutchman, it was made clear to Charles that his continued presence would make trade relations impossible between the two countries; so, prompted by the Marquis of Montrose, he rejected the terms of the Scottish commissioners which would make him a puppet in the hands of the Kirk and a Parliamentary clique, raised some money with the help of the Prince of Orange, and left

Holland for France, being well received on the way at Antwerp and Brussels, then part of the Spanish Empire.

He was met by Louis and the Queen-Regent at Compiègne, where he discovered that he was still expected to woo Mademoiselle de Montpensier. But she was shocked by his levity. He seemed to take no interest in public affairs. While he could talk in passable French with the young King about dogs and horses, his knowledge of the language deserted him on the themes of love and politics. Further, his gastronomic taste appeared to her indelicate. Instead of eating ortolans, he 'threw himself upon an enormous piece of beef and a shoulder of mutton, as if there had been nothing else'. When they were left alone together he made no soft advances; and though he declared that he could not understand how a man with a pleasant wife was ever able to give a thought to another woman, the sentiment failed to impress her. Altogether she found him unsatisfactory as a suitor, which no doubt accorded with his own desire.

On joining his mother at St Germains he mingled his tears with hers over their common loss, the dreadful fate of her loved husband having prostrated her with grief and driven her into a convent, from which she had emerged in order to counsel her son. But she found that he did not need her advice, that he had chosen his councillors without obtaining her sanction, that he was no longer dependent on her and would follow his own inclinations. She lost her temper, and with it much of his company. Charles wanted to put himself at the head of the army in Ireland, where the Marquis of Ormonde, a loyal and industrious adherent, was attempting the impossible task of uniting Catholics and Protestants in the King's cause; but the arrival of Cromwell in that country in August '49 decided the question, and though Charles insisted that his present existence was unbearably shameful and that he longed to die fighting with Ormonde, his advisers were able to convince him that the Parliamentary fleet would almost certainly capture him before he could achieve his wish.

Nevertheless he determined to leave France, where the Court

13

atmosphere was chilly, and return to Jersey, the governor of which still held the island for his monarch. On 12 September he set out from St Germains with his brother the Duke of York, their procession consisting of six coaches, sixty horses, and so many followers that many were compelled to walk. Accepting much hospitality on the way, they reached Jersey on the 17th, and here the winter was passed among a loyal population in pleasant circumstances and agreeable pursuits. Every Sunday, whatever the weather, they rowed over from Elizabeth Castle to St Heliers and attended the church service. They reviewed the native troops, wandered freely about the island, and Charles won the hearts of the inhabitants by his invariable amiability. But money was short, quarrels among his followers were frequent, and the news from Ireland was appalling. Ormonde's best troops were massacred at Drogheda and Wexford by Cromwell, whose bloodthirsty acts while crushing his opponents have made him a hero to many historians who would hesitate to crush a black-beetle.

The hopes of Charles were again centred on Scotland. He had encouraged Montrose to collect money and men from the rulers of Europe for a Royalist invasion of his northern kingdom, and the Marquis was now engaged in doing so. While at St Germains the King had written to Montrose that he was 'fully resolved to assist and support you to the utmost of my power', adding the assurance that his attitude to the Covenanters remained unchanged. The Presbyterians hated Montrose more than they professed to love Charles, much of their hatred being due to the fact that his loyalty to the late King made their treachery more humiliating by contrast.

James Graham, Marquis of Montrose, was a poet, a wit, and a born leader of men, whose chivalry and nobility of character, courtliness of manners and unimpeachable honesty, impressed both friends and enemies. Even the cynical Cardinal de Retz called him 'the only man in the world who ever realised for me the ideal of certain heroes whom one finds only in the *Lives* of Plutarch. He sustained the cause of the King of England in his country with a greatness of soul unequalled in this age'. His personal popularity and military ability were so remarkable that during the Civil War he united the mutually hostile Highland clans into an extremely efficient army, and within a year won a series of brilliant victories over the Parliamentary and Presbyterian forces which were three times as large as his own. He would have been able to conquer the whole of Scotland for the King if the Highlanders had not refused to march with him to the Lowlands, where his army of scarcely a thousand men was defeated by David Leslie at Philiphaugh. His services for the Crown having won him the implacable hostility of the Covenanters, especially their leader the Marquis of Argyll, he was excommunicated by the Kirk, proscribed and dispossessed of title and property by the Parliament; and when the King, who had taken refuge with the Scottish army, ordered him to stop fighting, he escaped to the Continent. Such was the man who now proposed to re-establish Charles II in the kingdom of Scotland against a large army of Covenanters, and afterwards in the kingdom of England against Cromwell.

The attempts by Montrose to obtain assistance on the Continent stimulated the Covenanters to make another effort to reach an agreement with Charles, and an emissary was sent to Jersey by Archibald Campbell, Marquis of Argyll, to treat with the King. The more extreme Royalists would have liked to repulse the emissary, but the moderates favoured an agreement between the King and the Scottish Parliament, and their influence was the stronger because 'of the king's gentle and sweet nature and disposition, or, to speak their own words, his Majesty's indifferency to all'. So wrote one of the King's intelligent followers, Lord Hatton, who put more truth in a phrase than most of them could cram into a speech. Placed between the buffetings of hostile and fanatical forces, Charles's gentle and sweet nature was already showing the inevitable effect of indifference to all. His one desire was for peace and unity, and his chief virtue in this war of hate and intolerance was a patience and moderation that appeased, at least

15

temporarily, the discord of bigoted factions. Argyll's emissary had to wait several weeks while Charles digested the conditions whereby he would be accepted as King by the Scottish Presbyterians, who had not meliorated their original demand: his oath to the Covenant with its egregious concomitants. Because the power of the Independents in England was steadily increasing, and the English Parliament had ratted on the Covenant when the Scottish alliance had served its turn, the northern Covenanters were more determined than ever that Charles should swear to enforce their religion throughout the entire realm, that he should abide by their civil and religious laws, and that Montrose should be forbidden to enter Scotland. Charles might again have rejected their terms if the news from Ireland had not been so bad. Cromwell had beaten down all opposition except for Ormonde's handful of men who were on the verge of starvation.

The only hope now was Scotland, and Charles called a meeting of his Council, at which, reported a participant, the violence of the members was assuaged by the King with 'such moderation, patience and judgment, as was admirable in a person of his years'. He calmed their fury, repressed the insults that were flying about, and at length got them all to agree that a treaty should be made with the Scots 'on honourable terms'. Charles wrote a letter in which he promised to meet the commissioners of the Kirk and Parliament at Breda the following March, under the mediation of the Prince of Orange; but he also urged his Scottish subjects to unite with Montrose and the Duke of Hamilton. At the same time he wrote to Montrose, appointing him a Knight and Companion of the Garter, sending him a copy of his letter to the Covenanters, and assuring him that 'we will not before, or during, the treaty do anything contrary to the power and authority which we have given you by our commission, nor consent to anything that may bring the least diminution to it'. Admitting that Montrose's efforts to obtain support on the continent had induced the Covenanters to reopen negotiations, Charles expressed the hope that 'your vigorous proceedings will be a good means to bring

16

them to such moderation in the said treaty as probably may produce an agreement and a present union of that whole nation in our service'. Montrose had permission to publish this letter if he wished; but another letter from Charles was private and promised Montrose his perpetual friendship: 'Nothing that can happen to me shall make me consent to anything to your prejudice. I conjure you therefore not to take alarm at any reports or messages from others, but to depend upon my kindness and to proceed in your business with your usual courage and alacrity. . . .'

Poverty was now becoming apparent in the clothes of the establishment and Charles decided that he must look as much like a king as possible when he met the Scottish deputation at Breda, his present garments being so soiled and spotted that he dared not be seen in them outside Jersey. He managed to borrow enough money to buy an embroidered dress with a belt and hat-band, together with a plain riding-suit and coat. Leaving his brother on the island, he landed in France towards the end of February '50, passed a night with the Bishop of Coutances, and went via Caen, St Lisieux and Rouen to Beauvais, where his mother awaited him. One form of Protestantism was the same as another to her, and she urged him to cancel Montrose's commission and arrange a treaty with the Scots, but not to take the Covenant. He ignored her advice, appearing to be apathetic on the subject. She did her utmost to gain his confidence, staying for a fortnight at Beauvais in the hope of winning him to her view; but she emerged from their last interview 'very red with anger', and on 16 March they parted coldly.

He continued on his way to Breda, being politely welcomed at every place except Ghent, where Charles, refusing the governor's offer of the castle, requested accommodation of the magistrates, who assured him that there were plenty of good inns in the place. Charles put up at the Golden Apple, peevishly declining to receive the magistrates, who were innocent of offence and sent a message that it was their habit to present visiting princes with two hogsheads of Rhenish wine, but that if he would rather have the equivalent in cash he was welcome to it. Charles considered this an additional affront, and his ill-temper resulted the following morning in a fierce altercation with the landlord over the size of his bill, closing with the heartfelt wish, fortunately delivered in English, that the innkeeper and all his fellow-countrymen would go to the devil. Having to pay for his lodgings was a serious matter for Charles, who was excessively hard-up. But an English merchant came to his rescue with a loan of £200, which enabled the royal cavalcade to reach Breda on 26 March 1650.

[3]

The Mad Pact

THE KING'S WISEST COUNSELLOR was Sir Edward Hyde,
who at this time was in Spain trying to collect money for the
cause. The moment he heard of the projected treaty he wrote that
the Scots would 'cozen' the King, and, when told that Charles
had nothing out of which he could be cozened, replied : 'When all
is lost, we may be cozened of our innocency.' We must take
Charles's age into account as well as his character in considering
what followed. When the negotiations were completed he was
just twenty, an age when most young men are about to enjoy life,
not to plunge into a maelstrom of lunacy. True, his youth had been
passed in the shadow of civil war, and he had already been
pestered by Puritans and Catholics ; but now for the first time he
was called upon to make a vital decision, himself the centre of a
tug of war between fanatical extremists. By nature he was much
more the grandson of his grandfather than the son of his father ;
and just as Henry IV of France had said that Paris was worth a
Mass, so Charles felt that his kingdom was worth the Covenant,
especially as he believed that once in power he could repudiate
what had been forced upon him.

But he did not give in without a fight. He had the patience of a
man not subject to feelings of indignation, but a patience trans-
cending that of Job was required to cope with the disputatiousness
of Scottish theologians, who harassed him continually in the
presence chamber, in his private rooms, in his bedchamber.
While waiting for news of Montrose, who had landed in the

19

Orkneys with a small force at about the period when Charles reached Breda, and still hopeful of a Royalist rising in England, the young King conciliated the Scottish commissioners as far as possible, though he once asked the ministers representing the Kirk how people knew the scriptures were the Word of God except by the testimony of the Church, an awkward question which lessened their confidence in him. They took their revenge by preaching to him on the sins of his father, his mother and himself; they upbraided him for dealing with the Irish Catholics and for encouraging Montrose; they urged him to sin no more and to humble himself before God for the crimes he had already committed; and as their sermons were very long and not very lucid, he was certainly made to atone for something or other.

The out-and-out Royalists wholly opposed the slightest concession to the Scots; the more moderate men, like the Duke of Hamilton and the Earl of Lauderdale, said that the King's mere presence in Scotland would rally the country and that the harsh terms of Kirk and Parliament would not be insisted upon; while his personal friends, the Duke of Buckingham and Lord Wilmot, advised him to accept all the conditions of the commissioners, as it would not dishonour him to give way in order to attain a position in which he could recover all in the end. Even the Prince of Orange urged him to make any promises demanded, and to keep as many or as few of them as he wished. Moreover the Marquis of Argyll, the most influential man in Scotland, recommended compliance. Charles knew that the Marquis was an opportunist who had been instrumental in selling the late King to the English Parliament. Clearly the man was now playing a double game, trying to keep on terms with Charles in the event of a Royalist reaction, with the Covenanters in case there was not. He offered his daughter, Lady Anne Campbell, in marriage to Charles, knowing that the union would please the Presbyterians; he promised that Montrose should not be sacrificed, that all the Scottish Royalists should be pardoned on laying down their arms;

and he implied that the warmth of the King's reception in Scotland would prevent the enforcement of the conditions. Such an opinion by a leading Presbyterian and Scotland's most powerful noble had a considerable effect on Charles, who, though he knew Argyll to be a trimmer, had reached a point where a little trimming seemed to be indispensable.

At the end of April, after much vacillation and backstairs diplomacy, Charles agreed to the terms of the commission in so far as Scotland was concerned; but he refused to break the Irish treaty. However, after listening to the insidious counsel of Argyll's representative, Lord Lothian, who assured him that when in Scotland he would not be subjected to the harsh terms of the agreement, and bearing in mind the opinions of his friends and the Prince of Orange that he could make and break as many promises as he liked, for what he was compelled to accept as an exile would be dishonourable to endorse as a ruler, Charles swallowed the Covenant and agreed the conditions. He still would not openly repudiate the Irish treaty, but gave one of the commissioners a private note in which he agreed to cancel all arrangements made with non-Covenanters and to persecute papists, should those actions be required of him by a free Scottish Parliament. Upon which he was officially invited to Scotland.

The moment it became known that he had surrendered to such preposterous demands, many of his best friends deserted him and all plans for a Royalist rising in England and Scotland were abandoned. Though it was perfectly clear to everyone except the insane promoters of the pact that Charles would never be able to establish Presbyterianism throughout England and Ireland, that he could not change his own religion and that of his family to order, that an oath to extirpate prelatists and papists would totally exclude him from the crown of England and Ireland should the rule of the Puritans come to an end, and that his recognition of the absolute supremacy of the Scottish Kirk and Parliament made him a puppet instead of a monarch, yet his pretended acceptance of conditions that could not possibly be realised was regarded by many of his loyal supporters as a betrayal of his kingship and his cause, and many felt that to win a crown he had winked at blackmail. Charles himself believed that the instant he set foot in Scotland there would be a Royalist rising throughout the realm, and he would be able to do as he liked. He regarded the representatives of Kirk and Parliament, not without reason, as mad, and he treated them as lunatics by soothing their whims. He probably considered his oath as a certificate to their insanity. It was not so regarded at the time, but he was in advance of his age.

To show that he had no intention of implementing the treaty, he wrote advising Ormonde to stop fighting and leave Ireland, adding that he would do nothing prejudicial to that country, for he did not consider any promises made to the Scots with regard to English and Irish affairs as binding. He sent the same advice to Montrose, promising to re-instate him as soon as possible, begging his forgiveness, and supplying him with money. The bearer of this letter, Sir William Fleming, was charged to explain to the Marquis all the circumstances of the case, and to approach Argyll's agent about the future employment of Montrose and the well-being of his followers. Before Fleming could leave Breda it occurred to Charles that the Covenanters would have it all their own way if Montrose's army were eliminated; so he countermanded Fleming's instructions and now counselled Montrose to act as he thought best, keeping his forces intact if he distrusted Argyll. But before Fleming could reach Scotland disaster had befallen Montrose.

The news of the treaty between Charles and the commissioners at Breda had taken the heart out of the Royalist movement in Scotland. The Highland clans held back, the Lowland lairds wavered; the promises of continental help had not been fulfilled; money was not forthcoming; and a boat carrying nearly a thousand men was lost. When Montrose disembarked a small force at Kirkwall in the Orkneys everything depended on a rising in Scotland. But he was disappointed, and his army was little more than two thousand strong when he marched south from the coast of Caithness, his cavalry consisting of a small party of personal friends. Penetrating Sutherland to the borders of Ross, he found that the Mackenzies would not join him without their absent chief, and circumstances compelled him to make for the east coast. At the end of April his army was routed at Corbiesdale by a strong force of Presbyterian cavalry. Badly wounded, Montrose escaped, taking refuge with Macleod of Assynt, who sold him to his enemies.

Argyll, who had the coward's loathing of a brave man and the time-server's resentment against an honest man, gloated over his prostrate foe.[1] The nobility and serenity of Montrose's bearing affected to tears the crowds that witnessed his humiliation, which was so borne as to make his judges look despicable, and stern Covenanters were impressed by his courage and dignity. Without trial Parliament sentenced him to be hanged and quartered, and the hangman wept without restraint as he discharged his hideous office. The last words of Montrose on the scaffold showed his true spirit: 'I blame no man, I complain of no man. They are instruments. God forgive them . . . I leave my soul to God, my service to my Prince, my goodwill to my friends, my love and charity to you all.'

Charles was ignorant of these events until about a fortnight after the murder of his loyal lieutenant, and to the annoyance of the Scottish ministers at Breda he passed much of his time at balls, dancing until the dawn. He further aggravated them by attending the Church of England service of Holy Communion. When he heard of the battle of Corbiesdale and the sacrifice of Montrose, he wrote to the Marquis's son, addressing him by the title that Parliament had repudiated and promising to 'provide for your subsistence with that affection you have reason to expect from your affectionate friend, Charles R.' Though the fate of Montrose

1. Later attempts to whiten Argyll's character have been made, but they won't wash. As the most influential man in Scotland, he could easily have saved Montrose, but he was void of chivalry and charity.

had been determined by the treaty of Breda, it is improbable that Charles felt himself to be the chief cause of the tragedy, as he was kept in ignorance of the utter inadequacy of the Royalist invasion and believed that the Highland clans would rally to the great leader who had led them to victory so often in the past. In his indignation over the execution of Montrose he declared that he would not sail for Scotland, but he calmed down after hearing what Lothian and the Prince of Orange had to say and agreed to go in a Dutch warship.

Meanwhile the Scottish Parliament, no longer afraid of Montrose, ordered their commissioners at Breda to exact more stringent terms. Many of the King's friends who were suspected of more loyalty to him than to the Covenant would not be permitted to land in Scotland; the Irish treaty was to be publicly broken, the Roman Catholic religion prohibited, the Covenant enforced throughout the realm, and all who infringed it were to be banished. Furthermore the Scots would make no efforts to restore Charles to the English throne unless they felt it to be necessary, while the promotion of his personal wishes, as well as the promises he had already received, were to depend on his obedience to Kirk and Parliament. Convinced that these new instructions would prevent the King from sailing, Lothian declined to impart them; but the other commissioners were more thorough, tracked down Charles from Breda to the port of departure and went on board his vessel. They did not break the news to him until the boat had sailed and owing to the wind was anchored off Heligoland. He promptly rejected the latest instalment of lunacy, saying he would land in Denmark and not proceed to Scotland on such terms. The argument continued until the Scottish coast came into view. The King declared that the laws of the Long Parliament, which had established Presbyterianism in England, were illegal because they had been passed without the royal assent, and that by signing the articles now proposed he would be violating the real laws of England. But the commissioners wore him down and bored him into acceptance, his action resembling that of a pauper compelled to sign a cheque for a million pounds.

Two of the men responsible for his taking the oath which he could never discharge were later to regret their part in the affair. One of them, a minister named John Livingstone, said that the real guilt lay with the Kirk and Parliament. The other, Alexander Jaffray, made an entry in his diary: 'We did both sinfully entangle and engage the nation, ourselves, and that poor young Prince to whom we were sent, making him sign and swear a Covenant which we knew from clear and demonstrable reasons that he hated in his heart; yet, finding that upon these terms only he could be admitted to rule over us, all other means having then failed him, he sinfully complied with what we, most sinfully, pressed upon him . . . In this he was not so constant to his principles as his father, but his strait and our guiltiness was the greater.'

It would have saved Charles a great deal of future anguish if a Scottish mist had not screened his vessel and prevented its capture by four ships of the English Parliament which sailed out of the Spey as he sailed into it. Instead, he landed at Garmouth on 24 June 1650, and plunged into the fog of Scottish theology.

[4]

An Asylum

THE PEOPLE SEEMED PLEASED at the sight of Charles and
gave him an enthusiastic welcome. Probably they were already
tired of hearing about God and felt that the King was an agreeable
substitute. But he was not permitted to enjoy his popularity. He
was at once surrounded by Argyll's minions and rushed off to the
Bog of Gicht (afterwards Gordon Castle, near Fochabers) then
garrisoned by Parliament. Here some of his companions, notably
the Duke of Hamilton, were ordered by the authorities to leave
him, as they were suspected of feelings hostile to the Covenant.
He then proceeded to Aberdeen, and as they crossed the river
Ury he remarked that the scene recalled his 'dear England'. The
citizens of Aberdeen received him with jubilation and bonfires,
and the magistrates in a fit of loyalty paid all his expenses and
gave him £1500, an act which was reprobated by Parliament in
a command that other towns should refrain from similar bene-
factions. It may be doubted whether Charles appreciated these
outward manifestations of joy, for the view from his lodgings
near the Tolbooth, perhaps chosen for the purpose, included a
dismembered part of Montrose's body, stuck up on the town
port. What he felt may be guessed but what he said has not been
recorded, none of Argyll's spies having overheard it. Leaving
Aberdeen he stayed a night at Dunottar Castle, two nights at
Kinnaird House, and three at Dudhope Castle, from which he
entered Dundee, being warmly welcomed and hospitably entertained by the provost and burgesses. At St Andrews he was made

26

to realise that life had its less diverting aspects, being forced to listen to a long oration in Latin, followed by a long sermon in Scottish. Pausing on the way at Cupar, where he patiently attended to another speech, he arrived at his royal residence, Falkland, early in July.

As usual the Marquis of Argyll was playing a cunning and dishonest game. He wanted to keep in with the King in case the country's sympathies suddenly placed Charles in a commanding position; and he wanted to keep in with Kirk and Parliament in case they maintained their power. In effect he became the King's gaoler, surrounding him with rigid Covenanters who preached at him and spied upon him, placing sentinels around his house, and not permitting him to converse freely with his friends, nearly all of whom were banished from his presence. But to outward appearance Argyll played the submissive courtier, anxious above everything to honour his master and treat him with all due ceremony, appointed his son Lord Lorne as Captain of the Royal Bodyguard, instructing him to gratify Charles in any way possible, and doing his utmost to strengthen his own position by pressing the political advantage of a marriage between his daughter and the King, who managed to evade an awkward engagement by saying that he must write to obtain the consent of his mother. The one intimate friend who was permitted to stay with Charles was the Duke of Buckingham, who curried favour with Argyll by assuring the King that his one hope was to rely wholly on the Marquis's loyal support. The rest of the royal party that had landed in Scotland were either sent out of the country or allowed to remain at some distance from the Court until their good behaviour warranted access thereto.

Apart from the fun of matching his wits against Argyll's, the King's life at Falkland was pretty gloomy. He had to attend numerous sermons, prayers and theological disquisitions of great length, when the crimes of his parents as well as his own were harshly censured and the godliness of the Covenant was passionately eulogised. Once he endured six sermons in succession, clamorous enough to keep him awake if he had dared to close his eyes; but his looks and gestures were closely noted. He was not allowed to walk abroad on Sundays, and received ministerial reproof if he smiled on the Sabbath. Card-playing and dancing were forbidden; and indeed everyday life in Scotland was a fairly good training for the Hell to which its non-Covenanting inhabitants were consigned. Argyll pretended to be out of sympathy with such domestic persecution, and he advised Charles to 'please these madmen for the present', as he would be able to shake off their yoke when he got to England. Charles was chiefly upset by the enforced absence of his companions, called 'malignants' by the Covenanters, in particular the Duke of Hamilton, to whom he wrote: 'Pray let all your friends know how sensible I am of their sufferings, knowing it is only for my sake, and that I am very much grieved that I am not in a better condition to let them see it; but I hope mine will mend, and then I am sure theirs shall be better.' Unpleasant though his experiences were, Charles turned them to good purpose in after years, as they supplied him with some of his funniest anecdotes.

Meanwhile the presence of a king in Scotland was agitating the Commonwealth of England, and stern measures were taken against anyone suspected of Royalist sympathies. An army was sent north under the command of Cromwell, who issued a proclamation from Berwick in which the Scots were urged to abandon the belief that all religion was 'wrapped up' in the Covenant and bitterly reproached for their dealings with Charles Stuart, whose sympathy with the Pope of Rome was notorious, etc., etc. A Scottish army under General David Leslie prepared to meet the invaders, and the usual appeals to Heaven were sent up by the opposing forces, each side assuming itself favoured by the Almighty. While Cromwell was crossing the border Charles was paying visits. Leaving Falkland for Perth towards the end of July, he received the freedom of the town, ate a heavy meal, and moved on to Dunfermline, where he stayed with the Earl thereof and met Anne Murray who had assisted his brother James to escape from England. On arrival at Stirling he received an invitation to visit the army, and in a state of great excitement dashed off to Leith against the advice of his wary counsellors, being welcomed by the soldiers in a manner that betrayed too much loyalty for the stomachs of stern Parliamentarians and inflexible Presbyterians.

The Scottish army of about 26,000 men under Leslie stood on the defensive between Edinburgh and Leith, its left wing protected by Edinburgh Castle, its right by a fortified position at Leith, its centre by a deep trench between the two, its rear by the river Forth, while outposts were on Arthur's Seat, Salisbury Craigs and the Calton Hill. The English army of some 16,000 men under Cromwell occupied Musselburgh, Duddingstone and Corstorphine, its supplies coming by sea, the ships unloading in the Forth. In August Cromwell was encamped on the Braid Hills, where he waited for a while, hoping that the Scots would rather make peace than risk an attack on their position, and encouraging the ministers of the Kirk with the suggestion: 'I beseech you, in the bowels of Jesus Christ, think it possible you *may* be mistaken.'

The King's popularity with the troops, again manifested when he entered Edinburgh, annoyed the ministers, and he was ordered back to Dunfermline on the plea that the men neglected their duties to gather around him. Closely watched, he could scarcely write letters to his friends, but he was able to get an uncensored line through to the Duke of Hamilton: 'The soldiers were so kind to me upon my first coming that the next day after the commission of the Kirk desired me to retire out of the army, pretending it was for the safety of my person; but indeed it was for fear that I should get too great an interest with the soldiers.' The ministers asserted that the army contained many 'wicked and profane' men who had served under the late King, and that the one hope of overcoming their enemies was to fight 'with a handful of elect and godly people rather than with mighty arms loaden with sin'. They therefore insisted on a great purge of 'malignants', the expulsion of whom was apparently essential to appease God and obtain the divine assistance; and as a consequence nearly a hundred officers who had fought well under Charles I and Montrose, and over three thousand men, were removed from the army, which was thus deprived of its best fighting elements.

Even so the commissioners were not satisfied that they had done everything possible for the Almighty, and they insisted that Charles should sign a declaration acknowledging his own sins and those of his father and mother, announcing his abhorrence of popery, prelacy and idolatry, and affirming his unqualified loyalty to the Covenant and obedience to its ministers. At first he refused to avow this latest promulgation of idiocy, saying that he would never again be able to look his mother in the face. But he was blackmailed into signing it by the threat that if he refused he would be handed over to Cromwell. Advised by Argyll to calm the madmen and rescind the declaration as soon as he could safely do so, he yielded; and as a sop to soothe his feelings the crown and sceptre were brought from Stirling, intimating that now he had become a puppet of the Kirk he would shortly be crowned as King. But he did not trust these godly men, and secretly arranged for a fishing smack to be in readiness at Montrose in case he found it prudent to leave Scotland suddenly. The merciless mental anguish to which he had been subjected would have turned a more acidulous nature into a Satanist; but Charles was a charitable young man, and all he said at the time was that 'it has done me a great deal of good, for nothing could have confirmed me more to the Church of England than being here and seeing their hypocrisy'.

While a ruffled Deity was being propitiated by his crazy ministers in the manner just described, Cromwell was trying to engage the Scottish army in open conflict. Leslie was a cautious warrior and kept securely within his lines; but Cromwell had not visited Edinburgh to enjoy the scenery, and as he was having difficulty in obtaining supplies he decided to fall back on Dunbar, feeling sure that Leslie would follow him. This was exactly what happened. Oliver wished the enemy to believe that he had been cornered at Dunbar, because he allowed them to surround him on the Lammermuir hills and even to cut off his retreat to England by holding the pass at Cockburnspath. He had an acute knowledge of human nature, especially of the religious variety, and he felt convinced that if the Presbyterian fanatics thought he would escape them by sea they would throw security to the winds, rush from their excellent position on the Lammermuir heights, and wreak their vengeance on these English breakers of the Covenant. Acting on their belief that he was trapped, they were entrapped by him. The ministers forced Leslie's hand, and against his judgment he descended to the low ground on 2 September. Cromwell wisely refrained from immediate action, but spent the night in careful preparation for frontal gun-fire and a flank assault by cavalry the moment dawn broke. He had no difficulty whatever in disposing of this sanctimonious mob of half-wits, his own brand of sanctimony being subservient to his military genius, and in about an hour an army nearly twice the size of his was put to the sword or captured, his own losses being two officers and some fifty men. At a blow southern Scotland was at his mercy. Edinburgh and Leith were taken, Glasgow fell in a few weeks, his horses were stabled in the kirks, and a new form of fire-eating gospel was thundered from Presbyterian pulpits. Edinburgh Castle held out until 24 December, but as it was merely a question of starving the garrison into submission Cromwell was too intelligent to waste much energy in attacking it. Describing the battle of Dunbar in his dispatch to the Speaker of the English Parliament, Cromwell declared: 'It is easy to see the Lord has done this.' And as the slaughter of the flying foe was as savage as many acts of butchery approved by Jehovah in the Old Testament, we can appreciate his point of view.

The King received news of the battle at Perth, and his feelings must have been mixed. On the one hand the Covenanters were thrashed, which was all to the good; on the other a victory had been won by the man chiefly responsible for his father's death and his present uncomfortable position. He experienced a glow of satisfaction that the canting humbugs who had made his life a misery had got their deserts, but he was wary enough to pretend a sorrow he could not feel and write a letter of condolence to Parliament in the sort of snivelling style that he knew would appeal to them. Needless to say, the Covenanters attributed their defeat at Dunbar to the King, because he had not fully repented the sins of his family, nor purged his Court of 'malignants'. This attitude annoyed some of their more moderate Presbyterian brethren and stimulated a movement favourable to Charles in various parts of the country. The men who had been purged from the army before the battle, together with many Highland royalists and a number of partisans in the eastern counties, made a formidable group; and Charles, while promising a dukedom and other favours to Argyll, and adopting a repentant attitude to the Covenanting authorities, was quietly arranging with his sympathisers to rescue him from Campbells and Kirk. Spied upon by the former, persecuted by the latter, and living constantly in dread of being sold to Cromwell by the Covenanters, he listened eagerly to optimistic reports from his personal adherents; and when he heard from his banished physician, Dr Alexander Fraser, that he could depend on a loyal force of sixty nobles, a thousand gentlemen and ten thousand followers, he made up his mind to join them in Fife on 3 October. In his absence Perth was to be captured by Highlanders, after which he would issue a proclamation explaining his ill-treatment by Argyll and Parliament, when it was hoped that the gentry and a large part of Leslie's newly-recruited force would come over to him.

The plan might have succeeded but for the treachery of the King's intimate friend, the Duke of Buckingham, who, believing that his future security depended upon Argyll, had been steadily gaining the favour and confidence of that nobleman. During a ride together on 3 October the King told Buckingham of his plans. Excusing himself, Buckingham promptly rode back to Perth and confided in Lord Wilmot. They decided to argue the King out of his design, and that evening a violent dispute took place with their monarch, who, tired and out of heart, at length agreed to drop the business. But to 'make assurance double sure' they told Argyll of the project, and he passed the information on to Parliament, the consequence being that the King's Horse Guards were cashiered and all the 'malignants' who had found their way back to the Court were given twenty days to quit the kingdom. Hearing from the Royalist leaders that their plans were too far advanced for withdrawal, and learning that Parliament would not forgive their action, Charles decided to join them, and after dinner on 4 October he rode off without any change of apparel, as if he were taking his normal daily exercise, ferried across the Tay, and arrived at Lord Dudhope's house near Dundee that afternoon. Advised to return, he declined to do so, and went on with a body-guard of eighty Highlanders as far as Clova in the Grampian Hills, where nightfall and weariness overcame the party, which had covered forty-two miles almost without a stop. Meanwhile Parliament had dispatched Colonel Montgomery in pursuit, and when that officer arrived at Clova he found the King in a dirty little room and ill at ease because he had not been joined by the promised force. An agitated debate took place. Charles said that his flight had been caused by Parliament's intention to hand him over to Cromwell. Montgomery denied the intention and vigor-ously protested his own loyalty. Dudhope urged a continuance of the flight, saying that a large force had collected in the hills a few miles off. Charles was perplexed, torn this way and that. But his mind was made up for him by the arrival of Montgomery's soldiers, and he was compelled to return, spending the night of the 5th at Huntly Castle. The next day he received a friendly and cautious letter from the committee of Kirk and State, asking him as a favour to return to Perth and telling him that he could hence-forth choose his place of residence.

This escapade, known to history as 'The Start', frightened Parliament into lenience. Charles was at last invited to join the Council and take a part in public affairs. In return for this con-cession he expressed regret for his recent action, pretended that he had been misled by wicked men, swore that he had never intended to leave, and 'trusted in God it would be a lesson to him all the days of his life'. The lesson he had been taught was that independent action often brings beneficial results, but he did not think it necessary to mention this. Asserting himself at once, he declined to order his supporters to lay down their arms until he was assured that they would not be penalised, and an Act of Indemnity was duly passed on 12 October. In spite of the relief felt by the Kirk and State committee, because they were no longer endangered by a Highland army of Scottish Royalists in addition to a Lowland army of English sectaries, Charles could not dodge the reproofs and sermons of sedulous Covenanters, who lectured him as if he had been a naughty boy playing truant. Like the naughty boy, he lied like a trooper over the whole affair, mendacity being the only answer to hypocrisy.

At the end of October there were four armies in Scotland. The centre of the country was occupied by a Presbyterian army of between ten and twenty thousand men under Leslie. This was for the King and the Covenant. The south of the country was held by an English army of much the same number under Cromwell. This was against both King and Covenant. The north was in the hands of an episcopal army of ten thousand under General Sir Thomas Middleton. This was for the King and against the Covenant. The west was dominated by a body of extremists under Colonel Gilbert Ker. This was for the Covenant and against the King. By the close of the year, the Highland army had joined up with Leslie on patriotic grounds, after its members had pretended to accept the Covenant; while Ker's fanatical force in the west had been destroyed by Cromwellian troops under General Lambert.

Following a number of public oaths, prayers, accusations, remonstrances, resolutions, excommunications, exhortations, repentances, and all the other afflictions quite inseparable from religious controversy, it seemed advisable in the interest of national cohesion that Charles should be crowned, and 1 January 1651 was fixed for the ceremony, to be preceded a few days earlier by a solemn fast for 'the sins of the King's family'. Charles gravely went through the process of mourning in public for the crimes of his father and grandfather, afterwards making the comment: 'I think I must repent, too, that ever I was born.' The coronation was solemnised at Scone, the anointment being left out as savouring of popery, prelacy and antichrist, and for the same reason the monarch was crowned by a layman, Argyll. The sermon was preached by the Moderator of the Kirk's General Assembly, Robert Douglas, whose remarks on the sins of Charles and his ancestors were far from moderate. The Covenants were read, the King swearing his approbation thereof and appending his signature to the oath. Much praying accompanied the holy farce, and it was observed that Charles went through the performance 'very seriously and devoutly'.

It may seem curious that Cromwell, at Edinburgh, made no considerable effort to interfere with the coronation; but he was far-sighted enough to await his chance in patience, and he must have guessed that Charles would eventually take an army into England, where it could be dispersed under more favourable conditions. Oliver had written to his wife, the day after the battle of Dunbar: 'I grow an old man and feel infirmities of age marvellously stealing upon me.' He was then in his fifty-second year and had no doubt strained his physique following the victory by singing psalms, pursuing fugitives, and cutting them down over eight miles of rough country. Perhaps as a consequence of this, with a winter at Edinburgh thrown in, he was unwell from February to June '51 and left the business of subduing southern Scotland to his lieutenants, who occupied nearly every town and fortress in the Lowlands.

While the English were making themselves comfortable in the south of Scotland, Charles was doing his utmost to unite the Scots in defence of their land. His chief job at the moment was not to fight Cromwell but to reconcile the warring elements, Cavalier and Covenanter, in his own force. The Scots fought one another for the sake of God far more enthusiastically than they fought the

English for the sake of their country. To those who had known him in the past, Charles seemed to become a different man after his coronation. He toured the midlands of Scotland, inspecting passes, fords, castles, fortifications, and putting new heart into the levies that were being raised in every county. He was a first-class recruiting-officer, his mere presence causing men of all sorts to join the army, which soon consisted of fanatical as well as moderate Covenanters, of those who hated the 'malignants' and those who sympathised with them. Cromwell quickly informed himself of the young man's doings and described him as 'very active and intelligent'. He never seemed to tire, rising early every morning and spending the day in the saddle, travelling from one town to another, settling disputes, addressing the soldiers, super-intending defences, compelling a Presbyterian like Leslie to work in harmony with a Royalist like Middleton, and displaying an ability and a tact with which no one had previously credited him. As his influence steadily increased, Argyll's as steadily decreased, and the tone of the sermons which he still had to endure became less minatory. His twenty-first birthday occurred on 29 May and was celebrated by the Scots with feasts, bonfires and peals of ordnance. By that time he had collected an army of twenty thousand men, and was in a position to do what he wanted.

In June his forces were centred on Stirling, while Cromwell's were mostly encamped on the Pentland Hills, though some were to the south of the royal army's headquarters. Charles was advised to be content with that portion of Scotland which he held; but his eyes were fixed on England, and he had been so miserable in Scotland that nothing could induce him to remain there longer than was absolutely necessary. He afterwards complained that no women were to be seen in Scotland, where the barbarism of the men was such that they thought it a sin to listen to the violin, and where he had been bullied and browbeaten and bored to an extent that his thoughts and actions became meaningless. Oddly enough Cromwell too was anxious that Charles should leave Scotland for England, and the moment Oliver's indisposition enabled him to take the field he did everything in his power to tempt the King in that direction. After making a series of feints in the neighbourhood of Stirling, the English commander crossed the Forth, marched through Fife, and captured Perth, thus cutting off the northern portion of the royal army under Middleton, preventing supplies from reaching the main army under Leslie at Stirling, and leaving the south open to the King.

Charles now had to take a definite course one way or another. He could turn and fight Cromwell in Scotland, or retire to the western Highlands, or march straight into England, the road having been cunningly left clear by Cromwell, who of course acted solely on clear instructions from the Deity: 'After our waiting upon the Lord, and not knowing what course to take, for indeed we know nothing but what God pleaseth to teach us of his great mercy, *we were directed*,' etc., etc. Argyll was cute enough to spot the danger of invading England, and on perceiving that his reasons were unacceptable he retired from public life. But Charles was panting for England almost as fervently as he was gasping to get out of Scotland, and on 31 July 1651 he set forth at the head of his army on the great adventure.

[5]

Escape

IT WAS OUT OF THE FRYING-PAN into the fire, but Charles would have preferred total destruction to slow torture. Not that he thought himself faced with such an alternative. He believed that England was still Royalist at heart, that risings in his favour would take place all over the country, and his upbringing had not helped him to form an accurate estimate of Cromwell's genius. For that matter it is common even now for military experts and historians to labour under the same disability, dislike of the man influencing their opinion of the general. Putting aside his peculiar gifts as a strategist and tactician, the notable points to remember about Cromwell are that he never lost a battle, that he was always matched against troops as zealous as his own, that his main victories were won against his own countrymen in their own country, not against mercenaries and half-hearted foreign conscripts, and that unlike nearly every other self-made absolute ruler in history he died in power and in bed. We need not admire Cromwell as a human being to recognise his greatness as a leader, nor regard him as a hero on account of his achievement as a soldier. Matched against him, the army of Charles had about as much chance of survival as an iceberg on the equator. Cromwell's Ironsides were the toughest troops in history. Dragooned into discipline, fired by fanaticism, and led by a man whose brilliance as a commander was backed by unflinching personal bravery, they would probably have gone through Caesar's Tenth Legion and Napoleon's Old Guard like a bradawl through butter. If every

Royalist in England had risen to fight for Charles, the result would have been the same. But many of them had lost their enthusiasm for the King because he had accepted the Covenant; some felt patriotically opposed to the invasion of their country by a Scottish army; while others had suffered enough at the hands of Parliament and knew what would happen with Cromwell in the field against them. It was nearly a decade of government by Puritans, closed by the death of a dictator, before England was ready for the son of Charles I. Nevertheless, though defeat was a foregone conclusion, the whole episode is exceptionally interesting to the biographer of Charles because it brought out certain salient features of his character and ended with an adventure which helped to mould his nature in durable form, making him the most sensible and popular of monarchs.

Not wanting to be encumbered with lukewarm troops, Charles practically echoed a sentiment given by Shakespeare to Henry V, who wished his army to be told

> That he which hath no stomach to this fight,
> Let him depart . . .
> We would not die in that man's company
> That fears his fellowship to die with us.

Many took Charles at his word and stayed behind; many more deserted before reaching the border; and a fortnight after the royal forces commenced their march to the south, the town of Stirling surrendered to General Monk. When Charles entered England his following had been reduced to about nine thousand foot and four thousand horse. At Woodhouse, on the border, he issued a proclamation of 'general pardon and oblivion to all his loving subjects' who would return to the obedience they owed to their lawful King, excepting only those who had voted for the murder of his father: Cromwell, Henry Ireton, John Bradshaw and others. He promised that 'this service being done, the Scotch army should quietly retire' and all armies be disbanded. A copy of the proclamation, sent to the Lord Mayor of London, was burnt by the hangman, and the English Parliament countered it with a declaration that Charles Stuart, his agents and abettors, were 'traitors, rebels, and public enemies'. Having plundered and preached its way south, the royal army reached Rokeby, where Charles was proclaimed King to the accompaniment of trumpets, drums and cannonades, a ceremony that was frequently repeated on the march. The town of Carlisle refused to surrender, but Charles had no time to pause and make the governor reconsider his decision. They passed through Penrith, Appleby and Kendal, but there were few signs that the English were glad to see them. Charles did his utmost to check the fanaticism and pillaging of his followers; but while the combination of religion and robbery irritated the English, the restraint on both enforced by the King discouraged the Scots, many of whom returned to their native land.

The Duke of Buckingham believed that the lack of enthusiasm in England was due to the refusal of the gentry to serve under Leslie, a Scottish general. Charles wanted to know who could take his place. Buckingham expressed his willingness to do so. Charles assumed he was joking. Buckingham said he was serious. But, objected Charles, the other was much too young for the job; to which the Duke rejoined that Henry IV of France had won a victory when younger than himself. The debate was closed by Charles, who claimed that the Commander-in-Chief was the King. Buckingham then sulked and refused to attend future meetings of the Council. There is little doubt that Leslie was incompetent and despondent, but if he had been removed from the command his troops would have refused to serve under a leader suspected of mere lip-service to the Covenant.

Meanwhile Cromwell, having informed a nervous Parliament that the situation was well in hand, sent some cavalry under Lambert to follow on the heels of the royal army, and another troop of horse under Harrison to hover on its eastern flank. The main force under Oliver moved southwards at a more leisurely rate, passing through Newcastle, Ripon, Doncaster, Mansfield and Nottingham. At Warrington the crossing of the Mersey by the royal army was disputed by Lambert and Harrison, but they were pushed back, or perhaps politely gave way, and Charles was the first man across the quickly-repaired bridge. At Stoke the King was reinforced by a small body under the Earl of Derby, and a march on London was advocated by the Duke of Hamilton. But Leslie gloomily opposed this, being of opinion that his men would not fight. Charles tried to cheer him up, as it was clearly useless to adopt any plan of which he disapproved, because his followers still formed the main part of the army and his depression would quickly be reflected by their inaction.

Having decided for the present to keep in the counties bordering on Wales, Charles continued his march, sending Derby into Lancashire to rouse the people for the King. But the Presbyterians in that county insisted that Derby should take the Covenant and renounce his Catholic associates. He refused, saying that 'if I perish, I perish, but if my master perish the blood of another Prince and all the ensuing miseries of this kingdom will be at your doors'. He then determined to fight with the small force at his disposal, some fifteen hundred men. Defeated and himself wounded at Wigan, he escaped to Boscobel, where he was hidden by the family of Penderel and soon managed to rejoin the royal army at Worcester.

On his way to that city Charles demanded the surrender of Shrewsbury, which was refused in a letter addressed to 'The Commander-in-Chief of the Scottish army', a designation which expressed the attitude of many who would otherwise have sympathised with the King's cause. The governor of Chirk Castle took no notice of the summons to surrender and seized his Majesty's messenger, who was subsequently hanged. Such dispiriting episodes were partly recompensed by the reception of Charles at Worcester, where a thoroughly Royalist population gave him a welcome that temporarily obliterated what had gone before. His soldiers were exhausted after their march of twenty-three days, and a halt was imperative. Moreover Cromwell now blocked the way to London, and the King's one hope was that his ranks would be swelled by the gentry of the surrounding districts; but the response to his appeal was disheartening.

He promptly took measures to defend the city against the attack which could not be long delayed with Oliver in the vicinity. The fortifications having been destroyed in the Civil War, he supervised the construction of earthworks, managed to repair a fort, and ordered the partial destruction of the bridge over the Severn at Upton, posting three hundred men there. He then stationed a large force at Powick bridge on the Teme, and assembled the remainder of his army to the south-west of the city in the vertex of the triangle formed by the junction of the Teme and Severn. He also enjoyed a short respite from Presbyterianism by attending divine service in the cathedral.

On 24 August Cromwell arrived at Warwick, where Lambert and Harrison joined him, and when he reached Evesham his force consisted of twenty-eight thousand men. He ordered his generals Lambert and Fleetwood to cross the Severn and cut off the Royalists from Wales. Owing to negligence, no sentinel had been placed at the partly-broken bridge of Upton, and Lambert managed to get his troops over the river by a single plank left for pedestrians. The Royalists were surprised and compelled to retreat towards Worcester. The bridge was repaired, and eleven thousand of Lambert's men were soon across it. But they were still confronted by the River Teme, and it was necessary to build a bridge of boats. While they were doing so, Cromwell arrived at Perrywood, a mile to the south-east of the city. Charles, hoping to surprise him, attacked by night with twelve hundred men, their shirts over their armour to distinguish them from their foes in the dark. But Cromwell was not the man to be caught napping; the Royalists were driven back with some loss; and Oliver dispatched a thousand men to construct a bridge over the Severn a mile below the city.

Early in the morning of 3 September, the anniversary of the

battle of Dunbar, Charles held a council of war on the top of the cathedral tower, where they had a good view of Oliver's dispositions. The chief danger spots were the bridge being made over the Severn and the bridge spanning the Teme. Charles visited both, leaving three hundred men to oppose the Severn passage and two thousand to hold the attack across the Teme. But Cromwell's guns, and lack of ammunition on the King's side, compelled the abandonment of both positions; the bridges were crossed, and with the desperation of condemned men the Royalists fought every foot of the way back to the city gate. Charles took instant advantage of Cromwell's presence on the western side of the river by leading a force of Cavaliers against the Parliamentary troops on the eastern side, and charging them with such energy that they gave way. Cromwell at once recrossed the river with reinforcements and drove the Royalists back to the city. It was a fierce engagement, during which the Duke of Hamilton was mortally wounded; and though nothing could have successfully resisted Cromwell, the casualties would have been far less severe, the retreat less ignominious, if Leslie had come to the King's assistance with three thousand Scottish horse. But Leslie felt convinced that his men would not fight, and he was not the sort of leader to enhearten his followers. Charles had one or two horses shot under him and got back with difficulty to Sudbury gate, where a capsized ammunition wagon barred the way. He managed to struggle through the wheels, flung off his armour in Friars Street, mounted a fresh horse, and rode through the city exhorting officers and men to put up a fight. But the Scots, overcome by theological controversy, were in no mood for physical exertion, and Leslie seemed dazed. 'I had rather you would shoot me than keep me alive to see the consequences of this fatal day!' cried Charles. But they were better at preaching than killing, and Leslie's horsemen maintained their attitude of malevolent neutrality.

Having reduced Fort Royal, which protected Worcester on the east, Cromwell put its garrison of fifteen hundred Scots to the sword and turned its guns on the city. The gates were then stormed, and at about six in the evening the Ironsides forced their way in. When Cromwell's soldiers entered a city at one gate, the wisest course for their opponents to pursue was to leave it by another; but on this occasion the plight of those within the walls was made more unhappy by the entry of the victors from two sides, east and west. A frightful hand-to-hand and house-to-house conflict took place, panic making the Royalist soldiers mistake friends for foes. Soon the streets were a shambles, echoing with screams and groans, slippery with blood. Charles fought with the rest, and one of his followers testified that 'a braver Prince never lived, having in the day of the fight hazarded his person much more than any officer in his army'. But with the coming of night he knew that further resistance was futile, and taking advantage of the plundering proclivities of the victorious troops he traversed the city by unfrequented lanes, passing through St Martin's gate in the company of Leslie and his three thousand horsemen. They had ridden in some confusion for half a mile when Charles pulled up at Barbon's Bridge with the intention of rallying the troop for a final charge to victory or death. But Wilmot pointed out that the men had caught the spirit of their leader, and Charles had to admit that the same soldiers who had deserted him when in good order were not likely to fight for him in defeat. So for the sake of safety he determined to part from them. This was easier to resolve than to accomplish, and he said : 'Though I could not get them to stand by me against the enemy, I could not get rid of them now I had a mind to it.' However he contrived at last to quit their company.

Cromwell called the battle of Worcester 'as stiff a contest for four or five hours as I have ever seen . . . Indeed it was a stiff business . . . The dimensions of this mercy are above my thoughts. It is, for aught I know, a crowning mercy'. Those of the King's forces who were not killed were captured, and many of the Scots were sold as slaves for transportation to the American planta-tions, where perhaps they had less time for argument about the nature of God. The Earl of Derby was captured and executed, saying just before his death that Charles was 'the most godly, virtuous, valiant, and most discreet King that I know lives this day'. Buckingham escaped to Scotland, thence to France. Leslie and his troop were soon taken as they made their way north, and Leslie himself was imprisoned in the Tower of London until the Restoration. The subjugation of Scotland followed the taking of Dundee by General Monk, who massacred the entire population, men, women and children, possibly because he did not wish to be thought less zealous in the Lord's work than Cromwell had been in Ireland. Argyll of course cringed to the conquerors.

On the whole God's 'crowning mercy' was more apparent to the English Puritans than to the Scottish Presbyterians.

[6]

The Flight

NO MONARCH IN HISTORY, born in the purple, has had so good a lesson in democracy as Charles, and it is doubtful if any other would have profited as much as he did from such a lesson. His natural kindliness was deepened, his liberality of temperament broadened, by his experiences as a fugitive and an exile. Under circumstances of extreme danger, acute discomfort, corroding poverty, persecution and neglect, his inborn sympathy, geniality and mildness of character were untouched by rancour or resentment and became more pronounced when he emerged from the ordeal; though his disposition suffered from the obverse of these qualities, indolence and compliance.

The most curious aspect of his escape from England after the battle of Worcester was that, with all the apparent vigilance of his pursuers, he was able to make it. His height, his appearance, were well known; a full description of him was circulated throughout the country, and no disguise could sufficiently transform him; the majority of the population were keeping a sharp look-out for him; Cromwell's espionage system was extremely efficient; every Royalist sympathiser was carefully watched: yet Charles managed to mix with and pass through numbers of Parliamentary soldiers, to stop at inns and ride through towns and villages, without receiving much more than a cursory glance or a casual query. A thousand pounds was offered by Parliament for his capture, and the Royalists were outraged that the value of their King was estimated at so niggardly a figure; but, taken with the circumstances already noticed, this relatively small sum suggests that Parliament was not over-anxious to have the blood of another Stuart king on its conscience. As Cromwell always declared his actions to be in harmony with the will of the Lord, it cannot be doubted that if Charles had fallen into his hands the Lord would have been mightily perplexed, for Parliament could not possibly have evaded the responsibility it had usurped: Charles would have had to be executed as a traitor to the Commonwealth, and the deed would have shaken the State to its foundations.

It is amusing to speculate on what might have happened if a zealous army officer had reported the apprehension of the King to Cromwell and claimed the reward. He might have been promptly offered double that amount to escort Charles safely to the coast, arrange the necessary transport to France, and keep his mouth shut on pain of death ; or he might have been compelled to witness Noll praying and struggling to get into tune with the Almighty, after which the too-ardent officer might have left the General's presence under an armed guard. But such speculations are for the dramatist, not the biographer, who is merely entitled to wonder whether the authorities took every possible precaution to prevent Charles from leaving England. Those who succoured him were certainly in grave danger, and quite a few of them suffered for it, but all willingly ran the risks of torture, imprisonment, death and ruin; while the chance of making a thousand pounds must have sorely tempted the poorer people who were in the secret or suspected it.

When Charles had managed to disencumber himself of Leslie's horsemen, by the simple process of leaving them on the main road to the north and following a track to the right with his friends, he confided in Lord Wilmot that he wished to reach London before the result of the battle was known there. They passed through Ombersley towards Hartlebury, and leaving Kidderminster on their left they arrived at Kinver Heath. On the Earl of Derby's suggestion they made for Boscobel, where he had lain concealed before joining the King at Worcester, a native of those parts, Charles Giffard, acting as guide along with a servant, Francis Yates, who was afterwards hanged for refusing to confess where he had left the King. They passed quietly through Stourbridge in the darkness, stopped at an inn for ale and bread two miles farther on, and arrived at the old Cistercian convent of Whiteladies at the break of day. They were admitted by a servant, George Penderel, one of five brothers, all Roman Catholics, who lived in the vicinity, the others being: John, a forester on the Whiteladies property; Humphrey, a miller of the same place; Richard, who lived with his mother at Hobbal Grange near by; and William, who occupied Boscobel House with his wife. Whiteladies itself had been let by the owner to various families who occupied apartments. The Penderels were small farmers, wood-cutters, etc., and looked after the estate. All of them were soon on the spot, and having given the travellers refreshment, bread, cheese and sack, they attended to the King's disguise. His long hair was cut off with a knife by Wilmot, and his face and hands were rubbed with soot from the chimney. The Penderels provided him with a coarse noggen shirt, breeches of rough green cloth, darned grey stockings, a well-worn leathern doublet, patched shoes which had to be slit before he could get them on, and a long greasy steeple-crowned hat. Then Richard completed the trimming of his hair with a pair of shears.

His safety was now dependent on the absence of followers, and the lords who had accompanied him so far left Whiteladies, begging him not to tell them of his plans 'because they knew not what they might be forced to confess' if captured. Wilmot alone knew of his wish to make for London, and the two arranged to meet there at the Three Cranes in Thomas Street by the Vintry. The rest departed for the north and rejoined Leslie's troop, which was soon overtaken and routed by a small body of horse, 'which shows', said Charles, 'that my opinion was not wrong in not sticking to men who had run away'. Buckingham escaped, but the rest were captured.

The Flight

Alone at last, Charles, armed with a hedger's bill-hook, accompanied Richard Penderel to a part of the neighbouring woods named Spring Coppice. While hidden there some horsemen arrived at the village, were told that the King had passed through, and continued their pursuit without attempting a search. It rained all day, and the protection of a large tree did not save Charles from a drenching. Richard provided a blanket for greater comfort and asked his sister Elizabeth to bring some food to the wood. She arrived with 'a mess of milk and some butter and eggs', her sudden appearance startling Charles, who believed that women were by nature too communicative. 'Good woman, can you be faithful to a distressed Cavalier?' he asked. 'Yes, sir, I will die rather than discover you,' she answered. He spent part of the day in learning from the Penderels how to walk and talk like a native of the western shires, and in making plans for the future. London now seemed out of the question, and he thought he had better cross the Severn and get into Wales, as no one would suspect him of going that way and he remembered 'several honest gentlemen' who would help him there. When evening came he went with the Penderels to Hobbal Grange, where he ate eggs and bacon, took Richard's daughter on his knee, and spoke with the mother of the Penderels, who 'blessed God that had so honoured her children in making them the instruments, as she hoped, of his Majesty's safeguard and deliverance'.

As soon as it was dark the King and Richard Penderel started off for Madeley, where they hoped to cross the Severn by ferry with the help of one Francis Woolfe, whose house contained hiding-holes for priests. Though the distance was only nine miles, Charles suffered agonies from his shoes, which he threw away, and then suffered worse agonies in bare feet from thorns and stones. Several times he flung himself on the ground and said he would go no farther until it was light enough to see where he was stepping. But Richard prevailed upon him to keep moving, sometimes hinting that the worst was over, sometimes that they were nearly there. At about nine o'clock they came to the mill at

Evelith, and a sound they made drew forth the miller. 'Who's there?' he shouted. Richard replied that they were neighbours going home. 'If you be neighbours, stand, or I will knock you down!' threatened the miller. As they believed there were other people in the house, they did not stay to be identified. Running up a deep and dirty lane as fast as they could, with the miller bawling 'Rogues! Rogues!' and some soldiers, as they thought, chasing them, they went on until they were exhausted. Then they stopped to listen, heard nothing, and pursued their way. Sometime afterwards they learnt that several Royalist fugitives had been hidden in the house, and that the miller had mistaken them for Cromwell's men.

Francis Woolfe, nearly seventy years of age, was in a state of much trepidation when Richard knocked on his door late that night. Charles had decided not to appear until he knew it would be safe, and remained hidden by a hedge. Asked whether he would give shelter to a gentleman who had escaped from the recent battle, Woolfe replied that it was dangerous to harbour a well-known person, and that 'he would not venture his neck for any man, unless it were the King himself'. Richard took the risk of saying that it was the King himself; upon which Woolfe declared that he would venture all he had in the world to secure his monarch. On hearing this Charles did not much like the word 'secure', but as it was beginning to get light he had to run the hazard or expose himself to greater danger. Entering the house by a back way, he was received by Woolfe, who said he was very sorry to see the King because the village was full of soldiers, the ferry was closely watched, every stranger was interrogated, and the hiding-places in his own house had been discovered. After eating some cold meat, the King and Richard retired to the barn, where they spent the hours of daylight concealed in the hay. When night came on Woolfe and his son brought food to the barn and discussed the next move. They told Charles that he could not possibly get over the Severn, as every place where the river could be crossed was under the closest observation; so he decided to go back to William Penderel's home at Boscobel, and again thought of finding his way to London. After supper in the house, his face and hands were stained by Mrs Woolfe with the juice of walnut-leaves to give him a weatherbeaten appearance.

He and Richard started off in the dark, and many years later Charles recalled an incident on their way: 'As we came by the mill again, we had no mind to be questioned a second time there; and therefore, asking Richard Penderel whether he could swim or no, and how deep the river was, he told me it was a scurvy river, not easy to be passed in all places, and that he could not swim. So I told him that, the river being but a little one, I would undertake to help him over. Upon which we went over some closes to the riverside, and I entering the river first, to see whether I could myself go over, who knew how to swim, found it was but a little above my middle; and thereupon, taking Richard Penderel by the hand, I helped him over.'

Although Woolfe had supplied Charles with shoes and stockings, his feet were raw and blistered, and on arrival at Boscobel House he was in great pain. But he did not go in until Richard could report the place free of soldiers. To his delight he met a valued comrade in the Worcester fight, Colonel Carlos, who wept with joy at the sight of his King, who wept at the joy of his faithful subject. A good meal of bread and cheese, followed by 'a posset of thin milk and small beer', braced the fugitives, and then William Penderel's wife washed the King's feet, cut the blisters and dried his stockings. It was unsafe to remain any longer in the house, and Carlos proposed that they should pass the day in a large oak tree where they could watch without being seen. The King agreed, and taking with them some bread, cheese, beer and a couple of pillows, they climbed into it. Not too soon, for the wood was shortly being patrolled by soldiers, whose words were audible to the two men hidden above their heads in a leafy screen:

> And far below the Roundhead rode,
> And humm'd a surly hymn.

But Charles was much too tired to bother about Roundheads or their hymns. He slept most of the day with his head on the Colonel's lap. At one period he moved slightly and his head rested on the Colonel's arm, which became so numb that it could hardly support the weight. As the Colonel dared not speak for fear of being heard by the soldiers, and as the King would certainly fall out of the tree if he failed to shift his position, Carlos took the liberty of pinching his Majesty; the situation was readjusted, and the peril passed.

The long day drew to a close, and they descended stiffly from the oak. Back in the house they heard from Humphrey Penderel that he had been to Shifnal, where an officer had informed him that the penalty of concealing the King was death, while the reward of delivering him up was a thousand pounds. Charles was a little alarmed, for such a sum of money was a great temptation to poor people; but he was reassured by Humphrey and Carlos that 'if it were one hundred thousand pounds it were to no more purpose'. That night he slept, or failed to sleep, in a hiding-place too small for one of his stature. The next day was Sunday 7 September, and owing to the Puritan love of psalms, prayers and sermons, it was felt that the house would be free from molestation. Charles had expressed a longing for mutton, and William Penderel, not daring to buy such a luxury, stole the sheep of a neighbour, killed it, skinned it, 'and brought up a hind quarter to the King, who presently fell a-chopping of the loin to pieces, or, as they called them then, Scotch collops, which the Colonel clapped into the pan, while the King held it and fried it'. The rest of the day was spent by Charles reading the scriptures in an arbour near the house, perpetual watch being kept by the Penderels on the neighbouring roads and tracks.

Charles was extremely anxious to know the whereabouts of Lord Wilmot, whom he had arranged to meet in London, and now learnt that, the journey having proved impracticable, Wilmot had taken refuge with a Roman Catholic, John Whitgreave, at Moseley Hall, where a priest, Father John Hudleston, also

CHARLES II AS A YOUTH

EDWARD HYDE, 1ST EARL OF CLARENDON

resided. Having heard from the Penderels that Charles was in hourly danger at Boscobel, it was decided by Whitgreave, Hudleston and Wilmot that he should leave at once for Moseley Hall; and at eleven o'clock on Sunday night the five Penderel brothers and Francis Yates, armed with pistols and pikes, escorted the King to Moseley, leaving Colonel Carlos behind for greater safety. As they had some ten miles to cover, and the state of Charles's feet prevented him from walking, he rode on Humphrey's mill-horse. They went by unbeaten tracks, the muddy condition of which made progress slow, though the King attributed their tardy rate to his mount, saying it was 'the heaviest dull jade' he had ever ridden upon. But Humphrey stood up for his animal: 'My liege, can you blame the horse to go heavily, when he has the weight of three kingdoms on his back?' Charles was not the man to frown at such an answer. At Pendeford Mill, two miles short of their destination, it became advisable that he should make the rest of the journey on foot. Alighting from the jade, he went forward, momentarily forgetting that three of the Penderels were returning with the horse. But he soon came back with an apology: 'My troubles make me forget myself; I thank you all,' and they kissed his hand. Yates was shortly to be executed for his stubborn loyalty, but after the Restoration his widow was pensioned, and Charles handsomely recompensed all those who had succoured him in adversity.

Whitgreave received the others at the back door of Moseley Hall and would not have known which was the King if he had not known each of his companions. Bidding farewell to Yates and the other Penderels, John and Richard, who were refreshed in the buttery, the King went upstairs with Father Hudleston and embraced Wilmot, who fell on his knees overcome with emotion. Charles asked eagerly after Buckingham, Derby and the rest, but Wilmot knew no more than he. Whitgreave showed the priest's hole, and Charles said it was the best place he had ever been in. Then he sat down on the bed in Wilmot's room, while Hudleston washed his feet, which were 'most sadly galled', giving him slippers, stockings and a new shirt. Suddenly his nose began to bleed, but he remarked that it was habitual with him, and when the 'old coarse clout' given him by the Penderels was soaked he exchanged it for one of Father Hudleston's clean handkerchiefs. After his feet had received attention and he had been refreshed with biscuits and sack, he sat by the fire feeling a different man. 'I am now ready for another march,' he said; 'and if it shall please God once more to place me at the head of but eight or ten thousand good men, of one mind and resolved to fight, I shall not doubt to drive these rogues out of my kingdom.' The morning was now upon them and he retired to sleep in the priest's hole, Wilmot privately enjoining Whitgreave and Hudleston that 'if it should so fall out that the rebels have intelligence of your harbouring any of the King's party, and should therefore put you to any torture for confession, be sure you discover me first, which may haply in such case satisfy them and preserve the King'. Whitgreave promptly sent his servants out on various devised jobs, and told his two nephews and another boy, who as pupils of Hudleston lived in the house, to keep a sharp eye open for soldiers, as one of the priest's relations was in hiding there. This was a welcome change from lessons, and the lads spent a pleasant scouting holiday.

Nothing happened during the day, which Charles spent in talking quietly with Whitgreave's mother and planning his next journey, it having been agreed that he should go to Bentley Hall, where Colonel Lane would arrange his further movements. Having passed the day without alarms, Charles slept in Hudleston's bed that night. The following morning he looked out of the window and saw remnants of the Royalist army straggling by, some wounded, most in tatters, all starving. It was a saddening sight, and he spoke much of the battle, saying that the Scots had let him down. In the afternoon Whitgreave heard that soldiers were approaching. Instantly Charles was secured in the hiding-place, and Whitgreave went out to meet the men, who, he reported, 'were ready to pull me in pieces and take me away with them, saying I was come from Worcester fight'. But after much disputation he was able to prove, with the evidence of neighbours, that illness had kept him indoors at the time; and they left without searching the Hall. Charles had been glancing through Hudleston's books and manuscripts, and now asked to see the chapel in the attic. 'If it please God I come to my crown,' he declared, 'both you and all your persuasion shall have as much liberty as any of my subjects.'

At midnight Colonel Lane arrived with horses, and Charles, having prayed with the family and expressed his gratitude to them, started for Bentley Hall, where he arrived in the early morning of 10 September. But he could only snatch a few hours rest, for he now became 'Will Jackson', a tenant's son who served the Lanes. The plan was that he should conduct Jane Lane, the Colonel's sister, to Bristol, whence he might escape in a boat. Jane was on a visit to her cousin Ellen Norton at Abbotsleigh, between Bristol and the Severn estuary, and she had obtained a passport for the party, which consisted of her sister, brother-in-law, cousin, and 'Will Jackson', Jane alone of the company being aware of the latter's identity. The Colonel decided that 'Will' must look more like a farmer's son, and gave him a suit of grey cloth. Charles then accompanied the Colonel to the stables and received hints on how to assume his new character. Bringing the horse round to the front door, Charles stood motionless, hat under arm. 'Will,' said the Colonel, 'thou must give my sister thy hand.' Charles obeyed, but so clumsily that Jane's mother laughed and asked her son what goodly horseman her daughter had got to ride before her. Wilmot followed some distance behind with one or two others, accompanied by hawks and spaniels as if they were out for sport, having agreed to stay at different places and not to join Charles until they reached Abbotsleigh. After travelling for two hours, the horse on which the King and Jane were riding cast a shoe, and they had to stop at Bromsgrove to rectify it. While holding the horse's hoof, Charles asked the blacksmith whether there was any news. Only that Cromwell had routed the Scots and the King had got away, replied the smith.

'Perhaps he has got by byways back into Scotland,' suggested Charles.

'No,' said the smith, 'that is not very likely; he rather lurks secretly somewhere in England, and I wish I knew where he was, for I might get a thousand pounds by taking him.'

'If that rogue be taken, he deserves to be hanged, more than all the rest, for bringing in the Scots,' remarked Charles, and, thinking of the part played by his northern subjects, he meant it.

'You speak like an honest man,' approved the smith; and so they parted.

Proceeding on their way, the travellers came to Wootton Wawen, where they saw a troop of horse ahead of them, the horses eating the grass on the roadside, the men lounging about. Jane's brother-in-law at once refused to ride through them, as he had already suffered at the hands of the military. Charles whispered urgently to Jane to let him ride on, as it would be fatal if they were seen to turn back. But her brother-in-law was insistent, and they took another way into Stratford-on-Avon. As it happened they met either the same or another troop of horse in the main street of Stratford, just before crossing the bridge, but the soldiers allowed them to go through 'civilly giving hat for hat'. Jane's sister and her husband left them at Stratford for their home in Buckinghamshire, and the King's party, now reduced to three, rode another six miles that evening to the house of John Tomes at Long Marston, where they spent the night, and where 'Will Jackson' sat in the kitchen. Ordered by the cook to wind up the roasting-jack, he tried to oblige, but so awkwardly that she raged at him: 'What countryman are you, that you know not how to wind up a jack?' He excused himself: 'I am a poor tenant's son of Colonel Lane in Staffordshire; we seldom have roast meat, but when we have we don't make use of a jack.'

On Thursday 11 September they entered the Cotswold country via Chipping Campden, and came to the Crown inn at Cirencester, a distance of thirty-six miles. (Local tradition connects the visit with the Sun inn, where there is a 'King Charles's Room'.) After supper Jane's cousin Henry Lascelles, who by now knew that the poor tenant's son was the King, slept in a room at the inn with 'Will Jackson', for whom a truckle bed had been provided. But when they were left alone he insisted that 'Will' should occupy his own more commodious couch. Passing through Chipping Sodbury on Friday they arrived at Bristol, which they had to ride through. Charles was so desirous to see the alterations that had taken place in the city since he had been there that he looked about him with keen interest, 'and when he rode near the place where the great fort had stood, he could not forbear putting his horse out of the way, and rode with his mistress behind him about it'.

In the afternoon they reached Abbotsleigh, three miles west of the city, where Jane was greeted by her friends George and Ellen Norton, who occupied an Elizabethan mansion there. A bowling-green in front of the house was surrounded by people watching the game, and the first man the King saw was a one-time chaplain of his own, Dr Thomas Gorges, who now practised physic. The Nortons, though loyal folk, had not been told who 'Will Jackson' was, in case their manner towards him excited suspicion, and Jane eased the situation by asking the butler, John Pope, to take care of 'Will' and give him a private bedroom, as he suffered from ague. Pope did so, and brought food to Charles from the dining-room. Dr Gorges supped with the family, and seeing the care Jane Lane took to provide her tenant's son with soup and meat he asked after the young man's health. Supper over, Gorges went secretly to see the fellow, thinking he might need a purge. The King got well away from the candle to the dark side of his bed, and answered the questions put to him as briefly and rustically as possible, allowing the ex-chaplain to feel his pulse. But the strain was considerable and at last 'Will' said that he needed sleep. To his great relief Gorges took the hint and left him.

'The next morning,' related the King, 'I arose pretty early, having a very good stomach, and went to the buttery hatch to get my breakfast, where I found Pope and two or three other men in the room, and we all fell to eating bread and butter, to which he gave us very good ale and sack. And as I was sitting there, there was one that looked like a country-fellow sat just by me, who, talking, gave so particular account of the battle of Worcester to the rest of the company that I concluded he must be one of Cromwell's soldiers. But I asking him how he came to give so good an account of the battle, he told me he was in the King's regiment; by which I thought he meant one Colonel King's regiment. But questioning him further I perceived that he had been in my regiment of guards, in Major Broughton's company, that was my major in the battle. I asked him what a kind of man I was? To which he answered by describing exactly both my clothes and my horse; and then looking upon me, he told me that the King was at least three fingers taller than I. Upon which I made what haste I could out of the buttery, for fear he should indeed know me, as being more afraid when I knew he was one of our own soldiers than when I took him for one of the enemy's. So Pope and I went into the hall, and just as we came into it Mrs Norton was coming by through it; upon which I plucked off my hat, and standing with my hat in my hand as she passed by, Pope looked very earnestly in my face. But I took no notice of it, but put on my hat again and went away, walking out of the house into the field.'

Returning to his bedroom in half an hour, Henry Lascelles entered in a state of alarm and asked what they had better do as Pope had recognised the King. Learning that the butler had fought for the Royalists in the Civil War and had served under himself in the west, Charles decided that he must be trusted and sent for him. This was fortunate because Pope proved both loyal and helpful, saying he would go to Bristol that very day to see if there were any ships sailing for France or Spain. On hearing that Lord Wilmot was hourly expected at Abbotsleigh, the butler was dismayed, feeling certain that several unreliable people in the house would know him. He therefore went out, met Wilmot a mile or two away, took him to a nearby lodging, and at nightfall brought

him by the back entrance into Charles's bedroom. Pope's enquiries at Bristol were fruitless: no vessel would be ready to sail
for a month. It was dangerous for Charles to stay longer in the
house of the Nortons, though Jane had kept up the fiction of his
illness. Pope came to the rescue. He told Charles that he would be
quite safe in the house of Colonel Francis Wyndham at Trent, on
the borders of Somerset and Dorset, not far from Sherborne.
Charles knew Francis and his elder brother Edmund very well,
and the proposition pleased him. Wilmot at once set off for Trent
to prepare the family for the King's coming, and Jane Lane agreed
to start on Tuesday 16 September. But at the last moment
another obstacle was put in their way. Charles was equal to it, and
recounted it well:

'The night before we were to go away, we had a misfortune
that might have done us much prejudice; for Mrs Norton, who
was big with child, fell into labour, and miscarried of a dead child,
and was very ill; so that we could not tell how in the world to find
an excuse for Mistress Lane to leave her cousin in that condition;
and indeed it was not safe to stay longer there, where there was
so great resort of disaffected idle people. At length, consulting
with Mr Lascelles, I thought the best way to counterfeit a letter
from her father's house, old Mr Lane's, to tell her that her father
was extremely ill, and commanded her to come away immediately, for fear that she should not otherwise find him alive; which
letter Pope delivered so well, while they were all at supper, and
Mistress Lane playing her part so dexterously, that all believed
old Mr Lane to be indeed in great danger, and gave his daughter
the excuse to go away with me the very next morning early.'

They began the journey on the Bristol road, as if returning to
Bentley, but as soon as it was safe to do so they turned and rode
south through Bedminster to Castle Cary, near Bruton, where
they spent the night with Edward Kirton, steward to the Marquis of Hertford. Late the same evening Wilmot arrived at
Trent, and Colonel Francis Wyndham received a message that a
friend wished to see him in the yard. Stepping out of the house, the

Colonel at once recognised Wilmot in the dark because he had not attempted to change his appearance. 'I never could get my Lord Wilmot to put on any disguise,' remarked Charles, 'he saying that he should look frightfully in it'; so the King's danger was increased by his sense of humour. Wyndham was inexpressibly relieved to hear that Charles was still alive and wanted to hear all the details of the battle and his escape. He was willing to sacrifice his life, his family and his fortune for the King, for whose preservation he took every precaution, making up his mind to confide in six people out of a household of twenty: his wife, his mother, his cousin Juliana Coningsby, his man Henry Peters, and two maid-servants. Jobs and journeys were invented to get the rest off the premises; four rooms were prepared for the King, one of them communicating with a hiding-closet; and all was ready by nine o'clock in the morning of 17 September, when Wyndham and his wife went for a stroll in the fields as if they were taking an airing, and were soon addressed by an odd-looking youth on a horse with luggage tied to the saddle. 'Frank! Frank! How dost thou do?' cried the youth. He was followed by Jane Lane, now mounted behind Lascelles. The party were hurried into the house, and then into the King's private rooms, where, in the words of the host or hostess, 'the passions of joy and sorrow did a while combat in them who beheld his sacred person. For what eye could look upon so glorious a prince thus eclipsed, and not pay unto him the homage of tears?'

Next day Jane Lane and Lascelles bade Charles farewell. In a short while, being suspected of having helped the King, Jane managed to get a passage to France, where she remained until the Restoration. An incident during his stay at Trent remained in the King's memory: 'One day, I hearing the bells ring (the church being hard by Frank Wyndham's house) and seeing a company got together in the churchyard, I sent down the maid of the house, who knew me, to enquire what the matter was; who, returning, came up and told me that there was a rogue, a trooper, come out of Cromwell's army that was telling the people that he had killed me, and that that was my buff coat which he had then on. Upon which, most of the village being fanatics, they were ringing the bells, and making a bonfire for joy of it.'

While the villagers were rejoicing at the King's death, the Wyndhams were busy saving his life. The Colonel went to a tough Royalist named Giles Strangeways of Melbury, who could do nothing, all his friends having been banished, but he sent Charles a hundred pounds, which was all he had. Also he gave Wyndham the names of two Lyme Regis residents who might be able to help. One of them, Wyndham found, was away in Portugal, but the other, Captain William Ellesdon, was 'ravished' by the prospect of proving his loyalty. Making enquiries he learnt that the owner of a small vessel at Charmouth, one Stephen Limbry, was about to sail for St Malo, and as he was Ellesdon's tenant he would wish to oblige. Wyndham and Ellesdon rode by the seaside to Charmouth, where they interviewed Limbry at the inn, telling him that two of their friends who had fought at Worcester wished to escape across the Channel. At first Limbry raised objections, but when offered sixty pounds he agreed to bring his vessel from the Cobb at Lyme Regis to Charmouth Road, send the long-boat for the passengers at an agreed spot, and ship them off immediately the winds were favourable. Returning to Lyme, they remembered that a fair would be held there on the day they had fixed, which might mean that every inn in the neighbourhood would be filled with guests; so they sent the Colonel's servant, Henry Peters, back to Charmouth in order to secure the two best rooms at the inn, where Charles and Wilmot could wait until the long-boat arrived at midnight. Primed with a likely story, Peters set off, offered the landlady five shillings and a glass of wine, and melted her heart with the story of a nobleman who was deeply in love with an orphan girl, whose guardian opposed their marriage; so they were running away and would like to rest at the inn for some hours the following Monday night, leaving before daylight. The landlady took the money and swallowed the story with the drink. This matter

61

settled, Ellesdon showed Wyndham a country house belonging to his brother at Monkton Wylde in the hills behind Lyme and Charmouth, where the King was to be brought on the day arranged.

Returning to Trent, the Colonel had to deal with a tricky situation. He heard from the village tailor that his house was to be searched for Royalists. Thanking him for the information, the Colonel said that his only guest was a relation who had so little desire for concealment that he would probably be going to church that day. Not caring for the Puritan parson then in charge, Wyndham seldom went to church; but clearly his relation was of a different mind, and, Charles agreeing, they attended service together. The villagers were impressed, and there seemed no occasion for a search.

On Monday 22 September the runaway couple left Trent, Charles in the guise of a groom riding with the orphan girl, Juliana Coningsby, attended by her pretended lover Wilmot, in the company of Wyndham and Peters. They got to the rendezvous at Monkton Wylde, where they met Ellesdon, who told them that Limbry had described his passengers as a ruined merchant who was going to St Malo with his servant to retrieve some of his losses from the evil agent responsible for them. It would be as well, said Ellesdon, to discuss such matters before the sailors when they were on the boat. Ellesdon then returned to Lyme, the others going on to Charmouth, little realising that the tenant of the house they were leaving had recognised Charles and would have earned the thousand pounds reward if a neighbour had not appealed to his conscience or his superstition: 'It would be the price of blood and it would do no good.'

Soon after they reached the Queen's Arms at Charmouth they heard from Limbry that all was well and his boat would be ready for them at midnight. But Limbry's wife felt that all was not well, and having discovered that her spouse intended to sail without having loaded a cargo she forced him to admit that he was earning a goodly sum for taking a friend of their landlord to France.

Guessing that the passenger was a Royalist, and knowing the heavy penalties exacted for helping such an one, she locked the door of the room in which her husband was packing a few things, and the rest of their conversation was conducted in raised voices from different sides of the door. She made it quite clear that if he tried to escape she would report his intention to the authorities, and as his incarceration gave her the best of the argument he submitted.

In a state of acute tension Charles and Wilmot sat out the hours in their room, while Wyndham and Peters paced the shore waiting for the boat. With the coming of daylight Wyndham decided that they must leave Charmouth to avoid suspicion, and it was agreed that Charles, Juliana and himself should make for Bridport, leaving Wilmot and Peters behind to find out why Limbry had failed them and whether there was still a chance of leaving in the man's vessel. While Charles and the other two were on their way to Bridport the ostler of the Charmouth inn was confiding in the landlady that he believed the female of the party to be none other than the King. By this time she was probably aware that the story she had heard could not be relied upon, but she rebuked the ostler and told him to mind his own business. It happened that his business was to take Wilmot's horse, which had lost a shoe, to a smith, who remarked that the horse's other shoes had been set in three different counties, one of which was Worcestershire. Having returned the horse to its master, the ostler dashed off to see the local clergyman, whose name was Wesley, a name that would one day be made famous by his great-grandson John Wesley. But the parson was engaged in family prayers, which went on for such a long time that the ostler lost heart and returned to the inn. By then Wilmot had left and was following the King to Bridport; so the ostler again called on Wesley and this time found him free to listen. The parson hurried to the inn and facetiously addressed the landlady: 'Why how now, Margaret? You are a maid of honour now.' She asked him to explain his meaning. 'Why, Charles Stuart lay last night at your house,' said he, 'and kissed you at his departure; so that now you can't but be a maid of honour.' The landlady did not think this funny and replied that he was a scurvy-conditioned man to spread such news and bring her into trouble. 'But,' she added, 'if I thought it was the King, as you say it was, I would think the better of my lips all the days of my life; and so, Mr Parson, get you out of my house, or else I'll get those shall kick you out.'

Wesley disliked this answer and applied to a Justice of the Peace, who refused to believe the story. When however the ostler mentioned the matter to a captain in the army, swift action was taken, a troop of horse setting off in pursuit. Little realising what was happening at Charmouth, the King's party arrived at Bridport, finding it full of soldiers about to embark for Jersey and Guernsey, which Cromwell had decided to occupy. Wyndham was startled and wondered what to do. 'I told him,' related Charles, 'that we must go impudently into the best inn in the town, and take a chamber there, as the only thing to be done; because we should otherwise miss my Lord Wilmot, in case we went anywhere else, and that would be very inconvenient both to him and me. So we rode directly into the best inn of the place, and found the yard very full of soldiers. I alighted, and taking the horses thought it the best way to go blundering in among them, and lead them through the middle of the soldiers into the stable, which I did; and they were very angry with me for my rudeness.' The inn was the George, nearly opposite the Town Hall. Though it no longer exists, mention of it must be made here because the number of public houses at which Charles is supposed to have stopped almost equals the number of beds in which Queen Elizabeth is supposed to have slept, and our record aims at historical accuracy. Charles continued his account:

'As soon as I came into the stable I took the bridle off the horses, and called the hostler to me to help me, and to give the horses some oats. And as the hostler was helping me to feed the horses, 'Sure, sir,' says the hostler, 'I know your face?' which was no very pleasant question to me. But I thought the best way was to ask him where he had lived ? whether he had always lived there or no ? He told me that he was but newly come thither; that he was born in Exeter, and had been hostler in an inn there, hard by one Mr Potter's, a merchant, in whose house I had lain in the time of war; so I thought it best to give the fellow no further occasion of thinking where he had seen me, for fear he should guess right at last; therefore I told him 'Friend, certainly you have seen me then at Mr Potter's, for I served him a good while, above a year'. 'Oh,' says he, 'then I remember you a boy there,' and with that was put off from thinking any more on it, but desired that we might drink a pot of beer together; which I excused by saying that I must go wait on my master and get his dinner ready for him. But told him that my master was going for London, and would return about three weeks hence, when he would lie there, and I would not fail to drink a pot with him.'

After much difficulty Wyndham managed to get some mutton for dinner, and Charles shared the repast in a private room, from the window of which Juliana saw Peters arrive and beckoned to him. He told them that Wilmot, having seen them through the window, had gone to another inn, and would overtake them shortly on the London road. They left the George as soon as Charles could get the horses ready, and a quarter of an hour after their departure the pursuing troop arrived at the inn, found that the fugitives had left for London, and galloped on as far as Dorchester. But their quarry, finding the main road too popular, had turned off it towards Yeovil, and so avoided capture. As night came down Wyndham lost his way, and they stopped at a village to find out where they were. The host of the George inn came out and told them the name of the place was Broadwindsor; and since Wyndham recognised him as a reliable Royalist, they asked for accommodation that night, Wilmot being described as Wyndham's brother-in-law, Colonel Bullen Reymes. The inn-keeper gave them rooms at the top of the house, and his wife, who had once known Colonel Reymes, bestowed a caress on Wilmot, much to the delight of Charles. But they had little rest that night, for soon after their arrival some forty soldiers came to the village, most of them being billeted at the inn, an occurrence that would have been disastrous to those imprisoned in the upper storey if the attention of the military had not been directed to a woman in their company, who gave birth to a child in the course of the night. A terrific argument then ensued between the parish officers and the soldiers, the former wishing to be free from the burden of keeping mother and child, the latter considering that neither was fit for active service. The argument lasted until sleep overcame the soldiers, and before they awoke the lodgers in the attic had crept noiselessly downstairs and got safely away.

It now became advisable that the King should return to Trent; indeed he had no option; and on 24 September he and Juliana Coningsby and Colonel Wyndham rode there, leaving Wilmot to seek a Royalist, Colonel Robert Phelips, whose residence, Montacute House, had been sequestrated by Parliament and who was now residing at Salisbury. With his help it was believed that a ship could be procured at Southampton. Wilmot, piloted by Peters, put up at an inn kept by a Royalist just outside the Cathedral Close, the King's Arms, which was the common resort of Cavaliers. Phelips did his best, arranging with a sailor to take two men to France for £40, and the good news was dispatched to Trent. But almost at once the ship was commandeered to take supplies to the fleet off Jersey, and Phelips considered it would be safer to make the attempt from a less busy spot farther along the coast. He consulted a local clergyman living in the Cathedral Close, Humphrey Henchman, who told him that Colonel Gounter of Racton, near Chichester, could be relied upon, and suggested that the King be brought to Heale House, six miles north of Salisbury on the Amesbury road. A message to that effect was carried to Trent, and Charles agreed. His second sojourn with the Wyndhams lasted eleven days and passed without incident, except for the presence of some soldiers at Sherborne, when Charles spent the time in his hiding-place while the Wyndhams kept watch. But the men soon left for Jersey, and Charles occupied himself by preparing his own meals and by piercing holes in coins which he presented to those members of the household who had looked after him.

Robert Phelips reached Trent on Sunday 5 October, and at ten the following morning the King, again riding with Juliana as her groom, set off for Heale with Phelips and Peters. They went through Wincanton and stopped at Mere, where they dined at the George inn. The host, being known to Phelips, drank with them and raised the main topic of conversation. The men of Westminster, said he, 'were in a great maze', not knowing what had become of the King, though everyone seemed to agree that he was hiding in London, where many houses had been searched. Charles was seen to smile, and after dinner the host asked him in a jocular manner whether he was a friend to Caesar. 'Yes,' said he. 'Then here's a health to King Charles!' said the host, a sentiment which Charles pledged in a glass of wine. Continuing their journey they probably passed through Hindon, Fonthill, Chilmark and Dinton. At Wilton they must have separated from Juliana Coningsby and Peters, because we hear no more about them, and somewhere in that district they not only passed through a regiment of horse but met the Roundhead General Desborough on foot. Striking north across the river Bourne, they got to Heale House at dusk.

Their hostess Mrs Hyde was the widow of a cousin of the King's friend Sir Edward Hyde. She had once seen Charles marching through Salisbury with his father some years before, and knew him immediately he came to her door. She controlled herself with an effort, and at supper, the other guests being Henchman and her brother-in-law, she experienced great difficulty in refraining from helping Charles first. However her feelings got the better of her when, after giving the rest of the company one lark apiece, she placed two on the King's dish, and drank his health. Seeing that he was recognised, Charles took her into his confidence after supper. Having shown him a safe hiding-place, she said that her servants could not be trusted, and suggested that Charles and Phelips should leave the house openly the following morning, returning after dark, by which time she would have got rid of her staff on some excuse. They did as directed, and spent the day riding about Salisbury Plain, remaining some time at Stonehenge, where according to Phelips 'the King's arithmetic gave the lie to the fabulous tale that those stones cannot be told alike twice together'. They returned late that evening to Heale, where Charles lay concealed for several days, his food being cooked and brought to him by Mrs Hyde, while Phelips left for Salisbury to speed arrangements for the King's embarkation.[1]

All this time Wilmot had been busy. From Salisbury he went to Racton, where he found Colonel Gounter, who was shocked by his guest's effrontery in attempting no disguise and dismayed by the knowledge that the King was near at hand. Gounter's wife insisted on knowing all about Wilmot and why he was there, and yielding to a passion of tears the Colonel got Wilmot's permission to tell her, on which she subsided and wished them well. Gounter tried several places on the coast, but with no success. At last he met a merchant at Chichester named Francis Mansel, who traded across the Channel, and finding him in a friendly mood begged a favour. 'Anything in my power,' said Mansel. Thus encouraged the Colonel was brief, asking if the other could freight a bark, because he had two friends 'who have been engaged in a duel, and there is mischief done, and I am obliged to get them off if I can'. Mansel replied that he could provide a vessel at the fishing-village of Brighthelmstone (later to be known as Brighton). The Colonel wanted to fix it up at once, and next day they rode along the coast to the village, where they learnt that the skipper of the boat was at Shoreham. They sent for him on urgent business, and

1. Heale House still exists, with additions, in beautiful surroundings on the Avon. It is now under the direction of the Guild of Health and Welfare, whose hostess, Miss Pat Leeds, gave a most hospitable reception to the biographer, his wife and two friends. Miss Leeds said that the ghost of Charles had been seen flitting up the stairs to his old hiding-place. But such apparitions cannot be frequent, as there are so many other places to be haunted.

he was soon with them, agreeing to take the Colonel's friends to
France for sixty pounds, paid in advance, on condition that he
knew all about them. Mansel told him the Colonel's story, and
the sailor promised not to leave the place before the duellists
arrived. Another fifty pounds, plus out-of-pocket expenses, were
also promised by Mansel. The successful issue of these negotiations was quickly reported to Wilmot, and on 11 October Colonel
Phelips made haste to Salisbury with the good news. The same
evening Henchman took the tidings to Heale, and at 2 a.m. on
the 13th Charles walked some little distance with Henchman to a
spot where Phelips awaited them with horses.

They were to meet Wilmot and Gounter on Old Winchester
Hill beyond Warnford, and Gounter had borrowed a brace of
greyhounds from his sister Mrs Symons, to make it appear that
they were engaged in coursing, telling her that he would return
the dogs that night and quite possibly bring the party back with
him for refreshment at her house in Hambledon. Leaving his
cousin Tom with Wilmot on Old Winchester Hill, the Colonel
rode down to Warnford in the hope of meeting Phelips and the
King. He encountered them at the entrance to the village, but not
thinking it safe to notice them he rode on to an inn, where he
drank and smoked a pipe. Then he went back the way he had
come, and they all met at the top of Old Winchester Hill. Various
large houses where they might safely spend the night were suggested, but the King favoured the relatively small and secluded
residence of Gounter's sister and her husband at Hambledon,
which they approached from Broadhalfpenny Down.

Thomas Symons was not at home when they called, but his
wife Ursula received them hospitably. As they entered the King
pushed Phelips in front saying: 'Thou lookest the most like a
gentleman now.' They were shown into a small parlour where
there was a good fire. 'This was about candle-lighting,' recorded
Gounter. Having refreshed themselves with wine, ale and biscuits, Mrs Symons provided a good supper, which they were
about half-way through when Mr Symons turned up in a

thoroughly joyous, not to say bibulous, condition, 'he having been all the day playing the good-fellow at an alehouse in the town', according to Charles; or, in the words of his brother-in-law Colonel Gounter, 'as it plainly appeared, he had been in company that day'. Taking a stool he sat down with the rest, gaily observing: 'This is brave! A man can no sooner be out of the way but his house must be taken up with I know not whom.' He then welcomed them, but could not approve of Charles. 'Here is a Roundhead!' said he, peering into the King's face and noticing his cropped hair. Then, turning to Gounter, he added: 'I never knew you keep Roundheads' company before.' The Colonel replied: 'It is no matter; he is my friend, and I will assure you no dangerous man.' Whereupon Symons planked a seat down by the King, shook his hand with alcoholic warmth, and said: 'Brother Roundhead, for his sake thou art welcome.' The King played up to the part assigned to him, and rebuked Symons when he swore: 'Oh, dear brother, that is a 'scape; swear not, I beseech you.' Nevertheless brother Roundhead could not avoid being plied with liquor, which was quietly removed by one of his companions whenever Symons was not looking; and at ten o'clock Gounter decided that the King had had enough of it. A very wearisome day would be followed by another on the morrow, and he tried to find an excuse for Charles to retire. Realising that himself and Wilmot would have to make a night of it, he whispered to Symons: 'I wonder how thou shouldst judge so right; he is a Roundhead indeed, and if we could get him to bed the house were our own, and we could be merry.' It was the right note to strike; Symons cordially agreed, and the Colonel conducted Charles and Phelips upstairs to their bedroom.

After a good night's sleep the King bade farewell to Phelips, who was returning to Salisbury, and set out with Wilmot, Gounter, the Colonel's cousin Tom, and Wilmot's servant Robert Swan. Not knowing whether they would be able to get any food that day, Gounter put two neats' tongues in his pocket before starting. When they got as far as Stansted in Sussex, it was felt that the smaller their party the better, so cousin Tom went back home. Continuing by unfrequented ways, they came to the top of Bury Hill, where a gate led into Arundel Park. Here they met the governor of the Castle, Colonel Morley, out hunting. As they were about to negotiate a steepish descent, they were able to alight without exciting comment, and in this way they avoided the hunting party. The danger over, and the King being told who it was, he lightly remarked: 'I did not much like his starched mouchates.' They went on down the hill to Houghton, pausing for refreshment at the inn, where, without dismounting, they drank ale and ate bread with the neats' tongues Gounter had brought. The road then took them under the South Downs, through Storrington and Steyning, to Bramber, where they found the place full of soldiers who had temporarily quitted the bridge they were guarding for refreshment in the village. The soldiers spotted them, and Wilmot wanted to turn back; but Gounter objected: 'If we do, we are undone. Let us go on boldly and we shall not be suspected.' The King agreed: 'He saith well.' They passed through without question. A little later they heard the clatter of cavalry behind them, and it seemed that all was lost. But a troop of thirty or forty men galloped rudely by, almost unhorsing them in the narrow lane. They arrived at Beeding, where Gounter had arranged for the King to rest at the house of a Royalist while he surveyed the coast; but the strain of events, following the previous night's debauch, was beginning to affect the nerves of Wilmot, who insisted on leaving the road and riding with the King by a quieter way. They parted from Gounter, who said he would expect to hear from them at the George inn, Brighton. Wilmot and the King probably took to the Downs, while Gounter continued along the road.

When the Colonel arrived at Brighton he made for the George, which was on the east side of Middle Street. He saw no strangers in the place, engaged the best room, and ordered supper. While drinking a glass of wine he heard some guests arrive, and Smith the landlord gave them another room. Then he heard the King's

voice: 'Here, Mr Barlow, I drink to you,' that being the name
adopted by Wilmot. On the reappearance of Smith, the Colonel
said he had heard someone speak the name of Barlow, and asked
the landlord to find out whether that gentleman had been a major
in the King's army; because if so they had known one another. The
answer being what the Colonel expected, the parties drank wine
together, and as Gounter's room was the more commodious the
three of them agreed to have supper in it, being shortly joined by
the merchant Mansel and the skipper Tattersal. During the meal
Charles was in excellent spirits, in spite of his consciousness that
the sailor and the landlord were closely observing him. Afterwards Tattersal took Mansel aside, reproached him for unfair
dealing, and said that 'Mr Jackson' was the King. Mansel denied
it; but Tattersal's ship and several others had been captured by
Charles in the days when he had commanded his father's fleet,
and the sailor remembered that Charles had let them go again,
for he now declared that he would venture his life for the King and
set him safely on shore in France. Mansel broke the news to
Charles, who recalled an occasion when another sailor had been
forcibly confined by his wife and thought it would be prudent if
Tattersal were not allowed to go home. Virtue was not the only
reward expected by the sailor, who now asked Gounter to insure
his boat for two hundred pounds. The Colonel argued, but the
man insisted, and at last it was agreed. Then Tattersal demanded
Gounter's written bond, which was indignantly refused, the King
intervening with 'He saith right; a gentleman's word, especially
before witnesses, is as good as his bond'. Well provided with
witnesses, the skipper climbed down. Then it was the landlord's
turn. Finding Charles alone in the room, he suddenly kissed his
hand, saying: 'God bless you wheresoever you go; I do not
doubt, before I die, but to be a lord, and my wife a lady.' Charles
laughed; but he did not forget the landlord in the days of future
prosperity, nor indeed any other person who had helped him in
the days of past adversity.

These excitements over, Charles and Wilmot lay down in their clothes to rest for an hour or so. Gounter called them at two o'clock in the morning of the 15th, and they rode along the beach to Shoreham creek, where the vessel lay in low water. Taking an affectionate leave of Gounter, they went straight on board, and the tide coming up they sailed at eight in the morning, forty-one days after the battle of Worcester and only a few hours before some soldiers came to search for 'a tall black man, six feet two inches high'. The last difficulty had now to be overcome. The boat, loaded with coal, was supposed to be sailing for Poole, and for a while the skipper kept along the coast until at about five o'clock they sighted the Isle of Wight. Charles reported what then happened:

'The master (Tattersal) came to me, and desired me that I would persuade his men to use their endeavours with me to get him to set us on shore in France, the better to cover him from any suspicion thereof. Upon which I went to the men, which were four and a boy, and told them truly that we were two merchants that had some misfortunes, and were a little in debt; that we had some money owing us at Rouen, in France, and were afraid of being arrested in England; that if they would persuade the master (the wind being very fair) to give us a trip over to Dieppe, or one of those ports near Rouen, they would oblige us very much, and with that I gave them twenty shillings to drink. Upon which they undertook to second me, if I would propose it to the master. So I went to the master, and told him our condition, and that if he would give us a trip over to France, we would give him some consideration for it. Upon which he counterfeited difficulty, saying that it would hinder his voyage. But his men, as they had promised me, joining their persuasions to ours, and, at last, he yielded to set us over.'

Next morning the wind dropped and they were compelled to anchor some two miles off Fécamp. While waiting for the tide Charles saw what looked like an Ostend privateer. As France and Spain were then at war, and they might be suspected by the Spanish boat of trading with the former, they would probably be

73

plundered and then landed in England. Charles promptly suggested to Wilmot that they should row ashore in a little cockboat; and so, having experienced nineteen months of ignominy, defeat and peril, he returned to France in a skiff, a wiser if not sadder man.

[7]

Penniless Freedom

TWO MEN WHO LOOKED LIKE TRAMPS were carried ashore
by sailors at Fécamp on 16 October 1651, their appearance being
such that when they applied for lodgings at Rouen next day the
innkeeper, said Charles, 'made difficulty to receive us, taking us
by our clothes to be some thieves, or persons that had been doing
some very ill thing'. However they managed to find an English
merchant in the town, and not only was the respectability of their
characters guaranteed but they were made to look respectable by
the provision of new clothes. Having sent a message to his mother
that he was safe, Charles started for Paris with Wilmot on the
19th, spent the night at Fleury, and they were met at Moriceaux
by Henrietta Maria, the Duke of York, the Duke of Orleans,
and a number of nobles, all of whom accompanied them to Paris.
Next day the King entered the Louvre.

It was his firm intention, since gossip was rife and spies were
plentiful, not to mention the name of a single person who had
helped him to escape, nor any place where he had stayed, nor even
the districts through which he had passed as a fugitive, lest those
who had been faithful to him should suffer. To put people clean off
the scent, he invented all sorts of fantastic adventures and lied
with a good conscience about places he had never been near, such
as the northern extremity of Scotland, where he had failed to get
a ship, and London, where he had been hidden by a woman who
had lent him her clothes, which, with a besom on his head, had

75

enabled him to get clean away. One thing he said we may well believe. So dispirited and bored had he been in Scotland, he told Mademoiselle de Montpensier, that he felt the loss of Worcester battle less severely because of the hope of returning to France, 'where he found so many charms in persons for whom he had the greatest regard'. The persons of course were mainly of the feminine gender.

Before starting on his adventure he had sent representatives to various courts to obtain financial assistance, and he now learnt that their missions had not been attended with much success. The King and Queen of Poland, more generous with good wishes than hard cash, made a small donation. The Czar of Russia appointed a committee of nobles to discuss the matter with Charles's envoy, who had to endure the tedium of hearing their list of titles before they would listen to his requirements. He must have passed the ordeal without yawning because they voted twenty thousand roubles for his master. The rulers of Persia and Morocco were not given a chance to subscribe because the diplomatist sent to them was lost in a sandstorm. Sir Edward Hyde was one of the two ambassadors sent to Spain, where they were received politely and taken to a bull-fight which they thought 'barbarous'. Unfortunately, while they were in Madrid, the English Parliament sent their own envoy, who was murdered by English Royalists, and a complicated situation arose. The Spaniards sympathised with the act, but they were becoming alarmed over Cromwell's successes and dared not flout the request of the English Parliament that justice should be done on the murderers. Eventually the six offenders, who had sought sanctuary in a religious establishment, were arrested and condemned to death; but a compromise was effected with the Church and they were restored to the sanctuary that had been violated, all of them escaping therefrom, though one was recaptured and executed. The presence of Admiral Blake with the English fleet off the shores of Spain helped King Philip IV and his advisers to make up their minds. They hated the English Puritans but they feared the consequence of hostility on their trade, and after much wavering they came down on the side of commercial prosperity, Philip recognising the Commonwealth. This meant that the sooner Charles's representatives left the country the better, and they were politely but firmly ordered away, their departure being made less displeasing by the promise of fifty thousand 'pieces of eight' which would be paid to Charles in Flanders. The Royalist ambassador to Rome was less fortunate. At first the Pope promised to consider what could be done; but soon he heard that Charles had accepted the Covenant; and as it was not the policy of his Holiness to destroy the Roman Catholic faith, he refused to assist one who had sworn to do so.

Life for the exiles in the Louvre was austere. Henrietta Maria had to make a little money go a long way, and her son had to make less go all the way. Both were pensioned by the French Crown, but owing to civil strife and a tendency to peculate by officials the pensions were seldom paid with regularity and rarely in full, the sums coming at uncertain intervals in driblets. Henrietta again decided that Charles must marry the wealthy Mademoiselle de Montpensier; and although Hyde argued against it on the ground that a Roman Catholic union would prejudice the King's cause in England, Charles replied that he would use every penny of his cousin's fortune in an attempt to recover his throne. They met again, and this time Charles paid his addresses in fluent French, which made Mademoiselle wonder whether he had picked it up in Scotland. For some months he laid siege to her, and she obviously liked his attentions. He went almost daily to her receptions and paid her the compliments of a lover. But she was hunting bigger game, no one less than King Louis of France, and though her ambition was ultimately thwarted it became clear that Charles was wasting his time. The moment he perceived this, he decided to retire with dignity. Having previously remained on his feet in her presence, he now availed himself of his kingly privilege, and when next she came to the Louvre he conducted the conversation from his arm-chair, which greatly vexed her, the matter of sitting and standing being one of prodigious importance at the Court of France.

Charles next turned his attention to a beautiful widow, the Duchesse de Châtillon, and sent her a formal offer of marriage. The prospect allured her, until she discovered that she would not be received at the French Court as Queen of England unless Henrietta Maria gave her consent. This damped her enthusiasm; and when Hyde managed to persuade Charles that the union was politically unsuitable, passion ebbed on both sides, giving way to female vanity and male prudence.

Another civil war had broken out in France, due to the ambition of certain princes and their hatred of Mazarin. The King, Court and Cardinal left Paris; the Duke of York fought on their side under Turenne; while Charles and his mother remained in the capital, their poverty making life difficult and their loyalty to the French Crown causing them to be execrated by the mob, which was now anti-Royalist in feeling. After a successful campaign by Turenne, a halt was called, and Charles was asked to mediate between the two sides; but his attempts were frustrated by the refusal of either party to believe in the promises of the other, and as usual in such cases the friend of each was blamed by both. Paris wanted peace, and when the negotiations broke down Charles found himself extremely unpopular there. The mob, as is customary with mobs, believed whatever they wished to believe, and for some weeks it was dangerous for an Englishman to be seen in the streets. Charles and Henrietta were practically imprisoned in the Louvre, the rabble yelling that, having already ruined England, the exiles were now ruining France. In July 1652 the English Court decided to leave Paris, where they were in constant peril, the inhabitants having renounced their own monarch. It was not easy to leave the city through a howling mob, but they chose a dark and stormy night for the attempt. Charles rode by the side of his mother's coach, and they got safely to the gates, where the presence of two nobles enabled them to proceed on their journey. Farther on they were met by some of the King's soldiers, who escorted them with torches to St Germains, where they arrived at midnight on 13 July.

They were left in peace there for two months, but when the French Court wished to occupy the royal quarters they had to leave, returning at some risk to Paris, where the attitude of the mob was less hostile owing to the success of the French King's forces. A month later Louis himself entered his capital in triumph; the campaigns of the Fronde were speedily brought to a close; and in February '53 even the hated Cardinal was received with frantic joy by a populace that had longed to tear him limb from limb a short while before.

At first Charles was in high repute for his labours to pacify the warring factions, and Louis with his mother paid a ceremonious call at the Palais Royal to signify appreciation of their royal cousin, who had to be content with payment in thanks, for he got nothing else. The trouble was that France, weary of the long struggle with Spain, wished to conciliate her potential foe England, which meant being polite to Cromwell, which meant being impolite to Charles. In September '52, without bothering to declare war, Blake had smashed the French fleet, as a consequence of which Spain took Dunkirk, and Mazarin, alarmed, sent a Resident to London in order to arrange a trade treaty and indemnify his country for Blake's action. This implied a recognition of the Commonwealth by France, and Charles at once complained. But Mazarin was cunning enough to invent plausible excuses, his main object at the moment being to use the English King as a pawn in the game he intended to play with Cromwell, or, if the latter fell, to assist in the promotion of Charles from pawn to king. Charles was shrewd enough to see through the Cardinal's duplicity, and tried his luck elsewhere. Austria had always maintained a friendly attitude towards the Stuarts; so he sent an ambassador to Ratisbon, where the Imperial Diet met in April '53. The ambassador was his fellow-fugitive Wilmot, whom he had now created Earl of Rochester, and who was charged with all sorts of friendly messages concerning the Catholics. But the important thing was to raise money and to find out if any of the princes at the Diet would welcome Charles as a guest. Rochester had a good time at Ratisbon, where the meat and wine served at one meal would have lasted his impoverished master a week; but he was not an ideal man for the job, being casual when he should have been careful. Although the princes were living in luxury they complained of poverty, and none of them appeared joyful at the prospect of entertaining Charles. Eventually Rochester managed to extract ten thousand pounds out of the assembled rulers, but it took some time to collect the sum and a good deal was used to defray his expenses.

Charles next turned to Holland, his most hopeful ally because the Dutch were at war with the English Commonwealth; but they were too cautious to commit themselves. He then tried Denmark, with no better luck. His last chance seemed to have gone when an English fleet completely smashed the Dutch and killed their famous Admiral, Van Tromp. After that Holland wanted peace at any price with Cromwell, and the price Oliver demanded was considerable. Because the late Prince of Orange had helped Charles, his son and descendants were for ever to be excluded from the office of Stadtholder; and all enemies of the English Commonwealth were henceforth to be expelled from Holland, which meant that Mary, widow of the Prince of Orange, could not even invite her brother Charles to stay with her. The peace was promulgated in May '54, such being the fear of the Lord Protector of England that his government was soon recognised by all the European powers, and Charles was left friendless. But his greatest blow was the peace treaty between Mazarin and Cromwell, which also left him homeless.

There had never been much peace for him in that home. Life was a succession of quarrels. Two factions fought for supremacy. Queen Henrietta Maria with her chief adviser, Lord Jermyn, was at odds with Charles and his chief adviser, Sir Edward Hyde. Poverty exacerbated their differences. Though small sums from loyalists in England occasionally supplemented the pensions that were grudgingly doled out by the French treasury, the friends and followers of Charles were shabbily clothed, half-starved, badly lodged, and permanently in debt. Hyde and the Marquis of Ormonde could scarcely pay for one meal a day and in the winter shivered for want of fires and cloaks. Sometimes Hyde was too cold to hold a pen in his hand. 'I do not know that any man is yet dead for want of bread, which really I wonder at,' he wrote. In the spring of 1654 he said that Ormonde and himself wanted shoes and shirts, and that the King as well as his Court lacked food and warmth.

Their one hope of obtaining money lay with Prince Rupert, whose four ships were supposed to be taking prizes and accumulating wealth in the West Indies; but after an absence of nearly two years he returned with a leaky vessel and a single prize, the sale of which was barely enough to pay off the men.

Worse even than the discomfort of poverty were the jealousies, suspicions, rivalries and malicious tittle-tattle which were the main occupation of people who were mentally and physically unemployed, and Hyde wrote to a friend: 'Oh, to be quiet and starve were no unpleasant condition to what I endure!' Henrietta Maria disliked Hyde so much that she never spoke to him and would not even look at him. This was partly because as a loyal member of the Church of England he was strongly anti-Catholic, but chiefly because his influence over the King was far greater than her own. Hyde was an extremely able man, of which he was perfectly well aware, allowing his sense of superiority to be too apparent to those with whom he worked; and as he also had a caustic tongue, he was detested by everyone whose vanity could easily be ruffled. Charles liked and trusted him, but apart from Ormonde, who did not suffer from a feeling of self-importance, no one else had a pleasant word for him. He knew this, and informed a trusted correspondent that he had 'the good fortune to be equally disliked by those who agree in nothing else'.

Although Charles invariably paid attention to Hyde's advice, he was much too conciliatory by nature to follow it on all occasions. He would not 'make himself uneasy by unnecessary contestations', and not even Hyde could always convince him that a contestation was necessary; but when he personally felt it to be so, he could be firmer and infinitely more sensible than any of his advisers. In 1653 his Council consisted of the Chancellor of the Exchequer, Hyde, of Ormonde, Rochester, Buckingham, and the Lord Keeper, Sir Edward Herbert; also, to pacify Henrietta Maria, Jermyn, who engaged in a plot to disgrace and unseat Hyde. Both Presbyterians and Roman Catholics were in harmony on one point if on no other: a desire to damage Hyde's credit with Charles. To this end they planned a joint attack, drawing up two petitions to the King, one asserting that the Presbyterians were discouraged and hindered from serving him owing to their distrust of Hyde, the other stating that his Majesty's sole hope was to get the backing of the Pope, the Catholic princes and his Catholic subjects, but that owing to the hostility of Hyde to the Catholic religion none of them would assist Charles. Copies of these petitions were received by the King before their formal presentation. He saw through the plot at once, showed the copies to Hyde, thought them very funny, and ridiculed the whole affair at dinner before his mother and the Court. As a result the Presbyterians and the Roman Catholics had to think again. With the assistance of a man who had once been secretary to Charles, Henrietta Maria and Jermyn then started another intrigue against Hyde. This man asserted, on the evidence of one who had been in Cromwell's household, that Hyde was in the pay of the Lord Protector. The whole case was thrashed out in the presence of Charles, who declared the charge to be 'false and ridiculous', and Hyde's position as Chancellor became more secure than ever. At a much later date the King's ex-secretary confessed that the story had been a malicious invention.

One of Hyde's chief enemies on the Council was Sir Edward Herbert, who had been created Lord Keeper at the request of Henrietta Maria. In January '54 Herbert launched a final assault on Hyde, who had managed to irritate another member of the

King's Court, Lord Charles Gerard. During the previous year Charles had been recovering from an illness at Chantilly, and after dinner one day the party drove out to watch some setters at work. Hyde and Gerard, finding themselves apart from the rest, began to discuss politics, and Gerard spoke of the King's inattention to business and neglect of duty, advising Hyde to stimulate Charles and make him leave France where everybody was tired of him. Hyde replied that he was not responsible for the King's apathy, expressed a keen desire that he should leave France, and admitted that he was indisposed to business, taking too much delight in pleasure. Hyde's remarks were duly reported to Herbert, who declared that the Chancellor was not fit to sit on the Council. Proofs of this strange statement were demanded, and at the next meeting of the Council the conversation at Chantilly was reported by Gerard. At first Hyde looked a little uncomfortable, saying that he recalled the occasion; but he emphasised the fact that Gerard had started the topic by violently criticising the King's inertia and declaring that if he could find nothing else to do he should again try his fortune in the Highlands of Scotland. Hyde could not remember what he had said in reply, though he thought it unlikely that he should have spoken so freely to a man who was known to be unfriendly to himself. He would not deny having used the words imputed to him if Gerard would 'positively affirm' that he had said them; but even assuming he had spoken as reported, he left the King to decide whether 'such words proceeded from any malice in his heart towards him'. Herbert instantly claimed that Hyde's words were 'a high offence', and Hyde was about to withdraw when Charles, telling him to remain, staggered his Council by saying that he was quite willing to believe that the Chancellor had spoken in the manner related, 'because he had often said that, and much more, to myself'. Charles then admitted his fault, confessed he had no liking for business, but wondered whether Gerard's suggestion that he should become martially active again would be of much benefit to the cause. Having spiked the guns of Hyde's enemies, he declared his complete confidence in the Chancellor and commanded the Clerk of the Council to register it.

The idea of going to Scotland made no appeal to Charles. On hearing a rumour that he had found refuge there after the battle of Worcester, he exclaimed: 'I had rather have been hanged!' He was keeping in touch with a Royalist rising now being fomented in that country, but he was aware that, while the Scots would cut one another's throats with the utmost pleasure, it was almost impossible to unite them against a common foe, their leaders being more concerned over rank and religion than anxious to resist an invader. Nevertheless he told his Council that he would go to Scotland if they thought it expedient. None of them thinking it expedient to recommend such a course, he remained in Paris, the target of criticism by Catholics, Presbyterians and Anglicans alike, and of comment by Cromwell's spies, who clustered about the Court and kept Oliver in touch with all its doings. They were able to report that Charles was leading a thoroughly depraved life, that he preferred vice to virtue, and, what was more to the purpose, that he showed no signs of activity apart from intrigue. When Hyde received strictures on his master's licentious conduct, he touched an indulgent note: 'We must make the best of what we cannot help, and must always remember that Kings are of the same mould as other men, and must have the same time to be made perfect.' Henrietta Maria, enraged over her failure to discredit Hyde, maliciously suggested that her son James should head the Scottish rising. This annoyed Charles, because his brother had been gaining distinction under Turenne in the French civil war, and he answered that if it was fit for James it was still fitter for himself to go to Scotland, and that he would accompany his brother thither. Henrietta objected that it would be unwise to hazard both their lives. Charles retaliated that it would be more generous for James to hazard his life in Scotland than in the French wars, which did not concern him. That closed the conversation, and soon after it took place the future of Charles was decided by the political situation.

GEORGE MONK, 1ST DUKE OF ALBEMARLE

CATHERINE OF BRAGANZA

Penniless Freedom

The arrival of an English ambassador to represent the Commonwealth at the French Court made it difficult for Charles to remain in Paris, and the treaty between the two nations necessitated his withdrawal from France. Anxious to get rid of him, Cardinal Mazarin, normally a miser, became bountiful, and not only promised Charles a continuation of his pension, but gave him enough money to pay his debts, and advanced a sum for the ensuing half-year. Following a heated scene with his mother, who felt sore over his persistent refusal to take her advice, they parted frigidly, and Charles left France on 10 July 1654. Entering the Spanish dominion of Flanders on the 14th, he was entertained by the governor of Cambrai, but he received no official welcome because the Spaniards were still hopeful of avoiding conflict with Cromwell, though the treaty between England and France made it almost certain that the two countries would unite in the war against Spain. Going by Namur and Liège, he reached Spa, where he met his sister Mary of Orange, with whom he intended to spend a holiday.

Charles was one of those fortunate men who are able to forget their troubles at will. His situation at this time was sufficiently unenviable to draw from Hyde the despairing admission: 'The King is now as low as to human understanding he can be.' He was on bad terms with his mother and not on good terms with James his brother. France had ceased to recognise him as King of England and had practically expelled him. Spain could not acknowledge his sovereignty without precipitating hostilities with Cromwell. By compulsion from England, the Dutch had forbidden him to enter their territory and refused his sister permission to receive him on her own estate or to give him financial assistance. Even Sweden had concluded a commercial treaty with the Commonwealth. Look where he would, Charles could descry no gleam of hope. But instead of indulging in self-pity and complaints, he banished care and enjoyed the simple pleasures of a watering-place in the company of his sister.

[8]

Privy Conspiracies

BAD WEATHER kept everybody indoors for some days at Spa, but when the sun shone out they engaged fiddlers, learnt the latest dances, and pirouetted in the fields. Charles was surrounded by spies as well as courtiers, but as he was unaware of the former he relaxed gaily with his hangers-on, and Cromwell heard from a member of his secret service that 'there is not a day or night but there are balls and dancing. I think the air makes them indefatigable, for they dance the whole afternoon, then go to supper, and after they go into the meadows and dance there. None so much commended as our King, who indeed is grown a lusty and proper person; gains the affection of all by his affable and free carriage amongst them'. He drank the waters, both hard and soft, talked about sport, drove and rode about the neighbourhood, contented himself while dancing with fiddlers who made 'no difference between a hymn and a coranto', and was 'verie merrie'.

At the end of August one of Princess Mary's ladies died of smallpox, and the royal retinue moved to Aachen, where the following of Charles numbered above eighty. While here he received bad news from Scotland, but poverty prevented him from going there personally and trying to pacify the disputatious partners. The rising was of course abortive.

Their holiday over, he accompanied Mary on part of her way home early in October with the intention of visiting Cologne incognito. But he heard that the citizens thereof wished to give him a friendly welcome, so he submitted to a salute of thirty

86

cannon, the volleys of two hundred musketeers, a civic reception, and not a few presents. The burgomaster and two ecclesiastical dignitaries showed Charles and Mary over the cathedral, and the Tomb of the Three Kings was opened for their benefit, a rare privilege. They hunted, wandered around the city, attended receptions at various convents, and met the Papal Nuncio. Indeed Charles made himself so popular that he was invited by the magistrates to remain; and as he liked the place he determined to pass the winter there instead of at Aachen, especially as he hoped to obtain the money voted to him by the Imperial Diet which the German princes had not paid. A farewell banquet at the Town Hall was given the royal pair on 28 October, after which they proceeded by barge to Düsseldorf, where they were lavishly entertained by the Count Palatine of Neuberg. Brother and sister bade one another a weeping farewell on 5 November, and Charles returned to Cologne, where he passed the time walking about the city walls and trying to prevent his courtiers from quarrelling with one another. At least he was untroubled by debts, the burghers giving him 'house, firing, bread and wine'.

But another 'contestation' with his mother occupied the winter months. Henrietta Maria wished her children to become Roman Catholics, though her husband had begged her to make no effort to convert them. Only the youngest, Henriette Anne, born in 1644 at Exeter, had been reared as a Catholic, and though her brother Charles had protested against it he could only obtain a promise that the child should never enter a convent. Not that Charles was much concerned over religion, which, for all he could see, was merely a ground for futile wrangles and bloodshed, but he knew that his sole chance of regaining the Crown of England was to uphold the Established Church, and if any member of his family became a Catholic his own situation would be made more hazardous. It did not matter so much when the convert was a girl, but his two brothers were potential successors to the throne, and when Henrietta Maria tried to influence her son Henry to accept her faith Charles took a very stern line.

At the age of eighteen months the youngest son of Charles I, Henry Duke of Gloucester, was captured by Parliament. He and his sister Elizabeth were allowed to see their father in the days before his execution, when the King made his son vow that he would not desert the Anglican religion. After the tragedy the heart-broken Elizabeth died and Henry was called 'Master Harry Stuart'. His captivity at Carisbrooke in the Isle of Wight aroused the loyal emotions of those who saw him, and at last Parliament thought it advisable to get rid of him. A vessel and funds were supplied, and in February 1653 he sailed from Cowes and went to stay with his sister Mary in Holland. But Henrietta Maria longed to see her son, and in May of that year he joined her at the Palais Royal. When Charles left France in July '54 he permitted Henry to remain with his mother on the clear understanding that she should not try to change his religion.

But the understanding of a Catholic was not the same as that of a Protestant, and soon after the departure of Charles the young Duke was separated from his tutor and sent to live in the house of an *abbé*, who pointed out that his conversion would help his brother to recover the Crown, and tempted him with the prospect of becoming a cardinal. The lad was further informed by his mother that England was irrecoverably lost and that his only chance of doing well for himself was to change his faith. Henry stuck to his guns and wrote to tell Charles what had happened; but on Henrietta's instructions his letter was delayed in the post and pressure was brought to bear on the youth, whose mother assured him that he was to be instructed in the doctrines of the Roman Church. Henry replied that he had promised his father and brother to maintain the religion in which he had been brought up, and when Henrietta was reminded of her promise not to convert him she said that she had merely promised to use no force. Henry again wrote to his brother, and this time his letter was not delayed; but Henrietta also sent a letter in which she declared it her duty as a mother to reveal the true faith to her son.

When Charles at last tumbled to what was happening he acted

promptly. 'I never in my life saw the King our master in so great trouble and perplexity, nor of that quickness and sharpness in providing against a mischief,' wrote Hyde. The letter from Charles to his brother laid stress on the harm his conversion would do to their cause in England, and contained some shrewd advice: 'Whensoever anybody shall go to dispute with you on religion, do not answer them at all; for though you have reason on your side, yet they, being prepared, will have the advantage of anybody that is not upon the same security that they are.' He closed with an exhortation that the boy should remember the last words of his dead father, 'which were to be constant in your religion, and never to be shaken in it; which, if you do not observe, this shall be the last time you will ever hear from your most affectionate brother'. Charles wrote to brother James as well, conjuring him 'to hinder, all that lies in your power, any such practices, without any consideration of any person whatsoever'. Further he warned his mother that 'whatsoever mischief shall fall either upon me or my affairs hereafter will be laid upon your Majesty as the only cause of them and the undoer of your son'. Lord Jermyn, too, was told that if he did not use every endeavour to prevent the perversion of Henry, 'you must never think to see me again, and this shall be the last time you shall ever hear from me, being so full of passion that I cannot express myself'.

These letters were carried to Paris by Ormonde, who was instructed to see the King's commands carried out, failing which he was to bring the boy to Cologne. In the meantime Henry was subjected to a steady course of Catholic propaganda, which he sturdily withstood. When Ormonde arrived he experienced some difficulty in seeing Henry, and his conversation with Henrietta was unsatisfactory. But he persisted, and at length managed to interview the boy, whose mother then gave way, saying she would not prevent him from joining Charles at Cologne. However she knew that the French Court was on her side, and on 26 November both Mazarin and the Queen-Mother of France did their best to persuade Henry that he owed obedience to his surviving parent. Henry did not argue the point, but reported the occurrence to Ormonde. Two days later Henrietta played her last card. She tried to subdue her son with fond words and embraces, appealing to his affection for herself, and imploring him to enter the Jesuits' College. The *abbé* was then let loose, and for an hour Henry listened patiently to all the old arguments, on which he quietly observed that he was much afflicted by his inability to obey both mother and brother, but that the King's commands were 'more suitable to his inclination and his duty'. When Henrietta heard this, she lost her temper completely, telling Henry that she would no longer own him as a son, ordering him out of her presence, saying she would allow him nothing but his room to lie in, and adding that he must henceforth depend on Ormonde.

In great agitation Henry sought comfort from his brother James, who vainly appealed to their mother; and when the boy made a last gesture of remorse by kneeling before Henrietta on her way to Mass and begging for her blessing, she passed by without a word or a glance. The *abbé* attempted to sympathise, but the boy had now reached the limit of his endurance: 'What my mother says to me, I say to you; I pray be sure I see you no more.' 'Whither are you going, sir?' asked the *abbé*. 'To church,' was the challenging reply, and he went straight to a house where the Holy Communion was to be administered in accordance with the ritual of the English Church. Late that evening he returned to the Palais Royal to bid farewell to his little sister Henriette. But the child was distraught and could only utter laments. Henry found that the furniture in his bedroom and even the sheets on his bed had been removed, while his groom informed him that his two horses could not be stabled that night. One more attempt was made by the French Court to make Henry change his mind, but the Catholic method of persuasion had ceased to attract him, and the defeated authorities granted the passes for his journey. He wrote a final appeal for forgiveness to his mother, but she declined to read the letter, and he left without seeing her on 18 December in the company of Ormonde.

On their way to Cologne through Flanders the effect of all the spiritual turmoil to which the lad had been subjected became apparent, and at Antwerp he was prostrated by fever. Recovering, he spent some time with his sister Mary; but the serious risk of apprehension in Holland abbreviated his stay, and in May 1655 he reached Cologne. The attitude of Charles to the attempted conversion of his brother cost him the support of the Pope, who refused to send him money on that account. This was all the more annoying because the latest effort to win back the throne had just miscarried, and he could not raise money by fair means or foul.

For a year or more the Royalists in England were conspiring to overthrow Cromwell. Leaders in various towns and counties were appointed; sections of the army in England, Wales and Scotland, as well as part of the fleet, promised support; all kinds of religious fanatics, Presbyterians, Levellers and Fifth Monarchists, sympathised with the conspiracy; and Rochester went to England to gauge the chances of success and decide whether the rising should take place. Some of the keenest Royalists thought that their King's attitude to the plan was unsteady; at one moment his desire for its success overcame his scruples, at another his dislike of risking the lives of his friends was uppermost. But his fluctuating views were less a sign of weakness than intelligence. He knew that the Cavaliers were headstrong, the sectaries semi-demented, and felt sure they would never combine because they lacked singleness of aim. There was too much boasting, either of God or King, and too many people were in the secret.

Rochester travelled about the country assuming various characters, but he was not the right sort of man for the job and had many narrow shaves. 'If he had not been a man very fortunate in disguises, he could never have escaped so many perambulations,' wrote Hyde, 'for as he was the least wary in making his journeys in safe hours, so he departed very unwillingly from all places where there was good eating and drinking, and entered into conferences with any strangers he met or joined with.' The lack of unanimity and leadership, the abundance of traitors, and the activity of Cromwell's spies, brought about the collapse of the plot. It is quite on the cards that Cromwell encouraged it in order to lay his hands on the chief conspirators, for by the spring of 1655 the majority of them were imprisoned or arrested or on their way to Barbados as slaves. In anticipation of the rising Charles departed secretly from Cologne and remained for nearly a month at Middleburg in Zeeland, where he stayed quietly in the house of a Dutchman waiting for a call to England and quite unconscious that one of Cromwell's spies had tracked him down and was reporting his movements to the English authorities. Back at Cologne in May, he had the melancholy satisfaction of greeting Rochester and others who had managed to get away.

In the summer of 1655 there was a movement among the Presbyterians to influence the King against his chief adviser Hyde, and Charles had great difficulty in keeping peace between those who wanted a swordsman like Prince Rupert or the Duke of York and those who still believed in Hyde, the lawyer and man of words. 'Men would have they know not what, or anything but what is,' said an acute observer of the scene. 'I cannot but pity the poor King, who must be so perplexed with the factions and unreasonable humours of some people . . . his trials are above the strength of a man,' noted a sympathetic soldier. When the anti-Hyde party appealed for support to the group about Henrietta Maria at the Palais Royal, the King put his foot down, issuing an order that his mother and her followers 'should neither meddle nor make' in England. Certainly Hyde was no diplomatist. Having a high opinion of his own honesty and intelligence and a low opinion of other people's, he made no secret of it. Charles himself had sufficient intelligence to appreciate Hyde's, and never wavered in his loyalty to a man he could trust implicitly, warning a correspondent: 'I pray do not give credit to those people who take upon them to censure whatsoever I do, and have no way to appear wise but to find fault with whatsoever is done.'

The poverty of the exiles in the summer of 1655 became increasingly serious, and the King would have sold such Crown jewels as he possessed if they had not already been pawned past recovery. Money had been borrowed to meet current expenses, and the Court practically lived on loans. 'The King hath not money enough to provide meat for himself the next ten days,' reported Hyde. Only two of the German princes had paid their subsidies, and the pension from France was both sparse and tardy. Mary sent sums to her brother whenever possible, but these could not be depended upon. Nevertheless the King enjoyed a week at Düsseldorf and occasionally hunted. The state of his wardrobe occupied his attention, and he wrote to a friend in Paris: 'My clothes are at last come, and I like them very well, all but the sword, which is the worst I ever saw. I suspect very much that it was you that made the choice, therefore you have no other way to recover your judgment in that particular but to make choice of a better.' He asked for twelve pairs of shoes, six from his own shoemaker and six from another, of which 'three pair must be black and the other coloured, and a little bigger than those he sent me last.' Sometimes the gossip he sent to this friend was restricted: 'I have taken pills this morning, which hinders me from saying much more to you.' His letters were mostly concerned with fashions of one kind or another: 'Pray get me pricked down as many new corantos and sarabands and other little dances as you can, and bring them with you, for I have got a small fiddler that does not play ill on the fiddle.'

Mary spent two summer months with Charles at Cologne in 1655, and he announced that 'we . . . pass our time as well as people can do that have no money, for we dance and play as if we had taken the Plate fleet'. They visited Frankfurt together for the annual fair, meeting the eccentric Queen Christina of Sweden in the neighbourhood, and enjoying the trip all the more because two princes were reminded of their subsidies and paid what was due. But the expenses of their journey had been considerable, and not even the offer of an American that he should cross the ocean to become King of Virginia helped Charles to raise money on the prospect.

It had now begun to dawn on the Royalists that their only hope lay in the death of Cromwell, and they commenced to plot his assassination, though they did not dare tell Charles of their intention, knowing that he was out of sympathy with murder. Quite a few members of the King's circle travelled to England for that purpose, secretly as they thought, though Cromwell was well aware of their movements. The queer thing is that they were allowed to come and go with such apparent ease, but probably the Lord Protector believed he could learn more to his advantage from people at liberty than from those under duress. So effective was his secret service, and so disloyal were many of the King's followers, that after the Restoration the head of Cromwell's intelligence department, John Thurloe, said 'that if he were hanged, he had a black book which should hang half of them that went for Cavaliers'. As a consequence, instead of being hanged, he was frequently consulted by Charles II.

As it happened Cromwell agreed with the plotters that their sole chance of restoring the King lay in his own death; so he made arrangements to meet the peril. In 1655 he divided the country into eleven districts and placed a personal friend as Major-General over each, giving him absolute power and taxing the Royalists to pay for their own suppression by this means. 'The Supreme Magistrate,' declared Cromwell, 'was not to be bound by ordinary rules, and the preservation of the State necessitated the assumption of a dictatorship.' Although this method protected the Protector, it ensured the return of a monarchy after his death, for it united the liberty-loving elements in the country, whether sectarian or orthodox, against a government that ruled without laws and established Courts of Injustice. Needing much more money than he could wring out of the Royalists, Cromwell sent a fleet to the West Indies with instructions to seize the Spanish possessions and kill the settlers thereon. While the English fleet was busy capturing Jamaica, the Lord Protector was equally busy arranging a treaty with the Spaniards in Flanders; but when the news of the West Indian assault reached Europe in August '55, the treaty was dropped and war became imminent between Spain and England.

The attitude of the Spaniards to Charles quickly changed. His stock went up and it seemed advisable that he should open negotiations at Brussels. He heard that if he wished for Spanish help he must become a Roman Catholic, a fact that he could conceal in order to obtain the Crown of England, resting assured that the Pope and the King of Spain could be trusted to keep the secret. This was only a 'feeler', and Charles hoped for something more reasonable. Early in '56 the Spanish ministers in Brussels became more friendly with the King's deputy, which seemed to reflect the feeling of their ruler, Philip IV, and Charles decided to talk things over in person. He left Cologne in March; and though his sudden arrival in Brussels discomposed the Spanish ministers, they gave him a courteous reception. He then retired to Vilvord, about three miles from Brussels, to await events. Here he whiled away the time by reading Spanish, writing letters, and playing cribbage with Rochester. 'Pray send us as good news tomorrow as the wine and mutton was today,' he wrote to Ormonde, who had remained in Brussels to prepare the terms of a treaty, which was duly signed by representatives of the two monarchs on 12 April. It reaffirmed an alliance between the Crowns of the two countries, and arranged for the provision by Spain of a fully armed force of four thousand infantry and two thousand cavalry, together with transport and maintenance, whenever Charles could provide an English port for their debarkation. On his side Charles promised, when restored, to assist Spain in her fight against Portugal with twelve warships for five years, to relinquish the recent West Indian conquests, and to suspend the penal laws against Roman Catholics in Ireland, repealing them when possible. Charles could not officially remain in Brussels without an invitation from Philip and the expenditure of much money to keep up his state; so he retired incognito to Bruges, whence he wrote optimistically to Hyde: 'That which we have gotten already is more than I hoped for when I left Cologne, and which, if anybody could have assured us of two months since, would have made you caper in spite of the gout.'

[9]

Castles in Spain

THE CASH PREDICAMENT was always acute. There seemed
no possible chance of paying debts, though the news of the latest
alliance between the two monarchs enabled Charles to raise a
loan at Antwerp for current expenses. The pension from France
was stopped the moment Mazarin got to hear of the Brussels
treaty, and Charles could send no money to his establishment at
Cologne. With the arrival at Brussels of a new Spanish viceroy,
Don John of Austria, the situation improved, and Charles was
promised an allowance from Philip of six thousand guilders a
month (say five hundred pounds), while half that sum was assured
to his brother Henry. But promises are more easily made than
kept, and such sums as they received were meagre and delayed.
However, Charles was able to solace himself with the visits of
eminent foreigners, the friendliness of the Flemings, and the en-
dearments of a mistress. His Chancellor arrived in July '56 and
pressed the Spanish authorities to abolish the King's incognito,
to open the ports to his ships, and to arrange quarters for his
regiments, which were then being embodied from the many
Cavaliers who had been serving with continental armies. The
difficulty over the incognito was that the expense would be too
great if Charles were acknowledged as King, for in that event all
the ceremonies and pomp of royalty would have to be observed.
But Don John gave orders that all Royalist vessels should be
made welcome at the various ports, and after some delay permission was granted for the raising of several regiments which

would march with the Spanish army until needed by Charles and be partly maintained by Spain. It was agreed that the Irish soldiers then fighting with the French should be encouraged to join the King's forces in Flanders, and within a few weeks some eight hundred of them trickled over the border in small bodies of six or seven at a time.

A certain amount of jealousy existed between Charles and his brother James, and for a long time the latter would not leave France, where he had won distinction in the civil wars. His popularity with soldiers made Charles particularly anxious to have him with the troops now gathering in Flanders under the Royalist banner. Family discord increased when their sister Mary visited Paris early in 1656, being hospitably entertained by the French Court and enthusiastically received by her mother. It did not strengthen the fraternal feelings of Charles when Mary remained in Paris for close on a year, during which another treaty was concluded between England and France, Cromwell promising to send six thousand of his soldiers to serve against Spain in Flanders. But Charles's irritation with Mary was momentarily assuaged when James at last responded to his appeal, left France, and joined his brother at Bruges at the end of September '56. By this time the King's army was getting large and out of hand. Pay, food and quarters were not easily obtained from the Spaniards, and famished soldiers soon become a menace instead of a defence.

Apart from raising money Charles's main concern was the provision of an English port at which the invading army could disembark, because without that Spain would not move; and a blow to his hopes was delivered when Blake smashed the Spanish fleet, capturing their treasure ships. Another Royalist plot to restore him collapsed; while a vigorous attempt by the Levellers to occupy the ports of Plymouth and Portsmouth and engross the attention of the ruling power while Charles landed with Spanish forces elsewhere was thwarted. The Levellers were to be helped by a cashiered quartermaster, who intended to slay Cromwell in

Hyde Park with the help of forty men. The arrangements did not proceed as planned, and the next idea that occurred to the quarter-master was to hire a house at Hammersmith and pot the Protector from a window as he rode on his way to Hampton Court. This too fizzled out; and a further attempt on Oliver's life by the more comprehensive method of blowing up Whitehall Palace with gunpowder was baffled. Cromwell had every intention of dying what is usually termed a natural death, and the efficiency of his spies coupled with the devotion of his bodyguard enabled him to expire in peace.

By the close of 1656 Charles was in parlous plight. Somehow enough cash had been collected to redeem his dependants at Cologne, and his Court at Bruges now included all his chief advisers, physicians, chaplains, clerks, officers and servants, to say nothing of the retinues of his two brothers, James and Henry. 'We are wondrous merry and divert ourselves at home and abroad,' wrote Ormonde. But those who knew the King's situation were also wondrous moody. James became actively trouble-some when his brother wished to make changes in his staff, ran away from Bruges, and had to be coaxed back. Everyone felt rest-less and longed for home, one of the King's emissaries in Madrid pining for 'good old England, where one turf is worth all Spain'. It was impossible to get the money promised to Charles from the responsible ministers in Brussels. The Spanish officials were courteous, urbane, socially charming, but their procrastination and mendacity were maddening. 'All the devils in hell take them!' exploded Hyde, and Charles wrote: 'I have lost all patience, and give all men that have, or shall have, to do with money to the devil.' There was nothing for it but to sell his coach-horses, while those of his followers who had no possessions were imprisoned for debt, those who still had a few belongings pawned them to keep out of gaol, and the five ragged regiments of soldiers now embodied – three Irish, one Scottish, one English – mutinied, robbed, deserted, begged, and terrified their neighbourhoods.

Sheer anarchy might have resulted from Spanish supineness if

Cromwell had not come to the rescue. In May '57 his troops landed at Calais in new red coats and new shoes, the payment being ninepence a day for foreign service. Their object was to capture Dunkirk and Gravelines, which were at the same time blockaded by the English fleet. It had been stipulated in the treaty with France that the troops were to be wholly English, and that the first maritime town to be taken should be held by them. To save her trade Spain decided to make the army of Charles serviceable, with his brother as Captain-General of the Royalist regiments. As usual there was trouble with the Spanish authorities, who wanted James's help but were jealous of his prestige. Charles, who longed to lead his own troops, was humiliated by the appointment of his brother, and when he asked permission to appear on the scene of action his request was refused by the Spanish commander, Don John. Lack of money kept him in Brussels, to which he had recently moved; but at the end of August his persistency won a reluctant consent, and he joined the army as a witness of events. He exposed himself needlessly to gunfire, Ormonde's horse being shot as he rode by the King's side, and received a lecture from Hyde : 'I am not one of those who think you are like to recover your kingdom without being in danger of your life, but let it be when the adventure is of use, and there is a recompense in view.' Charles was sick of Spanish incompetence, of promises that were never kept, of begging for money he never received, and the thought of being killed was less grievous than the prospect of being a king only in name. So depressed was he by poverty that he asked his sister Mary to send him 'any jewel that I may pawn for £1500 sterling'. Though she sided with Henrietta Maria in the quarrel between Charles and their mother, she complied with his request.

Red-tape and indolence undermined the striking power of the Spanish forces, and the coastal towns were closely besieged by the French and English throughout the winter months of 1657-8 without the least chance of relief. During that period Charles and Hyde did their utmost to make Don John state what help he would give for an invasion of England. The methods of the dilatory Don made Charles lose his temper and even drove Hyde to despair. At last the Spanish viceroy announced that Ormonde should go to England, and if he reported favourably of the situation there an expedition would be sent the following spring. Ormonde accordingly went, using a hair-dye which gave a rainbow effect to the top of his head. He discovered that all the plotters distrusted one another; but as he doubted whether they would ever unite except under a monarch, and as their distrust grew with delay, he advised an early landing by Charles on the east coast while he himself caused a diversion in the west. Cromwell soon heard of the latest intrigues, sent a fleet to blockade Ostend and patrol the English coast, and ordered all Royalists and Roman Catholics to remain within five miles of their homes.

In January 1658 Oliver must have heard with some amusement that Charles had given Hyde the title of Lord High Chancellor of England in succession to Sir Edward Herbert, lately deceased. Hyde thought the title unnecessary until the Restoration, saying that the moment the appointment was known the King would be pestered for jobs, positions and the like. On the contrary, replied Charles, producing a sheaf of such pesterments, he had already received so many of them that he would much rather they were sent to the Lord Chancellor, to whom he could henceforth refer his correspondents. The King spent some weeks with his sister Mary at Antwerp that winter. The Earl of Rochester, who as Lord Wilmot had been his fellow-fugitive after Worcester fight, died early in '58; but Charles was not the man to indulge in unavailing grief, and on the day of the funeral went to a ball and banquet given by a leading citizen. Nor did it worry him much when Lucy Walter, who had not shown much discrimination in her lovers during his absence in Scotland, threatened to make known his letters to her. He had some difficulty in getting their boy out of her hands, but succeeded at last and sent the lad to Paris, where he received instruction in the Romish faith.

The private life of Charles in exile had vexed his two monitors,

Ormonde and Hyde, both of whom had spoken to him on the subject, gravely but without effect. His love-affairs were both numerous and productive, one of his sons being borne by a married woman whose maiden name was Elizabeth Killigrew, and a son and daughter by Catherine Pegge.[1] According to Samuel Pepys, the King's 'seventeenth mistress abroad' was Lady Byron, but this must have been hearsay evidence, as it is improbable that Charles's courtiers or even Cromwell's spies witnessed his amours. All the same his private behaviour was so well known to intimate friends that when, early in 1658, he told them of his intention to visit Brussels for the purpose of expediting the promised help from Spain, Ormonde wrote to Hyde: 'He must pardon me if I cannot believe it is that which disposes him to the journey, or will be his employment there . . . I fear his immoderate delight in empty, effeminate, and vulgar conversation is become an irresistible part of his nature.' In fact nothing could tempt Charles to live at Bruges, where he lacked feminine society, and in March '58 his belongings were removed to the capital.

The Flemish campaign reopened in the early summer of '58, when France and Cromwell's England fought for the possession of Dunkirk against Spain and Charles's England. The battle of the Dunes took place on 14 June, the only combatants to distinguish themselves being James, who led a gallant charge, and Oliver's soldiers, whose lustiness aroused the admiration of James. Eleven days after the battle Dunkirk surrendered to the French commander, who handed it over to Cromwell's general in pursuance of the treaty. By this time Spain could no longer afford a costly war, and made overtures to France. Directly Charles heard of it, he planned a journey to the Spanish frontier, where the conference would take place and the treaty would be signed, in the hope of gaining the help of both countries or at least of arranging something beneficial to himself.

His financial position was worse than ever, and in a mood of

1. Her son by Charles eventually became Earl of Plymouth.

despondency he left Brussels in August '58 for a border village named Hoogstraeten, where he hawked and hunted and became thoroughly bored. Then he made a short tour of the United Provinces, telling a story in the years ahead about a secret journey to see his sister at The Hague. He arrived with a servant at an obscure inn, and while the servant was absent with a message to Mary he received a visit from 'an old reverend-looking man, with a long grey beard and ordinary grey clothes'. Having locked the door the visitor discarded his make-up, fell on his knees, declared himself to be the English ambassador, George Downing, and begged forgiveness for past transgressions. Charles having pronounced pardon, Downing asserted that the King's arrival had been reported, that in accordance with the treaty between Cromwell and Holland his apprehension was inevitable, but that himself as ambassador would delay action until Charles was safely off the territory. Charles quickly made himself scarce, and Downing reported the King's presence on Dutch soil as soon as he could feel sure of his absence.

Having taken part in an incident that might later have appeared in *The Three Musketeers*, Charles went back to Hoogstraeten, where he again fell a slave to the charms of Henriette, daughter of the Dowager Princess of Orange and sister-in-law to Mary. They had been in love with one another for some time, but the girl's mother had refused to let them be engaged because the Dutch authorities would not have sanctioned their marriage. Now, however, an event occurred that seemed to remove the chief obstacle to their alliance. On 3 September 1658, the anniversary of the battles of Dunbar and Worcester, Oliver Cromwell died. A gasp of relief and a cry of joy went up from the three European powers with vulnerable seaboards, France, Spain and Holland, from which we may conclude that the might of England had been universally feared for the first time in history. Charles was playing tennis when he heard the news. He dropped the racket and took up a pen, making a formal request for Princess Henriette's hand. She was overcome with emotion and her mother proved tractable. The Dutch, who hated Cromwell as much as they feared him, changed their attitude to Charles; the French, whose loathing of Cromwell was tempered by awe, became conciliatory; and the Spanish, paralysed by a combination of abhorrence and terror of the Lord Protector, would have accelerated their preparations on behalf of Charles if they had not felt that France would now be quicker off the mark. But unfortunately for the exiles Cromwell had so thoroughly put the fear of God, or at least the fear of himself as God's instrument, into the English people that no one had the courage to strike a blow, and Oliver's son Richard became Lord Protector without a murmur. After several months of feverish anticipation Charles and his friends came to the conclusion that they were not wanted at home, and Hyde suggested a possible reason in the scandal of his monarch's private life, begging Charles to 'rouse up your spirit and do what you ought yourself, and then you will make us all do as we ought'. But the decline of his hopes, far more than his carnal offences, determined the Dowager Princess of Orange to renounce him and transfer her daughter to a German prince.

Charles had now reached the lowest ebb of his fortune. His outlook was bleak; his house was let; his courtiers were fighting one another; his belongings were sold or pawned; he ate what he could get; he was on bad terms with his mother, his sister Mary and his brother James; and, as a last straw, Holland and France renewed their alliances with the English Protectorate. But circumstances were achieving what conspiracies had failed to bring about. England was tired of the Protectorate, and the unpaid army, disliking the Parliament of the Protector, dissolved it by force, bringing back what was left of the Long Parliament after it had been purged by Cromwell, known vulgarly as 'the Rump'. That was in May '59, and the same month Richard Cromwell, wishful for a quiet life, abdicated.

In the general disintegration the one man who seemed to have power was General George Monk, who had been made head of the army in Scotland by Cromwell, and the agents of Charles tried to approach him. But he was an extremely cautious and secretive person, whose good opinion of himself was allied to a creed 'of that description which easily adjusts itself to worldly circumstances', for he had fought for the Royalists in the Civil War, and then, after meditating on the matter as a prisoner in the Tower, had transferred his allegiance; in short, a time-server who waited to see how the cat would jump. Charles had the wisdom to know that if his restoration were accomplished with the aid of foreign troops his reign would start off badly, and he hoped the English people would regain their King 'without owing those great obligations to foreign princes which they seldom yield without some advantage to their own interest'. He informed one of his agents in England that he would take any personal risk demanded of him, 'rather than expose my friends to the dangers which threaten them, and infinitely desiring to have no use of foreign force, if I can avoid it', and he sent an appeal to the Admiral of the English fleet urging a revolt of the navy.

A new Royalist plot was being hatched, and Charles secretly left Brussels for Calais, so as to be close at hand if needed. It was arranged that James should also land in England at a different place if all went well, and Charles sent him a letter telling him that everyone should receive a free pardon 'except only those who sat actually upon the murder of our father, and voted for it', but adding astutely: 'If any excepted person shall make offer to you of doing a very extraordinary service (which I do not expect that any of them will or can do) you may appoint some discreet person to treat with him, who may promise him that after he hath performed that service, he shall not be prosecuted by me, but shall have a time allowed to convey away his estate which shall not be seized by me, so that he withdraws out of my dominions, where he will never desire to live.'

At Calais it seemed as if the latest plot had gone wrong, for Charles heard that the county of Kent where he intended to land remained quiescent. He went on to Rouen, and then to St Malo, in the hope that the western shires would show more spirit and enable him to enter one of their ports. 'Sure never people went so cheerfully to venture our necks as we do,' he wrote to Hyde in August '59. But he heard at St Malo that the Royalists had been betrayed by one of their number, and all had come to naught. He made up his mind at once to go south to the Pyrenees, where the French and Spanish diplomats were negotiating a treaty of peace, and for some weeks his closest friends, starving in Flanders, were ignorant of his whereabouts. At Rochelle he and his companions waited for a favourable wind to go by sea to San Sebastian; but as the wind showed no sign of obliging them, the journey was continued through France on horseback. The trip seems to have been enjoyable enough to make them prolong it, because Charles did not write to Hyde until they reached Saragossa early in October: 'Our journey hitherto hath been very lucky, having met with many pleasant accidents and not one ill one to any of our company, hardly as much as the fall of a horse. But I am very much deceived in the travelling in Spain, for by all reports I did expect ill cheer and worse lying, and hitherto we have found both the beds and especially the meat very good. The only thing I find troublesome is the dust, and particularly in this town, there having fallen no rain on this side the Pyrenees these four months. God keep you, and send you to eat as good mutton as we have every meal.' Hyde was living a muttonless life, and the last line must have made him peevish.

Later in the month Charles arrived at Fuenterrabia, where the two nations were patching up their treaty. The Spanish ministers received him with elaborate courtesy, but Mazarin was too cunning to show him open hospitality, 'though he takes pains to let me know underhand of his good inclinations and intentions towards me'. Good intentions were almost all that Charles got out of the visit, in spite of his effort to win the Cardinal's support by offering to marry his niece, Hortense Mancini, an offer that was refused on the ground that the King should wed someone of greater distinction, Mazarin's true reason being that Charles's restoration was extremely problematical. Many years later

Hortense became Charles's mistress, a more satisfactory arrangement.

He left Fuenterrabia with a gift of seven thousand gold pistoles from Philip's representative, and the promise of a good reception at Brussels when he returned there. Then he went to see his mother in Paris and a reconciliation took place, marked by the title he bestowed on her most trusted counsellor, Henry Jermyn, who became the Earl of St Albans. But far more important for Charles was his meeting with his youngest sister, Henriette Anne, now fifteen years of age. According to an observer, 'Her Highness is so grown the King did not know her, for they brought his Majesty another young lady whom he saluted for his sister, and was in that mistake till my Lord Gerard undeceived him.' Perhaps it was not a mistake, Charles never being averse to kissing young ladies. But from the moment he saw his sister during this visit he became devoted to her. He called her Minette, and thereafter they corresponded regularly, with deep affection on both sides, and it is almost certain that he loved her more than any other woman in his life, their particular relationship, unimpaired by sexual passion, conducing to that end. His first letter to her after their separation displayed the feelings she had aroused in him: 'We shall never have any other quarrel but as to which of us shall love the other most, but in this I will never yield to you . . . In future, I beg of you, do not treat me with so much ceremony in addressing me with so many "Majesties", for I do not wish that there should be anything between us two but friendship.'

[10]

Journey's End

ONE EVENING towards the end of December 1659, the King entered Brussels in good health and high spirits. All sorts of rumours were flying about and people were proposing the maddest ideas, for example that he should marry the daughter of the Cromwellian General, John Lambert, who was temporarily in the ascendant as commander of the forces in England. Lambert was beginning to throw his weight about, and Parliament, not wishing to be at the mercy of another Protector, sacked him. Taking a leaf out of Oliver's book, Lambert sacked Parliament. That was Monk's cue. Announcing in the well-known Cromwellian style that he had a call from God, he marched an army of seven thousand men across the border. Lambert went north to check him, and they met at Berwick, where they began to tell one another about the Lord's purpose. While thus engaged Lambert's men discovered that Monk's troops were much better fed and more regularly paid than themselves, and the Lord's intentions were soon manifested by the increase of Monk's army and the diminution of Lambert's. The pseudo-Cromwell was soon cooling his heels in the Tower of London, and the field was left open for Monk, who continued his march to the south.

The Rump by that time was again sitting, and fearing another dictatorship they ordered Monk to send his army back to Scotland, inviting him to London with a following of five hundred men. He accepted the invitation, but felt that the Lord's affairs would be arranged more smoothly with a larger force. The Rump, backed by the City, began to put obstacles in the way, and shortly after his arrival in London, where he resided at Whitehall Palace, he ordered the re-establishment of the Long Parliament, the survivors of those members who had been purged by Cromwell returning to Westminster. Having conciliated the City with a show of power, he decided in favour of a free general election. The Long Parliament then dissolved itself, as an alternative to being dissolved by Monk, and the prospect of a new Parliament to be elected without military assistance drove the country mad with joy. Bonfires blazed, rumps were roasted in the streets in mockery of the recent political gang, and the King's health was freely drunk in public.

Even before the election it was clear that the new Parliament would favour a restoration of the monarchy; and when it was learnt in April '60 that the Commons were almost Royalist to a man, the public rejoicings became delirious. To the accompaniment of much bell-ringing the people toasted the King on their knees in the streets, 'which methinks is a little too much' reflected Samuel Pepys, and pictures of Charles were displayed outside houses, a form of decoration which a short while before would have ensured the hanging of their inmates. Butchers' boys went about yelling 'Will you buy any Parliament rumps and kidneys?' and when an honest pedestrian remarked that the King was not so handsome as he appeared in one of the pictures, he was nearly killed by those who overheard him.

As soon as he perceived which way the wind was blowing, Monk got into touch with one of the King's agents, who travelled to Brussels with the necessary instructions. Charles was to send letters to both Houses of Parliament, as well as a public Declaration to be enclosed in a letter to Monk, who outlined the terms of the various communications. As Spain was still officially at war with England, the King was told to leave Brussels and go to Breda in Holland. Charles obeyed, informing Monk that he desired with all his heart the peace, happiness and honour of his country, 'and whatever you have heard to the contrary, you will find to be as false as if you had been told that I have white hair or am crooked'. In his Declaration to all his subjects, he announced that he would uphold their liberties, restore justice and the laws, and be guided in all things by Parliament. He granted a free pardon to all who wished to be loyal henceforth, and promised that 'no crime whatsoever committed against us or our royal father before the publication of this shall ever rise in judgment or be brought in question against any of them to the least endamagement of them, either in their lives, liberties or estates . . . we desiring and ordaining that henceforward all notes of discord, separation, and difference of parties, be utterly abolished among all our subjects'. He added that certain people were to be excepted from this amnesty by Parliament, meaning the murderers of his father, though he did not say so. He also declared 'a liberty to tender consciences and that no man shall be disquieted or called in question for differences of opinion in matter of religion, which do not disturb the peace of the kingdom'. In his letter to the Speaker of the House of Commons, he expressed a hope 'that we have made that right Christian use of our affliction, and that the observation and experience we have had in other countries hath been such as we, and we hope all our subjects, shall be the better for what we have seen and suffered.'

His Declaration was read aloud in the Commons, the members standing bareheaded to hear it. A resolution of thanks was passed, and, more to the purpose, fifty thousand pounds voted for the present expenses of the King, who was asked to return unconditionally. Grants were also made to his brothers, ten thousand for James, five thousand for Henry. Public acclamation now passed all bounds. 'Good God!' wrote an observer: 'Do the same people inhabit England that were in it ten or twenty years ago? Believe me, I know not whether I am in England or no, or whether I dream.' Charles suddenly found himself extremely popular abroad. Spain wanted to have him back in Brussels, France wanted him in Paris, Holland invited him to The Hague. He was swamped with correspondence, begging for this, promising that, reminding him of that or this. The old enmity to Hyde broke out afresh, Catholics and Presbyterians hating him as much as ever. Buckingham helped to spread slanders about the Chancellor, whose return to England was opposed by Monk. Hearing a report from England that Hyde had lost his favour, Charles promptly suppressed it: 'The truth of it is, I look upon the spreaders of that lie as more my enemies than his, for he will always be found an honest man, and I should deserve the name of a very unjust master if I should reward him so ill that hath served me faithfully. Therefore I do conjure you to let as many as you can of my friends know the falsehood and malice of that report, and I shall take it as a service.' Monk withdrew his opposition both to Hyde and to Ormonde.

The King's clothes were as shabby as his debts were considerable when the English Parliament sent an advance of several thousand pounds in gold, the mere sight of which made him feel so jubilant that he called his sister Mary and his brother James to have a look at it before the cash was taken out of the bag. He had no cause to love the Dutch but when the States-General asked him to The Hague as a guest he accepted their invitation because it was 'the nearest and most commodious place from whence I may embark'. Accompanied by his sister and brothers, he travelled thither, being received with the roar of cannon. He was sumptuously housed and entertained, admitting some years after that he had never supped better than on the day he went to the Hague. The States gave him sixty thousand pounds, seven thousand five hundred to each of his brothers, and allowed thirty thousand for the expenses of his visit. Princes, ambassadors, notabilities of all sorts, flocked to see him and pay their respects. The committee of the English Parliament arrived with the money voted to himself and his brothers together with a 'humble invitation and supplication . . . that his Majesty would return and take the Government of the Kingdom into his hands'. The City of London sent ten thousand pounds, which pleased him so much that he knighted each of the fourteen citizens who brought it. The

only inharmonious note was struck when a number of Presbyterian divines tried to make Charles promise that he would suppress the Book of Common Prayer and the use of surplices in his
own chapel and elsewhere. This kind of thing had been steadily
getting on his nerves for years, and he tartly rejoined that in
giving liberty to others he did not intend to renounce his own.

The English navy had arrived off Scheveling, and James took
command as Admiral of the Fleet. On 23 May a huge crowd
gathered on the Dunes to witness the royal departure for England.
Salutes were fired from the ships and harbours, and the air was
filled with smoke as the King, escorted by ministers, ambassadors
and a conglomeration of citizens, left for the shore. At 11 a.m. he
went on board the *Naseby*, which was quickly renamed the *Royal
Charles*, and here he said farewell to his sister Mary, who wept
bitterly at the parting. He paced the quarter-deck in the highest
spirits, and for the first time gave his friends a truthful description
of his escape after the battle of Worcester. The fleet set sail at
4 p.m., and the English cliffs were seen in the evening of the next
day. Having breakfasted on the ship's rations of pork, pease and
boiled beef, and distributed five hundred pounds among the crew,
the King landed from the Admiral's barge at Dover about three
p.m. on the 25th. The moment he stepped on English soil he
dropped on his knees to render thanks, and though the gesture
was theatrically effective it doubtless expressed his intense feeling. Monk was there kneeling to receive the King, who raised
him, embraced him, and called him 'Father'. A minister of Dover
presented a large ornate Bible, which Charles took, saying that it
was the thing that he loved above all things in the world, a suitable sentiment for absorption by a nation of bibliolaters.

Greeted by the populace with howls of joy, Charles proceeded
to Canterbury, where there was much knighting and earling and
gartering. On 26 May he wrote therefrom to his sister Henriette:
'I was so plagued with business at The Hague that I could not
write to you before my departure. But I left instructions with my
sister to send you a little present from me which I hope you will

soon receive. I arrived yesterday at Dover, where I found Monk with a great number of the nobility, who almost overwhelmed me with friendship and joy at my return. My head is so prodigiously dazed by the acclamation of the people and by quantities of business that I know not whether I am writing sense or no; therefore you will pardon me if I do not tell you any more, only that I am entirely yours. C.'

On Sunday the 27th he went to the Cathedral and heard an Anglican service. The next night he slept at Rochester; and on his thirtieth birthday, Tuesday 29 May 1660, he entered London amidst scenes of such wild delight as have never been surpassed in the records of public rejoicing. The roads were strewn with flowers, the houses covered with many-coloured stuffs; the bells of every church rang out, the cannons thundered, and the fountains ran with wine. The procession took seven hours to pass through the city to Whitchall Palace, and the tumult of cheers, shouts and yells never ceased. Charles enjoyed it all, as he enjoyed most things, but he knew the value of popular acclaim, knew that it could change overnight into popular execration, and his sane attitude was expressed in the comment 'that it could be nobody's fault but his own that he had stayed so long abroad, when all mankind wished him so heartily at home'.

Shakespeare said that 'journeys end in lovers meeting'. Charles concurred, and while the populace were still revelling, the nobility still celebrating his restoration, he crossed the river to Lambeth, where he spent the night with his latest mistress, a voluptuous married woman named Barbara Palmer, who had followed in his train from Holland and would shortly become the chief influence at his Court.

[11]

The King's Own

IN THE DAYS NOT LONG PAST when the walls of Whitehall
Palace were hung with cobwebs instead of tapestries, a poet
named Martin Parker had written:

> But all's to no end, for the times will not mend
> Till the King enjoys his own again.

And the poet trusted his divinatory skill:

> Whereby I can tell, all things will be well
> When the King enjoys his own again.

The outburst of gladness showed how popular the monarchy had
become after an interregnum of politicians and Protectors; while
the release of the populace from religious gloom, social constraint
and dictatorial laws, seemed to suggest that the times had already
begun to mend. But much distress was to be endured before the
King's suppleness and sanity brought the country to a point when
his people could claim with some degree of accuracy that all things
were well.

For a year after his return everyone was so busy celebrating
the event that few had time to spare for any other business. The
general joy was unconfined, expressing itself in dancing, singing,
eating, drinking, swearing, gambling, blaspheming, whoring,

cock-fighting, dog-fighting, bear-baiting, bull-baiting, horse-baiting, bonfire-burning, gunpowder-exploding, and similar manifestations of national high spirits, which had been damped down during the Puritan régime. Whitehall Palace was besieged with loyalists whose one desire, apart from more material benefits, was to see the King and kiss his hand. They flooded the galleries there and he submitted freely to the operation. They watched him dining in state; they mobbed the chapel to see him pray; they yelled themselves hoarse when he rowed or sailed on the Thames, and the continuous rain failed to dispirit them when he visited the Guildhall to dine with the Houses of Parliament on 5 July 1660, the streets in the city being enlivened by much pageantry. Less picturesque but quite as pleasant was another kind of pageant, performed at the end of January 1661, when the bodies of leading regicides – Oliver Cromwell, his son-in-law Henry Ireton, John Bradshaw and Thomas Pride – were dragged from their tombs in Westminster Abbey to Tyburn, hanged in their coffins on the gallows from nine in the morning till six at night, and then buried beneath the gibbet, a process that did no one any harm and the enthusiastic onlookers a lot of good. The bones of Oliver's mother, Admiral Blake and nineteen others were also taken from the Abbey and dropped into a pit nearby, to the approval of the multitude. But another spectacle was denied them. It was felt by some that a public funeral of Charles I would deepen the sense of thanksgiving for the revival of the monarchy in the person of his son; but according to Hyde the royal body could not be found in the chapel at Windsor; so the public were deprived of their tears. However, much entertainment was to be derived from the trials of the living regicides in October '60, when twenty-nine were sentenced to death, ten of whom were publicly hanged, drawn and quartered, a sport greatly to the taste of the age, though not to that of Charles, who absented himself from London at the time and travelled through the provinces, where many country ladies, not content with kissing his hand, held up their heads to be kissed. His reputation as a lively lad with the lasses had been spread abroad since his journey through the shires dressed as a farmer's boy.

Apart from the acts of vengeance which he hated but was compelled to countenance, Charles had some domestic troubles in the autumn of '60. His young brother the Duke of Gloucester died of smallpox, and his other brother the Duke of York contracted a secret marriage with Anne Hyde, daughter of the Chancellor. As the Duke was next in succession to the throne, and should therefore have married a royal personage of political advantage to the state, Charles was worried. But he remained calm and asked his councillors, the Earls of Ormonde and Southampton, to tell her father. They broke the news gently by saying that the Duke of York was in love with his daughter, who was already pregnant. In a furious temper he declared that he would turn her out of the house as a strumpet and never see her again. This seemed a favourable moment for springing the further news that she was no strumpet but a married woman. Instead of being mollified Hyde was distraught with rage, saying he would rather she were the Duke's whore than his wife, that she should at once be committed to the Tower, cast into a dungeon, and decapitated by Act of Parliament, which he would very willingly be the first man to propose. The situation was eased by the arrival of the King, who sympathised with the Chancellor's predicament but pacified him with the assurance that as the thing was done they must accept it and make the best of it. In the belief that he was acting in the interests of all concerned, one of the King's friends, Sir Charles Berkeley, tried to blacken Anne's character by saying that he had lain with her. The Duke believed this, but the King declined to do so and treated the defamed woman with chivalrous respect.

Hearing the scandal, Henrietta Maria left France for England to prevent 'so great a stain and dishonour to the Crown'. She would not speak to the erring Duke, cut him dead, and said that if his wife were brought into the Palace by one door she would leave it by another. But suddenly she changed her tune and accepted the situation, prompted perhaps by Mazarin, who may

have scented some advantage to France. There was much gossip
that Hyde had engineered the business in his own interests, and
he was placed in a very tricky position; so he offered to resign the
Chancellorship. The offer was refused by the King, who showed
his confidence by making Hyde a baron and giving him twenty
thousand pounds. When more money was pressed upon him,
Hyde declined it on account of the envy it would arouse in others;
whereupon the King gave him a word of advice: 'I tell you,
Chancellor, that you are too strict and apprehensive in those
things, and, trust me, it is better to be envied than pitied.' Hyde
was a born constitutionalist, and his anger against his daughter
can be explained by the fact that her marriage may have endangered, or at least injured, the monarchy which he had done so
much to preserve. Had he known that his daughter's daughter
would one day be Queen Anne of England, it is unlikely that his
attitude would have softened.

Henriette, the beloved sister of Charles, whom he called
Minette, came to England with their mother, and he saw as much
of her as he could. At a meeting of the Council one November
day he told Hyde that he was just off to stay with her at Tunbridge Wells. 'I suppose you will go with a light train?' queried
Hyde. 'I intend to take nothing but my night bag,' Charles
assured him. 'Yes, but you will not go without forty or fifty
horse,' persisted the Chancellor. 'I count that part of my night
bag,' was the reply. The meeting of Charles and Minette was
followed by tragedy, their sister Mary of Orange dying of smallpox before the end of the year. Minette was soon to marry the
Duke of Orleans, brother of the French King, and Charles was left
in England with no near relative but the Duke of York, who
caused him as much annoyance as Minette gave him happiness.

In the early months of 1661 he was too busy to think of
domestic sorrows and joys. Preparations for his coronation were
in full swing, and the question of his marriage was being debated.
The coronation took place on St George's Day, 23 April 1661.
Early on the morning of the 22nd the King went by water from

Whitehall Palace to the Tower of London, whence at 10 a.m. the procession started through a coloured city, the streets of which had been strewn with gravel, the houses hung with every sort of decoration, from flags to carpets. The cavalcade and coaches glittered in the sunshine, and 'so glorious was the show with gold and silver that we were not able to look at it, our eyes at last being so much overcome with it', noted Samuel Pepys. At three in the afternoon the King reached Whitehall. Next day the royal suite walked on blue cloth from the Palace to the Abbey, where a sermon was preached in Henry VII's chapel. Then came the ceremony, the King being anointed by Dr Juxon, Archbishop of Canterbury, who had attended Charles I at his execution. Once the crown was on his head, Charles must have recalled the days when a price was on it, and there was plenty of time for reflection while the Garter King of Arms issued the customary proclamations, the Chancellor read a general pardon, and the congregation scrambled for the silver medals that were flung at them.

The next item on the agenda was a banquet in Westminster Hall, where Charles I had been tried. The King's Champion, Sir Edward Dymock, now took the floor on horseback in full armour, and a herald announced 'That if any dare deny Charles Stuart to be lawful King of England, here was a Champion that would fight with him'. The Champion then flung down his gauntlet, but in the whole history of England there was never less likelihood that anyone would take it up.[1] For two days the weather had been glorious, but shortly after the King left Westminster Hall for his palace a terrific thunderstorm broke out, and some people remembered that there had been an earthquake on the day his father was crowned. But the torrents of rain and flashes of lightning did not restrain the universal enthusiasm, displayed in bonfires, yelling multitudes and national inebriation. The King's health was drunk with such fervour that the health of the drinkers was affected. The streets were full of vomiting men and women, and

1. The Champion and the banquet were last heard and seen at the coronation of George IV.

Pepys admitted that he had never been so 'foxed' in his life, waking up next morning to find himself 'wet with my spewing'. Altogether a memorable occasion.

Arrangements were already being made for the King's marriage. Many suggestions had been put forward, and he spoke of 'a whole litany of princesses' provided for his consideration. The idea of marrying a German specimen was very distasteful: he described Teutonic females as 'dull and foggy', and when he heard that a certain French duchess intended to marry a German prince he wrote to Minette: 'If she knew the country, that's to say the way of living there, and the people, so well as I do, she would suffer very much in France before she would change countries.' So he concentrated on a Portuguese alliance, especially as Louis, anxious to increase the opposition to his father-in-law the Spanish monarch, was willing to advance fifty thousand pounds if Charles would marry the Portuguese Infanta, Catherine of Braganza. In return for a promise of military assistance by England against Spain, Catherine's dowry would include the port and island of Bombay, the port of Tangier, and about £330,000 in sugar, money, and Brazilian mahogany.

The marriage treaty was settled by August '61, Charles having already referred to his forthcoming nuptials in a speech to the House of Commons: 'The mention of my wife's arrival puts me in mind to desire you to put that compliment upon her that her entrance into the town may be with more decency than the ways will now suffer it to be; and, to that purpose, I pray you would quickly pass such laws as are before you, in order to the mending of those ways; and that she may not find Whitehall surrounded with water.'

Catherine landed at Portsmouth with a retinue of women and priests on 14 May 1662, and on the evening of the 19th Charles, delayed by business, set off to receive her, leaving a note for his Chancellor, who had been created Earl of Clarendon: 'I shall have one conveniency in it too, that if I should fall asleep too soon when I come to Portsmouth, I may lay the fault upon my long journey.' On the 21st he reported his arrival at two in the afternoon of the previous day, finding his wife in bed with a cough and a fever, 'which was caused, *as we physicians say*, by having certain things stopped at sea which ought to have carried away those humours' (in other words, she had not been seasick). He continued: 'It was happy for the honour of the nation that I was not put to the consummation of the marriage last night; for I was so sleepy by having slept but two hours in my journey, as I was afraid that matters would have gone very sleepily. I can now only give you an account of what I have seen a-bed; which, in short, is: her face is not so exact as to be called a beauty, though her eyes are excellent good, and not anything in her face that in the least degree can shock one. On the contrary, she has as much agreeableness in her looks altogether as ever I saw; and if I have any skill in physiognomy, which I think I have, she must be as good a woman as ever was born. Her conversation, as much as I can perceive, is very good; for she has wit enough and a most agreeable voice. You would much wonder to see how well we are acquainted already. In a word, I think myself very happy; but am confident our two humours will agree very well together. I have not time to say any more.'

On the date of this letter to Clarendon they were twice married at Portsmouth, first by a Roman Catholic *abbé* and next by the Archbishop of Canterbury. Apparently the marriage had not been consummated by the 23rd, for Charles wrote that day to his sister Minette: 'I hope I shall entertain her at least better the first night than he did you,' the reference being to her husband the Duke of Orleans, whose homosexual proclivity may have made him unsatisfactory as a lover. At the same time Charles announced his approval to Catherine's mother, the Queen of Portugal: 'I am the happiest man in the world and the most enamoured, seeing close at hand the loveliness of her person and her virtues, not only those which your Majesty mentioned in your letter—simplicity, gentleness and prudence – but many others also . . . I cannot sufficiently either look at or talk to her.' And on 25 May a line to Clarendon hints that she had passed the final test: 'I cannot easily tell you how happy I think myself; and I must be the worst man living (which I hope I am not) if I be not a good husband. I am confident never two humours were better fitted together than ours are.'

All seemed to promise well for the future, but on their arrival at Hampton Court Palace the new Queen's old-fashioned attire and rigidly respectable attendants provoked the derision of the young bloods and beauties of the King's entourage; and when one day Catherine graciously received an attractive young woman led by Charles into her presence-chamber, the ill-concealed mirth of the courtiers proved to the Queen that she was not abreast with Court news.

The female thus introduced was none other than Lady Castlemaine, who as Barbara Palmer had first attracted the King's notice, since when she had been his mistress. She was born in 1640, her family name being Villiers, and her father Lord Grandison had died of wounds in the Civil War. Her amorous life began at the age of fifteen, when she conceived a passion for the Earl of Chesterfield, aged twenty-one, who took advantage of it. He served two terms of imprisonment during the Commonwealth, and it occurred to her that she could indulge her whims with greater security if she were married. She chose a man whom she could easily hoodwink, Roger Palmer, and after their marriage continued her liaison with Chesterfield. In '59 the Palmers, along with many other Royalists, visited the Court of Charles at The Hague, and it was not long before she transferred the rights of Roger and the claims of Chesterfield to the King. She was a lascivious beauty, with blue eyes, dark hair, a fine figure, and her own carnal desires being intense she knew all the tricks of arousing and satisfying sexual appetite. She was as greedy for power as for passion, using each to gratify the other. The King was quickly enthralled, and she soon became the most important figure at his Court, her husband having been compelled to accept the Irish earldom of Castlemaine. Charles dined with her every day and supped with her every night of the week before going to fetch his Queen, and one evening they weighed themselves, her state of pregnancy tipping the scales. She was deeply dejected when he left to welcome his bride and probably extracted a promise from him which he intended to fulfil.

Catherine had heard about Lady Castlemaine, though she did not associate her with the woman whom the King had just presented. But the moment she realised what had happened, she changed colour and burst into tears, her nose bled and she fainted. Having recovered, she was faced with something worse. The King's mistress had just given birth to a son, and Charles was determined that she should have an official status at Court. This was only possible by making her a Lady of the Queen's Bedchamber. But when Catherine saw Lady Castlemaine's name on the list of her ladies-in-waiting, she erased it. At first Charles was indignant, but a softer mood prevailed and he begged her to grant his request, saying that he had not been intimate with Lady Castlemaine since their marriage and would never again be guilty of intimacy but would be a faithful husband. Catherine was shocked and distressed, refused to discuss the subject, and lost her temper. Charles now believed that if he did not get his own way he would be ruled by his wife, and not a few of his courtiers backed his opinion. It seemed to him that his independence was at stake, and though considerate by nature he determined to win the battle of wills. But there were two sides to the question, and he found that his Chancellor was against him. As might have been expected Clarendon was hostile to the power Lady Castlemaine exercised over the King and was doing his best to destroy it. His refusal to let Charles give an English title to Roger Palmer had compelled the King to make the fellow an Irish peer, and it soon became apparent that he opposed the appointment of Palmer's wife to the Queen's bedchamber. Charles was angry and sent a letter to his Chancellor:

'I wish I may be unhappy in this world and the world to come if I fail in the least degree of what I have resolved, which is, of making my Lady Castlemaine of my wife's bedchamber. And whosoever I find use any endeavour to hinder this resolution of mine (except it be only to myself) I will be his enemy to the last moment of my life. You know how true a friend I have been to you. If you will oblige me eternally, make this business as easy as you can, of what opinion soever you are of, for I am resolved to go through with this matter, let what will come on it; which again I solemnly swear before Almighty God. Therefore, if you desire to have the continuance of my friendship, meddle no more with this business, except it be to beat down all false and scandalous reports, and to facilitate what I am sure my honour is so much concerned in. And whosoever I find to be my Lady Castlemaine's enemy in this matter, I do promise, upon my word, to be his enemy as long as I live.'

Clarendon was not accustomed to this tune from his monarch. As a rule it was the Chancellor who exhorted the King to a course of duty. Now the King exhorted the Chancellor to approve of licence. It was an awkward situation for a highly responsible Chancellor, and it became a disagreeable one when the King asked him to smooth matters over with the Queen. The request being tantamount to an order, he approached Catherine on the subject, but she gave vent to torrents of tears and he retired saying that he would attend her when she was more capable of listening to what he had to communicate. Again waiting on her, he spoke like a father, saying that, though he knew she had been very little acquainted with the world, 'yet he could not believe that she was so utterly ignorant as to expect the King her husband, in the full strength and vigour of his youth, was of so innocent a constitution as to be reserved for her whom he had never seen, or to have had no acquaintance or familiarity with the sex'. She hinted that the King was still attached to the woman in question. Clarendon answered that 'he had authority to assure her that all former appetites were expired', that henceforth the King dedicated himself entirely and without reserve to her, and that her future happiness depended on meeting her husband's affection with the warmth and good humour which she knew so well how to express. So far, so good; but the moment he raised the topic of Lady Castlemaine's appointment, the Queen lost control of herself and said that, if the King persisted, she would return at once to Portugal.

Clarendon reported what had occurred to Charles, who went straight to the Queen and reproached her for stubbornness and want of duty, which she countered by reproaching him for tyranny and want of affection. He closed the scene with the threat that he would dispatch all her Portuguese servants home, as they were responsible for her attitude. 'The passion and noise of the night reached too many ears to be a secret the next day,' related Clarendon, 'and the whole Court was full of that which ought to have been known to nobody.'

For a short period the King and Queen ignored one another. But Charles soon tired of such unsociable behaviour and ordered his Chancellor to settle the matter at once. Summoning up all his knowledge of human nature, especially female nature, Clarendon made a last attempt. In a long interview he was extremely diplomatic, saying among other things that 'her Majesty had too mean and low an opinion of her person and her parts if she thought it could be in the power of any other lady to deprive her of the interest she had a right to'. He went on for some time without arousing her fury, and at last she remarked that 'the King might do what he pleased, but that she would not consent to it'. The Chancellor left her with the warning that 'she would hereafter be sorry for her refusal'. He then recounted his failure to Charles and begged that 'he might be no more consulted with nor employed in an affair in which he had been so unsuccessful'.

The King in a pet ordered the Portuguese attendants to return home, which subdued the Queen to the point of entreating that she might retain a few of those whom she found most useful, as she did not wish to be left entirely in the hands of strangers. He granted her request but showed his displeasure by an aloof manner. Lady Castlemaine continued to appear in Court every day and exhibit herself in the Queen's presence. Taking their tone from the King, the courtiers ignored his wife, who sometimes signified her sense of the affront and retired. The incessant cheerfulness and unconcern of Charles at last wore her down. She saw how gay everyone was except herself, how universal the mirth except among those in her company. Quite suddenly she changed, talked to Lady Castlemaine, became friendly with her, and joined in the laughter. Her transformation did not at once conciliate the King, who thought her previous rage must have been assumed and esteemed her less for obliging him than for defying him. But he could not resist her friendliness for long, and soon they were on good terms, which, apart from occasional ruffles, were never afterwards dispelled.

The behaviour of Charles in this affair was so much at variance with his usual kindliness that we must pause to consider his singular nature.

[12]

The King's Character

SOME PART OF A MAN'S CHARACTER is determined by his height. It often happens that short men make up in energy for what they lack in inches, and as often that tall men lack agility on account of their build. But physical measurement may seriously affect psychological make-up, giving one man a sense of superiority, another a feeling of inferiority, tranquillity to one, perplexity to another. The subject has never been satisfactorily dealt with and remains hypothetical, though if we compare Charles II with his father it could be argued that smallness of stature made Charles I solicitous and busy while the tallness of Charles II made him indifferent and lazy. If this appears to reflect on the son, it should be added that his apparently negative qualities were far more effective in the long run than his father's positive qualities, and that he was successful as a ruler while his father had been a failure.

Our Charles was at least six feet tall, in those days an exceptional height, very lean but perfectly proportioned. All his movements, whether walking, riding, dancing or playing tennis, were easy and graceful. In youth his face was handsome, but the privations and anxiety of his early manhood had given him a saturnine and sometimes even a fierce expression, emphasised by his swarthy complexion, like that of a man who would have had a large black beard if unshaven. His somewhat forbidding countenance was relieved by a pair of large, luminous and lively eyes, which softened the expression of his face and wholly counteracted

126

its harshness in conversation, which was made more pleasing by his sonorous voice. His hair, plentiful, black and shiny, curled naturally in large rings, being described by a contemporary as 'a very comely ornament'. He did not think much of his personal appearance, writing to his sister Minette, who had reported that her baby resembled him: 'I hope it is but a compliment to me when you say my niece is so like me, for I never thought my face was even so much as intended for a beauty.' And when he saw a portrait of himself by Riley for which he had sat, he exclaimed: 'Is that like me? Then, odds fish! I am an ugly fellow.' But however alarming the cadaverous effect of his features, he seemed to be transformed in personal intercourse. There was a gentleness in his tone and style of speech that reassured all who spoke to him, putting them completely at their ease. He listened patiently to what they had to say, and was so amiable that they spoke quite freely, confiding in him as if they had been familiar for years. He was as easy of access as he was pleasant and friendly in manner; and this was no pose on his part, for he liked people, loved to hear them talk, and never lost a sense of his and their common humanity. He was perhaps the only king in English history who would have charmed everyone as a commoner.

The character of Charles may be read in his sensual mouth and projecting chin. It embraced self-indulgence and resolution in about equal degree. That feature of his disposition which gave colour to all the rest was a desire to take life easily. He was indolent, frivolous and pleasure-loving. As a consequence he hated anything that added to the trials and tribulations of life. Furious arguments, malevolent actions, exhibitions of temper, intolerance, resentment, jealousy, theological disputes, war-mania: the passions that moved others were alien to his nature. He actually wanted and expected people to be happy, perhaps the rarest feeling in the human soul. The ordinary frailties of the flesh were in his view harmless compared with the sins of the spirit. 'There is nobody that hates disputes so much as I do, and will never create new ones,' he confided to Minette, and when he heard of her ill-treatment by her husband he thought of his own relations with his wife and wrote: 'I shall have by this a better opinion of my devotion for the time to come, for I am of those bigots who think that malice is a much greater sin than a poor frailty of nature.' He hated cruelty and the evil generated by mendacity, saying, 'Falsehood and cruelty I look upon as the greatest crimes in the sight of God.'

Many people are inclined to assume that their tastes harmonise with those of the Creator, but Charles was not of their number. He never pretended to speak from divine inspiration and distrusted those who did. In matters of religion he was out of step with his earnest contemporaries, but it was as well to be out of step with human beings who closely resembled the Gadarene swine. In England, as before in Scotland, he was a sane man in a lunatic asylum, untouched by the sectarian venom of his time. On the whole he preferred the Roman Catholic faith to the others because 'no creed matches so well with the absolute authority of kings', and he once remarked that 'for my part, rebel for rebel, I had rather trust a papist rebel than a presbyterian one.' But that was about as far as he went: 'I am not priest-ridden. I will not venture a war nor travel again for any party.' And when one of his subjects, Sir John Warner, became a papist and a recluse, he refused to let the man's property be transferred to the next of kin. 'Sir John at present is one of God Almighty's fools,' said he, 'but it will not be long before he returns to his estate and enjoys it himself.' He adopted the same attitude to the Anglican faith. Learning that a clergyman to whom he had given a living in Suffolk had converted many nonconformists to the established church, he expressed surprise: 'What he could have said to the nonconformists I cannot imagine, except he believed that his nonsense suited their nonsense.' His view of Presbyterianism had been coloured by his early experiences, and he came to the conclusion that it was 'not a religion for gentlemen'. In short, his was a sceptical nature. He was much too intelligent to believe that any creed had the monopoly of truth or that any institution

could provide a rational or mystical explanation of creation that
was mentally and emotionally satisfying; and he was much too
kindly by temperament to accept the petty, punitive deity conceived by the littleness and revengefulness of human beings. He
was tolerant of all beliefs, and indifferent to all, preferring
personal honesty to any profession of faith; so much so that when
he was strongly advised to remove a firm Presbyterian, the Earl
of Crawford, from the office of Treasurer in Scotland, he flatly
refused. While others had renounced the Covenant in order to
gain favour, Crawford had remained loyal to it. Charles admired
the Earl's sincerity and confirmed him in his office.

Though not in concord with his subjects over religion, he
shared their love of sport. 'I am going to take my usual physic at
tennis,' he notified Clarendon at eight o'clock one morning. He
was an excellent player, and supervised the building of new courts
at Whitehall. Disliking flattery as a rule, he was amused by the
way his courtiers piled it on whenever he won. Sometimes he
would weigh himself before and after play, and the fact that on one
occasion he lost about four and a half pounds shows the energy he
put into the game. He loved yachting and popularised that sport
on the Thames. He was a keen huntsman of foxes and stags, out-
riding the field and exhausting the others. Horse-racing aroused
his enthusiasm, and some years after his accession he regularly
attended the spring and autumn meetings at Newmarket, where
he hawked, coursed, hunted the fox, and took part in the races as
a gentleman-jockey. He was the only good dancer at his Court
until his natural son the Duke of Monmouth grew up, but most of
his dancing was done elsewhere, possibly because whenever he
took the floor at Court all the ladies including the Queen had to
stand up. His less energetic periods were spent in fishing at
Windsor or Datchet, and often with the Queen at Hampton
Court. But his vigour in the first half of his reign was a cause of
discomfort to his courtiers. He rose early, sometimes at five or
six in the morning, and usually walked for three or four hours a
day, the length of his stride and the speed of his progress being

such that those who tried to go at the same rate were soon out of breath. People said that he walked fast in order to prevent petitioners from keeping pace with him. There may have been some truth in this; but he was naturally a quick mover, and when his nephew Prince George of Denmark complained of a tendency to corpulence since his marriage, Charles gave him a few hints: 'Walk with me, hunt with my brother, and do justice on my niece, and you will not be fat.'

Like his countrymen in another respect, Charles was devoted to dogs. They followed him in his walks, accompanied him to meetings of the Council, sat in his coach, and lay in his bedchamber, where they distressed the courtiers by whelping and suckling their young. Occasionally an animal was stolen and the King advertised for its return, one of them being described as a black dog, a cross between a greyhound and a spaniel. 'The dog was better known at Court than those who stole him,' ran the advertisement. 'Will they never leave robbing his Majesty? Must he not keep a dog? This dog's place (though better than some imagine) is the only place which nobody offers to beg.' Many such entreaties were printed at different times, the King's pets being much coveted by loyal citizens anxious to be in the canine fashion.

His fondness for dogs signified a desire for giving and receiving affection, matching his fondness for women. It was customary for Kings in those days to have a fairly wide assortment of mistresses, Louis XIV of France setting a normal example of marital infidelity. In the case of Charles there was a deeper reason than fashion, the variety and number of his mistresses implying a search for something he could not find. He had never known the sense of security and comfort imparted by an affectionate mother and father. Men often seek for what they have missed in life, and Charles's attempt to find someone whose disinterested affection could make up for what he had failed to experience caused a succession of applicants for the post of King's mistress. He probably knew in his heart that the search would be fruitless, partly on account of the instability of his emotional nature due to a loveless childhood and partly because no one in his position could be certain of any woman's love being given to the man instead of the monarch. The unity of all life to which human beings aspire can only be felt by two people in love, and a happy married life is the sole human condition that can impart a sense of permanence to an impermanent state. It was a condition for which Charles might have sacrificed all his mistresses and become a monogamist; but he was never deeply in love with anyone, and his procession of concubines exhibited his vain attempt to find someone who could appease his yearning for what he had never known. Add to that spiritual privation his innate sensuality and his amorous career became inevitable.

He had a deal of French blood in his veins, his mother and a paternal ancestor being French, and it is easy to see why the grandson of Henry of Navarre had inherited so much gaiety, common sense and concupiscence. Another virtue deriving from the same source was a fairly shrewd judgment of his fellow-men. He made a close study of physiognomy, reading men's characters in their features. 'There's no art to find the mind's construction in the face,' says a king in Shakespeare, but it was not the opinion of King Charles. He applied to books on the subject, and felt himself able to read the lines that nature had stamped on the human countenance. Clarendon thought that Charles was 'apt to think too well of men at the first or second sight'. But Clarendon lacked sympathy with others, had none of his master's detachment, and disliked the type of man whose social qualities appealed to Charles. If the Chancellor had referred to women instead of men, he would have hit the mark. In that respect the King's judgment was at the mercy of his senses. All he wanted from women was coddling, beauty and sexual attractiveness. He disliked female busybodies who tried to interfere with state matters, and he had what Clarendon describes as 'an aversion from speaking with any woman, or hearing them speak, of any business but to that purpose he thought them all made for'. Though surrounded and

seemingly enslaved by courtesans, his Court was never a porno-
cracy, for he refused to let any woman influence or advise him in
matters of policy.

Generally thought to be a weak king, both by contemporaries
and historians, he was firm enough to do what he wanted, and
wily enough to wait for the right moment to do it. Along with his
usual kindliness there went a streak of obstinacy, partly innate
but largely the result of early experience as an impoverished
exile and a reluctant Covenanter, when he had been compelled to
submission and humiliation. Having regained his kingdom at the
universal desire of parliament and people, he resolved that he
would never again be affronted within the domain of his personal
authority, and this resolution became operative when his wife,
his Chancellor or his parliament defied his wishes or attempted to
thwart his policy. In 1668 he wrote to tell Minette that 'whatsoever opinion my ministers had been of, I would and do always
follow my own judgment, and if they take any other measures
than that, they will see themselves mistaken in the end'. In order
to win in the long run, he often had to give way when parliament
was exercising its rights; but this came easily to him because he
loved England without being patriotic, his strong will was not
fortified by moral courage, and his kind-heartedness did not
involve self-sacrifice. He was a born diplomatist who had arrived
at exactly the right moment to display his gifts.

[13]

An Unsettling Settlement

IN THE REORGANISATION of the country that followed the restoration of the monarchy it was inevitable that many people should be disappointed. Those who had done least demanded most, and many who had made the greatest sacrifices had to be content with the knowledge of their virtue. The fines on Royalists during the Commonwealth and Protectorate had resulted in the loss of some of their lands, and as these had frequently been purchased by people who were in no sense responsible for their forfeiture it would have been unfair and impracticable to restore the properties to the original holders. After much acrimonious debate in the House of Commons, certain bills were passed which had the effect of restoring whatever had belonged to the Church, the Crown, and certain privileged people, while securing those lands that had been privately bought to the present possessors, mostly tradesmen, soldiers and merchants who had built new houses. Naturally the Royalists who had been compelled to part with their estates were not pleased with this arrangement. The Presbyterians also had some cause for discontent. They had helped to restore the King, who had sworn to abide by the Covenant, and now their ministers were compelled to give place to Anglican parsons. But it would have been impossible to please every political and religious group in the country; and considering the magnitude of the task, parliament did its job fairly well, at least well enough to avoid another revolution. Petitions from everybody with a grievance poured in from all parts of the realm, and had to be dealt with by parliament, council or king, appeals from prisoners, cripples, revenue officers, printers, purveyors, soldiers, sailors, dons and debtors. The King could not go for a walk without being pestered by petitioners. Like vultures descending upon a dead body, from the four corners of St James's Park they flew at the monarch who had suddenly decided to stretch his legs in that area. Though always considerate and willing to listen when he could not avoid it, he was a marathon walker and the supplicants had so much to say that they were soon outdistanced and out of breath.

The King himself was the leading petitioner of his kingdom, for the national finances were in such a parlous condition that he had great difficulty in obtaining an income. Parliament's first consideration was to pay off and disband a large part of the army and navy, and when that was done the exchequer was empty. At length the King's annual revenue from customs, excise and other sources was estimated at over a million pounds, but he only received about two-thirds of that sum and remained an appellant for the rest. At first he had nothing but good words for his parliament. 'I know most of your faces and names, and can never hope to find better men in your places,' he said, preparatory to asking for necessary expenses. He courteously dismissed them when they displayed signs of weariness: 'My Lords and Gentlemen, I perceive by the thin appearance of the members of both Houses this day that it is high time to adjourn.' And four years after his accession he addressed them in words that may not have come from a warm heart but certainly proceeded from a level head: 'I need not tell you how much I love parliaments. Never King was so much beholden to parliaments as I have been; nor do I think the Crown can ever be happy without frequent parliaments.'

Charles begged for other things besides money, above all that parliament should pass an Act of Indemnity and Oblivion. Revenge was in the air and everyone seemed desirous to punish someone. Royalists wished to chastise Cromwellians; Presbyterians wished to injure both; Charles wished to appease all. 'This mercy and indulgence,' he informed the House of Lords, 'is the best way to bring them to a true repentance and to make them more severe to themselves when they find we are not so to them.' He requested the Lords 'to depart from all particular animosities and revenge or memory of past provocations', and entreated the Commons not to remember anything of the late ill times 'which, you know, we are all obliged to forget as well as to forgive'. Such was his christian spirit that he would probably have pardoned even the men who had condemned his father to death if his hand had not been forced. When the newly-elected House of Commons discussed a bill for executing nineteen more regicides in July '61, he said to Clarendon: 'I must confess that I am weary of hanging except upon new offences,' and at his request the bill was dropped, while the sentence of hanging, drawing and quartering passed on Sir Henry Vane, who was unfortunate enough to incur the wrath of Cromwell as well as Charles, was mitigated by the King to beheading.

He did his utmost, but without success, to moderate the Act of Uniformity which deprived of their livings all those clergy who would not accept the new Anglican prayer-book. This Act was more political than religious. Conspiracy against the monarchy and dissent from the doctrines of the established church were regarded as synonymous, and the Clarendon Code which enforced the Act in detail, though not drawn up by the nominal author, represented Clarendon's attitude to the subject and caused the rift between himself and the King which steadily widened, Charles being for tolerance, his Chancellor supporting the intolerance of parliament and saying of the dissenters: 'Their faction is their religion.' Alone among the public men of his time, the King stood for toleration in its widest sense. He wished to suspend all penal laws against religious dissentients of whatever denomination, so long as they would live in peace with their neighbours, and in February '63 he addressed parliament: 'I am in my nature an enemy to all severity for religion and conscience, how mistaken soever it be, when it extends to capital and sanguinary punishments, which I am told were begun in Popish times. . . . If Dissenters will demean themselves peaceably and modestly under the government, I could heartily wish I had such a power of indulgence to use on such occasions as might not needlessly force them out of the kingdom, or, staying here, give them cause to conspire against the peace of it.' But the Commons were against his Declaration of Indulgence, and he had to give way.

His chief minister Clarendon sided with the Anglican extremists not from belief but from policy. In the opinion of the Chancellor anything that weakened the Church weakened the State. Oddly enough Charles agreed, saying: 'He that takes one stone from the Church takes two from the Crown,' but that did not affect his wish that men should be left alone to worship God in whatever form they chose. Clarendon's attitude made him disliked by Roman Catholics, Presbyterians, and all who could not subscribe to Anglican orthodoxy, and his unpopularity with these portions of the community became general when it was known that Dunkirk had been sold to the French. As he negotiated the sale the populace believed him to be responsible for the act; but the transfer was due to the cost of keeping it garrisoned, roughly £130,000 a year. The English were proud of having a foothold on the continent, and even proud of Cromwell for having obtained it. But Charles needed money more than prestige, and his Council favoured the deal. Louis XIV gave half a million pistoles in specie for the surrender of Dunkirk and Mardike, and the patriotic people of England assumed that Clarendon had not only advised the transaction but made something out of it. He happened at the time to be building a mansion in Piccadilly, and the mob christened it Dunkirk House.[1]

Nevertheless, in spite of disagreements on church policy,

1. This was built on ground now covered by Albemarle Street and its neighbourhood. After Clarendon's fall from power it was occupied by General Monk, who had been created Duke of Albemarle.

Charles remained on intimate terms with his Chancellor in the early years of the reign, and at Council meetings they were in the habit of passing private notes to one another, few of which would have amused the subjects of their exchanges. We may glance at three of them:

'What do you think of my Lord Berkeley's being Deputy of Ireland, if we can find no better?' scribbled the King.

'Do you think you shall be rid of him by it? For that is all the good of it,' returned the Chancellor.

'The truth of it is, the being rid of him doth incline me something to it; but when you have thought round, you will hardly find a fitter person,' rejoined the King.

A born schemer, Berkeley eventually became Lord Lieutenant of Ireland.

One day the Chancellor requested the King to give an audience to Lord Broghill, and added: 'If you will give him leave to attend you tomorrow morning at eight of the clock, I will give him notice of it.' Charles consented, but could not resist a dig at his minister: 'You give appointments in a morning to others sooner than you take them yourself; but if Lord Broghill will come at nine, he shall be welcome.'

At another meeting the Chancellor must have felt in need of sustenance, throwing out a hint: 'Will you put us to deliver our opinions in this matter this night? It will take much time. My Lord Dorchester must be very long, and my Lord Anglesey as long . . .' His Majesty sympathised: 'If those two learned persons could be sent to supper, we might despatch it now; but by my Lord of Dorchester's face, I fear his speech will be long, which will be better for a collation than a supper.'

Such comments helped Charles to bear the boredom of business. Thoroughly disliking the duties of statecraft, he was nevertheless a first-rate man of affairs, having an instinctive grasp of public concerns which served him in place of industry. In a comparison between him and his brother the Duke of York, it was remarked by Buckingham that 'the King could see things if he would, and the Duke would see things if he could'. But it was difficult for a lazy and humorous man to take government seriously, and when attending the House of Lords, the debates in which he sometimes thought 'as diverting as a play', he often left the throne to stand by the fire, where he was joined by the less sedate members who enjoyed his audible asides on the solemn pronouncements of the speakers. His speeches to parliament were delivered in a perfunctory manner, and on being asked why he read them, though he complained of clergymen who read their sermons, he replied: 'Because I like to have something to hold in front of me. I've asked those damned fellows for money so often that I am ashamed to look them in the face.'

This was indeed his main public preoccupation, and eventually the refusal of parliament to supply his needs, especially for the defence of the country, forced him to adopt tricky methods of raising money. As early as June '63 he warned the House of Commons that 'if our friends think we can do them no good or our enemies believe we can do them no harm, our condition is far from being prosperous.' He said that if they gave him no money to obtain peace and security, he would spend a very melancholy summer, and uttered a pious wish: 'God knows, I do not long more for any blessing in this world than that I may live to call a parliament and not ask or receive any money from them; I will do all I can to see that happy day.' To show that he was willing to practise economy, he cut down the expenses of his household, restricting the number of dishes per meal for his own and the Queen's consumption to ten, while Prince Rupert was allowed six, the Maids of Honour seven, with enough fire and candles for all, above and below stairs. There came a time when money was so short that he would have resorted to any shift to procure it, and he jumped at an idea suggested by his friend Henry Bennet, Lord Arlington, that Roman Catholics and nonconformists should pay for the privilege of exercising their religion. Clarendon opposed the scheme in the House of Lords and it was dropped, much to the King's chagrin.

Often Charles had to borrow money for current expenses and extravagances, the interest charged by the bankers varying from six to ten per cent. The bankers were a new race of men; there were only five or six of them, all of whom were aldermen, and two or three of whom had been Lord Mayors, of the city of London. 'They were a tribe,' wrote Clarendon, 'that had risen or grown up in Cromwell's time, and never were heard of before the late troubles, till when the whole trade of money had passed through the hands of the scriveners: they were for the most part goldsmiths, men known to be so rich, and of so good reputation, that all the money of the kingdom would be trusted or deposited in their hands.' When a clamour was raised against them, they were called 'cheats, bloodsuckers, extortioners', and accused of being responsible for want of money throughout the kingdom. But Charles found them useful and depended on them when cash was short.

He made the best of everything and seldom complained of anything. 'Pray do not be alarmed so soon by political coxcombs, who think all wisdom lies in finding fault,' he cautioned Minette, and it is no exaggeration to say that he was incapable of being alarmed. He chose his ministers as well as he could and stood by them when their policies were disastrous. 'My Lord, be of good comfort; I will not forsake my friends as my father did,' he said to one of them, and to another: 'I will stick by you and my old friends, for if I do not I shall have nobody stick to me.' He never forgot how treacherously Charles I had flung Strafford to the wolves: 'I will never part with an officer at the request of either House. My father lost his head by such compliance, but as for me I intend to die another way.' Yet he was well aware that his ministers lacked his common sense. Late in his reign he asked the Earl of Rochester, son of his old friend Wilmot, to write his epitaph. The young man obliged:

> Here lies our sovereign lord the King,
> Whose word no man relies on;

Who never said a foolish thing,
And never did a wise one.

Charles explained the apparent contradiction: 'The matter is
easily accounted for; my discourse is my own, my actions are my
ministry's.'

Unfortunately, in the bestowal of ministerial offices, his judgment was influenced by his personal predilections and he was
sometimes unfortunate in his choice of instruments. The best of
his counsellors were inherited from his father, Clarendon and
Ormonde. The latter, created a duke after the Restoration, was
made Lord Lieutenant of Ireland, which he ruled with understanding and equity. The claims of Cromwellian soldiers who had
been given property, of investors in land, of Protestants and
Catholics, were so large that Ireland would have had to be the
size of the British Isles in order to satisfy them; but many papists
had their estates restored, many soldiers their holdings confirmed, the inhabitants were as reasonably treated as was
humanly possible, and there was less active discontent in the
country than it had known in the three previous reigns.

Scotland was not so fortunate. Charles had taken a liking for
John Maitland, Earl of Lauderdale, who had repented of his part
in selling Charles I to the English parliament, had fought for the
son at Worcester, was imprisoned in the Tower until the Restoration, and then became secretary of state for Scotland. He was an
able man, but a sycophant, and the combination of cleverness and
servility appealed to Charles, who was further entertained by the
ease with which Lauderdale could be turned into an object of
bawdy ridicule. His appointment was the gravest political error
of the reign for which the King was solely responsible, and it
suggests that Charles harboured resentment for the boredom and
humiliation he had suffered in Scotland. It was not in his nature
to nourish hostility for a considerable period, and this single
instance of it gives us the measure of his mortifying experiences
in the north. Lauderdale, a one-time zealous Covenanter, now

did his best to stamp out the Covenant. Episcopacy was enforced on an anti-prelatic country; the Anglican prayer-book was foisted on Presbyterians; absolute authority was vested in the Crown; Argyll was executed; and a time-server, James Sharp, was made Primate as Archbishop of St Andrews. But the Scottish ministers were not so adaptable as many of the English parsons, whose accommodating natures were later to be celebrated in a song called 'The Vicar of Bray', commencing with a famous phrase: 'In good King Charles's golden days.' Some three hundred Scots resigned their livings, and the seed was sown which was reaped in blood after Lauderdale, raised to a dukedom, had ruled with all the ferocity of a renegade.

While the people of Scotland were in a state of agitation, the English were settling down to relative quiescence. Reaction followed the celebrations of the King's coronation, and there was a dazed period when people wondered what was going to happen next. The Court enjoyed itself, the government relaxed, the public offices were dormant, and the life of the nation seemed to be suspended.

[14]

Court Circular

LIFE in the Court of Charles II was more Egyptian than English, more like that of Antony and Cleopatra than that of his father and mother. 'To be easy oneself and to make everybody else so,' was his definition of a gentleman, and his own behaviour encouraged the courtiers to be free as well as easy. One of them burst into his bedroom at a moment when he was amorously employed, but this was carrying liberty too far and the fellow came out as quickly as he went in. Gambling, drinking and flirting were the three freedoms, and all were indulged without restraint. The King was not an enthusiastic gambler, and he discouraged the practice among his female favourites, perhaps because he knew that he would have to pay their losses. Nor was he much addicted to alcohol. Sometimes he got drunk with a few choice spirits, but he perceived that drink and women did not blend, and he knew which he preferred. All the same, drunkards amused him and he never checked their orgies. A French ambassador reported that drinking at the English Court was a sport, and that a good drinker was esteemed as highly as a good player of any fashionable game. Charles was even tolerant of rogues, admiring their daring and deftness. Once he noticed with interest a gentleman calmly abstracting a gold snuff-box from a peer's pocket. Aware that his act had been noted, the thief gravely winked at the monarch. Charles did nothing at the time, and soon enjoyed the fun of watching the peer hunting in all his pockets for the snuff-box. 'You need not give yourself any more trouble about it, my Lord,' said the King; 'your box is gone. I am myself an accomplice. I could not help it. I was made a confidant.' Another picturesque personage named Roux, who tried to pass himself off as someone of consequence, was exposed and sent packing to the continent, Charles providing him with money for his journey.

From all of which it is clear that, short of making an unpleasant scene in the presence-chamber, the courtiers could do and say what they liked. Blasphemous, lewd and bawdy conversation was encouraged if witty and not discouraged when vapid. A good crack at the expense of religion was as well received as a subtle jape in the cause of cuckoldry. The courtiers showed no reverence for the King, their conversation being as licentious as their manners were careless. Charles himself was contemptuous of formalities and once criticised the etiquette of the Spanish Court, where, said he, the King 'will not piss but another must hold the chamber-pot'. He set an example of laxity in his own Court by kissing and toying with the women he fancied *coram populo*. One of his statesmen remarked that his love of women had as little of the *seraphic* part as ever man had, while another referred to that 'known enemy to virginity and chastity, the monarch of Great Britain'. His dissolute conduct and the profligate atmosphere of the Court were soon known throughout the country, for White-hall Palace was almost a public promenade, the galleries being filled with people who wandered about freely, curious to see the notabilities of the Court, to hear the gossip, to relish the scandal, to watch the King and Queen at dinner, to enjoy the music. It was rumoured that his Majesty spent fortunes on his mistresses, and one of the reasons why the Commons were reluctant to grant him subsidies was a belief that they would not be spent on men-of-war but on women-of-the-town.

His chief mistress, Lady Castlemaine, was certainly in receipt of large sums, but not from parliamentary grants to the King. As Clarendon refused to allow her money from public funds, she had to be given Irish property, with the bestowal of which he had nothing to do. In addition she managed to collect some £6,000 a year from the excise, about £3,000 a year for each of her bastard children, and later on £4,700 a year from the Post Office; apart from which the King frequently paid her debts and gave her presents. In the early years of the reign she infatuated him. Supping with her four or five times a week, he used to sneak back to the Palace early in the mornings, arousing comment from the sentries. Pepys spotted him once 'coming privately from my Lady Castlemaine's' and thought it 'a poor thing for a Prince to do'. In July '62 she quarrelled with her husband, and gathering all her valuables together she went to her uncle's residence at Richmond. When Charles persuaded her to return, she was given chambers near his own in Whitehall Palace. Her husband was a Roman Catholic and insisted that their child should be baptised in that religion. This led to their separation, and the child, born in '62, was rebaptised at St Margaret's, Westminster, in the presence of the King, being christened Charles Fitzroy. The paternity of the infant was a little uncertain, both King and husband claiming it, though Chesterfield may have been responsible.

Nearly every year Lady Castlemaine 'slipped a filly', as the saying was, and some of them were acknowledged by Charles, one being born in the chamber of a Fellow of Merton College, Oxford, where the Court temporarily resided. Pepys noticed in the summer of '64 that Charles was still supping every night with Lady Castlemaine, who 'has lately slunk a great belly away, for from being very big she is come to be down again'. The five children recognised by the King as his own became in later years the Dukes of Southampton, Grafton and Northumberland, and the Countesses of Sussex and Lichfield. But he repudiated several others she tried to foist upon him.

He needed a harem as manifold as Solomon's in order to find a woman who could satisfy all his needs. Lady Castlemaine's vitality and lasciviousness appealed urgently to one part of his nature, but he was repelled by her rapacity, her wantonness and her vulgarity. Her tall handsome figure, her auburn hair, her blue almond-shaped eyes, and her seductive methods, were irresistible and captivated his senses; but her extravagance, her deceitfulness, her meanness and utter indifference to everything that did not feed her vanity, lust and greed, eventually alienated him. Hating discord in any form, he could not endure her storms of rage when thwarted. Trifling vexations made her hysterically furious and venomous, and she screamed at him like a fish-wife, careless of other people's presence. By threatening to print all his letters to her, she blackmailed him into paying her debts. She gambled frequently, and it was said that she had won £15,000 at a sitting, losing £25,000 at another. Their quarrels and reconciliations were the chief news items of the Court. One day it was noticed that the King and Queen were riding hand-in-hand while Lady Castlemaine was being ignored. In a fit of spleen she dashed off to Richmond. Next morning the King said he would spend the day hunting. But the deer he hunted was found at Richmond and soon returned to Whitehall, where he showered more presents on the animal.

This emotional seesaw was perpetual. Now she was in favour and the courtiers solicited her smiles; now she was out of favour and the courtiers cared not if she frowned. A woman of whims, no one knew what she would do or demand next. A close student of human nature, Charles never ceased to be intrigued by her rapid changes of mood, though her lightest caprice had to be gratified. Having ordered a shin of beef for the King's supper, she was informed that the cook could not roast it as the kitchen was inundated by the high tide in the river. 'Zounds! she must set the house on fire but it should be roasted,' she cried. It was taken elsewhere to be done. But she was just as capable of annoying as of pampering him. The Queen happened to say that her husband caught cold by staying out so late at the house of Lady Castlemaine, who promptly rejoined that he always left her betimes and must go somewhere else before returning home. The King, suddenly entering, overheard this remark and ordered the speaker to leave the Court. She did so, angrily, but they soon made it up.

Her favourites were pushed into soft jobs carrying sound emoluments, and she sometimes disposed of these to the highest bidders, making money out of what she did for flattery. She even compelled the King to make her uncle the Bishop of St Asaph. Pepys described him as 'a drunken swearing rascal and a scandal to the Church'.

Wherever Charles went, Barbara went too. At the theatre she was more splendidly bejewelled than the Queen and Duchess of York together. The price of what she wore was once estimated at £40,000. When their Majesties drove round the ring in Hyde Park, it was noticed that each time their coach passed that of Lady Castlemaine greetings were exchanged. The ring was a piece of ground some three hundred yards in diameter with a balustrade round which the vehicles went. The Queen grieved that Charles scarcely ever supped with her, but nearly always with Lady Castlemaine, and this seemed to be generally known. The King was vexed if his mistress were insulted, and when she fainted because a nobleman in St James's Park reminded her that Edward the Fourth's mistress Jane Shore had died on a dunghill, Charles ordered everyone in the Park to be arrested. Owing to the congested state of the area, identification was impossible. It is not recorded whether he laughed on reading 'The Poor Whores' Petition to the most splendid, illustrious, serene and eminent Lady of Pleasure, the Countess of Castlemaine', which purported to be drawn up by ladies of her profession whose houses had recently been pulled down, but which was devised by some humorists who were not popular with the Countess and who also concocted her reply, supposedly 'Given at our Closet in King Street, Westminster, *die Veneris*, 24 April 1668'. We merely know that when a magistrate reported a riot, its object being to demolish a number of brothels, and described them as one of the nation's grievances, the King asked: 'Why do they go to them then?'

He probably smiled over the Petition because by that time he had wearied of Lady Castlemaine and decided to bring their sexual intimacy to a close. In spite of her exacerbating behaviour, he had been too weak to end the relationship before. Their natures were uncongenial and as soon as her physical attraction lessened he experimented elsewhere. In a letter to Minette at the beginning of '64 he said that he had been unable to converse with the French ambassador because the man was so much taken up with his new wife. 'But that fury continues not long, and I believe he will be as reasonable in that point as most men are,' concluded Charles, whose ardour for Lady Castlemaine now embraced one of her waiting-women, whom she promptly sacked, not to mention other more durable examples. He was particularly attracted to actresses and gave them many presents in exchange for what they had to give. Moll Davis was one of them, and her daughter, Mary Tudor, was acknowledged by him. Margaret Hughes was another. But his tastes were Catholic and his selections included the daughter of a clergyman, Jane Roberts, a singer, Mary Knight, a Maid of Honour named Winifred Wells, and two titled women, Lady Falmouth and the Countess of Kildare. He was generous to all of them. Winifred Wells, intimate with him for ten years, obtained the profits from the sale of underwood in certain parts of the New Forest, also the forfeitures of felons, and a pension of £200 a year; while Lady Falmouth received the dues from vessels and lighters moored in the Pool of London.

The children from these unions were many, and having exhausted such variations as Fitzroy and Fitzcharles the heralds had to fall back on Beauclerk, Lennox, Tudor, etc., Charles had a remarkable constitution. He was an early riser and must often have left his own bed very shortly after leaving someone else's. The courtiers called him 'Old Rowley', the name of a stallion in the royal mews, and he certainly did more than his share in procreating the new aristocracy that arose after the Commonwealth. Apart from the Duke of Monmouth, his natural son by Lucy Walter, and the five children by Lady Castlemaine already named, he begat sons and daughters who eventually became known as the Duke of St Albans, the Earl of Plymouth, and the Countesses of Yarmouth and Derwentwater. All his mistresses were pretty, unlike those of his Roman Catholic brother the Duke of York, who were so plain, said Charles, that they must have been given him by his priest for penance. No doubt a number of other children were begotten by Charles, and when a public appeal was made to him as 'the father of his people', the Duke of Buckingham whispered to a neighbour: 'Of a good many of them.'

Owing to the limitations of her sex, Lady Castlemaine could not compete with the King in the number of her offspring, but she did her best, being as faithless to Charles as he was to her. First of all she fell in lust with Henry Jermyn, nephew of Henrietta Maria's friend the Earl of St Albans. This infuriated the King. But Jermyn soon displayed a preference for another woman, which infuriated Lady Castlemaine, who tried to make out that her child by Jermyn was the King's. 'God damn me, but you shall own it!' she raged. He objected to her spending money on Jermyn, and on hearing this she gave vent to her feelings: 'It is certainly his place to cast such aspersions on the one woman in all England who least deserves them! Since his low tastes first declared themselves, he has never stopped picking unjust quarrels. With such degraded inclinations, he has no use but for stupid goslings like . . .' and she rattled off the names of several rivals. Late in '63 she announced her intention of becoming a Roman Catholic, possibly in the hope that Charles would be annoyed; but when asked to prevent her from taking such a step, he replied: 'I never interfere with the souls of women but only with their bodies when they are civil enough to accept my attentions'. After Charles had added two or three actresses to his seraglio, she retaliated by having affairs with actors, bestowing her charms in particular on a leading player, Charles Hart. From 1668, when her intimacy with the King ceased, she either kept salaried lovers or favoured those who took her fancy, such as John Churchill, the future Duke of Marlborough, whose affair with her started him on the ladder

HENRIETTE ANNE, DUCHESS OF ORLEANS

BARBARA, DUCHESS OF CLEVELAND

of fame,[1] and William Wycherley the dramatist, and Jacob Hall the rope-dancer, and so on. By threats and cajolings she made the King give her a title, or rather three titles, and in 1670 she was created Baroness Nonsuch, Countess of Southampton and Duchess of Cleveland. On borrowed money he also gave her the freehold of Berkshire House, the eastern boundary of its grounds being half-way up what is now St James's Street, the southern boundary being St James's Park, and the western boundary Upper St James's Park (now Green Park).[2]

Her cleverness in maintaining an influence over Charles was especially noticeable in the case of Frances Theresa Stuart, one of the Queen's Maids of Honour, a strikingly beautiful girl who drove the King to poetry. He raved about her, and in the summer of '63 appeared to be besotted, for he openly kissed and cuddled her and had no eyes for anyone else. He declared that her legs were the finest in England, and she obligingly lifted her skirts above her knees to prove the truth of his assertion. She was commonly known as La Belle Stuart and generally regarded as the loveliest girl at Court. She was painted by Sir Peter Lely as Minerva, and Charles insisted that she should be the model for the figure of Britannia on the coinage of the realm. Superficially she was childish, laughing at everything, giggling with delight over Buckingham's imitations of people's mannerisms and pro-nunciations, enjoying games like blind man's buff and hunt the slipper, loving to play with dolls and build card-castles, and watching with glee an aged peer who held a lighted candle in his

1. It was credibly reported that the future victor of Blenheim made a hurried retreat through the window when the King arrived unex-pectedly in Barbara's apartments, and that Charles leant out of the window to address the half-naked lover: 'I forgive you, because you do it for your bread.' But Churchill wanted plenty of jam on his bread.

2. In 1686 she had a son by a minor actor named Goodman. In 1705 her husband Castlemaine died and she married 'Beau' Feilding, who treated her badly; and when she discovered that he had a wife still living, their union was declared void. She died in 1709 at the later-named Walpole House, Chiswick Mall.

mouth without extinguishing it. In spite of her infantine frivolity, she was shrewd enough to keep the King in a state of suspense, denying him what he chiefly desired while permitting his caresses. He offered her whatever she cared to ask, even his fidelity, but she was businesslike enough to withhold the final favour from everyone except a husband. Charles said that he hoped he would live to see her 'ugly and willing'. Apparently he did, but in the meantime he tried to solace himself by writing three verses in her temporary absence:

> I pass all my hours in a shady old grove,
> But I live not the day when I see not my love;
> I survey every walk now my Phillis is gone,
> And sigh when I think we were there all alone:
>> O then, 'tis O then, that I think there's no hell
>> Like loving, like loving too well.
>
> While alone to myself I repeat all her charms,
> She I love may be locked in another man's arms,
> She may laugh at my cares and so false she may be
> To say all the kind things she before said to me:
>> O then, 'tis O then, that I think there's no hell
>> Like loving too well.
>
> But when I consider the truth of her heart,
> Such an innocent passion, so kind without art;
> I fear I have wronged her, and hope she may be
> So full of true love to be jealous of me:
>> And then 'tis I think that no joys be above
>> The pleasures of love.

His ecstasies were more than Lady Castlemaine could bear, and at first she indulged in tempestuous scenes and passionate tears. There was a trying moment when her Court supremacy was challenged. The King had been given a smart calash, and Frances

Stuart wished to borrow it for a drive in Hyde Park. Lady Castlemaine threatened to bring on a miscarriage if her request were granted. Frances Stuart countered this with the hint that she would never be in a condition to have a miscarriage if her request were refused. She duly appeared in the vehicle. Then Lady Castlemaine made a false move, refusing to let La Belle Stuart come to her apartments in the Palace. Upon which Charles said that he would not visit her unless the other lady were present. Perceiving her error, and anxious to cover up one of her own intrigues, Lady Castlemaine made the best of a difficult situation by forming a close friendship with her supplanter. Soon the two were inseparable, and once, when Charles discovered them in bed together, Lady Castlemaine asked him to join them, a request he felt it would be ungallant to refuse. At last, however, Lady Castlemaine had her revenge. The Duke of Richmond doted on La Belle Stuart. He was a heavy slow-witted man who also doted on the bottle, but he wished to marry the beauty. Informed by one of her spies that the Duke was visiting Frances Stuart in her bedchamber, Lady Castlemaine passed the information on to Charles, who discovered the two together and ordered the Duke to leave the Court. Temporarily in disgrace, Frances Stuart told the Queen what had happened and engaged her sympathy. On a stormy night at the end of March '67 La Belle Stuart escaped from the Palace with the Duke and went to his country-seat, Cobham Hall, near Gravesend, where they were married.

For the only time in his life Charles completely lost control of his temper. His vanity was touched at a very sensitive point. The girl to whom he would have given everything except a wedding-ring had rejected him for a loutish drunkard who bought her for just that. She was banished from the Court; and when Minette, who had been responsible for the appointment of Frances as a Maid of Honour, pleaded for her, Charles replied: 'You know my good nature enough to believe that I could not be so severe if I had not great provocation, and I assure you her carriage towards me has been as bad as breach of friendship and faith can make it.

151

Therefore I hope you will pardon me if I cannot so soon forget an injury which went so near my heart.' The following year Frances went down with smallpox, and when she got up she was no longer La Belle. Charles instantly relented, telling Minette: 'She is not much marked with the smallpox, and I must confess this last affliction made me pardon all that is past, and cannot hinder myself from wishing her very well.' In short she had become willing if not ugly, and so well did he wish her that he rowed alone down the river to her residence and clambered over the garden-wall so as not to disturb the doorkeeper; 'which is a horrid shame', thought Samuel Pepys, overcome by a mood of monogamy.

It almost seemed as if the only woman of the King's acquaintance incapable of giving him a child was the Queen. He treated the matter lightly and jokingly told his mother that Catherine had admitted she was pregnant. 'You lie,' said Catherine. This amused him, and he taught her to say in English; 'Confess and be hanged.' She tried the waters of Bath and Tunbridge Wells in the hope that they would assist nature; but fecundity was only granted to certain Maids of Honour, by the visitors not the waters. As the years went by Charles thought that Catherine was incapable of providing him with an heir, and after she had suffered two miscarriages in '68 and '69 he abandoned hope. But he never ceased to treat her with respect and consideration, and his fondness was shown when she fell ill with spotted fever in the autumn of 1663. For a while she lay near to death. Her priests prayed, her doctors prescribed, both parties believing firmly in their nostrums. The priests covered her shaven head with a miraculous nightcap; the doctors placed the bleeding carcasses of pigeons at her feet. In her delirium she believed she was giving birth to several children. Charles remained for hours by her bedside. He wept freely, and she wept to see him weep. At last he became convinced that between them the priests of God and Galen were killing her, and he ordered them away. She was conscious of his desire that she should live, and this may have helped her to do so. He reported the stages of her illness to Minette. Early in November she was out of danger, though weak; the fever left her, but for some days her mind wandered. When well enough to get up, she was too weak to stand on her legs; but by 10 December she had recovered. Throughout her illness he spent all the time he could spare from business at her side, though he supped every night with Lady Castlemaine and Frances Stuart.

Charles refused to judge between the claims of religious and medical experts that one or the other had been instrumental in cases of cure. When his sister Minette fell ill and got well, her mother attributed the fortunate outcome to a Mass, her doctor to pills. Charles reserved his opinion. When their mother Henrietta Maria returned finally to France in 1665, Charles continued to keep Minette fully posted with Court news, writing to her with a freedom that displayed his affection. 'You have my heart, and I cannot give you more,' he told her. One item of news aroused considerable interest at the time. The King's son by Lucy Walter, called James Crofts after the name of his governor Lord Crofts, came to England in 1662. He was a handsome lad, socially attractive, and quickly became his father's darling, receiving so much attention and so many favours that everyone thought he would shortly be acknowledged as a lawful son. Instead he was created Duke of Monmouth early in '63 at the age of fourteen, and married within a few weeks to Anne Scott, Countess of Buccleuch, aged twelve. On 20 April Charles wrote to Minette: 'You must not by this post expect a long letter from me, this being James's marriage day. And I am going to sup with them, where we intend to dance and see them a-bed together, but the ceremony shall stop there, for they are both too young to lie all night together.' As the boy grew up he became the Court's pet, and Lady Castlemaine sulked because her children by Charles were nothing like so fascinating as Adonis Monmouth. But his father was not deceived by the youth's charm, and realised even at this early date that his nature was weak, his mentality inconsiderable. It soon transpired that he was a fool, losing his head on the slightest occasion, and eventually losing it on a serious occasion.

Minette was kept in touch with all sorts of events, gay as well as grave. She heard that Charles and Catherine were going to supper with Lady Castlemaine, that he had just been to see 'a new ill play', that he was 'called away by very good company to sup upon the water', that having no news one very cold winter he 'did not think it worth your trouble and my own to freeze my fingers for nothing', that he was going to Bagshot to hunt the stag, that though a great many handsome young women had arrived at Court 'the passion Love is very much out of fashion in this country' because young men were marrying for money not beauty, and that there was only one way of dealing with long-winded preachers: 'We have the same disease of sermons that you complain of there, but I hope you have the same convenience that the rest of the family has, of sleeping out most of the time, which is a great ease to those who are bound to hear them.' Charles was a deep sleeper on these occasions, and his courtiers must have followed suit because Lauderdale was once loudly reproved from the pulpit: 'My Lord, my Lord, you snore so loud you will wake the King!'

In February '65 came the news that Minette was expecting a child and Charles hoped it would be a boy. The Duchess of York had recently been delivered of a girl:[1] 'I am very glad to hear that your indisposition of health is turned into a great belly. I hope you will have better luck with it than the Duchess here had, who was brought to bed, Monday last, of a girl. One part I shall wish you to have, which is that you may have as easy a labour, for she despatched her business in little more than an hour. I am afraid your shape is not so advantageously made for that convenience as hers is; however, a boy will recompense two grunts more, and so good night, for I fear I fall into natural philosophy before I think of it.'

Minette was as regular a correspondent as her brother, though one piece of information she thought more suitable for a member of her own sex. It seems that a lady at the French Court was in-

1. The future Queen Anne of England.

capable of having a child without a surgical operation. Charles was amused: 'The Queen showed me your letter about the operation done upon Mademoiselle Montausier, and by her smile I believe she had no more guess at the meaning than you had at the writing of the letter. I am confident that this will be the only operation of that kind that will be done in our age, for, as I have heard, most husbands had rather make use of a needle and thread than of a knife. It may be you will understand this no more than what you writ in your own letter, but I do not doubt you will very easily get it to be explained without going to the Sorbonne.' French manners and customs were followed slavishly in England, even the method of sealing letters, and Charles no doubt was charged to make a necessary enquiry: 'I desire to know whether it be the fashion in France for the women to make use of such a large size of wax, as the red piece you sent me. Our women here find the size a little extravagant, yet I believe when they shall know that 'tis the fashion there, they will be willing enough to submit to it.'

Sometimes Minette taxed her brother with slothfulness, and he admitted it: 'I will not deny but that naturally I am more lazy than I ought to be.' But he usually gave her a budget of news, and ended one copious communication with the words 'if you are but as sleepy at the reading of it as I am at the writing, I am certain you will think it long enough'. Again and again he expressed his deep feeling for her: 'I hope you believe I love you as much as 'tis possible. I am sure I would venture all I have in the world to serve you, and have nothing so near my heart as how I may find occasions to express that tender passion I have for my dearest Minette.'

War, Plague, Fire and Fall

THE POLITICAL HISTORY of the early part of Charles the Second's reign centres on the story of English and Dutch commercial rivalry. In spite of the achievements of the British navy under Blake during the Commonwealth and Protectorate, the United Dutch Provinces had by the time of the Restoration absorbed not a little of the colonial possessions previously shared by Spain and Portugal. With the decline of British sea-power after Cromwell's death, Dutch fishing fleets were busy catching herring in British waters; and though the House of Commons debated the trespass, they had no means of stopping it. The Grand Pensionary of Holland, practically the ruler of the country, was Jan de Witt, who had concluded a peace with the English Commonwealth whereby the Dutch republic renounced William of Orange, who was excluded from the office of chief magistrate or *stadtholder*. But William, a boy of eleven in 1661, had many partisans, among whom was his uncle Charles of England. Thus there was a lack of friendliness between the rulers as well as the peoples of the two nations, and as both countries were enriched by overseas trade the almost inevitable result of their mutual antagonism would be war. But not if Charles could prevent it.

His first act was not appreciated by the Dutch. The Resident at The Hague in Cromwell's time had been George Downing, who, as we have seen, did Charles a good turn. Partly perhaps on that account, but chiefly because he was an efficient man of affairs, Downing was restored to the post of Resident by Charles. This annoyed the Dutch, because Downing had as much business sense as any of them and could beat them all at a bargain. Clarendon described Downing as proud and insolent, a terrific talker who wrapped himself up 'in a mist of words that nobody could see light in' and who gave the impression that he understood 'the mystery of all professions much better than the professors of them'. At least he had an amazing grasp of detail and capacity for work, and eventually he was placed in control of the national finances of Great Britain, the street named after him still containing the official residence of the Chancellor of the Exchequer, not to mention the Prime Minister.

The early negotiations with the Dutch did not improve matters for England because Downing was not supported by Clarendon; and when Jan de Witt contrived to bring off an alliance with France, each country engaging to help the other if attacked in Europe, the position of England deteriorated. This Franco-Dutch agreement was particularly unpleasant for Charles, who had hoped from the beginning of his reign to arrange an alliance with Louis XIV and had begged Minette to act as go-between. Knowing that his country's future welfare depended on overseas markets, he also knew that the only real danger came from the Dutch, whom he anyhow disliked, not from the French, whom he liked and whose ambition for territorial aggrandisement did not conflict with England's for trade promotion. But, anxious though he was for an alliance with Louis, he would not sacrifice his dignity to obtain it, writing to Minette in December '63: 'There is nobody desires more to have a strict friendship with the King of France than I do, but I will never buy it upon dishonourable terms, and I thank God my condition is not so ill but that I can stand upon my own legs, and believe that my friendship is as valuable to my neighbours as theirs is to me.' A year later he wrote in the same vein: 'I would not be thought to seek anybody's friendship who is not ready to meet me half-way.'

Louis, too, would have liked an alliance with England. He had nothing in common with the Protestant and republican Dutch, who stood in the way of his conquest of the Netherlands; but the shadow of Cromwell's England still flickered over Europe and he feared that the islanders would be a thorn in his side. By his pact with de Witt he was able to keep Charles guessing and to move nearer to an alliance with England favourable to himself. His real desire was to see Holland and England engaged in a death-struggle, and when they were exhausted to step in and obtain what he wanted. But he underestimated the English King's ability as a diplomat.

In the earlier interchanges between them, it seemed to Charles that his wish for an alliance was being hampered by the behaviour of the English ambassador at Paris, Lord Holles, a gouty and cantankerous person, and the French ambassador in London, the Comte de Cominges, a capricious hypochondriac; but it is more than likely that Louis placed obstacles in the way of an early agreement. His was a far more efficient secret service than England's, and he knew how things were shaping. Cromwell had spent about £70,000 a year on his espionage system and knew the secrets of all the European rulers. According to Pepys, little more than £700 a year was spent on this service in the reign of Charles, whose diplomacy was necessarily guided by instinct instead of information. But Louis bribed anyone who could and would tell him what was happening in England and at the English Court. Peers and members of parliament received pensions from France, and the French ambassador sweetened Charles's mistresses with presents of Parisian gloves, ribbons, green silk stockings, silks, satins, and whatever else was supposed to be superior to home products. The ambassador thought that Lady Castlemaine was too furtive and fickle. True, she accepted his bribes; but as she also accepted bribes from anyone else, her information was unreliable. Secret intelligence was further obtained by opening letters in the post; but as this worked two ways the French ambassador arranged for his correspondence to be sent to the care of a Covent Garden surgeon, while Charles begged Minette to dispatch her letters whenever possible by someone who was travelling from Paris to London. At any rate Louis knew enough about the state of affairs in England to bide his time and wait for the unavoidable conflict between the two sea powers.

Practically a war was being waged without a declaration. Complaints were constantly being received in England of Dutch depredations and interference with British trade in various parts of the world, the damage being estimated at several millions. One of these complaints is of historical interest. For many years the English people on Long Island, in what was then known as the New Netherlands, had remonstrated against the harm done them by the Dutch, and Charles's Council appointed a committee to consider the question. As a result of its findings, the Council decided to take possession of the New Netherlands, and in March '64 the Duke of York received a patent bestowing upon him and his heirs the land on both sides of the Hudson river. Having obtained a royal charter and the sum of £4,000 for expenses, James resigned the district between the Hudson and the Delaware to Sir John Berkeley and Sir George Carteret, and the expedition under Captain Richard Nicholls seized New Amsterdam, after a stiff resistance, on 29 August 1664, renaming the town New York in compliment to the Duke. 'You will have heard of our taking of New Amsterdam, which lies just by New England,' wrote Charles to Minette on 24 October. ' 'Tis a place of great importance to trade, and a very good town. It did belong to England heretofore, but the Dutch by degrees drove our people out of it and built a very good town, but we have got the better of it, and 'tis now called New York.' By this stroke the Dutch lost their foothold in North America; New England was linked with Virginia; and the character of the future United States became decisively British. Naturally the act was condemned by the Dutch as grossly immoral, the two nations not being technically at war, but outside Europe they had been at one another's throats for some years.

In fact open warfare was taking place this year on the western coast of North Africa, where Captain Robert Holmes took Cape

Verde, from which the English had previously been ejected. When the Dutch ambassador insisted that it should be returned, Charles retaliated with a list of English grievances, adding: 'And what, pray, is Cape Verde? – a stinking place.' All the same he wished to avoid open war, and to placate the Dutch he put Holmes into the Tower, a mere formality, for the sailor soon resumed his patriotic labours on the high seas. De Witt ordered the famous Dutch admiral, de Ruyter, to regain what had been lost, and the various stations on that coast were soon back in Dutch hands.

By the autumn of '64 the English were spoiling for a war, and in parliament the wrongs done by the Dutch were heatedly discussed, redress being demanded. On 19 September Charles told Minette that 'except myself I believe there is scarce an Englishman that does not desire passionately a war with them'. But a Cavalier parliament did not wish to be thought less patriotic than its republican predecessor, and the King gave way. On 24 November he addressed them: 'I would not be thought to have so brutish an inclination as to love war for war's sake. God knows, I desire no blessing in this world so much as that I may live to see a firm peace between all Christian princes and states; but let me tell you . . . that when I am compelled to enter into a war for the protection, honour and benefit of my subjects, I will (God willing) not make a peace but upon obtaining and securing those ends for which the war is entered into.' He then begged them to use all possible expedition 'that our friends and enemies may see that I am possessed of your hearts, and that we move with one soul'. Parliament voted two and a half million pounds, and war was declared against the United Dutch Provinces on 22 February 1665.

Before the two fleets came to grips the Dutch thought they would have an easy victory. 'They brag very much that they will eat us up in the spring,' wrote Charles to his sister, 'and so they did some two months ago, but as yet we are all alive'. Certainly the Dutch had many advantages. The English and Scottish sailors were underpaid and the Dutch enticed some three thousand of them to serve in their navy. Moreover the press-gang collected a lot of men and boys who were unfit for the service, and after one great battle it was observed that many English sailors swimming in the sea wore their black Sunday clothes, showing that they had been seized on entering or leaving church. With such material did Great Britain go to war, and the Dutch were excusably contemptuous. One of them, walking with acquaintances at Bordeaux and discussing the subject, made a remark that came to the ears of the French Court and Minette passed it on to her brother, telling him that the English ambassador had requested that the man should be punished. 'An Englishman who was of the number,' she wrote, 'said that you would never make peace unless you were recompensed for all the expense of the war. A Dutchman was asked his opinion and said that the country was not rich enough for that, and that you ought to be paid with something which does not smell nice.' Unperturbed, Charles replied: 'I am sorry that my Lord Holles has asked justice upon a point of honour that I should never have thought of. You know the old saying in England, the more a T— is stirred the more it stinks, and I do not care a T— for anything a Dutchman says of me. And so I think you have enough upon this cleanly subject, which nothing but a stinking Dutchman could have been the cause of. But pray thank the King, my brother, and desire him not to take any notice of it, for such idle discourses are not worth his anger or mine.'

The Duke of York, as Lord High Admiral, did all he could to fit the navy for the encounter, and in May '65 the fleet put out to sea. The Dutch were slightly superior in the number of warships and guns. Having manœuvred for a couple of days off Southwold, each side trying to gain a favourable wind, the fight began some thirty or forty miles east of Lowestoft early on 3 June. The English had the wind-advantage; their gunners were more efficient; and by six o'clock in the evening the Dutch turned tail. Having given orders that the enemy should be pursued until the morning, the Duke of York retired to rest at about 11 p.m. But his secretary, Henry Brouncker, 'who', reported Clarendon, 'with wonderful confusion had sustained the terror of the day, resolved to prevent the like on the day succeeding', and the moment his master was sound asleep he tried to convince Sir William Penn, commander of the flagship, that it would be advisable to shorten sail and so avoid another encounter in which the Lord High Admiral might be killed. Penn replied that the Duke had given positive orders to the contrary, and that they must continue to chase the Dutch fleet. But Brouncker did not enjoy sea warfare and informed the master of the ship, Captain Harman, that 'it was the Duke's pleasure that he should slack sails, without taking notice of it to any man'. Assuming this was a direct order from the Duke, Harman obeyed, and when the morning broke the Dutch fleet reached harbour without further damage. His secretary's behaviour remained unknown to the Duke until a public enquiry took place in October '67, when Brouncker was expelled from the House of Commons in disgrace. The King, whose main weakness was to forgive everybody for anything, ultimately countenanced the fellow, who, according to Clarendon, stooped to the most infamous offices but played chess very well, which did more for him than any virtuous qualities would have done.

During the preparations for this naval victory Charles was writing to his sister about the latest fashion of waistcoat worn in Paris and the recent compositions of his Italian guitarist. Minette sent him some patterns, saying she felt sure 'that with your fine figure they will suit you very well.' He remained calm when everyone else in London was agitated by the sound of gunfire during the battle. As Clarendon testified, Charles always appeared most gay and self-assured when things were at their worst. The news of the victory drove the citizens mad with joy, and a mob broke the windows of the French ambassador because he had not caused a bonfire to be lit in front of his house, forgetting in their excitement that France was trying to mediate between the two warring nations and that rejoicing by bonfire was not the common policy of a neutral. The Dutch showed their displeasure over defeat by taking the extreme course of throwing one of their surviving admirals into the sea; but he lived to fight another day.

Whatever triumph Charles may have felt over the result was damped by the news that his greatest friend Charles Berkeley, Earl of Falmouth, had been killed. The King was deeply moved and shed many tears. Nearly everyone had a good word for Berkeley, who was loyal, generous, sincere, humble, good-natured, and without personal ambition. But he must have exasperated Clarendon, who described him as one 'in whom few other men had ever observed any virtue or quality which they did not wish their best friends without, and very many did believe that his death was a great ingredient and considerable part of the victory'. This view was no doubt coloured by the fact that Berkeley was one of the younger men who were gaining more and more influence with the King and gradually ousting Clarendon from his position as chief adviser and political panjandrum. Another of them, Charles Sackville, Lord Buckhurst, won fame by polishing off a song on the eve of battle:

> To all you ladies now at land
> We men at sea indite:
> But first would have you understand
> How hard it is to write—
> The Muses now and Neptune too
> We must implore, to write to you.

As in all wars, stories of atrocities were circulated by each side in order to excite enmity towards the other. But Charles was subject neither to war-hysteria nor to unnecessary falsehood; and on examining one of those who accused the Dutch of horrible cruelties to Englishmen in Guinea, he discovered the man to be a liar and told Minette so. 'There is no such thing as that news you heard of Guinea,' he said, scotching a bit of propaganda that might have done service to his country in France. The attitude of Louis remained uncertain. He sent several envoys to London with the

163

object of making peace between the belligerents, and for a while it looked as if he would remain neutral in spite of his alliance with the Dutch. Still hopeful of friendship with him, Charles sent a word of wisdom to Minette, who could be trusted to pass it on: 'According to the course of the world, those are better friends who see they have need of us than those whose prosperity makes them think we have need of them.' But Louis was cunning enough to wait until three events induced him to make an apparently pro-Dutch move. These were an English naval disaster, the intervention of the Bishop of Münster, and the Great Plague.

After the victory of 3 June, the King placed Lord Sandwich in command of the fleet, as he did not wish the Duke of York to risk death in another battle. Sandwich attempted to capture a number of Dutch merchant vessels in the neutral port of Bergen; but the guns in the forts were too much for the English ships, which had to retire. Though Sandwich was able to counter this disgrace by capturing some Dutch boats at sea, he made the mistake of giving part of the plunder to his officers without waiting for the usual legal processes to be observed, for which act he would have been impeached if the King had not stood by him, sending him to Spain as ambassador. Another setback was the futile invasion of Holland by the Bishop of Münster, who had received a subsidy from the English government. Christian Bernard von Galen, the son of a murderer, had somehow managed to become a canon of Münster and had given a banquet at which all the other canons were so drunk that they elected him as Bishop. Brutal and unscrupulous, he waged war ruthlessly with some sort of fiery projectile which was more spectacular than serviceable.

Far more serious for England than the Bergen and Bishop episodes was the outbreak of the last and worst of the plagues which were a feature of the seventeenth century. Insanitary conditions probably caused most of these epidemics, but the one that now decimated the population was bubonic, brought by rats and spread by fleas. In May 1665 forty-three people died, in June about six hundred, in July thousands, in September above thirty thousand. A total of seventy thousand perished that year in the capital alone, where the population scarcely reached half a million. Not only London was affected. Norwich, Newcastle, Portsmouth, Southampton and Sunderland were the principal sufferers in the provinces, and the poor supplied nearly all the victims. Each house visited by the plague was signified by a large red cross with the words 'Lord, have mercy upon us', and all the inmates were imprisoned therein, thus ensuring the infection of all. Food was handed in by constables. Friends and relations were not allowed to attend the burials which took place by night, when carts filled with bodies emptied their loads into huge pits. It was a dreadful visitation, and many preachers saw in it a punishment of the people for breaking the laws of God. They had certainly neglected the laws of hygiene. The rich were able to escape from the pestilence, and the Court moved to Salisbury, then to Oxford, where parliament assembled in November.

That autumn Philip IV of Spain died, and Louis claimed the Spanish Netherlands in his wife's name. His real object now became clear. While the English and Dutch were fighting for their lives, or rather their trade, he could walk into the country that was later to be known as Belgium, a first step to occupying the United Dutch Provinces as well. The English poet laureate at that time, William Davenant, described war as 'the sport of kings', and Louis was about to entertain himself and his Court with the pastime. Disconcerted by the state of affairs, the English statesman who was supplanting Clarendon in the administration of foreign affairs made a commercial treaty with Spain. He was Henry Bennet, now Lord Arlington, one of the King's most intimate friends. It was a short-sighted policy because it left England without allies, and the power of Spain was sharply declining. But all through history England's success has been partly due to the mistakes of her rulers, whose actions have been so silly that foreigners have thought them sinister and failed to take advantage of them. Arlington was even stupid enough to intrigue with the faction supporting William of Orange, in the hope that he could bring the Dutch to terms. As Denmark, Sweden and the German states feared the power of Louis, and the Dutch needed his support, he was in a favourable position when in January '66 France declared war on England, and Charles wrote to Minette: 'We had some kind of alarm that the troops which Monsieur de Turenne went to review were intended to make us a visit here, but we shall be very ready to bid them welcome, either by sea or land.'

Although parliament at that moment was more concerned over passing a Five Mile Act restricting nonconformist preachers than with voting money for a war, Charles was still able to match the Dutch fleet in the number of ships; but owing to a belief that the French fleet would sail up the Channel to join the Dutch, a considerable portion of the English navy was stationed at Plymouth under Prince Rupert to intercept them. The rest, under the Duke of Albemarle (Monk), engaged the enemy on 1 June with about forty ships against eighty of the Dutch commanded by Tromp, Evertsen and de Ruyter. Rupert had been hurriedly ordered to bring his squadron, and on the third day of the fight he arrived, the English fleet then numbering fifty-eight, the Dutch seventy-eight. By the close of the fourth day's battle both fleets were too shattered, their crews too exhausted, to carry on. It was a drawn contest, though the English suffered more from loss of ships and men. A conspicuous example of bravery was provided by an English admiral, Sir Christopher Myngs, part of whose throat was blown away in action. In order to make his voice heard bawling orders above the din, he had to thrust his fingers into the gaping wound, and so he continued until a bullet put an end to him. De Ruyter paid tribute to the valour and stubbornness of the English, which qualities were again exhibited two months later, when the fleets, quickly repaired, joined battle off the North Foreland on 25 July, the Dutch still superior in numbers, and Tromp, Evertsen and de Ruyter were defeated by Rupert and Albemarle. The victory was followed up in August by an action that enraged the Dutch. Captain Robert Holmes, now out of the

Tower, destroyed two of their warships, set fire to a large mercantile fleet, and burnt stores on several islands near their coast, the damage done being estimated at a million pounds.

These cheerful events were involuntarily celebrated by the largest bonfire in the history of London. Early in the morning of Sunday 2 September a fire started in the house of a baker named Farryner, situated in Pudding Lane, leading from Eastcheap to Lower Thames Street. The season had been dry, a strong east wind was blowing, many residents were absent, much combustible material was in the immediate vicinity, and the city's water-engine was in a state of disrepair. In a short while whole streets were ablaze. Panic seized the inhabitants and confusion reigned. Men, women and children rushed hither and thither in an attempt to save their goods, which were piled on barges or strewed about the fields. The crash of falling houses mingled with the shouts and shrieks of the people, who were too busy saving their belongings to help those who were trying to check the conflagration, which raged for five days. The Lord Mayor was begged to order the destruction of houses that stood in the way of the fire, but he replied that he could not do so without the consent of their owners. Fortunately the King took charge and ordered the blowing up of many dwellings where the flames were spreading. Accompanied by the Dukes of York and Albemarle, he rode and walked about the city, helping the people to save their property, encouraging those at the work of demolition, directing supplies, calming nerves, and maintaining order. Farmers from all the country districts were commanded to bring in provisions, tents were erected in the surrounding fields, the neighbouring towns and villages were charged to billet the homeless, and as in war-time there was soon an uprush of charity towards the needy. Unaided by the nobility, whose property was not endangered, the King and his brother risked their lives for the sufferers and did what should have been done by the city authorities. So tremendous was the blaze that the glow in the sky could be seen for forty miles, and a schoolboy at Westminster could read small print by the burning of St Paul's at night. The fire spread as far west as the Temple, as far north as Smithfield, as far east as the Tower; and the medieval city of London was practically reduced to a rubble-heap. Eighty-nine parish churches and over thirteen thousand houses were destroyed, while more than four-fifths of the city's area had been laid waste.

In a time of crisis any sort of story is believed, and rumour spreads like fire. The populace wished to revenge themselves on someone or something, and innocent objects must suffer to relieve a general sense of injury. Before long the French and the Dutch were held responsible for the catastrophe, and it was generally believed that fire had broken out at different and widely separated places. To their astonishment many French and Dutch merchants who had lived for twenty or more years in London were seized, cursed, kicked, and thrown into prison. The next rumour accused Roman Catholics of whatever nationality, and they were subjected to similar treatment. Those of their English friends who denied their guilt were suspected of conspiracy, and the usual lies of people who had witnessed things happen with their own eyes were accepted as infallible proof that the things had happened as witnessed. For instance, a servant of the Portuguese ambassador was actually *seen* to throw a fire-ball into a shop. All he had actually done was to pick up a piece of bread and put it on the window-ledge of a nearby house, a custom observed in Portugal. The King was much concerned over this manifestation of hysteria, made the Council sit morning and night to sift the evidence, and ordered the Lord Chief Justice to London for an examination of the allegations. Needless to say, the evidence was as fantastic as the accusations were freakish, and the victims were set at liberty.

While the ruins of the city were still smouldering, the King issued a proclamation which prohibited the rebuilding of houses. He hoped that a much more beautiful city would be reared than the one destroyed, more sanitary too, and he intended to approve designs for the whole. The abatement of fogs interested him keenly. He read a pamphlet, *Fumifugium*, by John Evelyn the diarist and wished to get a bill through parliament that would approve methods of dissipating the fogs of London, one being to confine certain smoke-producing trades to a particular district. Like all plans, the one eventually adopted was quickly adapted. Beauty as usual was sacrificed in the cause of money; the plans of the great architect Christopher Wren were nullified by lack of funds, and his genius was confined to the churches. Nevertheless the new city of London was a cleaner, healthier, more spacious and handsome place than the aggregation of stinking alleys and disease-breeding hovels that made up the old one, and for this the King was chiefly responsible.[1]

Apart from what may be called his token war in alliance with the Dutch, Louis XIV felt that he could safely hurt England to his own advantage by attacking her West Indian possessions while she was otherwise engaged, and his forces captured the island of St Kitts in April '66, Antigua in November, and Montserrat in February '67. But his other preoccupations did not prevent Charles from hitting back, and his admiral Sir John Harman decisively beat French and Dutch fleets the following May and June. By this time England was weary of war and Louis felt indisposed to maintain his half-hearted support of the Dutch. In the autumn of '66 Charles told parliament that he had anticipated his own revenue in order to raise a fleet the previous spring, and he asked for money. A further £1,800,000 was voted him, but it could not be raised owing to the country's condition after plague, fire and war. Parliament also insisted that the King's accounts should be examined, and a note of irritation crept into his speech to both Houses in January '67: 'I am not willing to complain you

1. Walter Bell, historian of the Great Fire, states that 'London as it was created after the Fire owed more (always apart from Wren's individual buildings, which glorified it) to King Charles II than to Sir Christopher Wren. His was the active agitating mind. His hand was seen everywhere.' The time it took to make good the damage may be measured by the fact that the King did not issue orders for the rebuilding of St Paul's until May 1675.

have dealt unkindly with me in a bill I have now passed, in which you have manifested a greater distrust of me than I have deserved. I do not pretend to be without infirmities; but I have never broken my word with you; and, if I do not flatter myself, the nation never had less cause to complain of grievances, or the least injustice or oppression, than it hath had in these seven years it hath pleased God to restore me to you. I would be used accordingly.'

The failure to raise the sum granted by parliament made peace essential, and negotiations were commenced in Paris. There was no difficulty with Louis, who agreed to hand over his West Indian gains in return for England's promise not to enter into any alliance opposed to French interests for one year. After some haggling de Witt consented to discuss peace terms at Breda in the summer of '67. This gave him time to revenge his country's humiliation over the action of Captain Holmes the previous August. The prospect of peace lulled the English government, as de Witt thought it would, and he prepared a little surprise for them. Secure in the knowledge that for the sake of economy many English battleships were now laid up and the crews paid off, de Witt persuaded the Dutch admirals to sail up the Thames and destroy what they could not take. While Arlington and the rest of the Council were discussing the articles of peace to be shortly agreed at Breda, a Dutch fleet of some sixty vessels appeared off the North Foreland on 7 July '67. Even then it did not occur to the English government that the Dutch would have the audacity to strike at the heart of the nation, and feverish preparations were made to receive them at Plymouth, Portsmouth, the Isle of Wight, and Margate. But the incredible occurred, and on 11 June de Ruyter bombarded Sheerness, put eight hundred men ashore on the island of Sheppey, and dispatched a squadron to the Medway. The English were totally unprepared. Owing to bad organisation and corruption Chatham could scarcely be defended, and the chain across the river at Gillingham was burst. First-class battleships in docks were destroyed by Dutch fireships, and the flagship of the English fleet, the *Royal Charles*, was captured and taken off by a small boat and half a dozen men. The shore defence, rapidly improvised by Albemarle, could not prevent this crowning indignity, though it saved what was left of the English navy.

The Dutch crowed with delight, the English howled with mortification. Charles rightly disclaimed responsibility for having demobilised the greater part of the fleet, a policy forced upon him by parliament's inability to implement their vote for supplies. After such a triumph the enemy were in relatively pliable mood at the Breda peace conference in July. It had been an inconclusive war, but the Dutch were getting nervous over the slow advance of Louis in the Spanish Netherlands and were anxious to conciliate the English, who were equally anxious to be conciliated. The chief result of the peace agreement was that England retained New York, New Jersey and New Delaware, which laid the foundation of her western empire. Charles did not escape public censure for the Dutch invasion, the frivolity of his Court being held responsible for the success of the action. Pepys noted that on the night the Dutch were wrecking the English navy, with Louis quietly absorbing Flanders, Charles was supping in the company of Lady Castlemaine, the entire party being engaged in chasing a moth; but whether Pepys expected the monarch to be singing anthems or saying prayers or firing a culverin at de Ruyter, he does not say. At least Charles restrained the panic that broke out at Court when the news came through; and though there was nothing to prevent the Dutch from sailing up the Thames and bombarding London, he declined to consider the frightened appeals of his courtiers to leave the capital, busying himself instead with the raising of troops.

Nevertheless a sacrifice was demanded for the propitiation of the people's wrath. Public fear breeds public vengeance, and ignorance always creates a villain, the sins of the many being absolved by the immolation of one. In this case the Court, the Commons and the populace agreed that Clarendon should be the scapegoat. Quite wrongly the mob still attributed the sale of

Dunkirk to him, and now they erroneously believed that he had been responsible for the war. Their feelings were expressed by breaking the windows of his house in Piccadilly, rooting up the trees he had planted in front of it, and making the day hideous with their hooting. The House of Commons disliked him because he considered them incapable of dealing with high matters of state and wished to curb their authority. The courtiers disliked him because of his rigid and pompous manners, his disapproval of juvenile high spirits, and his severely moral attitude to most questions. His air of authority and admonition had increasingly grated on the King; while the ambitious younger men in the royal circle hated his domination and were jealous of his power. An instance given by himself will explain how he was alienating the King and why Arlington was gaining favour. One day Clarendon and Arlington were discussing the growing licentiousness of the Court when the King suddenly entered the room and asked what they were talking about. Clarendon at once replied that they were speaking of him, 'and, as they did frequently, were bewailing the unhappy life he lived, both with respect to himself, who, by the excess of pleasures which he indulged to himself, was indeed without the true delight and relish of any; and in respect to his government, which he totally neglected, and of which the kingdom was so sensible that it could not be long before he felt the ill effects of it'. Clarendon went on like this for some time, the King listening with his usual imperturbability ('for he was a patient hearer', said the Chancellor) and at length admitting that there was too much truth in what the other had said. At this point Arlington, anxious to spare the King's feelings and bored by the Chancellor's homily, began to treat the whole subject as a joke, which annoyed Clarendon so much that he proceeded to paint his monarch's weaknesses in darker colours.

It is doubtful whether Clarendon perceived how much he was disliked by the pushing young men at Court, the touchy men in the Commons, and the disgruntled men in the street. He had the offensiveness of a self-righteous person, creating unwilling esteem, subconscious envy and active resentment. But he might have withstood his other enemies if he had not antagonised and then insulted Lady Castlemaine. He steadily refused her the grant of Crown property and did his utmost to get her removed from the Court. That was bad enough, but worse was to follow. The King complained that the Chancellor's wife was not courteous in returning visits and civilities to those who paid her respect, adding that he expected his friends to be kind to those he loved. The reference being solely to Lady Castlemaine, Clarendon replied that he could not stoop to such a condescension as to have the least commerce with 'persons infamous for any vice for which by the laws of God and man they ought to be odious', and he declared his firm resolution that his wife should not be of those who paid respect with their lips to what they loathed in their hearts. There can be little doubt that the object of his disapproval got to hear of this, and from that moment, with the active assistance of the Duke of Buckingham, the Duke's creature and dependant Sir Thomas Osborne, Arlington and others, she worked incessantly for the Chancellor's downfall. Her unwitting allies were the proletariat and the politicians, both of whom normally hated her, and the conspiracy against Clarendon issued in a motion to impeach him in the House of Commons at the end of August '67.

Charles advised his retirement, at the same time telling him that 'never King had a better servant'. The Chancellor replied that if he delivered up the seal he would be accusing himself and admitting that he deserved impeachment. He went on to say that parliament could do nothing if the King decided in his favour, but very ill-advisedly mentioned the hostility of Lady Castlemaine, which displeased Charles. At the conclusion of their interview Clarendon noticed that Lady Castlemaine and Arlington 'looked together out of her open window with great gaiety and triumph, which all people observed'. The one person of note who stood by him was his son-in-law the Duke of York.

On 30 August the King sent his secretary with a warrant to

receive the great seal, which the Chancellor surrendered; but he refused to leave the country, saying that he 'would not give his enemies that advantage as to fly from them'. The King, though vexed by his attitude, tried to stop further proceedings against him; but early in November the articles of impeachment were drawn up and Thomas Osborne attacked the Chancellor in the Commons. The charges were largely fanciful, hinging on corruption and the arbitrary misuse of power, the only ground for an accusation of treason being that he had disclosed the King's intentions to the enemy, a palpably false indictment. The House of Lords refused to commit Clarendon, and a bitter dispute took place between the two Houses, exacerbated by the Duke of York's support of his father-in-law, who wrote begging the King to 'put a stop to this severe prosecution against me'. Charles did not reply, but sent the Bishop of Hereford to advise him to leave the kingdom. Clarendon replied that he would do so if he received the King's personal command, which came to him by the Bishop of Winchester; and on Saturday night, 29 November, he left Erith by boat, reaching Calais three days later. He sent a long letter to the House of Lords, the truth in which was expressed in a priggish manner that irritated the peers, and it was burnt by the hangman. Charles explained to Ormonde his own part in the expulsion of Clarendon: 'The truth is, his behaviour and humour was grown so unsupportable to myself, and to all the world also, that I could not longer endure it, and it was impossible for me to live with it and do those things with the parliament that must be done or the government will be lost.'

Clarendon's arrival in France created an awkward situation for Louis, who ordered him to leave at once. But he was prostrated by gout and other ailments, and could not move without assistance, telling the messenger 'that he must bring orders from God Almighty as well as from the King before he could obey', and 'that though the King was a very great and powerful prince, he was not yet so omnipotent as to make a dying man strong enough to undertake a journey'. Minette interceded for him; and when it became clear that Charles would raise no objection, he was left in peace at Montpelier, where he occupied himself by composing his autobiography and replying very fully to all the charges brought against him. Charles was glad to hear of Minette's kindness, writing that 'my displeasure does not follow him to that degree as to wish him anywhere but out of England'.

During his exile Clarendon experienced one keen regret. He felt ashamed of the large sum he had spent on the building of his Piccadilly house, which he knew had contributed more than anything else to the envy of his enemies. Yet now, when advised to sell it for the payment of debts and the support of his children, he remained, in his own words, 'still so much infatuated with the delight he had enjoyed that, though he was deprived of it, he hearkened very unwillingly to the advice, and expressly refused to approve it until such a sum should be offered for it as held some proportion to the money he had laid out; and could not conceal some confidence he had that he should live to be restored to it, and to be vindicated from the brand he suffered under . . .'

Clarendon's two sons were in the King's service, and Charles remained kind to them, refusing to remove them when urged to do so by the Chancellor's enemies. But the two Houses of Parliament passed an Act of Banishment on Clarendon, whose exile finished with his death at Rouen in 1674.

16

Literature, Scandal and Politics

IN THE SAME YEAR that Clarendon was dismissed, John Milton's *Paradise Lost* was published, to be followed eleven years later by John Bunyan's *Pilgrim's Progress*; and it is an odd fact that the two most famous literary works of the reign should have been written by men who were wholly out of tune with the spirit of their age. Milton's active support of the Commonwealth and open admiration of Cromwell were easily forgiven by Charles, and the poet spent his last years in peace. Without the least appreciation of Bunyan's religious zeal, Charles would unquestionably have opposed his imprisonment, being all for toleration. But the writers of genius who were a part of the age in which they lived, their works admired by King and Court, were Samuel Butler, Edmund Waller and John Dryden. The first wrote the best burlesque poem in the language, *Hudibras*, which exposed the hypocrisy of the Puritans, who

> Compound for sins they are inclin'd to
> By damning those they have no mind to.

The King carried the poem about with him, constantly quoted from it, gave copies to innumerable people, and a sum of money to the author. It seemed certain that Butler would be offered some lucrative employment, but his gift of satire in ordinary conversation may have displeased the bestowers of office, and he died poor after telling the Court of King Charles what he thought of it:

'Tis a strange age we've lived in, and a lewd,
As e'er the sun in all his travels view'd . . .
Twice have we seen two dreadful judgments rage,
Enough to fright the stubborn'st-hearted age;
The one to mow vast crowds of people down,
The other (as then needless) half the Town . . .
In all as unconcern'd as if they'd been
But pastimes for diversion to be seen . . .

Edmund Waller was a very different sort of poet, who wrote some exquisite lyrics, a *Panegyric* on Cromwell and a *Congratulation* to Charles II on his accession. As a man of wealth, Waller managed to face both ways with some success, and he was abject and clever enough to keep out of trouble. When Charles asked him why the *Congratulation* was generally thought inferior to the *Panegyric*, he replied: 'Poets, sir, succeed better in fiction than in truth,' a remark that would have pleased without convincing the King.

John Dryden made a greater name for himself than any other writer of the time, largely because he stuck to the drama, which began to flourish after the long suppression of the theatre by the Puritans. He is the great transitional figure in the history of the drama between the Jacobean and the Restoration playwrights, and in his prefaces he revolutionised prose style. The bawdy and brilliant plays of Sir George Etherege and William Wycherley, produced during the reign of Charles, owed something to Dryden's influence, as well as those by Congreve, Farquhar and Vanbrugh in the succeeding generation. But the French plays[1] and fashions that appealed to Charles II influenced the whole Restoration drama, and in this way the King may be said to have changed the direction of theatrical art in England more than any single individual. He had a great admiration for Dryden and

1. Many of them were translations or adaptations from the comedies of the Spanish dramatist Lope de Vega, Molière's works appearing after the accession of Charles.

sometimes suggested episodes for his plays, *e.g.*, the principal incident in *Aurengzebe* and the plot of *Secret Love*. He gave Dryden money, and made him poet laureate after the death of Davenant. But the poet did not always find it easy to obtain his salary as laureate, and sometimes had to content himself with 'the pension of a prince's praise'. He wrote plays regularly for the King's Theatre in Drury Lane, the only other theatre in London for most of the period being the Duke's (Duke of York's) in Portugal Row, which was managed by Davenant and later by the great actor Thomas Betterton. Like many famous dramatists Dryden was often accused of plagiarism, but when Charles heard it he expressed a wish that those who complained of the theft would always steal him plays like Dryden's. The King was too good-natured to mind being ridiculed on the stage, too easy-going to draw the line at licentious wit, and this resulted in a form of entertainment that ultimately caused a violent reaction. But it exactly expressed the laxness and frivolity of the Court; and as the theatre in those days was solely dependent on the patronage of the royal circle and the nobility, it was free from the censorship of Puritan or plebeian. Another spur to the dramatists was the knowledge that the one thing Charles could not endure at a play was boredom. This brightened up their wits amazingly, and in their efforts not to be dull they were often silly.

Dryden is chiefly remembered today for his *Absalom and Achitophel*, the greatest verse satire in English, with its stinging portraits of Buckingham and Shaftesbury, containing lines that have become common quotations. Shaftesbury will appear later in our story, but Buckingham was the leading figure at Court during the first decade of the reign. We have already seen him as the tricky and treacherous companion of Charles in Scotland, as well as a selfish and sullen collaborator during the invasion of England. But such was the magnanimity of Charles that he forgot these things, and Buckingham started the reign with a clean slate. Having little vanity or self-pity, Charles had no malice in his heart, and his memory for slights and injuries was short, especially if those who hurt him possessed qualities he liked, which was eminently the case with George Villiers, second Duke of Buckhingham, whose father the first Duke had been the favourite of James I and Charles I. There is little doubt that our Buckingham would have done as much harm to the state as his father did if Charles had been as susceptible and foolish as his predecessors. But however lax in his Court, Charles was prudent in his Council, and he knew where to draw the line in matters of policy.

Buckingham was given the utmost licence in personal behaviour. A born mimic, he parodied the speech and manners of his peers, to the unspeakable delight of all but the victims of his caricatures. His wit was malicious and profane, and he ridiculed Anglican preachers in a manner that reduced the Court to hysterics. No one, not even the King, was exempt from his drollery and sarcasm. In religion he affected to side with the Dissenters, as previously with the Presbyterians, but that did not restrain him from making jokes at their expense. His public actions were solely dictated by private likes and dislikes, which were capricious. He led a depraved and dissolute life, 'more by night than by day' reported Clarendon, and did his best to lead his young companions along the same path. But his comicalities of behaviour, sprightliness of conversation and bawdiness of humour, amused Charles, until he overstepped the mark by expressing very disloyal and scandalous sentiments about the King in disreputable company. Thereupon he was deprived of his office as Master of the Horse and a warrant was issued for his arrest, which he managed to evade for some months by sleeping in the daytime wherever he was hiding and changing his quarters by night. At length he was caught and taken to the Tower. Lady Castlemaine, who was then plotting with him to ruin Clarendon, begged for his release, whereat the King called her a whore and she called him a fool. But Charles soon relented and Buckingham was set at liberty.

A few years later the Duke produced a play called *The Rehearsal*, in which fun was made of Dryden. It was probably more the work of Samuel Butler and other collaborators than of Buckingham, and it was popular enough to be revived at intervals during the two following centuries. This piece of raillery may have sharpened Dryden's satirical portrait of Buckingham, by which George Villiers lives in literature:[1]

> A man so various, that he seem'd to be
> Not one, but all mankind's epitome.
> Stiff in opinions, always in the wrong;
> Was everything by starts, and nothing long:
> But in the course of one revolving moon
> Was chemist, fiddler, statesman and buffoon;
> Then all for women, painting, rhyming, drinking,
> Besides ten thousand freaks that died in thinking . . .
> Railing and praising were his usual themes,
> And both, to show his judgment, in extremes:
> So over violent, or over civil,
> That every man, with him, was God or Devil.
> In squandering wealth was his peculiar art:
> Nothing went unrewarded but desert.

He was as fascinating as he was versatile, and women found him irresistible; though if he had not been a duke and a king's favourite, they might have been able to resist him. Married women were more to his taste than single ones. He made an art of adultery, and his bastards were plentiful. But one woman at least was unimpressed by his accomplishments, and when he found himself alone in the King's antechamber with Nell Gwynn, whom he tried to kiss, his ear was soundly boxed.

By that time Nell was one of the King's mistresses. Born in an alley off Drury Lane in February 1650, her father may have been

1. He also lives in brick, Buckingham and Villiers Streets in the Adelphi commemorating the fact that he once built himself a mansion there. See Walter Scott's *Peveril of the Peak* for a picture of Buckingham during his structural operations.

NELL GWYNN

GEORGE VILLIERS, 2ND DUKE OF BUCKINGHAM

a fruiterer in Covent Garden. She started to earn a living by serving drinks to the customers of a brothel, and then by selling oranges in the pit of the King's Theatre, where she kissed the males who took her fancy, cursed aloud when the house was half-empty, and talked freely with anyone. Soon she became notable for the quickness and neatness of her repartees, and sometimes she caused more gaiety in the audience than the actors were able to provoke. At about the age of fifteen she became the mistress of a leading actor, Charles Hart, who coached her for the stage. Before the Restoration women's parts were played by men, and William Davenant was responsible for the introduction of female performers as well as scenery. But the delight of the audience was boundless when they saw a woman playing the part of a man, which Nell did to perfection in Dryden's *Secret Love*, having 'the motions and carriage of a spark the most that I ever saw any man have', recorded Pepys, who went into ecstasies over her acting. This was in December '66, her first appearance having been early in the previous year. She was first-rate in comedy, feeble in tragedy. Her personality exuded humour; she laughed with the whole of her face, so that her eyes became almost invisible. Her vivacity, her wit, her mirth, were infectious. 'Pretty, witty Nell' Pepys called her. Her features were not pretty in the conventional sense, but her face was alive, alluring, and full of character. Her figure was good, and she had small feet; but her real attractiveness lay in her expressive vitality, her fun and good nature.

In the spring of '67 she left Hart for Charles Sackville, Lord Buckhurst, who in his early years led a riotous life, painting the town red. Once he was with two friends, Sir Charles Sedley and Sir Thomas Ogle, getting steadily drunk at the Cock tavern in Bow Street, 'and, going into the balcony, exposed themselves to the populace in very indecent postures', wrote Dr Johnson. 'At last, as they grew warmer, Sedley stood forth naked and harangued the populace in such profane language that the public indignation was awakened; the crowd attempted to force the door, and, being repulsed, drove in the performers with stones, and broke the windows of the house.' Buckhurst was always getting into trouble, and, because the King liked him, getting out of it. But he helped many poor writers, including Butler and Dryden, wrote poetry himself, and was generally regarded as one of the four wittiest men at Court, his satirical comments lacking the cynicism of Charles, the immorality of Buckingham, the thoughtlessness of Rochester. On the death of his father he became the Earl of Dorset.

He and Nell and Sedley were staying next door to the King's Head inn at Epsom in the summer of '67, and keeping 'merry house', after which Nell returned to play several of her parts, her success with the aristocracy being sufficient to annoy some of the older professionals, one of whom, Beck Marshall, a clergyman's daughter, was rash enough to call her Lord Buckhurst's whore. Nell's answer did not encourage Beck to repeat the charge: 'I was but one man's whore, though I was brought up in a bawdy-house to fill strong waters to the guests; but you are a whore to three or four, though a Presbyter's praying daughter!' Pepys thought the repartee 'very pretty'.

During 1668 the King fell under her spell, sent for her several times, and arranged her transference to him, appointing Buckhurst a groom of his bedchamber with a pension of £1,000 a year. She left the stage in 1670, after giving birth to a son by Charles, but she did not desert the theatre, where Pepys saw her in a box enjoying a play, 'a bold merry slut, who lay laughing there upon the public'. The King gave her a freehold property on the south side of Pall Mall with a garden touching St James's Park.[1] She retained his affection to the end of his reign, and he was fonder of her than of his other mistresses, two reasons being that she showed no sign of avarice and never attempted to meddle in public affairs. Many attempts were made by politicians and ambassadors to bribe her, but whatever she knew she kept to herself,

1. Roughly where Marlborough House now stands. It was not destroyed until the reign of Queen Victoria, when it was occupied by the Society for the Propagation of the Gospel in Foreign Parts.

describing herself as 'a sleeping partner in the ship of state'. She remained faithful to Charles, one of her virtues being fidelity to the man who kept her. She was kind-hearted, never cruel, benevolent in spirit and in purse, outspoken and honest. Although Dr Johnson described Aphra Behn's dedication of a play to Nell as 'the meanness and servility of hyperbolical adulation', one phrase in it was undoubtedly true: 'You never appear but you glad the hearts of all that have the happy fortune to see you, as if you were made on purpose to put the whole world into good humour.'

It was her good humour that made an especial appeal to the King, whom she called '*my* Charles the Third', her first having been Charles Hart, her second Charles Sackville. And it was his good humour that attracted her, the result being a friendship founded on understanding, mutual confidence, and the sharing of each other's troubles. As in everything else, he was the opposite of his brother, whose lack of humour made Nell call him 'dismal Jimmy'. The nature of her companionable relations with the King was disclosed when she gave a concert in her house at which Charles and his brother were present. The music over, Charles spoke highly of the performance. 'Then, sir,' said Nell, 'to show that you do not speak like a courtier, I hope you will make the performers a handsome present.' The King declared that he had no money about him and asked the Duke of York to lend him some; but the Duke regretted that he only had a guinea or two. Nell turned to the rest of the company: 'Odds fish! what company am I got into!' Having no ambition for herself, unlike his other mistresses, she never pestered Charles with requests for a title or a sinecure; and as he was not the man to bother himself when not bothered by others, their son was known simply as Charles Beauclerk until the age of six. But as the children of other mistresses were ennobled almost at birth, Nell decided to give Charles a hint, and one day called to the boy in his father's hearing: 'Come hither, you little bastard!' When Charles remonstrated she retorted: 'I have no better name to call him by.' The lad was quickly made Earl of Burford, and seven years later, on the death of Henry Jermyn the Earl of St Albans, he was created Duke of St Albans, receiving the profitable posts of Registrar of the High Court of Chancery and Master Falconer of England.[1]

Some years after her retirement from the stage Nell and other actresses were indirectly the cause of an incident that terminated in an Act of Parliament. Through the influence of Charles, the players at the King's Theatre were amalgamated with the Duke's company, and thenceforth both played at the house in Drury Lane. An entertainment tax was proposed in the House of Commons. This practically amounted to a vote of censure on the King, and one of his friends, Sir John Birkenhead, rose to oppose the project, saying that the players were the King's servants and 'a part of his pleasure'; upon which the member for Weymouth, Sir John Coventry, asked 'whether the King's pleasure lay amongst the men that acted, or the women'. This was a hit at Nell Gwynn and Moll Davis in particular, and the tax proposal was rejected. Soon afterwards Sir John Coventry, on returning to his lodgings in Suffolk Street one night, was attacked by a gang of ruffians. He defended himself with a sword in one hand, a flambeau in the other, and wounded several before he was disarmed, when his nose was slit to the bone and he received several flesh wounds, being laid up for some weeks. The Commons at once introduced a bill of Pains and Penalties, designed to prevent maiming and mutilation, and when passed it was known as the Coventry Act. The ringleaders of the assault were banished, one of them being a lieutenant in the Duke of Monmouth's troop of guards, which suggested that the King's natural son had something to do with it. The story told by Bishop Burnet that the Duke of York believed Charles himself to be responsible may be dismissed as an episcopal lie or a fraternal fiction. As we know, Charles was impervious to insult, repelled by violence, and incapable of revenge.

The House of Commons, though sternly critical of the King's

1. Nell's second son by Charles died early, her own death occurring at the age of thirty-seven.

expenditure, contained many members whose private lives were not open to inspection, and Coventry's ironic question cannot have pleased them. About the year 1669 Andrew Marvell, M.P. for Hull, drew up a list of what he called the 'Pensionary Parliament', his object being to show how many members had 'a lick at the bribe pot'. It was a sort of Who's Who, or rather Who's What, of the then House of Commons, and a few of the items may explain why the compilation was restricted to private circulation. For example, Sir Winston Churchill, M.P. for Weymouth and Melcombe Regis (which returned four members) is described as 'a pimp to his own daughter'; Sir William Bicknell, M.P. for Liverpool, is 'now a farmer of the Revenue of England and Ireland on the account of the Duchess of Cleveland, who goes snip with him'; Sir George Downing, M.P. for Morpeth, 'keeps six whores in pay, and yet has got £40,000'; while Sir Stephen Fox, M.P. for Salisbury, seems to have been even more expert in finance than Downing, for he was 'made Paymaster to the Guards, where he has cheated £100,000'. It must not be assumed that all the members were corrupt, for some were incorruptible and others were not worth corrupting, but a sufficient number were open to bribes by the French King or the English Court, and a good deal of their indignation over Charles's expenditure was due to their own inability to spend on the same scale.

The business of obtaining grants from parliament was always troublesome. Many sources of royal revenue had been pilfered during the Civil Wars, and most of the King's income was now dependent on the House of Commons; so, after the war against France and Holland, he was compelled to raise money for the defence of his country by any means open to him. If parliament continued to be niggardly, he would apply to his cousin Louis. In diplomacy, too, he would have to adopt a tortuous policy for the sake of his kingship and his kingdom. Should Holland be doing too well, he would make overtures to Louis; should Louis be getting too strong, he would become friendly with Holland; in fact he would adapt himself to any emergency. Needless to say,

France and Holland were quite capable of looking after their own interests at the expense of his, and it was simply a question of who could beat the others in the art of duplicity. In the end Charles won hands down because he was cleverer than anyone else and his wits had been sharpened by adversity: he never became the tool of France, he never truckled to the Dutch, he was never at the mercy of his own parliament and never ensnared by his ministers or mistresses, some of whom were bribed to spy upon him. But there were to be many obstacles in the rough and winding road of his long journey.

The main object of Louis in forming an alliance with Holland had been to gain a firm treaty with England beneficial to himself; for which reason he had done nothing to help the Dutch except to keep a fleet hovering off the Channel, and, solely for his own advantage, to attack England in the West Indies. In the result he was checkmated by Charles, who followed the signing of peace at Breda by entering into an agreement with Holland. The steady advance of the French army in the Spanish Netherlands had alarmed the Dutch, who were thus in a mood to make an ally of their recent enemy, and the two countries forced a peace between France and Spain by agreeing to declare war on France if Louis continued his conquest of the Netherlands. They obtained the backing of Sweden, and, faced with this Triple Alliance, Louis capitulated. Charles was careful to explain in a private letter to Louis that his actions were not in the least inimical to France, and that the Alliance was in everybody's interest. His exceptional common sense was shown during the negotiations when a French naval captain named de la Roche seized two Spanish boats in English waters. Charles at once sent an order that Sir Thomas Allin should anchor by the French boats, and, *if he judged himself to be the stronger*, compel de la Roche to deliver up every British subject on board the ships under his command.

The manner in which Charles had curbed the French King's designs by forming the Triple Alliance aroused the admiration of Louis, who was now more anxious than ever for an alliance with

England; and in 1668 envoys passed between the two Courts. Minette played her part as unofficial agent, and complained of one envoy, Sir John Trevor, receiving an apology from Charles: 'I am extremely troubled that Trevor carried himself so like an ass to you. I have sent him a chiding for it. I can say nothing for him, but that it was a fault for want of good breeding, which is a disease very much spread over this country.' It is possible that Trevor and his like were out of sympathy with Gallic good breeding. Frenchmen had swarmed in the Court at Whitehall ever since the Restoration, and as they affected to despise all fashions but their own, treating the English 'as if they were foreigners in their own country', the latter were occasionally incited to exhibitions of bad breeding.

In the eyes of Louis the Triple Alliance appeared to stand in the way of a treaty between France and England, and he wished Charles to forgo it; but his English cousin was much too cunning to break an alliance before he had made a better, and sardonically replied to Minette: 'I am sure the King my brother would not have me violate upon any terms, since he has given me the good example of being a martyr to his word,' a nasty crack for Louis, whose alliance with Holland had ranged him against England in the recent war.

Early in 1669 the Duke of York became a Roman Catholic, and it was related that at an interview between the two brothers Charles had shed tears while expressing his sorrow that circumstances prevented him from following suit. The tears may have been induced by a memory of the kind Catholics who had helped him in the dark days after Worcester fight, but it is more likely that they expressed a sensation of relief. Here was a way of touching the heart, and consequently the pocket, of Louis. A promise from Charles that he too wished to join the ancient faith would please the French King beyond words and result in a close alliance of great benefit to England and her monarch. The subject had no doubt been carefully weighed by Charles before his brother's disclosure, which however provided solid ground for negotiations. But the plot 'craved wary walking', and very few were let into the secret. Buckingham, though at the height of his Court influence, was not to be trusted, and to keep him quiet it was arranged that he should negotiate a commercial treaty with France, which would be practically the same as the secret treaty but would contain no reference to the King's conversion. His vanity thus appeased, he could be led to believe that he was solely responsible for the arrangements, while the serious business was being quietly done behind his back by two or three men, including Arlington, whom the King could trust implicitly. Charles was perfectly well aware of the danger he ran; he knew that if his secret were betrayed there would be a revolution in the country; but he took the risk because the support of Louis would not only free him from dependence on parliament but enable him to beat Holland, the object of both monarchs being to smash the power of the Dutch, who stood in the way of France's territorial designs and England's commercial aims.

Minette as well as Louis believed that Charles was sincerely desirous to become a Roman Catholic, and an *abbé* was sent over to impress the coming convert. Unfortunately the *abbé* was an astrologer, who found Charles at Newmarket and with the help of the stars predicted that certain horses would win their races. The Duke of York took the *abbé's* tips and lost a lot of money because none of the astral favourites won. Charles was sceptical and advised Minette: 'I give little credit to such kind of cattle, and the less you do it the better, for if they could tell anything 'tis inconvenient to know one's fortune beforehand, whether good or bad.' The attitude of Charles to the religion he had promised to embrace was frivolous enough to make anyone but Minette lift an eyebrow. Their mother was proverbially unlucky in her sea voyages, and when she sent a gift to Charles he was not surprised to hear that the bearer was drowned: 'I hear Mam sent me a present by him, which I believe brought him the ill-luck, so as she ought in conscience to be at the charges of praying for his soul, for 'tis her misfortune has made the man miscarry.'

While Arlington and two or three trusted Roman Catholics were arranging the secret treaty, and Buckingham was managing the commercial one, Louis confided the fact that de Witt had been secretly trying to get his agreement to a Dutch-French partition of the Spanish dominions; and as this gave England a moral excuse for breaking the Triple Alliance, Charles was able to tell his sister that 'there is all the reason in the world to join profit with honour when it may be done honestly', a pious sentiment that would have provoked appreciative laughter from anyone who could look at the world with the eyes of the writer.

One serious difficulty stood in the way of an agreement. The French King wanted a big fleet to extend his country's commerce. Charles had no intention of allowing another sea-power to rival his, and refused to consider an alliance until that plan was abandoned. Further, he claimed complete control of the naval warfare, and said that if his admirals were ordered on pain of death to obey foreigners they would refuse to do so. He got his way. In order to expedite matters and to gain further concessions, Charles said he would declare himself a Roman Catholic at once, knowing that this would alarm Louis, who had been informed that such a declaration would cause a Protestant rising in England and wreck the alliance. He wished Charles to defer his avowal until after the war had started. Charles agreed, and deferred it until his death. At length, after much haggling over the amount of cash to be paid, the secret treaty was settled. Shorn of its verbiage, Charles agreed to declare himself a Roman Catholic 'as soon as the state of his country's affairs permit', the exact time to be left to his discretion. The price of his conversion was roughly £160,000, to be paid within six months by Louis, who also undertook to provide six thousand troops if his cousin's subjects proved recalcitrant. Both monarchs were jointly to declare war on Holland, and neither was to make peace without the other. Louis would be responsible for the land campaign, assisted by six thousand British troops, while Charles would undertake the naval operations, reinforced by thirty French ships, all to be commanded by the Duke of York. As long as the war lasted Louis would make an annual payment to Charles of about £240,000. The terms of the public treaty, which were simply a blind to cover up the other and allay the suspicions of Buckingham and his fellow Protestants, were the same as those of the secret treaty except that the article dealing with the King's conversion was left out and the price to be paid for it was added to the first annual subsidy towards the expense of the war.

To discuss such questions as the date of the King's conversion and the commencement of the war, Minette travelled to England. She was only allowed to go as far as Dover and to stay a few days, because her husband the Duke of Orleans was insanely jealous of any prestige she might acquire from the visit. She led a wretched life with him, not even controlling her own house, which was run by his inamorato, the Chevalier de Lorraine; and he put every obstacle in the way of her trip to England. However she arrived at Dover in May 1670, Charles going out to meet her in a barge, the English fleet in attendance. Her household of some 240 people lodged in the cottages of the port, while she stayed with her brother in the castle. They had not met for ten years, Charles having decided never to cross the Channel again. The King was in good humour because parliament had recently voted him the wine tax for seven years, an annual yield of £300,000. He loved Minette almost as much as she loved him and he was greatly upset when she had to go. The secret treaty, known to history as the Treaty of Dover, was signed on 22 May by Arlington and three reliable Roman Catholics, Lord Arundell of Wardour, Lord Clifford of Chudleigh and Sir Richard Bellings, with the French ambassador, Colbert de Croissy. Charles gave Minette many presents of money and jewels, and begged her to leave behind one of her jewels as a keepsake. But when she heard that the jewel he coveted was one of her Maids of Honour, Louise de Kéroualle, she refused, saying that she was responsible to the girl's parents. At the parting of brother and sister Charles was seen in tears. He accompanied her some distance on the sea, returning to her boat three times to bid her farewell, perhaps with a presentiment that it would be their last. Within a month of her return she died, and Charles grieved so deeply that several days passed before he again appeared in public.

After the signing of the counterfeit treaty of commerce at the end of 1670, Louis felt that the time had come for Charles to take some preliminary steps towards his conversion. But Charles did not seem in a hurry and said that he must first consult the Pope in order to obtain concessions that would make his conversion acceptable to his people. His next excuse was that he had no suitable envoy to carry on such delicate transactions. Louis suggested one of his own bishops. Charles seemed delighted, but eventually decided that his envoy should be English. Having found one, matters were delayed by the drawing up of instructions. Then he explained that existing conditions were unfavourable, the present pontiff being old and sickly and unfit for such a serious confidence. When Louis became pressing, Charles had the brilliant notion of making proposals which he knew would be unacceptable at the Vatican, such as the celebration of the Mass in English, and the administration to the laity of wine as well as bread at Communion, it being understood that he would do his best to convert his own people. No doubt he would have had further ideas of an equally scintillating nature, but the Dutch war started, Louis became preoccupied with military matters, and Charles had something more interesting to occupy his attention than the condition of his soul.

[17]

Fun and Fury

THE SECRET AGREEMENT between Louis and Charles, though it appeared at the time to be a master-stroke of French policy, was in reality a triumph for the English King. Louis wanted to destroy Dutch power on land, and failed to do so. Charles wished to weaken Dutch power at sea, and succeeded in doing so. The result for France was a series of campaigns which ended in her defeat by Marlborough in the next generation. The result for England was a great increase in maritime strength and commercial expansion, which enabled Pitt to build the British Empire at France's expense in the next century. As to the ethics of these proceedings, all that need be said is that sound morality has never been the basis of material advantages. Charles was the most astute politician of his age. Had he not been, it is more than likely that the English monarchy would have perished along with the trade that supported it. The virtues and vices of most people seem contradictory; with Charles they seem complementary. His merits easily shaded into defects, which were not the opposite but the obverse of his good qualities. His imaginative nature made him gentle, but also weak. His intelligence made him tolerant, but also indifferent. His rational disposition made him considerate, but also negligent. His sense of loyalty made him generous, but also extravagant. His mental balance gave him humour as well as irresponsibility. His natural charity brought indolence as well as callousness. And his native shrewdness would declare itself, according to need, either in prudence or in cunning.

This last characteristic came to the surface in his instructions to Sir George Downing, his ambassador at The Hague, just before war broke out. In negotiating with the Dutch ministers Downing was ordered to 'insist upon having my flag saluted even on their very shore' and 'having my dominion of these seas asserted', such demands being an incitement to bellicose feelings in Holland. 'Notwithstanding all this,' continued Charles, 'I would have you use your skill so to amuse them that they may not finally despair of me, and thereby give me time to make myself more ready and leave them more remiss in their preparations.' Downing was further commanded to play the spy and report on the condition of the Dutch warships and how soon they could be put to sea.

The singular thing about Charles was that the opposite qualities in his nature were manifested simultaneously, and in creating an impression of surrender he was only giving way to prepare for resistance. Though none of his ministers, and none of his mistresses except perhaps Nell Gwynn, recognised the fact, he never lost command of himself and always knew the direction he wished to take, however devious the road he was compelled to follow. He lost ground in one place to win it in another; he yielded in order to retain; he pampered while thwarting his advisers. His attributes of strength and weakness were nowhere more clearly marked than in his dealings with the other sex. He gave them everything a woman is supposed to want, money, titles, luxuries, personal attention and consideration; but denied them what they really wanted, power to control events. This was especially so in the case of Louise de Kéroualle. After his sister's death, he renewed his request that Louise should come to his Court and be made one of the Queen's ladies-in-waiting. The daughter of a Breton gentleman, she was ambitious and willing, and it occurred to King Louis that she could sustain two roles: by forming a liaison with Charles, she could act as liaison between the two monarchs, in other words do the work of a spy. Charles was solely concerned with her performance in one capacity, and in 1671 eagerly dispatched a yacht to fetch her across the Channel. She became a Maid of Honour and received apartments in the Palace. At the age of twenty she had a pretty babyish face, dark hair, a cream and rose complexion, a mischievous look, and a slight cast in one of her eyes, all of which concealed a tough nature. In time she put on weight, becoming so plump that Charles called his yacht *Fubbs* in her honour, but at the period of her arrival she had an attractive figure, an innocent appearance, and a coy manner.

Although she soon occupied the position of chief courtesan after the retirement of Lady Castlemaine as Duchess of Cleveland, she was excessively vexed by Nell Gwynn's hold on the King's affection; and Nell took an instant dislike to her, calling her 'Weeping Willow' or 'Squintabella', and suggesting to Charles that, as his parliament had recently passed an Act forbidding the importation of foreign commodities that were prejudicial to the growth of English trade, he ought to apply it to the latest French importation. Nell could not help making fun of Louise, mimicking her, making faces at her, being witty at her expense, and boasting openly when Charles had spent the night in Pall Mall instead of at the Palace. When Louise went into mourning for a French prince, Nell wore black for the recently deceased Cham of Tartary, and upon being questioned about her connection with that potentate she replied that she was as closely related to him as Mademoiselle de Kéroualle was to the French prince. Naturally Charles enjoyed these pleasantries and was amused to hear that the populace, a trifle shaky on French vowel sounds, called Louise 'Mistress Carwell'.

Apparently there was a mock ceremony of marriage between Charles and Louise in October '71 at Lord Arlington's country seat, Euston, in Suffolk. The King was then at Newmarket, where he rode the winner of the Plate and incidentally visited Oliver Cromwell's fourth son Henry, who ran a farm at Spinney Abbey near Soham. But every second day of his fortnight's sojourn at Newmarket he went to Euston, and Evelyn entered in his diary:

'It was universally reported that the fair Lady Whore was bedded one of these nights and the stocking flung, after the manner of a married bride.' Ten months after the stocking had been flung Louise bore the King a son, Charles Lennox, who became the Duke of Richmond, and shortly after his birth Mademoiselle de Kéroualle was transformed into the Duchess of Portsmouth. Thenceforward she did her utmost, by backing one minister or attacking another, to influence the course of events, always in the French and Catholic interest; but though she frequently seemed to be in a strong position, and was much cultivated by those who wished to gain or retain power, she proved a nonentity whenever Charles determined on a stroke of policy unfavourable to France.

Her arrival in England happened to coincide with all the secret arrangements that were being made between the two monarchs and the appearance in London of far more Romish priests than the English people liked to see. In order to obtain money for the equipment of his fleet, Charles softened the Commons with a proclamation ordering Jesuits and priests out of the country, and then got rid of parliament for almost two years by a series of prorogations. If, during that period, he had followed the advice of his chief counsellors, he would have kept his word with Louis, become a Roman Catholic, and precipitated a revolution. But he was wiser than those around him, and tried to unite his countrymen on the eve of war against Holland by issuing a Declaration of Indulgence, whereby Roman Catholics were allowed to hold services in their own houses and nonconformists were permitted to hold services in public if they procured licences. But the latter, while welcoming their own freedom, strongly objected to freedom for papists, and Charles was soon made to realise that he was too far in advance of his age. However there was always hope that a successful war would achieve what 'the cankers of a calm world' prevented.

The Dutch having refused to take umbrage at the demand that every English ship should be saluted 'even on their very shore', it became necessary to goad them into action by stronger measures, and Captain Robert Holmes seemed the right man for the job. He was ordered to obstruct the passage of a large Dutch fleet off the Isle of Wight. Striking with a much inferior force, he was badly mauled and crept back to port with a few captured vessels. This seemed a good excuse for further action, the Dutch having dared to fight back, and on 17 March 1672, forty-eight hours after Charles had published his Declaration of Indulgence, a declaration of war against Holland was made by his government, the Duke of York being ordered to seize all Dutch vessels and to fight, sink, burn, or otherwise destroy any that resisted. Accompanying this order was the characteristic clause, denoting the King's personal wish, that all prisoners must be treated with fairness and humanity.

The English and French navies numbered ninety-eight warships against seventy-five of the Dutch. It is interesting to recall that the English first-rates of 2,000 tons, like the *Sovereign*, the *Charles* and the *Prince*, were equipped with 110 guns and carried crews of about 800 men. The Duke of York commanded the allied fleet, the French admiral D'Estrées being subordinate to him, while the Dutch were under de Ruyter. Hostilities commenced at the end of May with a sternly contested fight off Southwold Bay, resulting in heavy losses on both sides. Claimed by each as a victory, it was a drawn battle, which might have ended differently if D'Estrées had not disobeyed the Duke's orders. His conduct strengthened the distrust and dislike of the French that was steadily growing in England. While the sea-fight was raging, Condé and Turenne successfully attacked the Dutch on land. The Rhine was crossed on 30 May, and Holland asked Louis for peace terms, which were more than they could stomach. In their desperate plight they reinstated William of Orange as Stadtholder, and murdered Jan de Witt and his brother. Charles took advantage of his nephew's elevation by proposing peace. But William felt that his countrymen were behind him, and the suggestion that he should be made a sovereign under the protection of England and France, the alternative being extermination, made no appeal to him. 'Nothing can get us a better peace than the appearing ready to continue the war,' wrote Charles to his brother in August. But William was not to be frightened by the embattled monarchs; and having checked Louis by breaking the sea-dykes and deluging his country, he prepared to continue the maritime war.

In England there was a financial crisis, averted by Charles who assured the bankers that the government's indebtedness to them would be paid in full. But it was clear that he would have to summon parliament again if he wished for supplies to carry on the war, Louis having refused to grant a loan. In February '73 the Commons met in sombre mood, which reflected the anti-Catholic and anti-French feeling in the country. Charles did not dissipate their gloom by stating at once: 'I will deal plainly with you, I am resolved to stick to my Declaration' [of Indulgence]. After provisionally voting him enough money for prosecuting the war, or obtaining a reasonable peace, the Commons showed that they had no intention of tolerating toleration. There were stormy scenes in both Houses, members claiming that the King had no right to suspend penal statutes in ecclesiastical matters; and in order to prevent civil war, Charles was compelled to give in. On 8 March he rescinded his Declaration, and later that month the two Houses passed the Test Act, which made it impossible for anyone to take public office who refused to swear the oaths of allegiance and supremacy, to receive the Anglican sacrament, and to repudiate the doctrine of Transubstantiation. Thus Charles had to pay heavily for his supplies, temporarily sacrificing his conscience in the cause of commerce; but he was playing a lone hand in a long game.

The Test Act forced the Duke of York as a Roman Catholic into private life, and Prince Rupert was made Lord High Admiral. In May '73 the fleets were ready for action, and this time the fighting took place off the coast of Holland. A series of murderous engagements, accompanied by innumerable acts of heroism on both sides, and a spasm of timidity on the part of D'Estrées at a crucial moment, proved nothing except that the English and Dutch were invincible warriors, and that the former could not land troops on their enemy's territory. The cost of the war and the prevailing francophobia were creating disunion and distrust among the King's ministers, and the two historic political parties of Great Britain were born in 1673, when the office of Lord Treasurer was bestowed on Sir Thomas Osborne (created Earl of Danby the following year) and the office of Lord Chancellor was taken away from Ashley Cooper, Earl of Shaftesbury. The first, a cautious climber, had a genius for organisation and ultimately founded what came to be known as the Tory Party. The second, a born schemer, had a talent for publicity and originated what was to be called the Whig Party. The terms 'tory' and 'whig' were at first abusive nicknames, a tory being an Irish Catholic outlaw, a whig being a Scottish Covenanting fanatic. Danby as Treasurer got the country out of its financial straits due to the war, but he was helped considerably by a large increase of revenue during a commercially prosperous period. Shaftesbury, whom the King thought weak and wicked, nearly managed to wreck the monarchy some years later. He was one of the most significant figures of his time and demands some notice here.

Born in 1621, he fought for Charles I in the Civil War, until the moment when a change of sides seemed advisable and he fought for the parliament. During the Commonwealth he sat in parliament, supporting the government when it suited his purpose and opposing it when it suited Cromwell's purpose. Having a wonderful weather-sense, he could tell when a gentle breeze would become a strong wind, and he was foremost among those who brought back Charles II, to whom he quickly made a present of money. Good-looking and witty, his conversation was entertaining but superficial. He believed in astrological predictions, and thought that after death the souls of human beings 'went into stars and animated them'. His vanity was excessive; he could not have enough flattery, and Bishop Burnet tells us that he 'turned the discourse almost always to the magnifying of himself'. Proud even of the dexterity and success with which he had changed sides, he bragged of his skill in treachery. He was one of those portentous figures who are only able to feel self-confidence by the exercise of power over others and the winning of their admiration, any means to attain these ends being excusable, and in his own case meritorious. His sole interest in life was himself, his sole concern being his own advancement, power and glory. Such was the man characterised by Dryden as Achitophel in memorable phrases:

> Of these the false Achitophel was first,
> A name to all succeeding ages curst.
> For close designs and crooked counsels fit,
> Sagacious, bold, and turbulent of wit,
> Restless, unfixed in principles and place,
> In power unpleased, impatient of disgrace . . .
> Great wits are sure to madness near allied,
> And thin partitions do their bounds divide;
> Else, why should he, with wealth and honour blest,
> Refuse his age the needful hours of rest,
> Punish a body which he could not please,
> Bankrupt of life, yet prodigal of ease?
> And all to leave what with his toil he won
> To that unfeathered two-legged thing, a son . . .
> In friendship false, implacable in hate,
> Resolved to ruin or to rule the State . . .

From the moment of Shaftesbury's dismissal as Lord Chancellor, he became more dangerous to the King than a combination of foreign enemies.

But indeed Charles was in an extremely vulnerable position just then. The Duke of York's wife, Anne Hyde, by whom he had two daughters (later to be Queens of England), died in '71, and in September '73 he married a Roman Catholic, Mary of Modena, who brought a handsome dowry from King Louis and the approval of the Pope. Parliament assembled in October, and the Commons, ignorant of the accomplished fact, voted that the Duke should marry a Protestant princess, and refused supplies for the war until they were assured that the country was no longer endangered by Roman Catholicism. The belief was gaining ground that the war was being fought for the Pope, and the grievances of the Commons included their monarch's 'evil counsellors'. Louis came to the rescue with half a million pounds and a bribe for Shaftesbury. But not even Louis could bribe a whole nation, and the Commons wished to be enlightened on the full extent of the agreement between the two Kings. Charles got out of his difficulty by offering to show them the bogus treaty and telling a spanking lie: 'I assure you there is no other treaty with France, either before or since, not already printed, which shall not be made known.' Parliament seemed to think that a public fast to propitiate the Deity would be advisable, and Charles raised no objection. Receiving inspiration from that quarter, the Commons pressed for the removal of the King's advisers. Accusations were launched against Lauderdale for raising an army in Scotland, against Buckingham for visiting the French King and for crimes of so odious a nature that they could not even be discussed in Rome; also against Arlington for embezzlement, war-making, and sympathy with papists. Vindicating themselves before the Commons, Buckingham laid all the blame on Arlington, who laid all the blame on Buckingham. The King was advised by York and Osborne to save the situation by dissolving parliament. But Charles acutely perceived that, with the anti-French feeling in the country, he might get a more critical parliament in exchange, and instead of a dissolution he took both Houses into his confidence, asking them to approve his proposed peace-terms to Holland. Having agreed them and thanked him, the Commons ventilated grievances against a standing army, popery, and the bribery of members of Parliament; though they dropped the latter when it became clear that too many members were in the pay of Holland as well as France.

The Dutch were anxious for a peace, and a treaty was signed between the two countries in February '74, whereby England received an indemnity of something like £200,000 and Charles's pride in his navy was fortified by the Dutch concession that his ships should be saluted in British waters, i.e., from Spain to Norway. He once said that he would rather lose his crown than abandon the salute at sea, but the statement was rhetorical, since his main ambition, or rather intention, was to remain on his throne and never to go on his travels again. But ceremonial distinctions appealed to the histrionic side of his nature, and he insisted that the coach of his ambassador in France should precede the carriages containing the princes of the reigning house. Though Charles did his best to reassure the French King of his friendly intentions, Louis was naturally furious that England should have made peace with Holland, leaving him to continue the war alone. But nothing could so well have suited British commerce. New York, which had been recaptured by the Dutch in '73, was handed back to England as a result of the treaty, and the steady colonisation of North America went apace. While France and Holland were engaged in a death-struggle during the next few years, England's expanding trade enabled her to emerge from bankruptcy into prosperity; and though the Commons became more and more irksome, the King's personal popularity gradually increased.

There were many reasons for this, the chief being his personal fascination and his love of sport. He talked freely with all classes of the community and always in a good-natured friendly way, imparting his own enjoyment of life by the readiness and joviality of his conversation, and turning gravity into gaiety. A remark in one of his letters to Minette suggests his mirthful manner: 'I am sorry to find that cuckolds in France grow so troublesome. They have been inconvenient in all countries this last year.' Bishop Burnet, who knew him well and had some hard things to say of him, reported that he was 'civil rather to an excess and has a softness and gentleness with him, both in his air and expressions, that has a charm in it'. He could refuse a request so agreeably that the applicant was more pleased than if another had granted it. He entertained a poor opinion of men and women, thinking them wholly governed by self-interest; but being sensible enough to know that disinterestedness was not a noticeable feature of his own character, he did not like them any the less on that account. 'He has the greatest art of concealing himself of any man alive,' said Burnet, and this enabled him to be familiar with all sorts and conditions of people without ever giving himself away. Above all he loved to be at ease and to make others feel easy. He knew a good deal about most subjects, and could debate scientific matters with scientists as fluently as he could discuss poetry with Dryden, music with Henry Purcell, painting with Peter Lely or Godfrey Kneller, inventions with William Petty, mathematics with Thomas Hobbes, and horse-racing with jockeys.

In a country where sport occupies the minds of the majority, his position was assured. He was a great walker, thinking nothing of a stroll from Whitehall to Hampton Court, and at a time when rulers were seldom seen by their people, except on horseback or in a coach or palace, the peripatetic habits of Charles must have made his subjects feel that he was one of themselves. The pastimes of the period were chiefly hurling, a fearsome forerunner of Rugby football, falconry, archery, bowls, fencing, horse-racing, billiards and cock-fighting, the last as popular as fox-hunting became a century later. An attempt to introduce bull-fighting was abandoned late in the reign during the political excitement that followed the Rye House Plot. In all these diversions the King took an interest, especially horse-racing. The first of his regular visits to Newmarket occurred in October '68, and after that he usually spent a few weeks there every spring and autumn. He bought Audley End in Essex, where the Queen often stayed when he was at Newmarket. He raced, hunted (sometimes by torch-light), and occasionally spent week-ends at the houses of neighbouring noblemen. Samuel Pepys noted that once, at Culford in

Suffolk, the Duke of Buckingham amused the King with a bawdy sermon on Sunday, while his host, Lord Cornwallis, tried to get him a pretty whore. Another time his Majesty was so drunk at the residence of Lord Crofts, Little Saxham, near Bury St Edmunds, that he was unable to give an audience to Lord Arlington. It was not often that he gave way to such orgies, but at a Cranborne hunting-party the cool relationship between himself and his brother of York was warmed by alcohol, his equerry saying 'By God, sir, you are not so kind to the Duke of York of late as you used to be'. 'Not I? Why so?' 'Why, if you are, let us drink his health.' 'Why, let us.' 'Nay, sir, by God you must do it on your knees!' So Charles and the rest of the company knelt to drink the Duke's health, after which, related Pepys, 'all fell a-crying for joy, being all maudlin and kissing one another, the King the Duke of York, and the Duke of York the King, and in such a maudlin pickle as never people were; and so passed the day'. Though naturally solemn and serious, the Duke occasionally entered into the lively mood of his brother, and they were once observed laughing together as they watched the copulating geese and ganders in St James's Park. 'Now you shall see a marriage between this and that,' said the King, who enjoyed simple pleasures like the mating of birds and the debating of lords.

At last Charles decided to have a house at Newmarket, and got Wren to design one in the High Street. When completed, he thought the rooms too low, Wren having considered the building in relation to its neighbours. The architect, a short man, walked through the rooms, and said: 'I think, and it please your Majesty, they are high enough.' Charles lowered himself to Wren's physical level and replied: 'Aye, Sir Christopher, I think they are high enough.' The King loved Newmarket, where he cast off the cares of state – not that he ever allowed them to make him careworn – and felt free to do just as he liked. The jockeys enjoyed his company as much as he enjoyed theirs, and the atmosphere generated by him made everyone forget that there were turmoil and distress elsewhere, the quarrels of kings, the jealousies of politicians, the hatreds of christians.

The example of free behaviour set by the King was sometimes carried to excess by his courtiers. Once the Duke of Buckingham and the Earl of Rochester took an inn on the Newmarket road and while pretending to act as publicans did their best to seduce the respectable women in the neighbourhood, with what success we do not know. Rochester was the son of the King's old friend and fellow-fugitive Henry Wilmot. He was born in 1647; and Oxford having made him a Master of Arts at the age of fourteen, he travelled in Europe. Then he served in the navy during the Dutch wars with distinction and bravery, once volunteering to take a message from one ship to another in an open boat while a battle was raging, going and returning amidst a hail of shot. At Court he quickly won a reputation for sparkling wit, loose principles, obscene verses, lewd talk, heavy drinking, and general viciousness. In the execution of mad escapades he out-bucked Buckingham. He went about the streets disguised as a beggar, made love as a porter, harangued the populace from a stage on Tower-hill as a mountebank doctor, and disguised as a tinker collected the pots and pans of the housewives at Burford, damaged instead of mending them, and was thrust into the stocks and eventually rescued by his servants, who got him home by transporting the stocks as well. For five years he was perpetually drunk and never out of mischief. One of his hobbies was the writing of libels. Burnet relates that 'he found out a footman that knew all the Court, and furnished him with a red coat and a musket as a sentinel, and kept him all the winter long every night at the doors of such ladies as he believed might be in intrigues'. Having collected enough material, Rochester then retired into the country for several weeks in order to compose scorching verses at the expense of his victims. These were distributed about the Court and caused much merriment, unless they got into the wrong hands; which occurred when he accidentally gave the King what in his alcoholic condition he believed to be a libel on certain ladies

but was actually a defamatory assessment of the monarch himself
and included such lines as these:

> The bad we've too long known, the good's to come,
> But not expected till the day of Doom;
> Was ever Prince's soul so meanly poor,
> To be a slave to every little Whore?

The King loved his company but not his character, and frequently
sent him to cool his head in the Tower because of the objection-
able nature of his sallies on the female favourites at Court. Un-
repentant and unrebuffable, he emerged from these temporary in-
carcerations whenever the King wanted a good laugh, returning
to the Tower after a few months' freedom had resulted in some
unpardonable burst of ribald rhymes.

His debaucheries sometimes laid him low and he suffered from
remorse, 'for he was guilty both of much impiety and of great
immoralities', wrote Burnet; but having recovered 'he turned
again to his former ill courses'. Between his bouts of what Johnson called 'drunken gaiety and gross sensuality', he took an
interest in the drama, helped Dryden, and occasionally wrote
lyrics of some charm. He also fell in love with a pretty girl, or
coveted her fortune, and abducted her. But she was retrieved by
her family, and Rochester had to wait two years before marrying
her. The French ambassador called him 'the man in all England
who has least honour and most wit'. Charles continually forgave
his scathing sarcasms for the sake of his lively conversation, and
when bored by business would send for Rochester to cheer him
up, or cheer the Court up when important Dutch or German
visitors had to be entertained. In his case the King probably used
the Tower as a sort of inebriates' home. The patient entered it
dead drunk and came out of it relatively sober. One of the com-
mittals was due to a satire containing a phrase that has stuck to
Charles ever since:

Fun and Fury

A merry monarch, scandalous and poor,

he truth of which was confirmed when the merriment of the King
called for the restoration of the jester. But

The gods are just, and of our pleasant vices
Make instruments to plague us.

Rochester having, in Johnson's phrase, 'blazed out his youth and
his health in lavish voluptuousness', was reduced 'to a state of
weakness and decay'. He died of ulcers at the age of thirty-three,
penitent, pious, and full of good resolutions.

[18]

Double-Crossing

AT THE GAME Charles was now to play for seven years, from the peace with Holland in '74 to the dissolution of parliament in '81, he was a master, and he had need to be. He was up against the unscrupulous Louis, the suspicious William of Orange, the corrupt Spanish ministers, the hostile States-General of Holland, Catholic bigots, Puritan fanatics, and above all the growing Country Party or Whigs in his own House of Commons. That he kept his head as well as his crown, that he surrendered little and left England prosperous, was due to his superiority over all his clever scheming enemies in the craft of opportunism. His patience and knowledge of human nature were part of his inheritance from his maternal grandfather Henry of Navarre, developed by his own rough experiences up to the age of thirty. No monarch ever had so good a training in fortitude, the sharpening of wits and the necessity of guile. He has been judged harshly by many historians because he was not stupid enough to lose his head as his father had done before him, or silly enough to lose his throne as his brother did after him. They have accused him of selling himself or his country to France. What he did was to take money from Louis for the security of England when the Commons would have 'left her naked to her enemies', to give nothing in return, and to make France in effect the instrument of England's commercial welfare. Considerable cunning and mendacity were necessary to achieve his ends, along with the qualifications already named. Surrounded by tricksters, he outwitted the lot,

207

and won the last trick.

His acute insight into human motives was reinforced by a method which no respectable historian could approve. From 1668 onwards the page of his bedchamber was one Will Chiffinch, a polite and pleasant person who must have been a born actor, hiding his craftiness beneath a mask of honesty and inviting confidences by an ingratiating manner. He was the King's most trusted servant, acting as pimp, pawnbroker and privy spy, the chief needs of Charles being girls, money and secret intelligence. Though the cash that passed through his hands and the scandal that came to his ears could have made Chiffinch the richest and most influential man of his time, he remained loyal to Charles and did not even keep a diary. His chief value lay in his ability to find out whatever his master wanted to know. People came to his office, masked and by the backstairs, either to have a private talk with Charles or to impart useful information to Chiffinch. If they seemed nervous about telling what they knew, their tongues were loosened with drink, into which Chiffinch sometimes found it necessary to add 'salutiferous drops', when tongues wagged without restraint. 'Well-breathed at the sport himself,' reported Roger North, 'he commonly had the better, and discovered men's characters which the King could never have obtained by any other means.' With Chiffinch in command of the backstairs department, and the good rate of payment to eavesdroppers who brought spicy news, Charles was kept well abreast of plots and usually knew all about secret matters before they were brought to his notice by some well-meaning and well-posted courtier.

Needless to say, Chiffinch did not have to stint himself of life's pleasures. He had a country residence at Witney in Oxfordshire, where he kept a pack of black beagles, and took part in royal hunting parties or picnics on the Thames. The King loved the river, and in good weather bathed or yachted continually, often being seen at Chelsea and Putney, and passing as much time on the water when the sun was shining as he spent making experiments in his laboratory when it was wet. Deeply interested in chemistry, one of the excuses he made to Louis for delaying his conversion to the Roman Catholic faith was that he must receive instruction from a theologian who was also a chemist, as he was troubled by certain questions which could only be resolved by an expert in that science. Following every impulse, he moved about so freely, on boat or foot or horseback, and talked with such a curious assortment of people, that his ministers were often alarmed for his safety, and after one attempt on his life he agreed to have a regular bodyguard for use in times of danger. Thus the British standing army was established, the Foot and Life Guards, together with the Coldstream Guards, being recruited largely from Monk's old regiments, the Horse Guards from Cavaliers who had fought in Flanders, and later the Royal Scots, Dragoons and Scots Greys; the total force, including the Yeomen of the Guard, numbering some seven thousand men.

Parliament was always in a state of panic about this standing army, their nerves not having yet recovered from the sight of Oliver's redcoats, and the troubles of the years 1674–81 were exacerbated by the friction between the members and their monarch on this subject. 'I must let you know,' he addressed them sharply in June '75, 'that whilst you are in debate about your privileges, I will not suffer my own to be invaded.' The two parties in parliament were fairly evenly matched, Danby leading the Court Party (Tories) and Shaftesbury the Country Party (Whigs) abetted by Buckingham. Whenever the situation got out of hand, Charles prorogued parliament, but he refused every attempt to make him dissolve it and risk another election because he preferred the Cavalier devil he distrusted to the possible Presbyterian devil he detested. At the end of '75 he prorogued the Houses for fifteen months, and early the following year he made a secret treaty with Louis, whereby each king agreed not to help the other's enemies and not to make a treaty without the other's co-operation. Louis was much more direct in these negotiations than his cousin of England, who once told a French ambassador: 'Since I have come back to my kingdom I have nearly forgotten the French language, and in truth the trouble I have in looking for my words allows the escape of my thoughts. I must needs have delay in order to be able to reflect and meditate upon things proposed to me in that language.' But Charles was direct enough when in need of money. An instalment of his wife's dowry arriving in the form of dried fruit, he declared that he would have preferred fewer currants and more cash. He took little interest in any sort of present that could not instantly be converted into coin, and a gift of two lions and thirty ostriches from the Sultan of Morocco caused him to say that he would return the compliment with a flock of geese. He used Louis solely as a milch cow; and while Louis thought he was spending money for temporal gain and spiritual glory, his bribes ultimately helped to defeat the ambitions of France and the Papacy. Until the game was played out, Charles was nearly always one move ahead of his cunning cousin.

Yet he continually added to his liabilities. One addition appeared in the shape of Hortense Mancini, Duchess of Mazarin, who was given apartments in St James's Palace on her arrival early in '76. It will be remembered that her uncle, Cardinal Mazarin, had rejected Charles's proposal of marriage to Hortense, one of many females who might have become Queen of England if their relations had been gifted with prevision. A well-matured fourteen when Charles asked for her hand, she was a fully-seasoned thirty when he welcomed her to England. Her life had been intolerable and enjoyable in equal measure. The Cardinal married her to Armand de Meilleraye, the wealthy son of a French marshal, who shortly after their union went mad. One of those curiously unbalanced folk who suffer from alternate spasms of lust and revulsion therefrom, he feverishly surrendered to passion, followed at once by fits of contrition, when he smashed statues, destroyed paintings, and exhausted himself with prayers and lamentations. Hortense endured his lunacy for seven years while she produced several children, and then ran away. He managed to have her shut up in a penitentiary convent; and while she was busy bringing a legal case against him to secure her personal property, he circulated accusations against her of abnormal behaviour with a eunuch, of incest with her brother, and of love-affairs with her own sex. Hortense won her case, but in the belief that her freedom would be imperilled, her social position jeopardised, she left France secretly with a female friend, both in male costume. The next few years were occupied with venturesome visits to various parts of Europe and amorous affairs with different sorts of people, with exciting escapes and dangerous journeys.

Having tasted life in all its variety, she wished to subdue the most susceptible king in Europe, and fulfilled her wish. Her handsome appearance forced a reluctant admission from the French ambassador: 'I never saw one who so well defies the powers of time and vice to disfigure.' Her personal fascination, the stories of her hazardous adventures, her wit and intelligence, made an instantaneous appeal to Charles, none of whose women up to date had mentally stimulated him. She provided him with an entirely new experience, for she appeared to be as clever as she was lovely, answering all his requirements. But sexual fidelity was not among her virtues, nor for that matter his; and when she fell in love with the Prince of Monaco, the King quickly exchanged desire for friendship, enjoying her exquisite suppers, her brilliant conversation, and the company of artists and philosophers who thronged her salon. Her reception at the English Court aroused suspicion in France, where she was thought to be in league with the faction that favoured a Dutch alliance; but Charles never allowed his sentiment to influence his statecraft, and Hortense took no part in the plots and counterplots of the time, receiving the friendly advances of Louis through his ambassador with affable indifference. Nevertheless the average courtier firmly believed that Charles's women dictated much of his policy. Walking in St James's Park one day with Lord Dorset (formerly Buckhurst) Charles asked why the church bells were ringing. On hearing that it was Queen Elizabeth's birthday and a public holiday, he thought it strange that she should be remembered while the birthdays of his father and grandfather were no more heeded than William the Conqueror's. 'Sire,' explained Dorset, 'she being a woman chose men for her counsellors, but men when they reign usually choose women.' Charles chose neither men nor women, but he did not mind either sex thinking he followed the other's advice.

His gravest liability, the man whose advice, had he followed it, would have cost him the crown, was his brother of York, whose conversion to the Romish faith caused Charles more trouble than all his women and all his public enemies put together. There can never have been much affection between the two, their natures being antipathetic; but James, as a solemn ass, provided some entertainment to justify his existence. 'I am weary of travelling,' remarked Charles; 'I am resolved to go abroad no more. But when I am dead and gone, I know not what my brother will do. I am much afraid that when he comes to the crown he will be obliged to travel again.' He was. One day Charles and a couple of friends were strolling across the road between Constitution Hill and Hyde Park. James, driving past, caught sight of them, stopped his coach, alighted, and warned his brother that he was needlessly exposing himself to danger. 'No kind of danger, James, for I am sure no man in England will take away my life to make you King.' Charles had as little reverence and superstition in his nature as a man can have, while James was full of both. Religion was a fact to James, a fancy to Charles, who once declared that the only *visible* church he knew was that of Harrow-on-the-Hill. When Louise, Duchess of Portsmouth, survived an illness in '77, Henry Savile wrote to Rochester: 'The King imputes her cure to his drops, but her Confessor to the Virgin Mary, to whom he is said to have promised in her name that in case of recovery she should have no more commerce with that known enemy to virginity and chastity, the monarch of Great Britain.' Charles thought much more of a man's behaviour than his beliefs. He had a high opinion of Dr Sancroft, dean of St

JOHN WILMOT, 2ND EARL OF ROCHESTER

LOUISE DE KÉROUALLE, DUCHESS OF PORTSMOUTH

Paul's, a gentle, tolerant, non-persecuting clergyman who had refused a bishopric, the best man, felt Charles, to place at the head of the Church. When informed that he had been appointed Archbishop of Canterbury, Sancroft said that he was not competent for the office and begged the King to confer it on someone more capable. 'Well,' replied Charles, 'whether you accept the Primacy or not, the deanery of St Paul's has already been given to Dr Stillingfleet.' Sancroft had no option.

Religion in those days was a potent force in politics, and Charles, with frenetic Catholics on one side and ferocious Protestants on the other, would have liked to civilise both parties with indulgence. But he was malignantly pressed on every side, and took refuge in idleness. A gentleman has been defined as one who is too indolent to bear malice. In that sense Charles was a model gentleman. But his indolence was a positive quality, perfectly adapted to the circumstances of his time and founded on a philosophy of life which told him that all action breeds reaction and all compulsion begets opposition. With wonderful tact, admirable inertia, and a histrionic genius for timing his actions, he created a kingship of his own unlike any other in history, but one that was bound to collapse without his genius behind it. He had a sense of reality shared by no statesman of his time, and knew in an instant what to do in any given situation (usually nothing) and how far he could go. While others laboured over apparently insoluble problems, his intuition enabled him to deal with these in a flash, most of his time at Council meetings being spent in listening to lengthy expositions of questions to which he already knew the answers. By attending to innumerable matters, he often gave the impression of being very busy; but what was exacting to others was easy to him.

The incidental benefits of his various agreements with Louis were of far greater value to his country than the subsidies he managed to squeeze out of the French King. For example, their secret treaty of '76 was followed by a maritime treaty between the two nations in '77, as a result of which English ships were permitted to carry Dutch cargoes without French interference. It is pretty certain that Louis had no idea of what this would mean to England's commerce in the long run. From that time the British mercantile service began to outdistance all competitors, especially Holland, whose ships were constantly sunk, their cargoes confiscated, by the enemy during the Franco-Dutch war.

The British parliament represented the country's feelings on the subject of Catholic France, and were beginning to agitate for a war in support of the Dutch. Louis bribed Charles with £100,000 to keep parliament from sitting in '76, and offered a similar bribe for the same thing in '77, and an equal amount for a like service in '78. But on hearing that Charles intended to summon parliament early in '77, Louis sent large sums to bribe the opposition to vote against supplies for a war with France. Shaftesbury was rapidly becoming a power in the land. He had moved from Exeter House in the Strand to Aldersgate Street and was busily conspiring with members of the Green Ribbon Club at the King's Head Tavern to control the city, challenge the crown, and intensify anti-French feeling. Parliament met in February '77, and Charles urged the necessity of building more ships for the nation's safety, adding a warning: 'If any of these good ends should happen to be disappointed, I call God and man to witness this day that the misfortune of that disappointment shall not lie at my doors.' A sum of £600,000 was voted for the building of warships. Buckingham, Shaftesbury and others spoke in the Lords for a dissolution of parliament, knowing that a new one would largely consist 'of their own supporters, and they quoted a statute of Edward III upholding their view that as there had been no session for over a year it was virtually dissolved already. But the Lords did not like to think of themselves as non-existent, and since the peccant peers refused to apologise they were sent to the Tower. Charles knew why the opposition were so rabid, saying that two classes of people pretended zeal for the public good, 'either such as would subvert the Government and bring it to a Commonwealth again, or such as seem to join with that party and talk loud against the Court, hoping to have their mouths stopped by places or preferments', a remark that defines the aims and objects of many zealots before and since.

Louis displayed a remarkable tendency to win battles without gaining his end, and in the spring of '77 he took a number of frontier towns, causing panic in the House of Commons and several addresses to the King demanding action against France. Instead he proceeded against themselves, adjourning both Houses for over a month. On returning to business parliament refused further supplies until Charles had made his intentions known and asked him to form an alliance with Holland. He declined to have his foreign policy dictated by parliament, which was adjourned for two more months, and after another brief session did not meet again until '78. Asked by the Dutch ambassador why he refused to meet the wishes of his legislature and join with Holland against France, he tossed his handkerchief in the air, saying 'I care just that for parliament!'

Well aware that Louis had bribed many English politicians to vote against war supplies, Charles decided to teach his cousin a lesson, and arranged a marriage between the Duke of York's daughter Mary and William of Orange. His explanation to the French ambassador that such an arrangement, by removing suspicions of his pro-French policy and creating public confidence in himself, would ultimately benefit Louis, failed to convince that wily monarch, who did his utmost to make the Duke of York and the Duchess of Portsmouth stop the marriage. Their efforts were useless. On being reminded that he had promised not to dispose of Mary in marriage without her father's consent, Charles exclaimed: 'True, but odds fish! he *must* consent.' The betrothal was proclaimed on 22 October 1677, and the wedding took place on 4 November. On their marriage night, when they were in bed, Charles entered their room, and drawing the curtains cried to the Prince of Orange: 'Now nephew. Hey! St George for England!' Louis might have considered the remark in bad taste and a poor return for so many subsidies.

But Charles's chief enemy was the House of Commons, not Louis. He was constantly being pestered to get rid of his standing army as well as Lauderdale. Offered a considerable sum by Louis to disband his army and dissolve parliament, he refused to do so. The Commons then played the game of Louis by insisting on the dispersal of the troops. Charles stood firm, and it was as well he did. Corruption was now at its height, or rather its depth. The French ambassador was bribing Shaftesbury, Buckingham and others (released from the Tower in February '78). The Dutch and Spanish ambassadors, aided by Danby, were bribing the Court Party. Nearly everyone of note was receiving payment for something, and most of them were facing both ways. Charles had to face every way and shift his angle continually. He did not want to fight Louis, nor did he want a Dutch alliance. The Commons wanted war with France, but they feared a standing army. Everything was at sixes and sevens. But when Louis captured Ghent and Ypres early in '78 and the Spanish Netherlands were at his feet, Charles obtained supplies from parliament and sent troops to Ostend in pursuance of an understanding with Holland to force a peace between France and Spain. Meanwhile Louis had not been idle. He had bribed the States-General of Holland as well as the parliament of England, doing his best to hamstring both William and Charles, and in May '78 he received a letter from the States-General agreeing to discuss peace terms. At the end of July the terms were settled, whereby France secured her position on the north-eastern frontier, and peace was signed at Nimeguen between Louis and Holland, followed in September by peace with Spain. The presence of an English army on the continent may have influenced Louis to forgo more victories. Its continued existence was certainly a victory for the English King over his parliament.

It had been a feverish year for Charles, with little comic relief, though one period of stress was lightened by a fight between two peeresses. Denied the use of more lethal weapons, they skirmished with candles, and a knee was damaged in the fray. The injured party petitioned the House of Lords for compensation; whereupon the King offered to assess the damage by inspecting the injured part. His Majesty's thoughtful offer was declined, the matter being referred to a court of law. His attention was about to be engaged by something less pleasant than a lady's knee.

[19]

Horrors Accumulate

IMPORTANT EVENTS in the history of the human race are usually supposed to be heralded by portents in the heavenly sphere, and the years 1677–8, which provided a comet and several eclipses of the sun and moon, satisfied the superstitious. One day in August '78 the King was walking in St James's Park when a man named Christopher Kirkby, employed as a chemist at Court, requested him to read some papers. The King told the fellow to speak to Chiffinch about it, and walked on. That evening Charles heard an extraordinary story, and Danby was ordered to investigate matters. What he heard was that the Pope had entrusted the Jesuits with the job of demolishing the English monarch and government; the Spanish Jesuits and the French King's confessor, Père La Chaise, were to finance the undertaking; arrangements had been made to shoot Charles or to stab him, and if these methods failed, to poison him, the instrument in the last event being the Queen's physician, Sir George Wakeman; there were to be a slaughter of Protestants and an invasion of Ireland by the French; while the Duke of York would be made King, his actions controlled by the Jesuits. Further details were revealed later, such as the appointment of leading Catholics to the chief governmental posts, and the fact that the entire plot had been agreed at a meeting of Jesuits in a Strand tavern on 24 April 1678. That was the story, the narrators of which were two clergymen: a doctor of divinity named Ezerel Tonge, rector of St Michael's, Wood Street, and Titus Oates, ex-chaplain to the

Protestants in the household of the Duke of Norfolk.

Tonge was a rather feeble, indigent, credulous and simple person, who interested himself in botany and chemistry and longed for promotion in the church. Though constantly on the look-out for Jesuit plots, he could have done nothing effectual if left to himself; but early in '77 he met a much younger and more vigorous man named Titus Oates, who infused him with purpose and convinced him that his worst suspicions of Catholic conspiracy were mild in face of the facts. Tonge may here be dismissed as a weak and willing subordinate in the tremendous affair now set on foot. Later, when Oates had focused all the limelight on himself, the two men quarrelled, but apparently Tonge died in the belief that the lies he had told under the hypnotic influence of Oates contained the truth.

In considering Oates we are faced with a curious problem. It is not possible to believe either in absolute evil or in unadulterated good; yet Oates makes the irredeemable villain of Elizabethan drama seem relatively pleasant. His excessive ugliness probably helped to make him what he was, and the explanation of his depravity may be that a longing for affection was thwarted by his repellent physical aspect, and hatred, coupled with a craving for notoriety, took the place of his softer desires. Whatever the cause, there is no more deplorable figure in history or fiction. His misery started in early childhood, a constantly running nose and slobbering mouth getting on the nerves of his Anabaptist father, who ordered his mother to 'take away this snotty fool and jumble him about'. The boy was expelled from Merchant Taylors' school, ejected from Cambridge university, and dismissed from a living. Ambitious to be a schoolmaster, he tried to become one at Hastings by swearing that the man whose post he wished to fill had committed an unnatural act in the church porch. But the biter was bitten. Accused of perjury, relates Burnet, 'he got to be a chaplain in one of the King's ships, from which he was dismissed upon a complaint of some unnatural practices, not to be named'. He then began to mix with Jesuits, determined to be a convert to the faith, and was received into the Society of Jesus on the first day of Lent '77. Later, when asked by Burnet why he had become a Jesuit, he laid his hands piously upon his breast and declared that 'God and his holy angels knew that he had never changed, but that he had gone among them on purpose to betray them'. He went to Spain, where he 'made himself master' of many secrets and obtained a doctorate of divinity at Salamanca university. Then he travelled to St Omer, where, though treated with disrespect by his juniors, he completed his discoveries. His inventive powers being considerable, the secrets he had discovered were easily twisted into profitable forms, and when he returned to England a grand design was forming in his brain.

Having got into touch with Tonge, the 'plot' was carefully planned and brought before the King. Unfortunately Charles was enjoying the Newmarket air when Titus was examined by the Council. Had he been present he might have destroyed the evidence at the outset; for at a later meeting of the Council, when Oates stated that Don John of Austria had promised to provide funds for the murder of 'The Black Boy of Whitehall', Charles asked: 'What sort of a man is this Don John?' and Oates replied: 'Lean, tall and black,' upon which the King smiled, knowing that Don John was short, fat and red-haired. Again, Oates having said that within his knowledge the preliminary stages of the plot had been arranged in the house of the Jesuit fathers close to the Louvre in Paris, Charles corrected him: 'Man, the Jesuits have no house within a mile of the Louvre!' But Oates was utterly unabashed. He had an answer for everything, and before his listeners had been able to consider one contradiction he was entangling them in another. The story soon got about, and people talked of nothing else.

But for his appearance Oates would have been an effective Prime Minister. Short of stature, his body was imposing and ultimately puffed out with self-importance and success, the expression 'a swollen head' being a physical fact, not merely a figure of speech. Roger North observed him closely and described him thus: 'A low man, of an ill-cut, very short neck; and his visage and features were most particular. His mouth was the centre of his face, and a compass there would sweep his nose, forehead and chin within the perimeter.' He had an enormous chin, little shifty eyes, and a grave prophetic utterance that impressed everyone except the few who were intelligent enough not to be influenced by pulpit oratory. But as the mania grew even these were deluded, and Charles remained one of the few sane men in the nation. He never believed a word of it, in spite of the fact that some of Oates's lucky shots hit the target and brought evidence to light that seemed to support the story of a vast conspiracy.

The chief evidence was found in the correspondence of Edward Coleman, a Catholic convert who had first been the Duke of York's secretary and now acted in the same capacity for the Duchess. Being an indiscreet enthusiast for his faith, his vanity made him talk too much and he became an obvious mark for Oates, who charged him with receiving an instalment of the money intended for Wakeman's part in poisoning the King. The secretary was arrested and his private correspondence with Père La Chaise and others was examined. Although his letters contained nothing about a plot, they dealt with the restoration of the Roman Catholic faith in England, and the cipher in which they were written made them appear sinister. Most of them were begging-letters. Money was required for 'the great design', whereby the intrigues of wealthy Protestant merchants were to be undermined and Catholicism re-established; the sums given by Louis to Charles would be laid out to far better advantage if given to James; the debaucheries of Charles were set against the merits of James; and a general conspiracy seemed to be proved beyond question when the Council read Coleman's words: 'We have here a mighty work on our hands, no less than the conversion of three kingdoms, and by that perhaps the subduing a pestilent heresy which has domineered over part of this northern world a long time. There was never such a hope of success since the death of Queen Mary as now in our days when God has given us a Prince who is become zealous of being the author and instrument of so glorious a work.' With the ferment in men's minds started by the lies of Oates this was easily construed into a plot by the Duke of York and the French King to overthrow the national religion, especially when a cardinal's letter to Coleman mentioned the appointment of a Roman Catholic bishop for England.

But these letters had not been fully deciphered and translated before an incident occurred that turned strong suspicion into firm conviction and drove the whole country crazy. Just before laying their information before the Privy Council, Titus and Tonge called on Sir Edmund Berry Godfrey, a well-known London magistrate, and 'to make assurance double sure' asked him to swear them to the truth of the accusations in the papers they presented. When the contents were revealed to him, the magistrate took their sworn declarations on 28 September. Sir Edmund was a successful merchant who had remained in the city during the plague and sternly arrested those who robbed the dead by entering the foulest places for that purpose, a service that had earned him a knighthood. He was generous, honest, kindly and tolerant, and though an Anglican he was on good terms with Presbyterians as well as papists, all of whom esteemed him. Greatly upset by Oates's disclosures, he spoke of them to Coleman, who did not heed the warning. Rumours of a dreadful plot were now spreading in all directions, and those who sympathised with the Catholics felt insecure, among them Godfrey, who disappeared from his home on 12 October and whose body was found five days later in some bushes on the south side of Primrose Hill. The evidence at the inquest went to prove that he had been strangled elsewhere, but that his body had been taken to the place of discovery and transfixed with a sword. A reward of five hundred pounds was offered for the detection of the murderers.

This brought on the scene a man whose past was as disreputable as that of Oates and who had also obtained information by pretending to be a Catholic: one William Bedloe, who appeared before a committee of enquiry and provided sensational evidence implicating more Catholic peers in the plot and further testimony whereby several innocent men were hanged for murdering Godfrey, whose assassination was generally believed to be part of the Jesuit conspiracy, because of the knowledge he had obtained of their intentions; though it is much more likely that he was the victim of certain Protestants who wished to foment the anti-Catholic agitation. An avalanche of lies, suspicions, false witness, court perjuries and mendacious propaganda now submerged the country. Shaftesbury seized the chance of bettering his position by backing Oates and obtaining the financial aid of many wealthy Protestants in the city of London. The new rich were easily persuaded that they would be robbed by those whom their fathers had plundered, and stopped at nothing to save their money-bags. Shaftesbury was entirely cynical about the so-called plot, which served his turn well, his chief desire being to ruin Danby and take his place. Asked by a friend how he could expect to convince men of common sense in parliament that such a farrago of nonsense was true, he replied: 'It is no matter; the more nonsensical the better; if we cannot bring them to swallow worse nonsense than that, we shall never do any good with them.' When it was proved to him that certain evidence was tainted and incredible, he said that it must nevertheless be supported 'and that all those who undermined the credit of the witnesses were to be looked on as public enemies.' He had now appeared as the great Protestant champion, and gravely supported stories by boys in their 'teens of what had been told them by an infant of six. He had the mob behind him. The greater part of the nation had suddenly surrendered to an epidemic of delirium, seeing spies, conspirators and pro-Catholics in those who were not similarly infected, and hideous possibilities in the most innocent occurrences. A man who sold fireworks was suspected of incendiarism; Christopher Wren spent some time inspecting the walls and vaults beneath the Houses of Parliament because someone had heard mysterious knockings at night; and houses were searched in every direction for signs of Romish villainy.

Such phases of popular insanity occur at intervals in nearly every country, taking different forms according to the period and the circumstances. A famous historian once wrote: 'We know no spectacle so ridiculous as the British public in one of its periodical fits of morality.' But though these outbreaks sometimes take the shape of moral indignation in England, they are due to the sudden release of primitive passions that have been held in check by the necessities of civilisation. For long periods the mass of mankind endure the constant frustrations of life, due to their social conditions or their inner natures, and then suddenly wreak their rage on some object that infuriates them or makes them afraid. Hatred, which is born and nourished by fear, quickly becomes the main passion of their lives, creating a moral 'right' and 'wrong' which excuses their behaviour and gives fervour to their witch-hunt. Opportunistic politicians and other publicists, when they do not initiate the disease, make these bursts of hysteria serve their own turn and keep them at fever heat until their object is attained. Such is the simple explanation of the Oates affair, which became the Shaftesbury affair, and every similar manifestation of monstrosity throughout history. Discontented humanity demands at times a whipping-boy, or a number of such, on whom to vent their fury with life, that is themselves.[1]

Relatively few people are wholly free from the violent feelings engendered by hate, but King Charles was one of them. His common sense told him that he must bend before the wind to save his throne, and he has been criticised for bending too far; but, as we have seen, his tolerance could amount to indifference, and watching the waves of bloodthirsty vengeance pouring over his kingdom he decided to float on them as the only alternative to

1. In recent history the Dreyfus case in France and the Oscar Wilde case in England were symptoms of the malady, while two wars and their aftermaths have provided more comprehensive examples. War is the usual method of loosening the disciplined inhibitions of mankind.

being drowned. Panic having seized the nation, the Houses of Parliament reflected it. The five papist peers named by Oates and his confederates were dispatched to the Tower; the rest were dispossessed of their seats in the Lords. Parliament insisted that the standing army should be disbanded, and as Charles had not the money to keep it in being he was forced to agree, though he managed to retain some of his Guards; but when the Commons passed a bill for placing the militia under their control, he vetoed it, saying that he would not let that command go out of his hands for even half an hour. He also insisted that certain Catholic officers who had served him well should remain on the pay-roll; and when the Commons sent the Secretary of State to the Tower for authorising the salaries, he taught them a lesson in manners, saying that he would show them a civility they had denied him, for they had imprisoned one of his servants without letting him know, but he would now let them know that he intended to set his servant free again.

Oates and Bedloe were lodged in state apartments and pensioned. The popularity of Oates reached heroic proportions. He was guarded wherever he went, treated with the deepest respect, and the more paranoiac his performances the greater the reverence he inspired. His slightest word of disapproval sent a man to prison and possibly the scaffold. He accused the Duchess of Mazarin of taking part in the plot, and then, on the evidence of Bedloe, he pitched on the Queen, who, they said, had agreed to help her physician to poison her husband. The King was promptly asked to remove his wife and the whole of her household from the palace. But here the men who were plotting the plot came up against the flint of the King's loyalty. Some eight years earlier it had been hinted to him by Buckingham that the Queen should be abducted and secreted away to the plantations, when he could divorce her for desertion. Burnet records that 'the King himself rejected this with horror. He said it was a wicked thing to make a poor lady miserable, only because she was his wife and had no children by him, which was no fault of hers.' Now he spoke to

225

Burnet of the latest attempt to get rid of her: 'He said she was a weak woman, and had some disagreeable humours, but was not capable of a wicked thing; and considering his faultiness towards her in other things, he thought it a horrid thing to abandon her. He said he looked on falsehood and cruelty as the greatest of crimes in the sight of God.' The Queen appreciated what he did for her, writing to her brother: 'Every day he shows more clearly his purpose and goodwill towards me, and thus baffles the hate of my enemies . . . I cannot cease telling you what I owe to his benevolence, of which each day he gives better proofs, either from generosity or from compassion for the little happiness in which he sees I live.'

The 'discoveries' and murders, both private and judicial, went on, and the national paroxysms were so formidable that the King could do nothing. 'I will leave the matter to the law,' he informed parliament. The law was in the hands of the Chief Justice, Sir William Scroggs, whose life, according to Burnet, had been 'indecently scandalous'. He was a drunkard who bullied and ranted from the bench and condemned many innocent Catholics to death with relish, becoming very popular with the mob. Later, when the wind began to veer, he veered with it, but in the early stages of the mania he presented a spectacle of justice in a fever. Perjury is common in a court of law, but with Scroggs in control palpable lies were received as indubitable truths and virtue appeared culpable.

Shaftesbury put the fear of the mob into the King's Court as well as the Court of Justice, and the two men he wished to ruin were soon cursed by the populace. In November '78 he delivered a violent speech urging the dismissal of the Duke of York from the Council. The King prevailed upon his brother to quit public life for the present and informed parliament that he would agree to any reasonable safeguards against the abuse of power by a Catholic successor on condition that nothing was done to impair the ancient legal principle of hereditary succession. In this way he managed to outmanœuvre the Shaftesbury gang, who were attempting to destroy the monarchy by hitting at its weakest point, a Catholic successor, but dared not attack the principle of kingship directly. Next came Danby, the Lord Treasurer, who had served the crown well and become extremely unpopular by serving himself well too. Louis XIV disliked him for his pro-Dutch sympathies and was willing to bribe any faction that could bring him down. A tool for the purpose was soon discovered. Ralph Montagu was English ambassador at Paris early in '78 during secret negotiations for a subsidy from France, and Danby had written him compromising letters on the King's behalf. Montagu's ambition was to be a secretary of state, and he had a grievance against Danby for appointing someone else to a post he coveted. His sense of injury turned into fierce animosity when he was expelled from his embassy and the Privy Council because he visited England without permission to clear himself of spiteful charges made by the Duchess of Cleveland, then in Paris. With the promise of a fat pension from Louis, he determined on revenge, and Danby's letters to him requesting a French subsidy were read to the Commons. In one of them Charles asked for three annual payments of six million *livres* 'because it will be two or three years before he can hope to find his parliament in humour to give him supplies'. Although Charles had approved the letters, the Commons decided that Danby was responsible and impeached him for various crimes; but the Lords would not commit him until the reasons given for impeachment were clearly established, and while the two Houses were wrangling over the question the King prorogued parliament on 30 December '79 with the words: 'I think you are all witnesses that I have not been well used.'

Neither populace nor parliament was using him well. Though he discredited the evidence of the prosecution witnesses against the Jesuits and those accused of Godfrey's murder, all of whom appeared before the Privy Council, he was totally unable to allay the blood-lust of the people, and terrified judges dared not help the innocent. Had Charles exercised his right of pardon, there

would have been a revolution, and though he delayed signing the
death-warrants for certain condemned Jesuits he 'left the matter
to the law', saying as he wrote his name: 'Let the blood lie on
them that condemn them, for God knows I sign with tears in my
eyes.' In his desperation he made another appeal for money to
Louis, but that monarch declined to be fooled again and thought
he held all the winning cards.

To save Danby from the wrath of parliament, Charles dissolved it on 24 January '79, and a new Commons was summoned
for 6 March. For eighteen years the Cavalier Parliament, as it
was called, had been in existence, and starting in a condition of
emotional loyalty had become as troublesome as its predecessor
in the time of Charles I. A policy of propitiation seemed to be
necessary before the election of the new parliament, so Charles
asked his brother of York to leave the country. James agreed on
condition that the Duke of Monmouth, whom the leaders of the
opposition were putting forward as a Protestant heir to the
throne, should be declared illegitimate. Charles agreed and
signed a statement that the only woman he had ever married was
the Queen. Much as he loved Monmouth, said Charles to Burnet,
he would rather see him hanged than his successor. As a final
gesture of compromise, Charles made it known that Danby would
shortly cease to be Treasurer.

For the first time in English history the general election of
1679 was a contest between two clearly defined parties, Whigs
and Tories as they were afterwards known, republican and monarchical as they were in effect. Louis of France sent money in
support of Shaftesbury, whose use of propaganda was something
new in politics; and Lord William Russell, a virulent censor of
the crown, let it be known in Bedfordshire that the Court party
disbelieved in the Catholic plot, which was tantamount to saying
they were traitors and blasphemers. The Country party were
elected by a large majority of seats, and Charles was now faced
with a parliament of critics. It cannot be said that the new
Commons represented the nation in a modern sense. Apart from

the severely restricted franchise, Cornwall returned ten members to Leicestershire's one; Devon returned eleven and Derbyshire one; Hampshire twelve, Warwickshire one; Bedfordshire nine, Cambridgeshire one; and so on. In short the people as a whole had no vote; but they manifested their feelings without restraint during the election, and their feelings were distinctly anti-Catholic and pro-plot.

When thieves fall out, another lot falls in; and when one gang of politicians is in the ascendant it behaves much as any other gang in office. Though each pretends to live up to its shibboleths, all that happens is that power passes from one class to another and a different crew of time-servers gets the pickings. The Whigs who had just been returned were as keen as their Tory predecessors on ruining Danby, excluding the Duke of York from the throne, and treating Oates as the saviour of the nation. The King had to get rid of his Danby-controlled Council and reconstruct it with his opponents, Shaftesbury being made President. But he soon made it clear that he would not be a puppet in their hands. 'They shall know nothing,' he remarked to a loyal friend. When the House of Commons elected a Speaker he did not like, he declined to acknowledge the election. They sent delegates to him, but his answer was always the same: 'You do but lose time; go back and do as I directed you.' At last they obeyed. Over the impeachment of Danby he was equally firm, informing the Lords that he had rewarded and pardoned Danby. He would pardon the Treasurer ten times over, said he, 'for I will secure him in his person and fortune, which is no more than I commonly do to my servants when they quit my service, as the Duke of Buckingham and my Lord Shaftesbury well know.' The Lords committed Danby to the Tower, where he remained in safety for some years. The Commons next turned their attention to the exclusion of the Duke of York from the succession and the removal of Lauderdale from Scotland; upon which the King, having passed the Habeas Corpus Act, prorogued parliament until August '79, dissolving it before it could meet again.

It happened that Lauderdale's repressive policy, backed by the bishops, brought insurgence to a head that summer. The one lesson Charles had failed to learn from his father's mistakes was that the Scots did not like bishops, and the attempt to enforce episcopacy on them had dismally failed except on the surface, much hostility being felt towards the church as established at the Restoration. It is possible that Lauderdale nourished this resentment as an excuse for keeping a standing army, for he gave a practical demonstration of such an attitude by quartering some six thousand Highland clansmen on the unruly population of the south, which was thoroughly plundered as a consequence. The Covenanters, denied their conventicles, met secretly in the hills, armed for defence, and Andrew Marvell wrote that 'the patience of the Scots under their oppressions is not to be paralleled in any history'. Torture was frequently applied to obtain evidence against malcontents; and when one unfortunate man named James Mitchell was both tortured and executed at the request of James Sharp, Archbishop of St Andrews, his co-religionists took their revenge. According to Algernon Sidney, the Archbishop had been 'remarkable for outrageous covetousness, besides other episcopal qualities'. Certainly he was, next to Lauderdale, the most hated man in Scotland. On 3 May 1679 his coach was crossing Magus Muir. A number of Covenanters were on the watch, stopped the coach and pulled him out. He begged for mercy and offered them money to spare him. Replying that he had shown no mercy and that his money would perish with him, they hacked him to death. The government swiftly retaliated. Many men, innocent and otherwise, were taken and tortured. The Covenanters hit back in June, about 250 of them defeating Royalist troops under Graham of Claverhouse at Drumclog. By the end of the month a large force under Monmouth moved on Glasgow, then occupied by the Covenanters, who were driven out. Acting on the advice of their ministers, the Covenanters rejected Monmouth's offer of mercy if they would lay down their arms. They were badly led, poorly equipped, and suffered as usual from divided counsels. Monmouth had no difficulty in routing them at Bothwell Brig on 22 June, following up his victory by saving as many prisoners as he could. His clemency was criticised by Catholics and Anglicans alike, but he managed to persuade the King, who never needed much suasion in such matters, to grant a pardon to the captured rebels.[1]

The popularity of Monmouth as a Protestant was enhanced after the battle (or walk-over) of Bothwell Brig, and on his return to London he was acclaimed as a hero. Shaftesbury decided to use him as a puppet and claim his right to the crown, while Charles confessed that if it were not for *'la sottise de mon frère'* he would be able to deal with such obstructions. Although he had done his best for the innocent victims of religious frenzy, Charles never risked his position by interfering with what was miscalled justice, and the executions due to perjury were much enjoyed by the London mob up to the middle of 1679. In those days the gangster type murdered for religion, nowadays for money, which perhaps denotes progress. Charles gave the gangster element all the rope it needed, knowing that the more extreme the violence the more certain the reaction, when the rope could be put to better uses. 'It was like the letting blood, which abates a fever,' remarked a contemporary. 'Every execution, like a new bleeding, abated the heat that the nation was in.' It may have been the example of Charles that inspired a saying by one of his counsellors, Lord Halifax, that 'many times the nearest way to cure is not to oppose them, but stay till they are trussed with their own weight'.

No one knew what was going on beneath the amiable and self-possessed exterior of the monarch, but we are sufficiently acquainted with his nature to feel sure that this was the most painful and lonely period of his life. In June '79, accompanied by his wife, he left the bestial yells of the populace and the nasty conspiracies of Shaftesbury for the peace and quiet of Windsor, where he was

1. One of the greatest novels ever written, Walter Scott's *Old Mortality*, deals with this phase of Scottish history.

making great improvements both in the park and in the castle and where he could forget human beings while catching fish. No doubt he wished that Shaftesbury, Russell and the rest were wriggling at the end of his line as he pulled it out of the water, but as that could not be he thought that the time had come to make them feel that he still held the rod. With this in view he prevailed on the less extreme members of his Council, such as Lords Essex and Halifax, to favour a dissolution of the already prorogued parliament, since a new one, however similar in composition, would not be committed to the exclusion of the Duke of York and the impeachment of Danby. He took another risk, for the changed attitude of Scroggs at the trial of Sir George Wakeman, the Queen's physician, suggests that he had received a hint that her Majesty's honour was at stake. The trial took place in July, and the Chief Justice actually had the temerity to doubt the evidence of Oates, who had implied that the Queen knew of the plot to poison her husband. To doubt Oates at that time was equivalent to doubting the truth of the Scriptures, and when Wakeman was acquitted Scroggs was execrated. Oates and Bedloe at once complained to the Privy Council that their evidence had been questioned and the jury misdirected, their attitude being that if they were not believed justice was undone and the heavens would fall.

A fortunate occurrence in August of that year temporarily changed the emotional atmosphere, the national interest being shifted from Oates and Scroggs to the King, who fell seriously ill. Following a strenuous game of tennis he had caught a fever by strolling along the river bank in the evening chill. His shivering fits were so long and so severe that the physicians thought he would die, and the Duke of York was secretly advised to come from Brussels, where he was in temporary exile. He arrived in disguise to find his brother sufficiently recovered to talk of visiting Newmarket. The cure was supposed to have been effected by the administration of Jesuits' bark, later to be called quinine, but it was more likely due to the King's temperament, as calm in sickness as in health. The Duke wanted to stay in England, but he agreed to go away again when the King removed Monmouth from his military command and sent him into exile too. Monmouth was becoming troublesome as the tool of Shaftesbury, who was busily pushing him forward as an alternative to James in the succession. The King's health having absorbed public interest to the exclusion of 'the plot', the anti-Catholic brigade thought of something to revive the mania. Their clever idea was to discover forged letters, conveniently stowed away in a meal tub, which were supposed to prove a Whig or Presbyterian plot, making things at first look very black against themselves. But evidence was soon forthcoming that it was another Catholic plot to discredit Oates and Co., and a further spasm of hatred, redirected into its pro-Protestant channel, shook the populace.

The King now decided to test the strength of the renewed monarchical feeling in the country aroused by his illness, and appointed the Duke of York as High Commissioner of Scotland in place of Lauderdale, whose bad health gave him an excuse to resign. The new parliament assembled on 7 October '79, but was prorogued at once and then suspended at intervals for a year while Charles was haggling over the amount of a subsidy from Louis. Having determined to fight the men who wished to exclude the Duke of York from the throne, he dismissed Shaftesbury from the Council, and when Russell and others asked to be excused from further attendance he assented 'with all my heart'. Essex and Halifax having also retired, he formed a council of courtiers, known as The Chits, chief among them being Robert Spencer, Earl of Sunderland, Lawrence Hyde, son of Clarendon, and Sidney Godolphin, of whom the King said that 'he is never in the way and never out of the way', clearly a born courtier and destined for the highest office under Queen Anne. While sounding Louis about cash advances, Charles was also negotiating with Holland and Spain, part of his policy of playing off one side against the other, and the French ambassador had to confess to his master: 'It would be very difficult to explain to your Majesty

what is the real design of the King of England and his ministers.'
Not long afterwards he gave up guessing and informed Louis that
the English were solely interested in horse-racing and cock-
fighting.

There was now open warfare between the King and Shaftesbury, the first determined that his brother should succeed him,
the second equally determined that Monmouth should be a
puppet-monarch. In the event there was little to choose between
the two. Both good-looking and mentally negligible, Monmouth
lost his head for the sake of the crown and York lost the crown
for the sake of his head. But at the time each stood for a party,
and Charles naturally belonged to his own, though he dealt with
the matter casually enough in conversation, saying that his
personal security depended upon his having a successor less
popular than himself; an odd reflection, since he was as much
loved as his brother was loathed.

Shaftesbury's present method of warfare was to organise huge
petitions for an early assemblage of parliament, and to arrange
the composition and distribution of libellous tracts denouncing
the Duke of York, in one of which the people were warned that
the usual custom of papists was to ravish wives and daughters,
dash little children's brains out, plunder houses and cut Protestant throats. In the annual procession to commemorate Queen
Elizabeth's accession on 17 November '79 Shaftesbury's 'brisk
boys' marched along with two hundred thousand others to a great
papal conflagration, the mimic show including the Pope accompanied by the Devil. After that Monmouth returned to England
without his father's permission; but the city gave him asylum and
he received regal honours there, being cheered to the echo
wherever he went. Meanwhile no one was safe from accusation,
and informers throve on their trade. Oaths were made, recanted,
and made again. Letters were 'planted' on innocent people, who
were then seized, searched and incriminated. Those who were
accused became informers and those who informed were in turn
accused. It was a golden age for the dregs and scum of humanity.

Apart from Oates, the leading lunatic in this madhouse was Shaftesbury. His soul delighted in propaganda, and effective lies founded on improbable stories seemed to satisfy his æsthetic sense. Having failed to plant the plot in Ireland, with the object of inciting Catholics there to revolt, he encouraged the Irish aptitude for picturesque prevarication by shipping to England a crowd of informers, who were coached by Oates and paid for their fictitious evidence against their betters. No doubt believing that the bigger the lie the better the pay, the Irish were so adaptable that at a later date their evidence against the Shaftesbury faction was as fluent as it had previously been in favour of it. The next item in the opposition programme took the form of a report that a certain black box contained the papers proving that Charles had been married to Monmouth's mother, Lucy Walter. Under Shaftesbury's skilful guidance this vague rumour soon became thought of as an indisputable fact, and Charles had to issue a public contradiction. Driven insensate by his desire for power, Shaftesbury obtained bills of indictment against the Duke of York and the Duchess of Portsmouth as papist recusants, but the judges, instructed by the Court, dismissed the juries called to deal with the matter.

Without a parliament to grant him money Charles was extremely hard-up in 1680, and for economy's sake spent that summer at Windsor. Again he caught a chill, which brought on fever, and upon his recovery someone who knew his habits wrote that his good health could only be preserved 'if he can be kept from fishing when a dog would not be abroad'. While he was taking life easily at Windsor the reaction against Oates and Shaftesbury for which he had been patiently waiting showed signs of setting in. Judges began to question the evidence of witnesses, and many intended victims were acquitted; upon which Shaftesbury, following a turbulent election, managed to get two of his followers chosen as sheriffs for the city of London, and as the appointment of juries was in their power this meant the verdicts would always be determined in advance.

At length, on 21 October 1680, the new parliament commenced its first and last session. The King's speech was intended to placate them; and after saying that he would agree to any measures for the safety of the national religion that did not interfere with the legal succession to the throne, he begged for unity: 'Let us therefore take care that we do not gratify our enemies and discourage our friends by any unseasonable disputes. If any such do happen, the world will see it was no fault of mine; for I have done all that was possible for me to do to keep you in peace while I live and to leave you so when I die.' The Commons replied by attacking judges who had questioned the evidence of the Oates brigade and voting all sorts of retributive measures. So pronounced was their hostility that the Court itself was shaken, and not only the Duchess of Portsmouth but the Earl of Sunderland ratted. Charles, as always, remained unaffected, telling one of his adherents: 'I will stick by you and my old friends, for if I do not I shall have nobody to stick by me.' Lord Chief Justice North showed acute discomfort under the threat of impeachment, but the King cheered him up, saying that he would not follow his father's example and desert his supporters. Naturally the Commons demanded the dismissal of the King's ministers. The King dismissed their demand.

Then came the Exclusion Bill, which prevented James from coming to the throne and proclaimed him guilty of high treason if he returned to England. It passed the Commons on 11 November 1680 and was carried to the Lords by a mob of M.P.s accompanied by the Lord Mayor and aldermen of the city of London and headed by Lord Russell, an assemblage which it was hoped would intimidate the Upper House. The chief gladiators in that place were Shaftesbury for the bill, Halifax against it, the duel between the two lasting for seven hours and being won by Halifax after his sixteenth speech, the Lords rejecting the bill by 63 votes to 30. At first stupefied, the Commons in the fury of their frustration described Halifax as a public enemy and demanded his removal. Then they fell on Scroggs, who had dared to doubt the statement of Oates, then on Lord Chief Justice North, and finally on Lord Stafford, one of the Catholic peers immured in the Tower, who they believed would be weak enough to save himself by inventing falsehoods against the Duke of York. But Stafford was uncompliant, and after a sufficient number of lies had been told he was judged guilty of treason by his peers. Russell angrily insisted that he should suffer the extreme penalty of the law, hanging, drawing and quartering, but the King commuted this to beheading.

At the end of November the Commons tried to bribe the King with a hint of supplies if he would agree to the exclusion of his brother. He declined the bait. Their next move was to accuse Halifax of favouring Catholicism and to declare that anyone who lent the King money would be answerable to parliament. In a kind of frenzy they made all sorts of decisions relative to the Dukes of York and Monmouth and the Great Fire of London, which of course had been caused by papists. Their real intention was made plain when Shaftesbury told a friend that Charles should die the death of his father. Fighting for their own survival, the Commons resolved on 10 January '81, that anybody who advised his Majesty to prorogue parliament in order to prevent an Exclusion Bill from passing was a betrayer of the King and a papist in the pay of France. But Charles did not need advice. He interrupted their deliberations by proroguing them in person until 20 January, and dissolving them two days before their next meeting. He had begun to show his hand.

[20]

The Last Trick

THE POLITICAL SITUATION at the beginning of 1681 looked
extremely ugly, and civil war was confidently predicted. Even
Louis of France felt nervous, for he did not want to face another
hostile republic, his country having already experienced what
England could do as a Commonwealth. Besides, although it gave
him pleasure to make Charles uncomfortable, he was deeply concerned that the Duke of York as a Catholic should be the next
King, and the Commons of England had clearly determined on his
exclusion, which might compel Charles to nominate William of
Orange, husband of James's elder daughter, as his Protestant
successor. Thus Louis was in a more malleable mood when again
approached for a subsidy, and this time he promised about
£400,000, spread over three years on condition that Charles
would do nothing against his interests abroad, Louis promising
not to attack the Netherlands. Only Hyde and the Duke of York
knew of this secret treaty, which with his increasing income at
home made Charles relatively affluent. The growth of trade since
the last Dutch war had almost doubled the yield from customs and
excise, and Charles was now independent of parliamentary grants.
He could therefore face a new parliament boldly, whatever the
result of the general election.

The gloves were off and the party game was on. Whigs and
Tories, as each for the first time called the other offensively, used
bare fists and rude epithets. But there was no doubt of the result,

for the Whigs under Shaftesbury had a properly organised party which controlled the electoral corporations throughout the country. Their majority was reduced, but it was quite big enough to make the King tremble, if he were liable to tremors. Charles decided that parliament should meet at Oxford, where their deliberations would not be influenced by a bawling mob incited by Shaftesbury. Instantly the Whigs, who hoped to paralyse the Court with popular demonstrations, sent innumerable petitions against the move, claiming Westminster as the only place for a session of the nation's representatives. Charles intimated that petitions merely expressed the opinions of certain small sections of the community, and ignored them. But he took precautions. The London Oxford road was patrolled by a regiment of soldiers and many undergraduates were temporarily sent down from the university, accommodation for the Court being provided at Christ Church, Merton and Corpus Christi colleges, while the Commons were to debate in Convocation House, the Lords in the Geometry School (now the Bodleian).

The King arrived at Oxford on 14 March, and was received with acclamation by the populace, a speech by the Public Orator, and a bible from the Vice-Chancellor. Three days later he went hunting on the Cotswolds. Shaftesbury arrived with a guard of armed horsemen, and Monmouth made an equally spectacular entry, backed by a mob of yelling ruffians brandishing iron bars. Anyone who did not shout anti-popish slogans was likely to have his head broken, and it was probably here that a coach was mobbed in the belief that it contained 'Mrs Carwell', the Catholic Duchess of Portsmouth. The real occupant was the darling of the playhouse, Nell Gwynn, who put her head out of the window and cried: 'Pray, good people, be civil: I am the Protestant whore.' On the 21st the King opened parliament with a speech in which he declared his willingness to prevent the abuse of power by a Catholic successor, and went so far as to promise a regency under Mary of Orange, which would govern in the name of James; but he firmly stated his intention to abide by the laws of the land in the matter of inheritance. 'The unwarrantable proceedings of the last House of Commons were the occasion of my parting with the last parliament,' he said: 'for I, who will never use arbitrary government myself, am resolved not to suffer it in others.'

On the 26th the Commons debated the issue. It soon appeared that they objected to a regency, and they decided to introduce a bill disinheriting James and all other popish successors from the crown. That same day the King was present at the assembly of the Lords in the Geometry School. A paper was passed to him from Shaftesbury, proposing that Monmouth should be declared heir to the throne, so as to guarantee the Protestant succession and prevent civil war. The two men then conversed, Charles saying that his conscience would not allow him to act contrary to the law and justice, Shaftesbury replying that 'If you are restrained only by law and justice, rely on us and leave us to act. We will make laws which will give legality to a measure so necessary for the quiet of the nation'. But Charles, though he would do anything to maintain his kingship, refused to be a king only in name, and delivered Shaftesbury's quietus: 'Let there be no delusion. I will not yield, nor will I be bullied. Men usually become more timid as they become older; it is the opposite with me, and for what may remain of my life I am determined that nothing shall tarnish my reputation. I have law and reason and all right-thinking men on my side; I have the Church' (he pointed to the bishops) 'and nothing will ever separate us.'

Everyone thought that if the King did not give in, the country would be plunged into civil war; everyone except Charles, who had a conference with his Council in Merton College on Sunday 27 March, and on Monday the 28th he took his place in the Lords, crowned and robed, and summoned the Commons to appear. The mystery was all the greater because the crown and robes had been sent privately in a bag before his arrival; and when he was seen walking down to the Geometry School, his surrender to the demands of parliament seemed certain. Instead the rowdy Commons, excited over their coming victory, listened to his words with stupefaction: 'My Lords and Gentlemen: that all the world may see to what a point we are come, that we are not like to have a good end when the divisions at the beginning are such: therefore my Lord Chancellor, do as I have commanded you.' So completely taken aback were the lords and gentlemen that their dissolution scarcely evoked a murmur. Charles, in radiant mood, spoke to Lord Thomas Bruce, the gentleman-in-waiting who was unrobing him: 'I am a better man than you were a quarter of an hour ago, for you had better have one King than five hundred.'

The tables were completely turned. Charles had seized the psychological moment: the intuitive diplomatist had pulled his punches until the time came to deliver the knock-out blow. The Whigs never recovered for the rest of his reign from the totally unexpected dissolution of parliament just when victory seemed within their grasp, though they were still capable of resistance. They obtained one more victim before the utter collapse of the popish scare: Oliver Plunket, the Roman Catholic archbishop of Armagh, who had been accused by Oates of arranging the invasion of Ireland by a French army. Corroborative evidence against him was supplied by certain priests who, says Burnet, 'had been censured by him for their lewdness'. The Earl of Essex, who had at one time been an efficient Lord Lieutenant of Ireland, took part in the early stages of this evil business; and had he been less under the prevailing influence of the anti-Catholic aberration, he could have nipped it in the bud. But Plunket was condemned to death on utterly untrustworthy testimony, and Essex, now ashamed of himself, asked for the King's pardon, avowing that he knew the charge against the primate to be untrue. 'Then, my Lord,' exclaimed the exasperated Charles, 'be his blood on your own conscience. You might have saved him if you would. I cannot pardon him, because I dare not.' He had made up his mind to let the law take its course, and a pardon now would have convicted him of failure to exercise the prerogative in many earlier examples of equally innocent victims.[1]

The people were weary of faction by this time and seemed to be as angry with the House of Commons as they had previously been with the Pope of Rome. In April '81 Charles issued a Royal Declaration, which severely criticised the actions of his recent parliaments and was read in all the English churches. At once loyal addresses poured in from all parts of the country. The reaction set in so fiercely that Whig plots were now being discovered as fast as Catholic plots in the preceding years, and the paid informers changed sides. Shaftesbury was charged with an intention to use force if the Exclusion Bill were not passed, to start a rebellion and to establish a commonwealth. He was committed to the Tower, and much of the evidence against him was supplied by the Irish informers he had suborned. But the grand jury which heard the case consisted of Whigs and they rejected the indictment. At once it became apparent that unless the control of local governments by the Whigs were changed, the King would remain powerless against his chief adversaries. It was necessary to demand the surrender of the charters held by towns and cities and to issue new ones, whereby the corporations could be remodelled to exclude Whigs and to have mayors, sheriffs and juries chosen who would support the crown. With the influence of the territorial magnates in the various districts, most of the charters were resigned without protest; but wherever, as in London, there was resistance to this interference with freedom, a *quo warranto* was issued and the lawyers did the rest. Not even a Tudor monarch had dared to strike so mortal a blow at local liberties, and the fact that it all passed off without much friction shows that the personal popularity of Charles had reached a point where the King could do no wrong.

·1. Louis XIV avenged the Catholics of England when he revoked the Edict of Nantes in 1685 and the Huguenots of France were persecuted and hunted down in similar fashion. In the matter of religious gangsterism there was little to choose between Catholics and Protestants, both behaving like devils in the name of Christ.

Also he was for the first time backed by the sort of propaganda previously monopolised by the Whigs, the country being flooded with tracts and pamphlets in support of the monarchy, while in November '81 appeared Dryden's masterpiece *Absalom and Achitophel*, which, by exposing the national insanity of the previous years, showed the educated portion of the community that they had been making fools of themselves, a perception that changed to conviction when Shaftesbury's admirers celebrated his acquittal by distributing a medal bearing his head, and Dryden produced his next poem in March '82, calling it *The Medal*. The idea was suggested to him by the King when they were walking in the Mall one day. 'If I was a poet,' said Charles, 'and I think I am poor enough to be one, I would write a poem on such a subject in the following manner,' which he then sketched out. Grateful for the hint, Dryden once more ridiculed Shaftesbury, winning the admiration of his readers and 'a hundred broad pieces' from the King. We must not however overrate the effect of poetry on the multitude, which was more affected by thriving trade than by rousing verse. The population of England at that period was between five and six million, half of whom were agricultural labourers, London containing some five hundred thousand inhabitants, Bristol and Norwich coming next with about thirty thousand each. It is doubtful whether Dryden's satires were read by more than ten thousand people, who may have learnt from him that the Catholic plot was really a Protestant plot but who did not accumulate wisdom by the knowledge, for they swung easily and quickly from one form of idiocy to another, and led by the Anglican clergy began to persecute dissenters and quakers as they had previously been harrying the Catholics.

It goes without saying that James, Duke of York, should have proved his stupidity in Scotland by brutally ill-treating the Covenanters, but the more ruthless element in England was soon engaged in Whig-hunting, and the nonconformists who showed a disinclination to accept the Anglican sacrament were imprisoned, fined, and practically outlawed. It was a strange revulsion of feeling that now swept the country, and Charles followed his regular policy of leaving the law alone, hoping as usual that reaction would result in equilibrium. But meanwhile the leading Whigs were still causing trouble. Shaftesbury complained that the witnesses against him were suborned by the crown. The King heard this and said to Burnet that 'he did not wonder that the Earl of Shaftesbury, who was so guilty of those practices, should fasten them on others; and he used upon that a Scotch proverb very pleasantly, "At doomsday we shall see whose arse is blackest." ' Shaftesbury showed no interest in doomsday. In August '82 he discussed a rising with Monmouth, Russell and others; but the moment his great stronghold, the Corporation of London, fell to the crown that autumn, he realised that he would not stand a chance of acquittal if tried by a Tory-picked jury, and went into hiding at Wapping. Then, disguised as a Presbyterian clergyman, he sailed from Harwich at the end of November. His bad health and disordered state of mind made it impossible for anyone to deal with him. 'Fear, anger, and disappointment had wrought so much on him,' said Essex to Burnet, 'that . . . he was much broke in his thoughts: his notions were wild and impracticable,' and Essex was glad he had left England, 'as he had done them already a great deal of mischief and would have done more if he had stayed'. Ill and distraught, he reached Amsterdam, where he died in less than eight weeks.

While suffering from Whigs at home, the King extricated himself from an awkward position abroad. Louis was again on the rampage, and ignoring his verbal agreement with Charles that he would not disturb the peace in Europe he calmly took possession of Strasbourg and another town. As Charles had promised Holland that if Flanders were invaded he would summon parliament and oppose France, it looked as if he would have to break with Louis. Made aware of the situation by his ambassador, Louis offered Charles £75,000 for keeping quiet if the French occupied Luxemburg. Having pocketed the bribe Charles ex-

HORTENSE MANCINI, DUCHESS OF MAZARIN

ANTHONY ASHLEY COOPER, 1ST EARL OF SHAFTESBURY

plained his difficulty to the French ambassador when he was pressed by Holland to hinder the designs of Louis on their neighbouring state. 'You know what devils my members of parliament are,' said he : 'for God's sake get me out of this fix, or I shall have to summon parliament.' The trick worked. Louis had no desire to see another English parliament voting supplies for a war against him, and promptly raised the siege of Luxemburg. Charles received full credit for compelling the French King to retire; and as he had also received a handsome cash payment for doing nothing, he could congratulate himself on a neat bit of work.

Soon after this diplomatic triumph he experienced a return of the fever, again caused by his love of fresh air at inappropriate moments, and this attack diminished his usual vigour. He walked less, hunted less, and sometimes fell asleep in his chair at the conclusion of dinner. He seemed for a while less high-spirited than usual, but this may have been partly due to the childish behaviour of his beloved son, the Duke of Monmouth, who at Shaftesbury's instigation had got into the habit of making semi-royal progresses through the shires and obtaining the enthusiastic suffrages of all true Protestants, some of whom proclaimed him the rightful heir to the throne, hailing him with 'God bless the Protestant Duke!' In the autumn of '82 he spoke plainly of rebellion and made another grandiose visit to the west country, where he increased his popularity at horse-races by winning prizes as a jockey. At Liverpool he actually played the monarch by touching for 'the King's evil' and received the freedom of the town. Cheshire and Staffordshire welcomed him with rapture, but his indulgent father had ceased to smile at his exploits and he was arrested at the very moment a warrant was issued for Shaftesbury's apprehension. The latter escaped, but the King's protection enabled Monmouth to be bailed out; upon which he commenced a progress in the southern shires, where however the Whigs were not in favour, and at Chichester the sight of the high sheriff with a troop of horsemen made Monmouth swear 'bloodily', while an unsympathetic sermon in the cathedral caused him to quit the city.

It can scarcely be doubted that before their leader's escape there had been much talk of armed revolt between the chief Protestant exclusionists: Monmouth, Shaftesbury, the Earl of Essex, Lord William Howard of Escrick, Lord William Russell (son of the Duke of Bedford), John Hampden (grandson of the famous parliamentarian), and Algernon Sidney (son of the Earl of Leicester). Though all of them intended to do their best, if necessary by force, to change the succession and make certain of Protestant heirs to the throne, perhaps Shaftesbury was the only one who would not have stopped at assassination to secure this end. As plotters they were a poor lot, and the brains of the enterprise vanished with Shaftesbury. But in some way or other they had become connected with several men who meant business and who had every intention of killing not only the Duke of York but his brother the King. A few of these were old Cromwellian soldiers, others were disgruntled schemers, all well versed in conspiracy and sedition, and it is probable that the careless talk of the Shaftesbury clique had brought the two groups together. People like Essex, Russell and Sidney were in no way responsible for what was about to happen; but they had been seen in bad company; they had encouraged, or not discouraged, a rising in the Protestant interest; and they were judged accordingly.

One of the more vigorous Cromwellians was Captain Richard Rumbold, whose home was the Rye House at Hoddesdon, near Ware, on the direct road between London and Newmarket. It was arranged by the assassins that as the coach containing the King and his brother passed the moat of this house it should be obstructed by a hay-cart and the occupants killed by musket-fire from concealed marksmen. Unluckily for them a conflagration that laid part of Newmarket in ruins caused the King to leave it a week earlier than he had intended, and neither hay-cart nor musketeers were ready to receive him at the Rye House. Two months later one of the conspirators, an Anabaptist named Josiah Keeling, revealed the plot, which was soon substantiated by others who feared that if they did not get in first they might be informed against. Charles personally examined the various witnesses, from whose involved stories emerged the larger plan of the Shaftesbury set for a Protestant rising against the Duke of York's succession. Except Monmouth, all those who were named by the informers, Russell, Sidney, Howard, etc., were arrested, along with the Rye House desperadoes.

To save himself, Lord Howard gave evidence against Russell and Sidney. The King would have liked them to escape. According to Burnet, most of whose friends were Whigs, a messenger from the Council walked about for some hours before the front-gate of Russell's house, 'and it was looked on as done on purpose to frighten him away, for his back gate was not watched, so that for several hours he might have gone away if he had intended it'. Essex too was given plenty of time to leave the country, but did not take advantage of it. None of them seemed to think there was serious evidence against them, since they had only acted indirectly, talked vaguely if carelessly, and felt themselves innocent of the charge of treason. Essex cut his throat in the Tower before he could be tried. When the King heard of it, he said: 'My Lord of Essex needed not to have despaired of mercy, for I owed him a life,' his father having perished on the scaffold for the father of Charles. Russell was sentenced to death for high treason, but the King extended a mercy which Russell had done his best to deny Stafford, and instead of being hanged, drawn and quartered, he was beheaded by Jack Ketch. The King was strongly advised to pardon him and 'lay an eternal obligation upon a very great and numerous family' which would never forgive his execution. 'All that is true,' answered Charles, 'but it is as true that if I do not take his life, he will soon have mine.' Sidney was also executed, largely because his unpublished writings were treasonable in intent; John Hampden was fined; and the lesser fry ended their careers hideously at Tyburn. Charles had no vindictiveness in his nature, but his enforced quiescence over the judicial murder of so many innocent Catholics may have left in him a slight sense of guilt, and he did not feel in a charitable mood when those who had condemned them stood in need of clemency.

But his affection for his son Monmouth preserved the young man's life. He sent Lord Bruce to arrest the Duke at Toddington in Bedfordshire; but Bruce, divining the King's true feelings, did not go, and it was given out that the Duke had fled to Flanders. Charles liked being persuaded to do what he wished, and was soon reconciled to Monmouth, on condition that he would confess to the conspiracy. Having obtained his pardon in advance, Monmouth agreed, and in the presence of the Duke of York verbally confirmed the evidence of Lord Howard, named the other conspirators, and mentioned the threats of Lord Russell. The King wanted all this in writing, so Monmouth signed a confession which included the following: 'Your Majesty and the Duke know how ingenuously I have owned the late conspiracy, and though I was not conscious of any design against your Majesty's life, yet I lament the having had so great a share in the other part of the said conspiracy . . .' Hearing from several of his accomplices that his written statement would condemn them to death, he begged the King to let him have it back again. Charles demurred, but Monmouth insisted and at length got his way, the King telling him to go to hell. He went to Holland instead.

Shortly after Danby and the Catholic peers were freed from the Tower, the man who had been mainly responsible for their incarceration was prosecuted. Titus Oates had called the Duke of York a rogue and traitor, and the judges who had once crawled before the eminent Protestant now insulted him. Instead of regarding the charge as a tribute, the Duke asked for damages and was awarded £100,000, which meant perpetual imprisonment for Titus. When the Duke came to the throne, the one-time hero was tried, heavily fined, and sentenced to life-imprisonment, a whipping, and an annual exposure in the pillory. But with the accession of William III, Titus was released and pensioned. *Fiat justitia* was his watchword.

[21]

A Good Ending

IN THE LAST FOUR YEARS of his reign Charles achieved a popularity unique among rulers, unique because it had sprung from no spectacular quality, neither deeds nor words having contributed to it. He was too fond of a quiet life to be ambitious, or, as his counsellor Halifax put it: 'That some of his ministers seemed to have a superiority did not spring from his resignation to them, but to his ease. He chose rather to be eclipsed than to be troubled.' And yet, in a tranquil negative sort of way, he personified all that was best in the English character; and having passed through a series of emotional crises, his people obscurely felt that his calmness and reasonableness were preferable to the violence and partisanship of politicians. Lacking passion, he stood for toleration. Having no malignity, he typified charity. Hating retribution, he desired reconciliation. Such qualities were appreciated when commercial prosperity began to soften religious animosity. Another feature that contributed largely to his popularity was his friendliness with men of all degrees. With the possible exception of his grandfather, Henry of Navarre, no other sovereign in history could be described as a comrade-king. Halifax expresses this too in a dry unimaginative way: 'His wit was better suited to his condition before he was restored than afterwards. The wit of a gentleman and that of a crowned head ought to be two different things.' In other words Charles did not play the prince. He disliked solemnity, formality, ceremony, pretentiousness, and all the other outward signs of royalty; and his people recognised him as a man first, a monarch afterwards. Had it been possible, he would no doubt have liked to be a rich and independent commoner; but in his case the choice was between the crown and poverty, so the crown it had to be.

In a Puritan country it may seem strange that his amorous dalliance did not provoke popular odium. But the healthy openness, engaging honesty and refreshing shamelessness of his behaviour attracted a nation that had recently passed through a period of cant, humbug and hypocrisy in sex matters; and perhaps the sporting sense of the race responded to a king who would rather spend his time in the enjoyment of feminine society that in talking politics with ministers of state. It was known too that he did not cast off his mistresses as other monarchs did: he pensioned them off, and remained on friendly terms with them. It was not in his nature, said one of them, to be cruel to any living thing. With every woman he entered into a human relationship, and did not have to satisfy his pride by proving his potency.

That he was an all-round sportsman made a strong appeal to his people. He hunted, hawked, played tennis, walked, shot, swam, rowed and raced with the vigour of one who had no thought beyond the exercise of the moment. And he was an enthusiastic sailor. In all sorts of weather he encountered the sea with his yacht, sailing from Greenwich to Chatham, Sheerness, Southampton, Portsmouth, Plymouth, and inspecting the fortifications wherever he stopped on the way. He displayed as keen an interest in the fleet and the naval ports as in mathematics, medicine, and the experiments in his laboratory. The width of his sympathies was evinced by the creation of the Mathematical School at Christ's Hospital and the Observatory at Greenwich, to say nothing of the planning and rebuilding of London after the Great Fire; his concern for science led to the foundation of the Royal Society in '62; while his solicitude for old and disabled soldiers was manifested when he laid the first stone of the Royal Hospital at Chelsea in the spring of '82.

In those days the English were very fond of singing, dancing and music, not only to hear and see but to perform, and again the King shared their taste. He occasionally wrote songs and always had music at dinner, either vocal or instrumental. He was in the habit of humming his favourite ditties and beating time when they were sung. The anthems in his chapel pleased him, and he sometimes lent his violinists and French singers for the celebration of Mass in the Catholic chapel which was attached to the French embassy by diplomatic privilege. A favourite song of his was the *Récit du Sommeil*, rendered by French voices and accompanied by flute and clavichord. Another favourite in later years was James Shirley's

> The glories of our blood and state
>   Are shadows, not substantial things;
> There is no armour against fate;
>   Death lays his icy hand on kings.

Few kings would have chosen such a poem for a lullaby, and to suit the nature of Charles the last two lines,
>   Only the actions of the just
>   Smell sweet, and blossom in their dust,

should have run

>   Only the actions of the kind
>   Smell sweet, and blossom in the mind.

Indolent though he was by disposition, he got through an enormous amount of work in less than half the time another man would have taken. A witty courtier once said to him that his affairs could speedily be put in order if only he would employ one man for the job, namely himself. This was undoubtedly true, for he had the whole craft of government at his finger-tips and understood foreign affairs better than all his ministers put together; but when asked to attend to the business of the day, he could easily be persuaded by a fellow like Henry Savile that the really serious business of the day was hard drinking. Many of his jolly companions at Court flattered themselves that they were his intimate friends. But, as he owned to his loved sister, there were 'so few persons in the world worth a friendship', and not even his real friends knew his inner thoughts or were aware of his intentions. The tricky Buckingham, though restored to favour after Shaftesbury's death, was never admitted to the King's confidence; nor for that matter was anyone who had the least tinge of religious fanaticism. During one of Buckingham's absences in France on a diplomatic mission, the President of the Royal Society, Sir Robert Moray, a man with leanings towards Presbyterianism, asked the King when he expected to see the Duke again. 'On the Day of Judgment in the Valley of Jehoshaphat!' gravely returned Charles, adept at giving indirect but suitable answers to direct but unsuitable questions.

He enjoyed talking, and conversed with great charm and humour, but was usually careful to speak of things that had no reference to the political present. For this reason he chiefly entertained the company with details of his past experiences, making much fun out of his sojourn in Scotland and much drama out of his escape from Worcester and the part he had played in Paris during the French civil war. Bishop Burnet informs us that, though these exploits were recounted in a very graceful manner, Charles repeated them so often and with so many embellishments 'that all those who had been long accustomed to them grew very weary of them, and when he entered on those stories they usually withdrew: so that he often began them in a full audience, and before he had done there were not above four or five left about him: which drew a severe censure from Wilmot, Earl of Rochester. He said he wondered to see a man have so good a memory as to repeat the same story without losing the least circumstance, and yet not remember that he had told it to the same persons the very day before. This made him fond of strangers, for they hearkened to all his often repeated stories, and went away as in a rapture at such an uncommon condescension in a king'. Without perceiving it, the Bishop was paying the highest possible compliment to Charles, who was not egotistical enough to assume that he was of importance to anyone but himself, but was diplomatic enough to keep his discourse on the past. Any other king would have been furious if his courtiers had showed boredom with his stories, and it is difficult to think of another king good-natured enough to find pleasure in telling them to strangers.

His invariably pleasant manners, which signified his consideration for others, enhanced his popularity with the people. A witty instance of this occurred when he interviewed William Penn, to whom he gave a charter granting the famous Quaker a large tract of country west of the Delaware river in America, and later more territory on the right bank, which resulted in the settlement of Pennsylvania, founded in 1680–2 as a refuge for Quakers. Penn went to see Charles, and according to the custom of his sect kept his hat on while they talked; upon which Charles removed his own. 'Friend Charles, why dost thou not keep on thy hat?' demanded the Quaker. ' 'Tis the custom of this place that only one person should be covered at a time,' politely rejoined the King. It had also been the custom of that place to follow the sartorial fashions of France; but early in his reign Charles set a new style for clothes, and instead of the pink and white vests of his courtiers, which he said made them look like magpies, he wore one of plain velvet, and they followed suit. After 1663 he began to wear a periwig, therein acknowledging the French fashion, possibly because in that year, as Pepys noticed, his hair had become 'mighty gray'. The actors at Drury Lane did not go out of their way to compliment him. His own wig being black, he once exclaimed: 'Pray, what is the reason that we never see a rogue in a play, but odds fish! they always clap him on a black periwig, when it is well known one of the greatest rogues in England always wears a fair one?' The reference may have been to Shaftesbury or Oates.

From '63 to '81 he had trouble enough to make him go bald; but after 1681 both himself and the country, no longer agitated by parliaments, were at peace. Trade flourished, merchants got rich, the demand for ships grew, the New England confederation (Massachusetts, Plymouth, Connecticut and New Haven) throve, and the King's revenue steadily increased. The only colonial failure of the reign was Tangier, part of the Queen's dowry. It was isolated, subject to constant attack by Berbers, and useless as a trade centre. Charles tried to sell it to France, but Louis would not have it; then to Portugal, without success; so he decided to abandon it owing to the cost of upkeep. In 1683 an expedition was sent out to destroy the mole, erase the fortifications, and bring home the garrison. Apart from that, the other ventures overseas more than repaid the money spent on them; and by keeping the peace whenever he could, and so creating commercial prosperity, Charles, perhaps unknowingly, enabled the country to generate the force which encountered and smashed the continental designs of Louis in the coming generation.

Charles was comparatively wealthy in his last years; but by a mysterious edict of nature the more money people acquire the more they complain of penury, and Charles deluded himself that he was unusually hard-up. This self-deception was due to a fresh commitment. In the summer of '82 he stayed at Winchester for the races. The neighbouring country appealed to him, and he determined to build a palace at the ancient capital of England. The site he chose was on the west hill overlooking the city, and he engaged Wren as architect. The front of the palace was to be 328 feet long, and from the terrace there would be an avenue some 200 feet wide, with fine houses on each side, leading down to the west end of the cathedral. There were to be two chapels in the palace, one for the Queen, the other for himself. The first stone was laid on 23 March 1683 and thereafter he visited the city as frequently as he could, to watch the progress of the building, to fish in the river Itchen, and to hunt on the downs. In those days half of England consisted of fen, heath and forest, and there was plenty of room for sport; but one of the largest royal preserves was the New Forest, where the few cottages were occupied by venerers and swineherds, and here Charles amused himself when feeling in need of strenuous exercise.

The first time he took his family to Winchester, a slight hitch occurred in the arrangements. The dean, Dr Thomas Ken, objected to Nell Gwynn's presence in his house, and other apartments had to be found for her. This would have vexed anyone but Charles, who however recognised the merit of Ken's unworldliness; and when the see of Bath and Wells became vacant, he asked for the name of that little fellow at Winchester who had refused to let Nell sleep in his house, and gave him the bishopric. Finding Ken to be of a humble saintly disposition, Charles did not mind speaking of his own weaknesses to the new bishop, though feeling confident, as he once said to Burnet, that 'God would not damn a man for a little irregular pleasure'.

The living issue of his irregular pleasure were a blessing to him, and he treated all his natural children with affection. When they were young he often visited their nurseries to play with them, and when they grew up he was a generous indulgent father. To one of them, Charlotte, Countess of Lichfield, we find him writing in April 1684, granting her permission to build her garden wall as high as she pleased, so that her grounds should not be overlooked from the windows of other houses: 'The only caution I give you is not to prejudice the corner house, which you know your sister Sussex is to have, and the building up the wall there will signify nothing to you, only inconvenience her.' The Countesses of Lichfield and Sussex were the daughters of Charles and Barbara, Lady Castlemaine, one of their sons being the Duke of Grafton, nominal Vice-Admiral of England, who had recently suffered from smallpox and about whom Charles wrote to his 'dear Charlotte' in September of the same year: 'Your brother Harry is now here and will go in a few days to see Holland, and by the time he returns he will have worn out in some measure the redness of his face, so as not to fright the most part of our ladies here. His face is not changed, though he will be marked very much.'

A Good Ending

From such matters Charles turned easily to affairs of state. His brother of York wished him to be an absolute monarch, but he was comfortable enough without a parliament, saying: 'A King of England that is not a slave to five hundred kings is king enough.' He wished his subjects to be happy, to 'live under their own vine and fig tree'. At the meetings of his Council he refused to side with any of those who took sides, always 'hearing everybody against everybody', which irritated nearly everybody but compelled peace. Occasionally he was bothered by William of Orange, who warned him that when the French had beaten all their continental rivals they would vanquish England; to which he replied that they would have to cross the Channel first and defeat the finest navy in the world. Orange having become dictatorial in his attitude to English policy, Charles gave his nephew 'a slap in the face' by arranging a marriage between his niece Anne and Prince George of Denmark, which occurred in July '83 and made possible another Protestant heir to the throne. No objection to the match came from Louise, Duchess of Portsmouth, because Denmark was one of the French King's paid allies.

Louise was again the chief feminine influence at Court, receiving countless favours and attentions from the King. In October '83 the diarist John Evelyn reported that he went with Charles and several others to the Duchess of Portsmouth's dressing-room one morning. They found her in a loose garment, just out of bed, her hair being combed by maids. The King and courtiers stood about her for some time exchanging quips and commonplaces. Evelyn was struck by the luxury which surrounded her, the costly paintings, tapestries, furniture, etc. Shortly after this episode the King, whose health was usually excellent, complained of aches and pains, which may have been caused by the weather, the winter of '83–4 being the coldest within living memory. The Thames was ice-bound, and even the sea was frozen for two miles from the land. The citizens of London lived on their river, across which went coaches, carts and horsemen. Streets of booths were erected on the ice, plays were performed, bulls were baited, and after the snow fell thickly coach races were run. Oxen were roasted, and the poor were fed at the King's expense. An outbreak of smallpox occasioned more distress than usual owing to the intense and protracted frost.

In the spring of '84 Charles took his usual holiday at Newmarket. The weather was wet, the main street filthy, and he advised a companion as they strolled through the town to avoid a cold by wearing thicker shoes. That summer was as hot as the previous winter had been cold, and the country endured months of drought. Following his customary stay at Windsor, the King went to Winchester, where he hawked over the downs and watched his palace slowly rising on the hill. Wren told him it would take a year to complete. 'A year is a great time in my life,' he said. In the autumn he reviewed his troops on Putney Heath, and spent some days of wind and rain at Newmarket. Anxious to pay his debts, he employed Samuel Morland to find out exactly how much he owed. 'I shall be able to pay the bankers' debts which I have so much at heart,' he confided to Lord Bruce, 'and if God gives me life I hope to pay at least some of the King my father's debts.' He never failed to help his children financially; and though he could not officially recognise Monmouth without making his brother of York angry, he secretly sent the young man money.

In the winter of '84–5 the King looked remarkably well. But one of his legs was out of order, with gout thought Burnet, with a running sore according to someone else, and for a few weeks he could not take his daily exercise of three or four hours in the park. Instead he spent more time in his laboratory 'running a process for the fixing of mercury'. On Sunday 1 February '85 Dr Dove preached before the Court, and after dinner the usual crowd of spectators wandered about the palace, among them John Evelyn, who recorded his impressions: 'I can never forget the inexpressible luxury and profaneness, gaming and all dissoluteness, and as it were total forgetfulness of God (it being Sunday evening) which . . . I was witness of, the King sitting and toying with his concubines, Portsmouth, Cleveland and Mazarin &c, and a French boy singing love songs in that glorious gallery, whilst about 20 of the great courtiers and other dissolute persons were at basset round a large table, a bank of at least 2,000 in gold before them, upon which two gentlemen who were with me made reflections with astonishment. Six days after was all in the dust.' More accurately the ladies were ex-concubines, their presence together testifying to Charles's unshakeable friendliness; and perhaps it did not occur to Evelyn that if, instead of this scene, the King had been discovered in prayer surrounded by bishops, or singing hymns with pious choristers, all would still have been in the dust six days after.

The King retired to bed that night in cheerful mood, telling Lord Bruce that it was the sovereign's fault when modesty in a subject went unrewarded, and speaking of his palace at Winchester: 'I shall be so happy this week as to have my house covered with lead,' a remark that provoked a later comment from Bruce: 'And God knows the Saturday following he was put into his coffin.' After a restless night, Charles must have had some sort of seizure in the early morning, because he could only mutter incomprehensibly to those who attended him and wander aimlessly in his closet for some time. On sitting down to be shaved he had a fit, and after that he was at the mercy of soul-curers and body-curers, the clergy praying, exhorting and warning, the doctors purging, bleeding and blistering. Between the two he had no chance to recover, had his constitution enabled him to do so, for they allowed him no sleep, 'tired Nature's sweet restorer'. When conscious enough to perceive what had happened, he asked for the Queen, who had watched so long by his side that she was exhausted. She sent an excuse for her enforced and temporary absence, and begged his pardon if ever she had offended him. On receiving the message Charles exclaimed: 'Alas, poor woman! She beg my pardon! I beg hers with all my heart.' Told not to talk, he remarked that such an order would be the death of his friend Harry Killigrew.

A Good Ending

The rumour spread that he had been poisoned; but it was fashionable in those days for kings to die of poison, a regal right so to speak, and his death was certainly hastened by the poison administered by the doctors as medicine. Under their treatment his resistance weakened. Though he seemed to rally on Wednesday, a mammoth dose of Jesuits' bark made him unconscious on Thursday, and those about him knew that his time was short. The Duke of York, possibly prompted by the Duchess of Portsmouth, asked the King if he would receive a priest. When Charles could understand the question, he replied: 'Yes, with all my heart.' Always sensitive to a solution which would please others without inconvenience to himself, he may have remembered that some of those he had loved most, Catherine, Louise and Minette, were of the Roman faith, and that at the lowest ebb of his fortunes his life had been saved by Catholics. Possibly too he was dimly conscious that a Protestant parliament had tried to break him, and that a certain debt to Louis of France was somewhat overdue. Father Hudleston was not at the palace by mere chance; and when Chiffinch introduced the priest, it must have comforted Charles to know that the man who had helped him in his flight after the battle of Worcester was ready to help him in his flight after the battle of life. Having made his confession, he received absolution, communion and extreme unction. When the courtiers were allowed back in the room, he admitted that he had suffered much, but said that his business would soon be done. He endured the agonies of dissolution with a fortitude and serenity that amazed everyone. On Thursday night, the last of his life, he spoke most tenderly to the Queen, begged the Duke of York to be kind to Louise and all his children, added: 'Let not poor Nelly starve,' and apologised to those who were about him: 'I have been a most unconscionable time dying, but I hope that you will excuse it.'

Early in the morning of Friday 6 February he made a last request: 'Open the curtains that I may once more see day.' Bishop Ken, who had remained by his side for many hours during these last days, still hoped that he would receive the Anglican sacrament; but before midday the sanest, most human and civilised of monarchs had ceased to breathe; and envy, hatred and malice, masquerading as religion, could touch him no more.

Selected Sources

Selected Sources

Of the sixty odd books I have read on my subject, the following have been most helpful:

Burnet's History of My Own Times, edited by Osmund Airy, 2 volumes, 1897–1900.

A Supplement to Burnet's History of My Own Times, edited by H. C. Foxcroft, 1902.

The Life of Edward, Earl of Clarendon, written by Himself, 3 volumes, 1827.

Charles II and Madame, by Cyril Hughes Hartmann, 1934.

The Letters, Speeches and Declarations of King Charles II, edited by Arthur Bryant, 1935.

King Charles II, by Arthur Bryant, 1931.

England in the Reign of Charles II, by David Ogg, 2 volumes, 1934.

After Worcester Fight, by Allan Fea, 1904.

The Flight of the King, by Allan Fea, 1897.

The Travels of the King, by Eva Scott, 1907.

The King in Exile, by Eva Scott, 1904.

The Diary of Samuel Pepys, edited by H. B. Wheatley, 8 volumes, 1893–9.

Diary of John Evelyn, edited by H. B. Wheatley, 4 volumes, 1906.

A French Ambassador at the Court of Charles II, by J. J. Jusserand, 1892.

Personal History of King Charles II, by Rev. C. J. Lyon, 1851.

The Private Life of Charles II, by Arthur Irwin Dasent, 1927.

The Story of Nell Gwyn and Sayings of Charles II, by P. Cunningham, 1852.

Memoirs of the Comte de Gramont, by Anthony Hamilton: Translated by Peter Quennell, 1930.

Charles II, by Osmund Airy, 1901.

Selected Sources

Character and Anecdotes of Charles II, by Charles Barker, 1853.
The Life of John Dryden, by Sir Walter Scott, 1834.
Samuel Johnson's Lives of Dorset, Dryden and Rochester.
History of England, by George Macaulay Trevelyan, 1926.
The Last Rally, by Hilaire Belloc, 1940.
The Stuarts, by Charles Petrie, 1937.
Dictionary of National Biography.

Index

Index

Act of Uniformity, 135
Albemarle, Duke of, 166, 167
Anglesey, Lord, 137
Anne, afterwards Queen, 256
Anne of Austria, 8, 11, 13, 39
Argyll, Marquis of, 15, 16, 20, 22–3, 26–8, 30, 32, 35, 45, 141
Arlington, Lord, 165–6, 170, 172–4, 189, 194, 200, 203
Arundell of Wardour, Lord, 190

Bedloe, William, 223, 225
Behn, Aphra, 183
Bell, Walter, 169*n*
Bellings, Sir Richard, 190
Berkeley, Lord, 137
Berkeley, Sir Charles, 116
Berkeley, Sir John, 159
Berkshire, Earl of, 4
Betterton, Thomas, 178
Birkenhead, Sir J., 184
Blake, Admiral, 76, 79, 98, 115, 156
Breda, 16–18, 19–23, 170, 171, 186
Brentford, 4
Broghill, Lord, 137
Brouncker, Henry, 161–2
Bruce, Lord, 248, 257
Buckhurst, Lord, 163, 181–2; then *see* Dorset, Earl of
Buckingham, Duke of, 20, 27, 32, 40, 45, 48, 82, 111, 137–8, 173, 178–80, 188, 189, 200, 203,

204, 209, 214, 216, 225, 229, 252
Bunyan, John, 176
Burnet, Bishop, 184, 201–2, 204, 205, 219–20, 226, 228, 241, 247, 252–3, 257
Butler, Samuel, 176–80
Byron, Lady, 102

Campbell, Lady Anne, 20
Carlos, Colonel, 51–3
Carteret, Marguerite de, 6
Carteret, Sir G., 6, 159
Castlemaine, Earl of, 121–2
Castlemaine, Lady, 121–5, 143–54, 173, 179, 194, 227, 255, 258
Catherine of Braganza, Queen, 119–25, 129, 138, 145–6, 151, 152, 154–5, 225–6, 232, 258, 259
Charles I, 1, 3–7, 9, 11, 118, 126, 139, 140, 198
Charles II:
  Compared with Charles I, 1–2, 126, 192 ff., 249 ff.
  Birth and infancy, 1–2
  His governors, 2–3
  First military command, 3
  Created Duke of Cornwall and appointed Generalissimo (under a Council), 4
  Flees to Scilly, then to Jersey and France, 6–7